C000318981

Guildford Institute Library
Withdrawn From Stock

Hamilton Public Library
Withdrawn From Stock

# Coming in with the Tide

*Also by the same author*

A Journey to the Interior
Agents and Witnesses
The Spirit of Jem
Mariner Dances
The Snow Pasture
The Loot Runners
Maria Edgeworth
The Young May Moon
The Novel, 1945-50
A Season in England
A Step to Silence
The Retreat
The Picnic at Sakkara
Revolution and Roses
Ten Miles from Anywhere
A Guest and his Going
The Barbary Light
One of the Founders
Something to Answer For
A Lot to Ask
Kith
The Egypt Story (with F Maroon)
Warrior Pharaohs
Feelings Have Changed
Saladin in his Time
Leaning in the Wind

# COMING IN WITH THE TIDE

## P H Newby

Hutchinson
London Sydney Auckland Johannesburg

Property of the
Guildford Institute

Copyright © P H Newby

The right of P H Newby to be identified as Author
of this work has been asserted by P H Newby in
accordance with the Copyright, Designs and
Patents Act, 1988

*All rights reserved*

This edition first published in 1991 by Hutchinson

Random Century Group Ltd
20 Vauxhall Bridge Road, London SW1V 2SA

Random Century Australia (Pty) Ltd
20 Alfred Street, Milsons Point, Sydney, NSW 2061, Australia

Random Century (NZ) Ltd
PO Box 40-086, Glenfield, Auckland 10, New Zealand

Random Century South Africa (Pty) Ltd
PO Box 337, Bergvlei, 2012 South Africa

British Library Catalouging in Publication Data
Newby, P. H. (Percy Howard) *1918–*
    Coming in with the Tide
    I. Title
    823.914 [F]

    ISBN 0–09–174664–7

Printed and bound in Great Britain by
Mackays of Chatham

*Remembering Flo and Percy*

# 1

In those days the weekly *Penarth Times* ran a curious column. Questions were asked, such as, 'What was the young lady with grey gloves thinking of when she dropped one in Plymouth Road last Tuesday? Did the young man who picked it up consider her very careless?' Or again, 'Why did the gentleman wearing brown boots extract no fewer than a dozen bars of chocolate from the machine on Penarth Station before taking the train to Cardiff?'

Another example: 'It has been noticed that a certain small boy never passes Piper's Penny Bazaar without being taken inside by his nursemaid to make a purchase. What can the future hold for someone so indulged?' And another: 'At the public library it has been observed that a gentleman in clerical attire has been borrowing the boys' adventure stories of Mr R.M. Ballantyne one after the other. Can he be over-exciting himself?' And the like.

Hannah was terrified that some reference to the Weston trip might appear, and when it did she knew at once who was responsible. Only Mr White could have supplied the information. 'What was the real purpose of the three young people, two ladies and a gentleman, in crossing the Bristol Channel recently? An innocent excursion would surely not have led to so much earnest talk from which one of the trio was excluded.'

But once Hannah had overcome her terror she was delighted. Her family noticed the lines (everyone read the column) and Hannah, her face beaming, cried, 'Oh, but you know what a silly made-up thing this "Town Talk" is. I wouldn't wonder the boatman was paid a shilling. Didn't you know that everyone who sends in a question is paid a shilling?'

'But it must have been based on something he had observed,' said her mother.

'Or something he had imagined, hoping it would earn him a shilling.' All the time she knew it was really Mr White.

Throughout her life Hannah always saw Mr White as he appeared on that day. A darkish, quick man. In spite of the changes – growing a heavy moustache, the wiry upright figure developing a stoop, the feathery brown hair turning pepper and salt and the nose sharpening – he was (until misfortune came and the War went on and on) always boyish, enthusiastic about ... well, everything. Food, clothes, work – the weather when it was doing something positive, like snowing or blowing a gale, lightning and thunder, or stupefying everyone with the glare and the heat. Above all, he was enthusiastic about her. And reading, reading, reading. He was enthusiastic about that too. He devoured books.

'We'll run away together.' He was always saying this, even after they had been married for years.

But the first time was on that summer day when they embarked on the *Lady Margaret* from the end of the pier on the dairymen's annual outing. Mr White was not a dairyman (he was a carpenter with ambitions to set up on his own as a builder), but he had somehow managed to buy tickets for himself, for Hannah and for Olive, her cousin who went along as chaperone. The weather was calm enough for them to sit on deck, on slatted wooden seats against the rail, with the sun in their eyes, well forward of the paddles and windward of the funnel in case there were fumes and falling smuts.

'Let's run away together, 'Annah,' he said soon after they had disembarked at the short landing-stage out on the headland where, it was boasted by the municipality, the tide was always in. Mr White had trouble with his aspirates. He dropped them, he struggled not to drop them and sometimes he popped them in where they were not needed. Hannah's family held it against him that he spoke as he did, real Gloucester (which is where he came from) because it showed no sort of background. No family. That Hannah should form an acquaintance with a young man who could not even say her name properly!

Society, it seemed to them, was disintegrating. As the century drew to an end the old loyalties broke up. There was no authority any more. Nobody was respected, not even the Ministers.

'Let's run away to Bristol,' said Mr White, keeping his voice low so that Olive, who was walking a dozen paces or so in the rear, could not hear. 'We could set up a – an establishment there. We could live in sin.'

Hannah laughed and raised her parasol as though to strike him. 'You told me you didn't believe in sin.'

2

'No more I do, 'Annah. Sin is a word people use when they want you to toe the line. Men, and women for that matter, are naturally good if only they're left alone to live their own lives. Men and women are good. No, they're perfect like roses. That's how God thinks of us. When I said we'd live in sin, we'd really be living in God's love and tenderness, that's God's grace, but your family would say we were living in sin. So I used the words because I wanted to show I understood the issue. 'Annah, let us live like roses.'

'Mr White,' said Hannah. 'Now that I've got over the seasick feeling, I should like something to eat. Wouldn't you, Olive?' She turned and called back. 'Aren't you starving? Mr White is going to treat us to shrimps.' Which previously he had not known.

Nobody could forsee what mood Charles White would be in. He was up and down, no matter the state of his affairs. When things were going well – during his early years as an independent builder, for example – he was capable of being what Hannah called moody. During bad times – and they had them – he might see fit to fool about and spoof. Sometimes the easiest course was to join in and agree that they really were going to emigrate. If it was to Canada they had to take decisions, such as whether it would be wiser to wait until they got there before buying fur coats and snow-shoes or whether they ought to build up their requirements more slowly on this side of the Atlantic and not wait until they arrived at some trading post where they might be fleeced. If emigration was no longer the plan of the moment but, say, rearing dogs or chicken farming, they had to make up their minds which kind of dog or chicken would be most profitable. When he suggested Bull terriers or White Wyandottes, it was in expectation that Hannah would have her own preferences. Fox terriers and Rhode Island Reds were possible. She had to show a proper response; she had to follow where his imagination took him.

In the early days, the trouble was that she could never be sure whether he was just playing games. When some grand scheme was dropped it could have been for some sound, practical reason (he never told her) or simply because it had ceased to amuse him. As time went by she realized that resistance on her part only made him the more emphatic that he was serious – they really *were* going to adopt black babies from Barry Dock or take up bicycling in a big way, he in knickerbockers and she in bloomers – so she dropped her doubts. Her imagination became coloured by his. Whereas his seemed to flourish, Hannah's perception of what was really happening and what was actually possible became intermittent and confused.

But not to begin with, as on that trip to Weston-super-Mare. The suggestion that they went off to Bristol and lived together both appalled and attracted her. It became almost irresistible when Mr White said they would send no message to her family for a whole month. Yes, they would live together without being married because it would show that he and Hannah were different. It all seemed real and shocking to her.

'You don't understand, I love you,' Mr White said. 'After our first meeting at the Tabernacle Baptist Chapel I was so excited I went for a long walk, almost as far as the cement works. All the sea and sky were in front. A great emptiness. Nothing between me and the limits of the universe, except a lot of constellations. I felt I was lifted up into them. Like a prophet.'

Hannah said she couldn't possible agree to giving Olive the slip because the girl was only 18 and she'd be so frightened and upset. Just think of her going back to Penarth with the dairymen and their wives to tell Hannah's family that she'd lost Miss Jones and Mr White! The girl took her responsibilities seriously.

'You've got to break out.' He had a way of taking both her hands in his and looking into her eyes voluptuously. 'And live.' He implied that Olive would secretly be thrilled to have played some small part in a romantic elopement; she would talk about Charles and Hannah for the rest of her life. They must cut through the callus that had grown over her flesh, her blood, her nerves, and release the real spirit that dwelt there. He saw it flying up as a white bird. For Olive, too, their running away would be liberating.

'You're common.' Hannah shook off the hand that he had now placed on her arm.

'That I am, and what's going to happen is that common men'll take over. For the last time. I know where the railway station is here in Weston. Are we going to make a run for it?'

He meant it and was not just teasing. Suppose she said, 'All right. Let's run for it.' If it was just his fun they would get so far, to the railway station perhaps, and then just as he walked up to buy the tickets he would turn back with a silly, bright smile on his face and confess he was having her on. What would the implications be? That she had confessed her readiness to go off with a man she was not even engaged to. What would he think

4

of her? No, he could not possibly have run the risk of exposing her to such a humiliation. He was serious about eloping and she did not understand why. Common he might be, but he was not evil and she could not believe he intended to ruin her. She was bewildered.

Whenever she ate a tomato in the years to come that bewilderment flickered again, because on that trip to Weston she had tasted one for the first time. Mr White bought three at a penny each from a shop on the front and they went to sit on the sea-wall to eat them. Hannah had expected the fruity sweetness of a plum and was unprepared for the special ripe tomato flavour that was not sweet enough for her taste. The juice and seeds spurted out when she took a bite, just missing her long grey skirt, so she sucked the tomato cautiously and ever afterwards the taste brought back the enormous level sands of Weston, the two islands anchored out in the sleek, brown Channel and even a touch of the anxious excitement which had been thrown up by Charles's behaviour. Tomatoes were fruit for adults and she could well understand why they were sometimes called love apples and were once thought to be poisonous. Their flavour reminded her of the innocence of that Weston trip and quickened her awareness of the complications, of womanhood and motherhood, that had taken its place.

Hannah sang in the chapel choir and on most Sundays Charles White, in their courting days, would sit among the body of worshippers looking up at her, trying to catch her eye, grimacing, opening and shutting his eyes explosively (you'd have heard the pluck if it hadn't been for the singing and preaching), trying to make her laugh.

The Tabernacle Baptist Chapel was enormous and impressive, particularly on a winter evening when to enter from the darkness was to come into a vast, brilliantly lit cave with an organ and its silver-grey pipes (like the fluted goffering she did in her dressmaking) occupying most of one end. The choir, sixty strong – the men in their whiskers, Sunday best and high, stiff throat-choking white collars, the women in dark gowns often with bosoms covered by winking sequins – sat in a kind of raised amphitheatre behind and around this organ. Mr Powell, the organist, sang and also conducted with one hand as he played. All centred on the desk where the Reverend David Llewellyn stood in his frock-coat and clerical collar to enthuse the congregation, as many as 500 of them seated in rows under gas chandeliers that popped and hissed when he paused for dramatic effect. Among all these faces, turned up like flowers to the sun, their minister, was Charles Havelock White's, 24 years of age, sitting in the third row back, right-hand section as seen by Hannah; an intelligent face, she thought, with a high forehead and crimped, fair hair parted in the middle, like the shavings she had seen curl up from his plane when she had watched him in the workshop, where the air was nutty with the smell of fresh sawdust. He opened his mouth wide and square to sing hymns (he had a sweet but wobbly tenor voice), seeming to draw on more oxygen than the rest of the congregation were enjoying. Just to look down at him was to get the spicy whiff of that sawdust again.

Even so, she was apprehensive as to what his religious beliefs really were. On their walks he sometimes spoke of God and Jesus in a familiar sort of way, as though he had known both of them back in Gloucestershire. It was a vulgar superstition that God was an old man who lived in the sky; he said this in a way that assumed she thought so too. But if God was not an old man in the sky, who was he? She was afraid to ask but felt on the edge of an abyss.

Charles was very taken by an account given, quite in passing, by Mr Llewellyn in the course of one of his sermons. It seemed that in the time of the Emperor Tiberius a ship in passage from Alexandria to Italy passed close to an island. The pilot of the ship was a certain Thamus. A mysterious voice was heard from the land calling Thamus by his name and telling him to pass on the news that 'Great Pan was dead'. There were those, Mr Llewellyn said, who thought this an acknowledgement by the pagan world of Christ's victory. A funny way to make it, Charles said. 'But you can just imagine it, 'Annah. This ship on the dark sea and a voice out of the trees. Knowing the pilot's name was a good touch. Course it doesn't mean anything really, it's just a story.'

Then there were the books and all that reading. The first time he told her he had not been to the workshop for three days but stayed in his digs reading books from the library, she was really brought up short and said, 'But what did Mr Minsky say about that?' Minsky was the builder who employed Charles. Hannah now learned that Mr Minsky was surprisingly tolerant of Charles's absenteeism, particularly when trade was slack, and even lent him books of Russian works in English translation. German books too. Not French – Charles looked these out for himself.

'What do you read?' Hannah asked, standing very upright, holding her reticule tightly. 'Not novels! You don't mean to say you read French novels! You don't mean you stay away from work and read things like that? Say you *don't*. Charles!'

'But of course I do, 'Annah. Mind you, I don't know any foreign language so what I read 'as to be translated. But yes, I've read Paul de Kock. But what I read mostly is history and science and political economy and philosophy and things like that. You've got to understand the world. You think I'm common. Yes, I *am* common. I'm ignorant, too. I left school when I was ten because the inspector came and found I could read already. That was enough for him. It was enough for my mum and dad, too, who got charity money to buy my tools so I could go apprentice. Two brothers and a sister, one sister died. As they looked at it, you just 'ad to get a trade and fast.'

'Reading foreign books won't get you a living. My Uncle Jim read novels and Mam said it led from one thing to another. He lived up in the valleys. Keeping racing dogs, whippets and exercising them on a Sunday morning over the mountain when he ought to have been in chapel. And drink. You can guess what that led to.'

'I'm not that sort, 'Annah. You know what my folk were?'

'I don't see what that's got to do with it.'

'Peasants. You can't get no more common 'an that. I remember my old granfer an' as a young 'un 'e 'ad 'is own bit of land 'ere and there in the parish and grazing rights on the common. And wood-gathering rights. You know what? They took it away from the ol' feller under an act of Parliament and he was lucky to get work as a cowman. They took away liberty.'

Hannah brushed all this aside. 'But you're working for Mr Minsky.'

'All you can think of is me sitting down doing nothing. Course I'm working for Minsky, but it's only books can tell me why I'm working for 'im and not in a Cotsal cottage salt-curing my own pigmeat. So I'm not doing nothing. I'm thinking. I got to read and think. It's drink to me. Your Uncle Jim went to the pub and I go to the bookstall.'

'You wouldn't want to be a labourer, then?'

'No, it's out in all weathers, being a labourer,' said Charles. 'I'm an intellectual.'

'What's that?'

7

'It's what Mr Minsky says I am. 'E says I'm no peasant. I'm a deprived intellectual. His way of 'inting I'm not much of a chippie, I reckon.'

*The Penarth Times* ignored Hannah for years, except to print for payment the announcement of her engagement and then, after an interval, her wedding which, however, was reported free of charge, including the information that the honeymoon would be spent 'somewhere on the north coast of Devon' which everyone knew to be Ilfracombe; that was where all honeymooners went. Then came the occasion when 'Talk of the Town' wanted to know, 'What did the fortune teller say that caused the lady in grey to walk back along the pier with the hint of tears in her eyes?'

Hannah's first thought was that Madame Isis had earned herself a shilling, but she abandoned the idea. Who would trust her discretion if Madame Isis was known to be reporting to the press? Bad for trade. So it must have been some alert nosey-parker out for a stroll that windy, wet morning when Hannah impulsively presented herself at the fortune-teller's booth in the expectation that no one would be about to observe her because of the weather. Come to think of it, there had been a number of men in leather-belted overcoats or oilskins fishing from the pier for dabs and flounders, so it might well have been one of them. A close observer, whoever he was, because he was quite right – there was more than a hint of tears, and it was not brought on by the wind either.

For some time Hannah had been worried that she might not be a proper woman. Madame Isis had touched the swelling at the base of her left thumb. 'That's the mound of Venus, my lady, but you 'an't got one. So you 'an't got a passionate nature, just the opposite. It's the hand of a nun. Oh, you'll hold your husband, all right. See, there's the strong nick quarter way up the life-line, but children's a different matter. The nicks aren't clear. You're very cold, my dear, which is a fine thing in itself but I wish you a man with enough blood for both of you in his veins.' Which Hannah feared might mean she was not a full woman and, when she was married, it would turn out that – like Sarah in the Bible – she was barren.

That is how it turned out. After three years she and Charles had a heart-to-heart with the result that they both began eating oysters. Expensive and revolting. Charles would prise an oyster

8

out of its shell while Hannah held her nose and opened her mouth. He would pop the oyster in, hold her lips together and tickle her throat as though she were a cat being encouraged to swallow a pill. He took his own oysters more manfully. By the time they realized the oysters were not doing what was wanted, Hannah and Charles had taken a liking to them; with a dash of vinegar and red pepper, they were appetizing. Literally. The oysters made them hungry, but they cost the earth. So the Whites turned to the local mussels (though they had to be cooked and seemed less likely to be procreative as a result) and cockles. From Minehead across the Channel came edible snails which they experimented with and found them chewy, not to say rubbery, and tasting of cabbage.

Hannah's mother made a purée of mistletoe berries one Christmas and Hannah was ill as a result of eating it. Both Mrs Jones and Charles took the vomiting as a good sign. A potion made from bladderwrack seaweed was no more effective. Laver bread was brought from Briton Ferry, but to no effect, though in the nature of things it took time to test the efficacy of these womb quickeners. Their experimenting was quite unscientific because the Whites didn't take them one at a time. They would be eating mashed banana laced with linseed oil, herring roe and marinated conger eel all within the week, and if one of them did the trick there would be no way of knowing which it was. That would have been important for future reference, as Mrs Jones said.

It was about this time that Hannah confessed to her cousin Olive that when they had gone on that famous cross-Channel outing to Weston Charles had asked her to run away with him.

'He never!' said Olive. From being rather a suety girl she had become a pretty, not to say twitteringly feminine or even flirtatious young woman. No doubt this was due in part to being trained by the Singer Sewing Machine Company to sell their products, which involved a course in dressmaking in Cardiff. She made her own dresses. Saucy, Hannah thought them, in light greys and pale blues with sleeves in the summer so thin and gauzy that her bare arms could be detected. She cut the skirts tight at the back to draw attention to the rear movement as she walked. What is more, she made sure her ankles would not only be visible but remarked on because she managed to find outrageously coloured stockings, bright blue, or even pink. Hannah assumed she bought white stockings and dyed them. It was Olive's belief that Hannah was childless because there was not enough passion in their marriage.

'*He never*!' Olive giggled and flashed her eyes in a way which Hannah thought, had she been a man, she would have found irresistible. 'You should have, Hannah. You'd have been pregnant within the month, take my word for it. You and Charles would have struck the right kind of sparks. But marriage damps everything down, don't it? I sometimes think I'd like to be carried off by a foreigner.'

'A black man!' Hannah was horrified by Olive's shamelessness.

'Of course not. I mean a French count, or even an Italian. I want to be worshipped and spoiled. I'm not like you, Hannah. I've got a hot nature.' She looked at Hannah with an expression on her face that showed she, even she, was appalled by what she was now going to propose. 'I think you ought to get Charles to surprise you. Say if he went away and you didn't know how long for and you found this strange man in your bedroom. See? It might be Charles and it might not be. He wouldn't say anything, he wouldn't smell like Charles. Oh, wouldn't it be *exciting*, Hannah?'

'I couldn't do anything like that.'

'Well, somehow you've got to strike real fire, you two, and I don't see anyone getting sparks out of oysters and mussels no matter how you hit 'em or with what.'

Hannah and Charles persisted in their diet and went on bicycle rides in the lanes round Dinas Powis, hoping the exercise would help.

All this had to be kept from Hannah's father, who was a chapel elder and a stationmaster to boot – true, only of Cogan, a minor station but a genuine junction to which Mr Jones rode on his bicycle every morning, feeling guilty that he was not taking the train from Penarth, the Cardiff line. The bicycle was quicker. He had to be told when Hannah and Charles decided to go to the Reverend David Llewellyn so that they could pray together. He turned a pink that made his moustache all the whiter. But he had to agree there were scriptural precedents. He also said, 'What about seeing Dr Brownlow?'

'Men can be sterile too,' said Mrs Jones coldly, but nobody took any notice of her. 'Everything is pinned on women.'

Dr Brownlow examined Hannah and said that she was a perfectly healthy female and there was no reason why she should not have children. Be patient. He agreed with Hannah's father about scriptural precedents. Doubtless, what Mr Jones had in mind was the Biblical Sarah who did not conceive until she was ninety years of age. And Abraham, her husband, was a hundred. The figures, said Dr Brownlow, had to be interpreted. In the first place, the ancient Hebrew year was made up not of twelve solar months but of thirteen lunar months. So Sarah was not ninety by modern standards. She was only about eighty-three or four. Then divide by three and see what happens. You get 28 – which is a good age for an oriental woman. One had to allow for the oriental love of hyperbole. All it meant was that Abraham and Sarah were no chicks. Hannah, he pointed out, was the same age as the Biblical Sarah. So, God's intervention apart, the moral for the Whites was to be ardent. He also advised Hannah to take Scott's Emulsion regularly – a creamy substance made from the liver of the cod, a fish that laid millions of eggs. Hannah took it, but still nothing happened. Charles took it too.

Frankly, Charles did not believe in magic, whether induced by the eating of oysters or by prayers with the minister, and he decided the time had come to stop playing games. If he could not make Hannah pregnant, so be it. But what he could do was take the great step of securing a guarantee from the philanthropic Minsky, which the bank manager accepted, so providing the financial basis for setting up in business of his own: Charles White, Builder and General Maintenance. All work guaranteed, he announced in the *Penarth Times*. Commitments undertaken. (Whatever that meant.) Prompt and courteous attention given to even the smallest commission. And to the largest? Unequalled professionalism!

He was lucky. South Wales was into an industrial boom just then. All the world wanted its steam coal. The low-lying, tall stacked colliers slipped out of Newport and Cardiff and Barry Dock and Swansea into the prevailing westerlies. Huge new steam-cranes discharged iron ore from Spain, the colour of dried apricots, into open railway trucks that clanked away to the steel-works. Banks opened up new branches, shipping companies built bigger offices, import and export firms took on extra staff.

Ambitious young men like Charles were drawn in from the nearer English counties not to work in the mines (that was an earlier generation) but to work in offices or as tradesmen. They wanted houses to rent or lease and the big business men, the mine-owners and the landed proprietors (like the

11

trustees of the Plymouth estate in Penarth) had the capital to build them.

Charles was sub-contracted to build a row of terrace houses behind the station; then another row of houses. He had been working out of Minsky's yard, but now he was able to rent part of a bankrupt brewery out beyond the allotments and set up his own yard with a couple of horses and two one-time brewery drays for transporting house bricks and scaffolding. He now had eight men on the regular payroll, bricklayers, carpenters and labourers; as many more – plumbers, painters and decorators – he hired casually as needed. And he had a foreman whose name was Chris. He and Hannah could move out of their two-up two-down house with an outside privy in Plassey Street to a double-fronted three-storey house in Arcot Street which had once housed a circulating library. And, as there was plenty of room, Hannah hired a servant girl.

Polly Mahoney was eighteen, with blue-grey eyes so wide open she seemed just amazed at everything, and all the time; a big girl with round cheeks and a red dab in both of them like top-quality strawberries. With her fair, yellowish hair and jerky way of walking, all knees and elbows, she looked as though she had modelled herself on one of those clockwork German dolls. She radiated good humour and confidence. Whatever happened she would keep on marching, shoulders back – her shoes steel-tipped on toes and heels to make them last longer, clicking on the cobbles of life, and never in the least bit sorry for herself.

Her father had been an Irish labourer who worked on the construction of Barry Docks. One dark night he walked out of the pub and over the quayside into eighteen feet of water where he drowned. 'It gave a great deal of satisfaction,' said Polly, 'especially to my Mam. Say what you like about strong drink, but there's times it's a blessing. If the ole man 'adn't been blind drunk and stepped over the edge, 'd 've gone 'ome as usual and battered 'er. Father Groat said 'e was sure the ole man's past life flashed before him and 'e repented of all his sins so 'e could go to 'is Maker clean, but I'm not so sure of that myself and anyway it was good riddance. I never went to Mass after what Father Groat said.'

Polly worked in a haberdasher's, then as a live-in servant in one of the Plymouth Road big houses. But when her Mam took ill she took a job at the cash desk in a men's outfitters and ship chandlers

12

in Barry, pulling handles to send capsules containing receipts and change along overhead wires to all the counters in the store. She loved this. But the main reason she worked there was because it allowed her to live at home and look after her Mam. When Mam died (of consumption) the landlord wouldn't have Polly as a sitting tenant, so the furniture went to Polly's sister who had made a grand marriage to a Bristol Channel pilot, and lived on Christchurch Hill in Newport. Polly had to find another live-in place until she found a Bristol Channel pilot of her own or, if that was too much to hope for, a tally-clerk would do.

Polly loved touching people – just a natural, instinctive way of behaving so far as she was concerned. To say anything she would come up close, look at you with those great wide eyes and touch you on the arm or the chest or even, if it was Hannah she was talking to, gently on the cheek. She became so much a part of the family and there was such natural, unselfconscious warmth between the two of them that they would sometimes stand talking with an arm round the other's waist.

She would touch Charles, too, and from touching it grew to tickling and general fooling around which not only Polly and Charles but Hannah also thought good fun. Charles reported that Carlyle had opined in one of his books that we touch heaven when we lay our hands on a human body. To this Charles added something of his own. Your life was what you had, it was all you could be sure of – that and knowing one day you would die – so enjoy what you have, be happy, stick a flower in your cap. Polly was an orphan. For all her high spirits she hadn't a relation in all the world but this hoity-toity sister on Christchurch Hill who had collared all the furniture. So it was God's providence they were all so happy together and laughing in what was once the town circulating library.

Charles bought a second-hand harmonium. He had a talent for music. Just playing by ear he could knock out any tune, but what mostly came out was not 'Billy Boy' or an old sea shanty (which was what he really liked) but chapel hymns and 'I know that my Redeemer liveth' from Messiah. In bitter winter there were cosy Penarth evenings when there were little black tabs on the bars of the grate, trembling against the red and yellow coals. Just bits of papery carbon, but each one of them signified the coming of a stranger into the house; a tally-clerk, Polly surmised. There were ways of seeing his face. Put a piece of crumpled paper on the red coals and, when it had burned out and was black, red sparks would run about like ants. Finally they would come together in a way that looked just like a face; but the face came and went so quickly that it was difficult to be sure you would recognize it again.

Then touching and tickling and cuddling. They all had flowers in their caps and such fun that Hannah's obsession (for that is what it had become) with not having a baby was overlaid by this sensual gaiety. Late one evening, in a frenzy, she took off her clothes and walked about the house naked as though, Charles thought, she was inviting a pagan god to descend and make love. He could quite see her radiance and that teasing smile successfully luring some deity down from the sky, and the very thought made him so jealous that he prepared to anticipate the visitor by kicking off his slippers and removing his jacket. Polly became hysterically excited and began tearing off her own clothes. Before his incredulous eyes the two women began to grapple until Charles could no longer restrain himself and removed as much clothing as he had time for before making his advance.

By now Hannah and Polly were wrestling and knocking over chairs and small tables before finally collapsing to the floor in a wild shriek. How irresistible they looked as they lay in each other's arms! Polly turned her head to stare wide-eyed at him, the tip of her tongue just showing like an April bud on a rose-bush. How good the world was ! How generous with its gifts ! How, with two such women to console him, could he ever be unhappy? There was no need of a pagan god; he was the god himself. No, he was not a god. He was mad with ecstasy to the point where he thought he could take them both, but it was Polly who turned her body to receive him. Hannah's hand was on his back, gently massaging as though to take part herself in the act of loving. That night they slept in the same bed and for many nights. For weeks there was innocence. Then Hannah, all solicitous, made Polly stay in bed in the morning while she blacked the grate and oven herself.

'Charles,' she said, 'Polly's going to have a baby. I wish it was me, but it's the next best thing.'

When Charles was sure by the size of her belly that he had done the trick, he took Hannah and Polly off to watch the Royal Welch Fusiliers receive the Freedom of the City of Cardiff, marching along St Mary Street behind the regimental band with colours flying, bare bayonets, scarlet tunics with blue collars and cuffs, sealskin caps and black tapes behind the collars like pigtails.

'It will be a boy,' Charles said, 'and a soldier. Look at those men, Polly. Drink it in. It's great. The drums and the band, take everything you see into your womb because that's what you've got to 'ave for the military influence. It's the greatest thing in life, war and the soldier's life. Nothing good or great in this world comes from anything but war. All these are noble men in a noble profession. Polly, this is what your son will be, and 'Annah's son.' He was so excited and full of laughter, so roused by the band, the drums and the marching men, in such a shiny wet sweat of pleasure that he was ready to talk any kind of nonsense. But when he had brought it out he wasn't so sure everything he said *was* nonsense. 'And *my* son,' he added as an afterthought.

'He'll be a Channel pilot,' said Polly.

'Battles are terrible,' declared Hannah. 'All those darkies and that charging and slashing.'

Charles seemed lifted on some invisible cloud. 'Ruskin said war was necessary for a nation to be great, that it brought out the best. No wiser men than Ruskin and Carlyle.'

This was wasted on Hannah and Polly, who had heard of neither of these sages. They tried to keep up with the soldiers by walking behind the crowds, but both of them had to gather up their skirts and trot. The noise and dust in the bright sunshine reinforced what Charles had said. This parading of brave men under bayonets lifted the heart to such a degree that you just knew there was nothing grander, not even storms of thunder and lightning.

You might think that some aspect of life in the White household would be the subject of query in 'Talk of the Town', but that would be to mistake the readership for which the *Penarth Times* catered. They could take sly jokes provided it was understood that everyone referred to was totally respectable and innocent of even imagining a naughtiness. Hannah, who had been agitated by the question about her pre-marital trip to Weston-super-Mare with Charles and her cousin Olive, was quite easy in her mind over Polly's pregnancy. If anyone had been presumptuous enough to send in some such query as 'What young lady in domestic service is letting her stays out and lies in bed while her mistress does all the work?', the handwriting would have disappeared under

15

the incredulous editor's eyes like lines of insects under snow: it was so unacceptable the question became a non-question. It did not exist. Hannah would not have put it that way but she was well aware that, if at all possible, the disagreeable should not be recognized.

# 2

Shortly before her confinement Polly declared she was a ruined woman (belatedly, most people would have thought), took herself off to the sister on Christchurch Hill and called for a priest. Neither Hannah nor Charles could understand this backsliding and felt intolerably deceived by her. Perhaps she had been enticed away by the Pope, for although Polly had shown no signs of relapsing, the priests were cunning beyond belief. What if one of them had accosted her in the street?

'Ruined?' said Charles. 'Only in her own mind, not in yours or mine, 'Annah. I really thought she was a superior sort of young woman, not 'aving low thoughts. I'm sadly disappointed. No, it's more than that! Did she say she *was* a ruined woman? Or did she say she'd *been* ruined?'

'Just as she was going out of the door with her bags she said it, whatever it was. Just ruined, I think.'

'*Been* ruined. If she said that it would have been insulting. If it was just 'ruined' you'd best go and fetch her back, 'Annah.'

Polly's sister was a big, pale lady in what looked like seagoing attire, a dark blue skirt and blouse with wavy blue lines running down her broad white collar. As soon as Hannah explained who she was and why she had come Mrs Smorfitt (for that was her name) refused to open the door any further. 'She won't see anyone but Father Gillespie: You're a bad woman, Mrs White. It wouldn't have been so wicked if you'd been Mormons and acted out of some religious belief, no matter how misguided, but you're just Baptists, as I understand it, and you think you can read the Jews' scriptures for yourself. You read them by the light of ignorance. The Devil can quote scripture, they say, to 'is own advantage. What's Abraham and Sarah to do with it? I'm glad to say I knew nothing about those two until Polly told me. Your old man'll have to pay for this in 'ard cash. Father Gillespie is going to 'elp 'er fill out the affliction order form.'

Hannah begged to see Polly.

17

'She won't see you, missis.' Mrs Smorfitt would have shut the door, but Hannah managed to hand over a little wash-leather bag contining five sovereigns.

'Say it's from Mr and Mrs White with their kind regards.'

This was the time when the miners demanded an end to the way their pay was linked to the price of coal and the owners locked them out, so families began to starve. Hannah had relations up in the valleys. Uncle Ted was a face-worker with a wife and three kids to support, and she took the train up to Abercam with two baskets of food for them: faggots and dried peas which could be boiled up, shin beef for making soup, condensed milk, suet, flour and Golden Syrup for a pudding. Hannah believed that in a crisis people should have not only the necessities of life but the sweetness too. She was surprised, though, when Auntie Meg said they didn't want charity – not unless they could be sure Hannah and her husband were on their side in the struggle against the coal-owners.

Hannah did not know what to say. Uncle Ted and his family were just relations who needed food, that was all that mattered. She had not asked Charles whose side he was on, the miners or the coal-owners, and she did not care to ask him now that he was so inflamed by the way Polly had deserted them.

'They locked the men out, didn't they?' said Hannah. 'It isn't as though the men went on strike.' She knew Charles was against unions and strikes but was pretty sure, now she came to think of it, that he would be against the coal-owners starving the men into giving in. Uncle Ted was up on the mountain, exercising his dog probably or sitting with a lot of other men gambling with cards, look-out men posted to shout if the police showed up because gambling was against the law. Anyway, he was not there to jolly Aunt Meg. She was political, like a man, and believed the Liberals were as bad as the Conservative coal-owners; the miners wanted their own leaders, men of their own class and outlook, who would set them marching on places like Newport, Cardiff and especially Penarth where there was a yacht club, nobody did any real work and everybody was stuck-up and two-faced. Aunt Meg was a small, quick, birdlike woman whose hands were always on the go, sweeping up imaginary crumbs or pushing out with the backs of her hands – as it might be to the starving – imaginary crusts of bread; a real, brown-eyed Welshwoman who had been born in the north somewhere and sang rather than spoke her English.

18

'When you've had a baby of your own, Hannah, you'll understand better the realities of life. But there are some as choose to
be selfish.' This with a look at Hannah's small grey outfit, with
its wide silvery lapels. She would not even let her into the little
terrace house and Hannah emptied the contents of her basket
on the doorstep (she was not going to leave the basket as well)
under Aunt Meg's grim but – but now that she could see just
what Hannah had brought – unprotesting scrutiny.

'That's the second door you've had shut in your face in a matter
of days,' said Charles when she reported. 'They're funny times we
live in, 'Annah, you know that? When every man's hand will be
turned against 'is neighbour. But there are more important things
to think about.'

So anguished was he by Polly's behaviour that he immersed
himself in a bout of really hard reading; Carlyle's *French Revolution*
as it happens, which he had picked up second-hand in Cardiff
market in two volumes, red covers, two closely printed columns
on each page, each volume costing a shilling. Quite a coincidence
this, he said, because it had a bearing on the industrial turmoil in
the valleys. Up there men and women, some of them, were bent
on revolution and Hannah must not go there again with baskets
of food. Send postal orders. There was food in the shops if there
was only money to buy it; and in that way Hannah would not be
exposed to insult. But for the time being his main commitment
was to reading, to sitting in his basketwork chair which creaked
with every breath he took, stupefying himself day after day with
Carlylean rhetoric. He did not go to the yard and Hannah was
given instructions to turn away Chris the foreman, telling him to
get on with the job as best he thought fit.

'But I've got to say why? You're not ill, so I can't say that.'

'Say I'm reading,' said Charles and plunged into an account of
Louis XV on his death-bed – 'Yes, poor Louis, Death has found thee
. . . he is here at thy very life-breath, and will extinguish it' – which
was as dramatic and awe-inspiring as anything he had heard on a
Sunday from the Reverend David Llewellyn. Charles was glad to
learn that Louis XV would not allow Death to be spoken of in his
presence, and that he avoided the sight of churchyards. Ever
since he had seen his own father's coffin lowered into a black
slot in a snowy churchyard Charles had been like that too, and it
comforted him to think he was not alone. Louis was a monarch
and advised by the most learned men whereas Charles had no

19

such advantages, but there they both were, averting their eyes and minds together. If anyone asked Charles (as his father had from time to time) why he had his nose always stuck into some book, he said 'Reading puts you in touch. And takes you out of yourself.'

During his worst bouts of reading (and this was one of them) he would read not one book at a time but – because the mixture excited him – two. After a couple of hours with *The French Revolution* he would turn to *The Voyage of the Beagle*. And back again. And so on.

Darwin was a hero too, because whereas Carlyle took a hold on Charles's emotions Darwin took a hold on his mind. When Darwin said there were sea-shells high in South American mountains (so they must have been under the sea once), or that a certain kind of ant enslaved colonies made up of another kind of ant, Charles felt he was being given glimpses of the real and incontrovertible. It was a truth about all animal creation, mankind included. Carlyle said the French peasants were slaves, but the claim did not strike home as Darwin's words did. Not that Charles wanted to choose between them. Carlyle was a raving and wonderfully articulate preacher; Darwin was a scientist who displayed his evidence in lucid prose and Charles wanted both of them.

For long periods Charles was so lost in his reading that he scarcely knew whether Hannah was in the house or not. He even went out reading on his bicycle, with the book in his left hand while he held the handlebars with his right. As Hannah refused to send postal orders to Uncle Ted and his family – it would give an impression that she was keeping an account and one day would produce it – she filled two more baskets with provisions and set off. First she took the local train into Cardiff and walked the short distance to the main-line station where she caught the train for Newport. On arriving she ought to have walked back along the platform to the bay where the three-carriage train was waiting to be pulled up the Western Valley by a chubby little green engine with a tall chimney. Instead, her mind being so much on Charles and his mad reading and on Polly, whose baby must now be due, she walked out of Newport station into the Commercial Road and took the omnibus to Christchurch Hill. The last hundred yards were too steep for the horses and Hannah had to walk. Not until she was outside Mrs Smorfitt's house did she realize she should not be there at all but on her way to Abercarn. She had been in a dream, and now that she had awakened she saw all the curtains in Mrs Smorfitt's house were drawn.

The significance of this did not strike her. It seemed all of a piece, this blank expression on the house with its curtained windows and the way Mrs Smorfitt had turned her away. Hannah was not going to be rejected for a second time. She had mysteriously been led to this house for some good reason and although the faggots, the dried peas, the suet and the rest were not the right nourishment for a girl about to give birth, they would keep and come in useful afterwards. She put the basket on the step, rapped the knocker and shot across the street to a point where she could see the door but pop out of sight as soon as it was opened.

It did not open and after five minutes or so waiting, Hannah abandoned the basket and walked all the way into Newport where she bought a £1 postal order and sent it off to Uncle Ted.

Back in Penarth some days later, she went to her own front door in response to a loud knocking and found an unmistakably Roman Catholic priest standing there in his funny hat, cassock and big black boots. For Hannah the sight was so unexpected and so menacing that she gave a cry which was not exactly a scream – it was too choked, she felt just as though this priest had taken her by the throat – but sufficiently loud and dramatic to shake Charles out of his book-induced stupor and bring him bustling into the hall where he was no less amazed than Hannah had been to see – in all his painted, posturing, incense-smelling, bell-tinkling arrogance – this Papist seeking admission to his house.

In reality Father Gillespie was nothing like that at all – in spite of his similarity to Henry VIII – but a mild man, firm though, with a square face and folds of fat under each corner of his jaw. To Charles, as soon as he saw the funny hat and understood its significance, the priest was a figure straight out of eighteenth-century France, fresh from elevating a wafer at the old King's deathbed in the Palace of Versailles. And had he been at their house before? Was this the emissary of the Whore of Babylon who had revealed himself to Polly when she opened the door to him one fine morning, only to be spirited away out of this loving home to the flinty care of her sister on Christchurch Hill?

'Mr and Mrs White?' said the cleric, peering short-sightedly at each of them in turn. 'Am I correct? Then this must be the house where poor Polly lived. I am Father Gillespie, come over from Newport.'

*Poor* Polly! 'We want her back, that's all.'

Father Gillespie looked at them in astonishment. 'You want her back? Has her sister not written to you?'

'No.'

'So you have had no news at all?'

'Mrs Smorfitt turned me away,' said Hannah, 'Has she sent you? What news is there? Has Polly had her baby?'

'Yes,' said Father Gillespie, 'and died to give it life.'

Hannah shrieked and Charles took a step towards the priest as though to grapple with him.

'I'm truly sorry to be the bearer of such news. You admit paternity? Under the Bastardy Act you are required to maintain the boy unless you deny and can prove you are not the father. In the circumstances, I trust there will be no wrangle.'

'Boy?'

'I baptized him the same day. I am truly sorry that Mrs Smorfitt has not been in communication, but she is shocked and upset. We are all shocked. I can see you are. It all happened so quickly.'

It was not the kind of conversation the Whites wished to conduct at their own front door with lace curtains twitching in windows opposite and passers-by slowing their pace and even stopping to gape. So, feeling that in some strange way Father Gillespie was arresting them without a proper search warrant, they invited him in and shut the door firmly behind him. They went into the big room which served both as sitting room and dining room, where the harmonium was, and Polly had sat watching strangers in the fire. Hannah began to cry and then Charles cried in a dry sort of way, no tears coming though he worked at his eyes with tightly clenched fists to squeeze out a few. But he howled like a lost dog until Father Gillespie put a hand on his shoulder. Charles shook it off and turned an enraged red face on the priest. 'We want Polly. We love 'er.'

Hannah sobbed and just let the tears run down her cheeks. 'Polly was one of us. We were all so close. She wasn't like a servant at all, just one of the family.'

'So!' Father Gillespie used this word frequently. It was his way of acknowledging a statement but giving notice that he did not accept it. 'She put herself in God's hands at the last and made a good death.'

'When?' Charles demanded.

'Let me see. In the middle of last week – the Wednesday.'

'That's nine days ago. So the funeral's been and gone.'

'In St Faith's churchyard at Malpas.'

'Why weren't we told? 'Annah and me's got rights.'

'The father of an illegitimate child has no rights.' Father Gillespie gave the impression he was speaking out of a wealth of experience. 'He has a legally enforceable duty to provide maintenance, and that's all.' Since he was obviously not going to be invited to take a seat Father Gillespie, who had rheumaticky knees, placed himself on the horsechair sofa. 'This is not how I expected matters to turn out. Mrs Smorfitt ought to have been in touch. Naturally I assumed she had, but she is her own woman. She was very loving to her sister. Quite bowled over by her misfortune. Quite. Shamed by it, in fact. *Shrivelled* was the word she used. But I explained that the poor girl had been more sinned against than sinning.' All this quietly and gently, as though he was telling a bedtime story.

'Sin?'

'That's all in the past. Her sins have been forgiven.'

'There is no sin,' said Charles. 'I reject this. We lived like roses in purity and innocence, didn't we, 'Annah? There was no wickedness in our thoughts at all.'

'So! Then why did Polly run away from you?'

'Because some bloody priest persuaded her.'

'That is not what she told me. She said her eyes had been opened by the Blessed Virgin Mary herself, who appeared to her in a dream and said she was ruined. The Blessed Virgin said she must return to the Church and repent. That brings me to another point of substance. The child has been baptized into the Roman Catholic Church and his soul, like his mother's, has been purified. He must have a Roman Catholic upbringing, which means by Mrs Smorfitt, his aunt. Or if for some reason she does not see her way to make this possible, in the Orphanage of the Sacred Heart at St Briavel's.'

'He is our child,' Hannah said fiercely. 'Isn't he, Charles? He will be brought up by us, flesh of our flesh, blood of our blood, and by nobody else.'

'So!' Father Gillespie looked up at her in amazement – for she and Charles were still standing. He had to remind himself that he had only recently – not more than ten years ago – arrived from Newcastle-upon-Tyne, and did not flatter himself he yet understood the local people down here in South Wales. If a Geordie fathered a bastard, his wife would take it badly; but

23

this woman seemed to have the morals of the farmyard. 'The child's name, by the way, is James. Why? He was born on the day of St James the Less. A big baby, nearly nine pounds and that was the main trouble, but the fever started too.'

'Oh, the suffering. How could your God let her suffer like that, terribly?'

The priest was worried that neither Charles nor Hannah would sit down amd made imploring gestures with his hands; he raised his eyebrows and smiled in what he thought was an ingratiating way. 'This is an uncomfortable meeting and I am not finding the right words. You are different from what I expected.'

'But you,' said Hannah, 'You, being an unmarried man, what do you know? You've no idea what goes through a woman's mind when she wants a baby and she can't get one.'

'I can see you're as sinful as your husband,' said Father Gillespie calmly.

Charles thought he could see which way matters were tending and, in spite of his anguish over Polly (which would intensify as the days went by and the numbness wore off), he spoke fiercely of his intentions.

'Nothing, nothing, nothing, not you or the Pope 'imself, not officialdom, or priests or - or principalities or powers - will shut us out from our son.' It was Carlyle's Biblical rhetoric still fermenting in his mind. Coming down to earth, he said, 'Certainly not Mrs Smorfitt.'

'So!' said Father Gillespie,

'If you thought we knew what had happened to Polly, why 've you come?'

'Money. Mrs Smorfitt would have nothing to do with money, being sensitive and highly strung and shamed as she was, poor woman. So I have here the hospital bill, the undertaker's account and my own little fee for presiding over the obsequies. Fifteen pounds, twelve shillings and sixpence all told. I'll take it in cash now if you will be so obliging.'

This was the beginning of a confused period when telegrams were sent and received, there was much hanging about in a solicitor's office, forms were filled in, torn up and new ones filled in again, even an appearance in a magistrate's court where Charles and Mrs Smorfitt met for the first time and where, as a consequence Mrs Smorfitt saw what likeness the infant James bore to Charles and realized the impossibility – no matter how satisfactory the financial arrangements – of rearing the child herself. She could not have constantly under her eyes the physiognomy of the man who had seduced her sister and brought about her death. As the years went by, the likeness would undoubtedly grow. Polly would not have wanted James to be surrendered to the virgin nuns of the Orphanage of the Sacred Heart. But what *would* she have wanted? It was at this point that Father Gillespie made a quite surprising revelation. In ordinary conversation, he asserted, not in confession, Polly had said she was quite willing to gift her baby to Mr and Mrs White, because she knew that in spite of everything they would love it as no one else could. And she herself would go to London and start a new life on the strictest religious principles as a chambermaid in a hotel. She did not foresee her death. Father Gillespie, on whose head Mrs Smorfitt had been pouring her doubts and anxieties, eventually told her what Polly had said and Mrs Smorfitt, looking grim, said, 'I always suspected there was more to Polly's story than what she told me.'

James, when he came from the lying-in ward to Christchurch Hill, was a restless and demanding baby who woke up Mrs Smorfitt and the Bristol Channel pilot every hour or so during the night. They were so worn out that Mr Smorfitt took to sleeping on his tugboat in the docks and Mrs Smorfitt, who was hand-feeding the child, made the mxture in the bottle that much stronger – ordinary creamy cow's milk to begin with, then Jersey full cream, then finally a patent baby food mixed with warm water and laced with the tiniest amount of brandy, this on the recommendation of a visiting midwife nurse who charged half-a-crown a visit and wore a white bonnet with streamers at the back. If this failed, she was advised to try a minute amount of opium, which in those days you could buy from the chemist. All this was to no avail, not even the opium, and Mrs Smorfitt being quite worn out – after all, she had her own children to look after – and thinking that medical science had been tested to its limits, began to believe there was a need for spiritual guidance and turned to Father Gillespie. Her suggestion that James was possessed by a troublesome demon was dismissed by Father Gillespie, although after he and Mrs Smorfitt had tried to pray beside the the cot while James lay there with a red and wrinkled face screaming like a trapped piglet the priest was tempted to wonder whether there was anything in Mrs Smorfitt's theory. To be honest he had little experience of very small babies, and he had no idea whether there was authority for believing the

25

never-ending squalling of an infant could be held as evidence of original sin. He blessed James three times in a week.

'This can't go on,' said Mrs Smorfitt. Her husband said she was damn right that it couldn't bloody well go on. So Mrs Smorfitt wrote to the Whites in Penarth and said it had been brought to her notice that Polly wished the baby to come to them. This could be arranged if Mrs White was prepared to collect the child, meet all the expenses Mrs Smorfitt had so far incurred and pay a handing-over fee of £10 to make it all legal and respectable. The total sum involved would be £25.14s.6d. In return for this Mrs Smorfitt would provide not only James but his birth certificate – which was complete in all particulars, including Polly's real name which was Mary, except for Mr White's Christian name which she had not known. So the registrar had written Mr White, builder and contractor of 21 Arcot Street, Penarth, which he said was all that was strictly necessary.

One hot Saturday afternoon the Whites arrived at Newport station with a basketwork cot, some bedding and a Gladstone bag. They took a cab all the smellier because the nag, head hanging, had been standing with it in the sun for hours. They trotted out past the old castle and over the swing bridge from which they could see the Usk shrunk to a stream of chocolate between the glistening flats and mud-banks exposed by the receding tide. Hannah wondered about throwing herself in. Hop out of the cab and throw herself over the rail and they would never get her back, she thought, but not seriously. Now that she and Charles were so near to taking possession of Polly's baby, Hannah was deeply anxious. Would she be able to look after it? She knew one end of a baby from another, but that was about all. At a time like this a young woman turned to her mother for guidance but relations between the Whites and Hannah's parents were cool, so cool that Mr and Mrs Jones knew nothing of Polly's pregnancy and would be astonished at the arrival of a baby in Arcot Street. She and Charles had not even discussed what story to tell them. Hannah panicked at the thought that she would soon be looking after a real live baby.

'He's a healthy child. Back to birth-weight already,' said Mrs Smorfitt. She was wearing her best going-out costume in sea-green with jet bead epaulettes – not only that but, although they were indoors, a black straw hat with imitation cherries, rather as though to her the occasion was no more than the church fête

26

where she was handing over a lottery prize, which happened on this occasion to be a human infant. The Bristol Channel pilot was not there and James, exceptionally, was fast asleep. Hannah and Charles saw him for the first time and they bent over the cot in controlled swoons. Yes, he was like Charles, the same distance between the eyes, the same little chin and, in fact, nothing of Polly at all. This saddened them, in a way, because they really did love Polly.

'That's it then, missis,' said Charles. He handed over twenty-five sovereigns, four half-crowns, two florins and a sixpenny piece, all of which Mrs Smorfitt immediately put in a tin-plated money-box which she locked with a key. 'A sad business, Polly going like that. We shall set up a stone. Welsh slate, we thought. To say: Polly Mahoney, dearest friend of Hannah and Charles White, mother of James. Something like that. When was Polly born?'

'June 25th 1877,' said Mrs Smorfitt. She spoke as little as possible, controlling her strong feelings. She wanted to spit at the Whites, but at the same time she wished only what was best for little James. 'We're Catholics. You know Polly would have wanted him brought up as a Catholic.'

'She was lapsed,' said Charles.

'If you don't bring him up as a Catholic, Father Gillespie will be on your doorstep. He'll haunt you. And Polly will haunt you too. To us Catholics, the spiritual world is the real world, and if the baby is not brought up as a proper Catholic you'll have your troubles. Do you want a receipt for the money?'

Relations between the Whites and Hannah's parents were cool because they had never taken to Charles. He spoke common Gloucestershire and took the Chapel services dryly, never warming to the sermon or singing with enthusiasm. They acknowledged it was to his credit that he had set up a business but now, as all could see, he was neglecting it. In spite of his neglect the business seemed to flourish, but how long could that last? 'Going bust' was an expression Mr Jones the stationmaster used from time to time though he himself, being an employee of the Railway Company, had taken the precaution of putting himself beyond the reach of the bankruptcy laws. One of his objections to Hannah's marriage was that Charles had not. Charles, he was astonished to learn from the *Penarth Times*, even read books when he was riding a bicycle.

The following entry had appeared in the 'Town Talk' column

of the *Penarth Times*. 'Which does one admire most, the love of literature or the velocipedic virtuosity of the gentleman who regularly reads a book as he bicycles about town?'

Many people in the town could have tipped off the *Times* about Charles's behaviour (the actual form of words was of course devised by one of those clever dicks in the office), but Charles took it into his head that Hannah's mother was responsible. 'Velocipedic virtuosity' would not have come naturally to a clerk in the office. She had been an uncertificated schoolteacher and in her time a great reader of the novels of Dickens. Charles thought her capable of writing the entry herself (which meant she received not 1/– but 2/– in payment) and, though he did not begrudge her the fun, did believe that going behind his back in this way showed she had a devious nature.

Hannah said her mother was not devious at all; she might be sly but she was not devious, and this difference of interpretation cast a slight shadow on the relationship between Hannah and Charles for all of the interval between high tea and Charles's evening stint on the harmonium, a period of at least an hour and a half. Hannah did not ask her mother whether she was responsible for this wounding entry in 'Town Talk'. The coolness made it the more difficult for her to tell her mother that she had taken possession of a small – no, rather large – baby boy, who stood in the same relationship to her and Charles as Ishmael did to Abraham and Sarah. Eventually they decided to tell Mrs Jones that they had adopted a baby, and this Hannah's mother believed until the moment she saw young James and realized what a resemblence he bore to Charles: the same widely separated eyes and long upper lip. She was embarrassed and fluffed up when, seeing how happy Hannah was, she subsided.

Charles was so amazed by Mrs Jones's quickness of perception and readiness to accept a convenient bit of make-believe that he thought he would take notes as Darwin did when observing the behaviour of insects and animals. Mrs Jones knew perfectly well that James was Charles's illegitimate son but it was in the interest of Hannah and, indeed, of all concerned (not forgetting Hannah's father, who could be imagined making off-stage groans of protest and outrage), that the fiction of adoption should be accepted and the disappearance of Polly put down to bettering herself in Birmingham or London. Charles thought that Mrs Jones could accept the unacceptable because, like most women of her class and generation, she did not think there was all that much pleasure in sex. If she had known what delicious fun it was, she would have been very angry indeed and thought Charles (and Hannah) very immoral. But her imagination was not fired by physical activities that took place below the level of the waist. There had been an irregular transaction, that's all. And like dust and minor refuse, irregularities could be brushed under the carpet.

'It's a good thing,' Mrs Jones would say to her small circle of friends, 'that people like Hannah and Charles are ready to bring up other people's children. Otherwise, who knows how the poor little things would suffer for no fault of their own? He seems intelligent, but it is a pity he's so ugly. Hannah seems happy with him, though. *That* is what matters.'

Up in the valleys Uncle Ted and the other miners were starved back to work, and that autumn a chip-basket of mountain whinberries and horse mushrooms arrived in Arcot Street. To show his appreciation of the food she had brought during the lock-out Uncle Ted spent a whole sunny day on the mountain (for the little widely-scattered and tiresome-to-pick tart blueberries) and on the lower pasture for the mushrooms – as big as dinner plates, rank-smelling and good for nothing but ketchup. But you could not buy the whinberries or horse mushrooms in the shops; hence the princely nature of the gift. Hannah thought the reason for her dizziness and nausea was the ketchup she had been in the habit of sprinkling over her scrambled egg. The nausea was a mushroom-tasting sort of experience. Her sickness began long after the ketchup was finished with, but she kept tasting the stuff, and every morning. She went to Dr Brownlow, carrying James wrapped up in a shawl and he – after certain mystifying tests which included looking into her eyes with the sun behind him – said he was sure she was pregnant but to be absolutely sure he would like a urine test which nurse would now arrange for. Two dates later he sent a note saying, with his compliments, that Mrs White was certainly pregnant and would she make a point of coming to see him in eight months' time?

Hannah and Charles were ecstatic. Hannah was sure it had something to do with the mushroom ketchup, but Charles said, 'No, no. It's young James there.'

'The baby? What do you mean?'

''E's like a sleepy pear, 'Annah. Know what I mean? Real ripe. And the way my Dad used to ripen hard green pears was to put a really sleepy one over against 'em. A *maller purr* is what 'e called it. *Maller* is sleepy. And that's what a sweet, ripe, maller, sleepy baby like our young Jimmy can do to a woman.'

Hannah began crying she was so happy.

'Polly would have been very 'appy too,' said Charles. 'We must go out to Malpas and tell 'er with a bunch of flowers.'

# 3

For Hannah, her own pregnancy brought home for the first time the enormity of their behaviour. They ought to have taken more thought of Polly's innocence and youth. Poor child! She was only eighteen and they had treated her as though she was as old as they were – nearer thirty than twenty – and, as the scriptures had it, she was a stranger within their gates. Barren women go mad. That is what Hannah had been, mad, and poor Charles had been driven mad too. Everybody in Penarth must be talking about the Whites.

When Hannah was three months pregnant the Whites, with baby James, went on a visit to Charles's widowed mother who lived in the Cotswolds, in Northleach, where they had a marvellous un-Penarth-like holiday. It was April. At Hannah's insistence they walked up out of the town on to the hills where primroses lit up under the hedges when the sun caught them, Hannah's buttoned boots and the bottom of Charles's trousers were whitened by the dusty lane and larks trilled out of the cloudless heights. Charles wanted her to sit and rest, but Hannah said she was not tired and in her condition exercise was important. They could go a little further. They could look back to see the great square tower of Northleach church apparently sinking into the earth as they walked away downhill.

'Can't we just stay here and not go back?' Hannah was quite serious about it. Charles laughed, but she said it again. 'Why *can't* we live here?'

Charles's mother was a tall stringy woman with hair hanging down over her eyes, her hands red from hot, soapy water, and wearing her dead husband's black boots. She did the cleaning at the grammar school, so she had her independence, though when she took Hannah up to show her the school she pointed out the Workhouse and said with a quiet cackle, showing her gums and her few remaining teeth, that that's where she'd finish up. She didn't care. She was religious, of Baptist persuasion, but had no

31

fixed ideas on what to believe and was ready to attend services in the rather grand parish church on such occasions as Queen Victoria's Diamond Jubilee, which seemed more natural there. 'What with the soldiers and their flags and trumpeters and all.'

A saying often on her lips was, 'The Lord will provide,' and as if to show how she gave Hannah and Charles the most extravagant teas on the two Sundays they were there with neighbours invited in. The men had tots of her own potato wine (to make them more agreeable, she said) and then there was tea from two brown pots which were repeatedly replenished from a great black kettle that steamed continually on the kitchener. There was buttered white bread, buttered brown bread, sultana bread, malt bread, pineapple chunks out of a tin with evaporated milk also out of a tin, sardines on toast, raspberry and blackcurrant jelly with custard, then scones with cream and dollops of strawberry jam. All this in a two-up, two-down terrace cottage in the High Street which was noisy with farm wagons, shouting boys on ponies and the grinding wheels of delivery vans, the baker's, the general carrier's and the like.

To Hannah it was very foreign, very strange, and she loved it.

'Charles,' she said, 'Can't we come and live here, please? I'm not happy in Penarth.'

'No future 'ere,' said Charles, 'You've got to go where the work is and where money's to be made. Tell you what. South Wales is like the Klondyke to me, but without the snow. We got to better ourselves. Another thing; seeing the old church 'ere makes me think. Per'aps we'd best give up the chapel.'

'Give up the chapel? But what would we do?'

'There's St Augustine's up on the 'ill. Even chapel people go to the churchyard there to be buried. Fine view over the Channel to Somerset. So why wait till we're dead?'

'I'm not leaving the Baptist Chapel,' declared Hannah.

'The Baptists don't baptize kids and I want our kid to be christened straight away, like James was – and I tell you what, I wouldn't mind asking Mr Minsky to be godfather.'

'You can't ask him. He's a Jew.'

'What's that got to do with it?' Charles hated to be caught out not knowing something, and he would not have confessed he did not know Minsky was a Jew. But secretly he was amazed. Jews existed, no doubt, and he thought well of them, but he had not come across one. None in the Cotswolds. Well, Minsky was a fine man and Charles was proud to call him a friend. Charles just did not like being so stupid that he hadn't guessed why Minsky had such a funny name. The moment Hannah said he was a Jew Charles knew she was right, but still he did not understand why Minsky couldn't be the kid's godfather.

'I'll speak to the old chap,' Charles said.

While they were out on their walks James was in his perambulator with its big wheels and tasselled canopy back in the cottage garden where his grandmother would go out and peer at him from time to time. She took no notice of his rages, not even so much as to rock the pram soothingly as Hannah had asked, but then she had not been given much information about this baby. She owed it to herself not to become too involved and asked no questions, not even when she was told Hannah was pregnant. Adopting a baby and then making your own baby was not the usual sequence of events, but if Charles and Hannah did not want to talk about it that was their affair. When it suited she could make her mind quite blank.

The nearest railway station was at Fosse Bridge six miles away, and when Charles and Hannah set out on their return journey as they had come – on foot with Charles pushing the pram, a leather suitcase on the hood just over the baby's feet and Hannah carrying a Gladstone bag and an umbrella because it was raining – old Mrs White came half-way, her skirt spotted white to the knees from the dirt road.

'Our Jack, as 'ad to be put down,' she said as they parted. 'I picked him out of the litter because he'd got such bright eyes and 'e kept them fixed on me wherever I went. The other puppies didn't. So I chose 'im. That's how we got Jack. You remember Jack, Charlie.' This very oblique statement was the nearest she ever got to asking about James's origins.

The next time she saw them Hannah had her baby, a girl called Agnes, and the Whites were out of the cavernous Arcot Street house and living in a fantasticated villa set on high ground near the Penarth Yacht club. It had a conservatory with orange trees in tubs that bore real oranges, no fewer than four water-closets – all with chains to overhead cisterns and lavatory pans so ostentatiously decorated with roses and irises that Hannah (who loved flowers) thought it indecorous to squat over them – but no bathroom. The garden had yuccas, pampas grass and, edging the little lawns, blue floss flowers smelling sweet and powdery. The villa (not a house) was built by a shipping agent some twenty years before and was solid red brick, but the architect had decided to flesh it out with a verandah on the ground floor, a balcony on the first (all painted white), and a tower room to house the shipping agent's telescope. When Hannah first saw the house, she was horrified: she could not live up to it, she said. Charles said it was what life owed them; what was more, now she was pregnant it was clear that the Life Force (an idea which he had picked up from his reading) was on their side. They must have a gardener and a nanny. It went without saying that they had a general servant. The cry was 'Forward!' Previously clean-shaven, Charles now grew a moustache.

He had plans for the tower room. The telescope had long since gone but the ships in the Channel – tramps, colliers and freighters – would still lie under inspection for hours, waiting for the tide that would take them into Cardiff Docks. There was more shipping than ever because the South Glamorgan boom went on and on. Miners who had emigrated to the States came back, some of them, to work in their old pits. As for the Bristol Channel itself Charles, to be honest, was dissatisfied with it. Real sea was what you saw on comic picture postcards, heavily blue in the sunshine with flashing white seagulls, not this brown Windsor soup dribbling up the shingle. It was not what he called top class.

'It's a real place, though,' was the sort of thing he would say to James long before the boy could understand. 'We've got to come to terms with it. What's pretty isn't always the best. Some parts of the world, they've got grottoes and porpoises playing in and out of them. But the folk as live there, they don't know where their next crust is coming from. As you'll know better'n me 'cause you're going to be clever. Books and your fossil collection and your rock collection, and shells and coins. That's what you'll 'ave in your tower room. You see, I'll put up shelves and tables. It'll be your own room and you can 'ave fish in a tank, mice, snakes, anything – even insects, I wouldn't mind. Nobody will go in there if you don't want them. Tell you what, it'll be your own domain like Robinson Crusoe's.'

James was about three when his father started to talk to him like this and it did no good at all. He grew out of his infant rages, but he became sullen and quarrelsome with other children. He had difficulty with reading and was put in the backward class at the Lansdowne Road Infants' School where one sunny morning

34

he realized the letters of the alphabet had sounds that could be linked together.

He said to the teacher. 'They wriggle like worms.'

'Worms?'

'*Kur Ah Tur* is joined together like a worm, and it says cat.'

So he was not really stupid. He was a poor learner because he could not bear to be told anything; if it was of any consequence, he would find it out for himself. Why America could not be seen from Penarth Head was one of the problems. It was because our eyes were not strong enough. He was something of a flat-earther all his short life.

He took against music and his father's playing of the harmonium. The reason lay in the tonic sol-fa system used to teach singing in school. Before each playtime Miss Edwards struck three notes on the piano, and the first child to say which notes they were on the scale was let out of class. James was always last to escape because he saw no connection between the notes struck and those silly do-ray-mees. Miss Edwards said he was tone-deaf, but this couldn't be right because in one of his boisterous moods he was capable of joining in the singing of the morning hymn. 'New every morning is the love', was his favourite. But mostly he kept his lips pressed together in an ostentatious, defiant way.

Charles's idea that they might switch from the Tabernacle Baptist Chapel to St Augustine's Church was taken no further, partly because of Hannah's lack of enthusiasm but also because they were where they were, living in this grand house (it was called 'The Lookout') which for some reason blunted the appetite for hymn-singing and sermons. It had to do with 'The Lookout' being in the part of town it was, not in the Tabernacle's natural catchment area; they were out of that. By rights the Whites should have gone to the Lavernock Road Chapel, but they didn't; they had heard the minister there was an enquiring not to say inquisitive man, who could be expected to contact the Tabernacle minister to inform himself on the Whites' family background and to Hannah the thought of it was terrifying. She became convinced that she and her family were the subject of malicious gossip in the Tabernacle area. She would not even set foot there, not even to visit her parents, who, as a result, had to trek over to the 'The Lookout' if they wanted to keep in touch. Charles's declining interest in public worship may have been hastened by conversations he had with Mr Minsky.

35

Minsky was a big, quiet man who took thought before he answered questions and then spoke slowly. When amused his lips trembled, his eyes danced and he might wag a gloved finger but he never laughed. He wore a hat with a wide brim. Charles was fascinated. This man's remote forebears had been slaves in Egypt and here he was in a leather armchair, in a green knitted waistcoat and a black frock-coat, a Jew, living and breathing! Charles was full of wonder. All the kindnesses, the books lent, the financial guarantees given, and now this! A figure out of the Bible! Charles had always thought him a bit odd. For one thing, although Mr Minsky was the boss he thought nothing of carrying a hod of bricks up a ladder when he visited a site. He always wore gloves because of a skin ailment, so he looked quite the toff. The gloves were mustard-yellow. But it was not until Hannah told him Minsky was a Jew that the old fellow became a sage and a marvel.

That had been a while ago, and Charles found no way of talking to Minsky about religious matters. Out of curiosity Charles had done some background reading and now knew all about pogroms in Russia. When he tried to bring the subject up, using the word pogrom, Minsky snubbed him mildly by saying that only on special occasions in the religious calendar was the mind strong enough to be brought to bear on darkness, and this was not one of them.

'Oh, don't exaggerate, Mendel.' Mrs Minsky spoke rather better English than her husband and she knew how to drag vowels out for effect. Exaaagerate! She was never much in evidence, but when she did appear everyone cheered up; she had a ready smile and liked to make other people smile too. 'No negative feelings. We live, don't we?'

The Minskys had a daughter, Ruth, who went to college in Cardiff. She wore her hair long, loosely knotted at the back, and held her head high with chin up, as though the lustrous black hair was tugging at her. Ruth was a pale girl but her manner gave the impression that was just how she wanted it to be; it was the pallor of a rose, just on the verge of pink.

But there did come a time when Charles and Mr Minsky were able to talk about the Bible and that was shortly after young James put a safety-match to some shavings in the carpenter's shop and his father's timber went up in flames.

The child rushed out into the yard screaming more in excitement than fear at what he had done. Nobody was hurt except one of the chippies whose hair caught on fire and had to be doused with a bucket of water. There were enough men around to make a chain to pass buckets of water into the shop, but they could not get water up to the overhead timber racks and they were flaring, crackling, spitting yellow and red under a wonderful up-climbing growth of smoke, quite lilac-coloured in the sunshine, before the galloping horses of the Fire Brigade were heard, only seconds before the engine was actually in the yard and firemen in flashing brass helmets were working the hand-pump and directing a jet of water on to the blazing roof.

'What the child was doing,' said Mr Minsky when Charles told him about the fire, 'was in all innocence, and I'm sure you won't be punishing him.'

'I strapped 'im. Mind you, not like my father did. 'E took off 'is belt and let me 'ave it with the buckle-end. I'm not like that.'

Mr Minsky sighed. 'Oh, that's bad anyway.'

'There's something defiant and strange about the boy.' And reflecting that he was talking to a Jew who would therefore understand, Charles told Mr Minsky how James had come into the world. Like Abraham he had a barren wife, so the servant girl bore him a son. That could not be wrong, could it?

Mr Minsky was distressed, not to say alarmed, by Charles's candour and went to close the sitting-room door with some ceremony, drawing the heavy curtain that was there to keep out the draught. He was covering not just a door but something or someone in need of protection.

'Well, could it?' repeated Charles.

'This child needs your love, that's all I know.' There was a long silence before Mr Minsky changed the subject. 'You can draw any timber you are needing from my yard for the time being. Keep a reckoning with my clerk. You were properly insured, of course?'

'Of course,' said Charles.

Some time later Mr Minsky was down at the yard viewing the damage for himself. He caught Charles at a bad moment because he had just learned that the timber store had a top insurance cover of £500, nothing like enough, and the company were sending an inspector to establish just how the blaze had started.

Light rain fell on the blackened carcass – all that was left of the rafters and uprights, and of the stacked timber – so water stood about in oily puddles and the air reeked of carbon and scorched brick.

'It's not the end of the world,' said Mr Minsky, looking around and wrinkling his nose. 'It was an accident. A small boy is not legally responsible for his actions, so it can't be arson.'

'They could say I put 'im up to it.'

'You have books. You're in a healthy way of business, Charles. Show them your books so they see how you're making money. You are not needing to raise cash; you're in a fine way of trade, and it will all be turning out well, you see. This is nothing! Think of real disasters and suffering. Think of the millions, so many you can't count them, in Asia, suffering and dying.' Mr Minsky had a habit of citing the sufferings of Asia so as to put misfortunes like Charles's into proper perspective. 'If you would allow me to mention that other subject we were talking about. I was meaning the domestic arrangements of the Patriarch.'

'I dreamed about him,' said Charles.

'About Abraham?'

'I dunno why, but I was sure he was Abraham, a real old bearded man with a stick which 'e used to point out caves and tunnels. In this dream we were looking for that bastard son of 'is, but we never found'n.'

The rain thickened and Mr Minsky put his umbrella up. 'It wouldn't surprise me if under that muck there's timber to salvage. £500 might do. If there's salvage, £500 might do.'

'Got too 'ot,' said Charles. 'I've poked about, trust me. Just charcoal. Sell it off for biscuits. But there's a thousand quid up the spout and that's Jimmy's fault, the young sod.'

'You mustn't talk like that.'

''E's got a devil. It's what was put into him because of the way he was made, a bastard like Abraham's bastard we were looking for. I looked it up. He was Ishmael – an outcast against everybody, and everybody's hand against 'im.'

'No, that is not Scripture.'

Charles spat. ''E'll be a wanderer on the face of the earth.' This saying, once he had uttered it, struck him as so picturesque that he cheered up. He saw the sunlit, pocked face of the earth with its rivers, rocks and forests; he saw young James stepping it out, and it struck him that that is what he himself would like to be doing too, stepping it out, a jolly vagabond or gypsy. He was marked out for a greater destiny than a tin-pot master builder. Maybe the fire in the timber yard was a sign! Maybe he was being quite unfair to James! Perhaps the time would come when

Charles White could look back to the fire and say, 'That was the time when I realized I was getting into a rut.' And it would all be thanks to young James there.

'Please be telling me one thing, Charles,' said Mr Minsky. 'Now, if you think I'm being too familiar, say so and I'll go. But I am having my own reasons for asking this question. When you were coming to the conclusion your wife was barren and that you would get a child with your servant-girl, was it because you were knowing the story of Abraham and thought you would be imitating him. Or was it *not* that at all? But that you were making this girl pregnant and, *after the event*, brought in Abraham to justify you? You are thinking carefully?' Charles realized that Mr Minsky, for all his learning and command of the English language, made mistakes about tenses. He didn't seem to know the difference between 'he went' and 'he was going' and the result was sometimes confusing. 'But you were loving your wife all the time,' said Mr Minsky.

The sunnier side of Charles's nature expanded still further when he was forced by Mr Minsky's question to think back. 'Everything was sweet and happy about it. 'Annah was absolutely tickled, I tell you. And tickled in more ways than one because it wasn't so long before she knew she was 'aving Agnes, and that after years of trying and trying real *hard*.' In order to be really emphatic he gathered himself to sound the aspirate. To make sure he said it again, '*Hard.*'

'What was happening to the real mother? Was she content?'

'Polly died.'

Mr Minsky made a curious kind of obeisance, at the same time lowering his umbrella, so that his face was completely hidden. He straightened up. 'You haven't been answering my question. Were you doing it because you read about it in Scripture?'

After some thought Charles said, 'No, to be honest it was all great sport and that's the truth of the matter. Abraham came a long way after.'

'So, young Charles. I see that. Good. It would be terrible to think Scripture could lead men into error.'

Hannah had now developed from being a fresh-faced, spindly sort of girl – but for her big bony hips – into an unmistakably handsome woman with a prominent bust and an erect, challenging, stance. She had a way of showing her profile (which someone had told her was Greek), turning her head and waving a hand, so that everyone could see her straight nose and the sharp indentation under her receding forehead. She wore brightly coloured blouses with a lower neckline and a green, blue or yellow velvet band at her throat, depending on the blouse; and pinned to it, at the front, a gold butterfly which Charles had given her on their tenth wedding anniversary. She wore her hair piled on top of her head, secured with long coral-headed pins, and when she looked at you she made it a real encounter, her gravy brown eyes *bent* (that seemed to be the word) on you, appraising and a bit defiant. I am who I am, they said, and who are you?

She had long ago slipped into the belief that James was her very own child, flesh of her flesh, and that Polly – when she thought of her, which was rarely – had played no part in the transaction. Exchanging confidences with a complete stranger, a woman next to her on a seat in the park, she said it had been a most difficult birth and she had been really frightened to think what might happen the next time. But Agnes's delivery had been so easy. A smaller baby, of course, and a girl. That made a difference. But, to get back to James. She sometimes wondered whether his difficult birth had anything to do with the way he had grown up to be so naughty. He was getting back at the world, and her in particular, for the pain and trouble he'd had coming into it.

'Poor little thing,' said the woman on the park seat, 'he wouldn't know anything about it.'

'Even before he was born he kicked me terribly. He was set on trouble right from the start, and before the start, but we don't love him any the less. That wouldn't be natural, would it?'

Born to trouble. She did worry a bit that James might continue as he had begun, giving pain and trouble not only to her but to Charles as well. She could see that Charles was far too busy to have such thoughts himself; he was expanding his business and doing paperwork late into the night.

The business expanded not because Charles was planning a great capitalist future but because he was carried away by an opportunity not of his making. The lease on his builder's yard came up for renewal, but the successors to the bankrupt brewery said it was no longer on offer because they had plans for the development of the whole site; and Charles had occupied only part of it. Finding another yard would not be easy, the way property was booming, and it might mean moving out of Penarth altogether – perhaps down to Lavernock – and what with the extra haulage and transport costs would go up. It wasn't good business.

Mr Minsky advised him to go and see the agent, a Mr Todd, and talk to him about Rugby football because Mr Todd had once been in the Penarth team. He was a bachelor and one of those strict teetotallers who carried pledge forms around in the hope of signing up the unwary. What nourished him spiritually was the Tabernacle Baptist Chapel and Rugby football, so Mr Minsky's advice was shrewd. Within minutes of meeting Mr Todd he and Charles were talking about the amateur game (which was what Welsh Rugby was supposed to be) and whether there was any truth in the rumour that Cardiff's phenomenal run of success had been due to the way players found sovereigns stuffed into their boots; that and this new scrum-half from Denbigh, Olaf French, who was so good he had been enticed south by the offer of a job in one of the Cardiff shipping offices.

'Money and power,' said Mr Todd. 'In our latter days these are the gods. Why do you think there are all these strikes? First it's the docks; then it's the railways; then the miners. There are agitators going round and about in the ways of this world, seeking whom they may devour. I seriously think we are nearing the end of the world.'

'Puts you in mind of the French Revolution,' said Charles.

'That's it,' said Mr Todd swiftly. 'You've hit the nail on the head. The ground we walk on seems solid enough, but you can almost see the steam and smoke coming up through the cracks from the inferno below.' Mr Todd said there was not the slightest chance of renewing Charles's lease. His company didn't want any more messing about – they were putting the whole site on the market.

This was where Charles was caught up and carried away, as it might be in one of those cable skips in the valleys which started low at the pit-head and then soared to the distant tip-tops before voiding their broken rock, shale and slag. All done by steam. The beautiful economy of this method was what caught Charles's imagination, that and the height to which they rose and the abyss which lay below. Ever since he had first seen the cable skips at work, on a visit to some of Hannah's relations up the Western Valley, his fancy had played with the thought of actually riding in one of them, as a man might ride in an Alpine cable car, soaring up to the sun and then ... well, he knew that anyone riding in one of these skips would be tipped out with the rubbish, but a clever man in a hard hat would survive. As in business. The sort of business Charles was now engaged upon was a bit like that, raising enough cash to buy the whole of the old brewery site and make use of the extra space to become not just a builder, and one of the leading builders in town, but what was even more of an achievement: a builders' merchant!

It cost him £5,000, so the £500 he picked up from the insurance company was chicken-feed. Charles was now in such funds that he could rebuild the carpenter's shop on a grand scale, making use of the extra space he had on the site. When it was all over, the contract exchanged and the bank manger – who was putting up most of the money on the security of the site itself and of 'The Lookout' – had shaken him by the hand, Charles went for a walk in the town in a bit of a sweat, convinced, to begin with, that he was mad and now ruined. As he walked and the sun shone through the horse-chestnuts and dappled the Plymouth Road pavement, his mood changed and he saw himself no longer as being helplessly carried up in some cable skip but as a man who, like Napoleon at the height of the battle, had seen an advantage which would have been missed by an ordinary man and thrown his weight into attack. He deceived himself into thinking that all the time it had been his deep scheme to take over the entire brewery site, and that he had waited until the expiry of his lease because that was the advantageous moment to make his bid. The fact that this was not true, that he would probably have secured the whole site earlier at a smaller price because, as a leaseholder, he had rights as a sitting tenant, simply indicated the state of excitement in which he now found himself.

The beauty of being a builders' merchant was that you could stack your pipes, bricks, sand, lavatory pans, hard core and other rainproof stuff out in the open, so there wasn't the expense of putting up a shed. You just had a man with a tall crane and an enormous ball of concrete at the end of the chain to swing against the old brewery buildings and there was a site, finally cleared up by half a dozen labourers, where all this stuff could be dumped. And a shed, with open sides like one of the barns Charles knew from Gloucestershire, where the timber and the dry cement could be stored.

One of the labourers was in his twenties, Ewart Paul, who came from Somerset and was more at home in a bakehouse than a buiders' yard. His father had been a master-baker in the Quantocks where from a certain hill, Ewart Paul said, you could

42

look out over the Channel to the Welsh coast and, at night, see the lights of Porthcawl, Barry, Penarth and Cardiff, strung out and glittering in the black. So when his father went bankrupt . . .

'Bankrupt!' Charles broke in. He had a horror of bankruptcy; it was a disease, perhaps a contagious disease, and the man from Somerset might be a carrier. Charles knew this was nonsense, but bankruptcy was a catastrophe he was superstitious about. He would have liked a sign against bankruptcy just as in Italy (so he had read) there were signs against the Evil Eye.

The young man ignored the interruption and continued.

'. . . so when I knew I had to get away to find work, Wales seemed the obvious place.' He had a pleasant low-pitched voice with an accent to show where he came from. He was taller than Charles with an open, wholesome-looking round face with brown, amused eyes. Something of a bumpkin, Charles thought, especially with all that curly hair on his cheeks.

He took up Charles's exclamation. 'Bankrupt? Yes, that's bad, but you've no idea what it's like over there. Bad times for the farm labourers and my dad let 'em 'ave credit. No end. Sometimes a man would pay with a poached rabbit – even a pheasant or a hare. Great poachers in Somerset. Most paid nothing and the debts put finish to him. It was the sight o' the kids he couldn't stand, famished some of them, thin and barefoot. What's he do now? Well, Mr White, he's an employed man driving a carrier's van through the villages to Bridgewater.'

'So your dad's an undischarged bankrupt?'

'And always will be unless I can put together a quid or two. I tried to join the police, but they wouldn't have me.'

'What about the Army?'

'Didn't fancy it and that's a fact, Mr White. Anyway, my dad wouldn't have been in favour. He was a pro-Boer in a quiet sort of way, quiet being a tradesman. And a churchgoer.'

'Church?'

'We've always been church people. Dad sang in the choir since he was a boy, but he had to go when he went bankrupt. Vicar wouldn't stand for it: said Dad would leave the choir and my mother was to give up her regular seat. Bankruptcy was that much of a stain – not so bad as burglary but somewhere in that category, said Vicar, because it meant depriving flour merchants and yeast merchants and landlords and the like, men of integrity he called them, of what was their due. He said there was a parable in the Bible as said as much, but I don't know about that. They'd both have to go, Vicar said, my Dad and Mam.'

'Well, 'e would, wouldn't 'e?'

'You don't find it surprising? After all, Dad was just victim to his own good nature and the way things were so bad.'

Charles reflected that this talkative young man was reminiscing in work time. 'It's not Christian, but it doesn't surprise me.'

'Tell you the truth, Mr White, I can't get over it. Mind you, Dad's a hard man too. He was boss in the family and was very strict. Teetotaller. Wouldn't let Mam go gallivanting about. Things were dull in the village. She was a lively woman, see? She'd have liked it here in Wales, all the lights and the bustle and the boats in the docks sounding their sirens at New Year. There's nothing like that back home, but Dad couldn't see anything wrong with the life. One summer she told him she'd got toothache bad and would need a tooth out in Bridgewater; so Dad gave her the money and she took me with her in the carrier's. Course, she didn't have toothache at all; she just wanted to see new faces and what was on show in the shops. But she was very honest – she had that tooth out all the same.'

'Even though it was sound?' Charles was incredulous.

'That's right, Mr White. I sat in the next room and heard her scream. The dentist wouldn't give her anything to kill the pain, not for what *she* could pay. I heard her scream and when she came out she had 'er hankie up to her mouth all bloody. She had to go through with it, see? If she hadn't she would have thought it very deceiving of my dad. Course she had deceived him telling a lie, and that, but she was straight; she accepted the consequences of that lie, because she was really upright and religious. She also knew Dad would look in her mouth when she got back.'

'Life was that dull?'

'To her, going to Bridgewater was as good as going to Paris for some other women. It's all a matter of what you expect from life and her expectations were pitched low. She was quick and bright, like a robin.'

'Was?'

'Still is, Mr White. Have I said anything out of turn?'

James came home from school to say he had been chosen to take part in the end-of-term play. It was based on the workhouse scene from *Oliver Twist* and he was to play the part of Oliver himself because 'he was on the small side and looked sorry for himself'. From now on there was quite a transformation in his character. He seemed to be unable to think of anything but the play and his part in it, particularly the 'asking for more' bit, which he thought so funny he couldn't utter the words without giggling. What amused him was the consternation they caused Mr Bumble (played by the biggest boy in the school), and he loved setting off this consternation rather as he had enjoyed putting a match to that piece of paper in the carpenter's shop, in anticipation of the display that would follow. He would cast his father, Charles, for an impromptu rehearsal in which Charles was expected to swell up and say, 'What did you say? More? Oh, you make me feel faint.' (Some liberties were taken with the Dickens text.) And Charles found he was quite able to fall in with what James wanted, to roar the words out in mock horror and cling to the banister, or the harmonium, whatever came to hand, for support.

As time went by and rehearsals proceeded James grew calmer because he was more and more identifying with Oliver and thinking, yes, there was something very wrong with the world when a poor, starving pauper boy like himself could suffer under a bully like Mr Beadle. It no longer satisfied him that Mr Beadle was outraged; James wanted Mr Beadle to suffer and thought quite seriously of kicking his shins on the great day. But he did not – dressed as he was as a pauper boy in torn shirt and trousers. And whereas the biggest boy in the school, playing Mr Bumble in a top hat and painted-on moustache, wore boots and leather leggings, James was barefoot.

But his performance was really rather special. Charles and Hannah sat in the audience and watched, Charles with a tingling feeling in his scalp (he was that aroused) as young James established a strange ascendancy over the other actors, over the audience as they sat on their benches in the school hall, so that when he came to the plaintive words, 'Please, sir, I want some more,' there were gasps, indrawings of breath at the glowingly heroic figure he cut – such was the authority with which he put over the audacity of his request. The big boy in the top hat and painted moustache might puff himself up and squeak. 'More? That boy will be hanged, I know he will,' but he seemed irrelevant as though young James, his eyes raised to some point over Mr Beadle's head, was addressing himself to a wider audience.

After the performance Charles found himself in conversation with Mrs Dover-Davies, the teacher who had produced the play and who was quite ecstatic over James's performance. She said he had great natural talent and only regretted she had not asked her friend in Cardiff, the one who worked in the professional theatre (he was a stage-manager in the Empire) to come along and see for himself. The room was so crowded that Charles and Mrs Dover-Davies were pushed up close to each other and he could feel her hot breath, smelling of cachous, on his face, and her eyes – so near and bright – had a curious dazzling effect upon him. She had a white, narrow wedge of a face with thin lips that were put in brackets by two lines which appeared on either side when she pressed the lips together, as she had a habit of doing. If her nose had been bigger, brown and hooked and if her ears had stood up to a point and had hair in them, she would have looked just like a screech-owl. Charles knew all about owls; there were lots of them in Northleach. He could just imagine Mrs Dover-Davies on silent wings, swooping out of the darkness, talons and beak at the ready for some scampering field-mouse or, as it might be, himself. For Hannah, on the other hand, Mrs Dover-Davies was not like an owl at all. She was medical, in some sinister, not to say clinical way, like one of those nurses you read about who poison elderly patients for their money. Either way Mrs Dover-Davies had made quite an impression on the Whites and, later, they talked about her from time to time and what sort of a body she was.

For Charles the impression went quite deep and he had a recurrent dream of Mrs Dover-Davies's face coming closer and closer, her breath quite steamy and her enormous eyes hypnotic. He was her helpless prey. This he rather enjoyed and although he had met her on only two other occasions she stirred his imagination to the point where he began looking to her for appreciation of his achievements in life. He had worked his way up from chippie to master-builder and now to the previously unthought-of splendour, that of being master-builder and master-builders' merchant, the holder of that great cornucopia out of which flowed the bricks, the timber, the cement, sand, pipes and lavatory fittings for the supply of all the builders in Penarth – and wider afield, Cogan, Lavernock and Dinas Powys. Needless to say, Mrs Dover-Davies's appreciation and admiration existed only in Charles's mind, but that was quite enough for him. Hannah had become too matronly, too statuesque to fire his imagination in a way that allowed him to flatter his self-esteem by voluptuous daydreams. For a time Mrs Dover-Davies did that very effectively (it would have shocked and amazed

46

her had she known), standing as a wraith at Charles's side to inspect his accounts, to admire the new warehouse and stables he was building and to say she had never seen such magnificent creatures as those barrel-chested work-horses with their smart white fetlocks and their way of striking sparks from the pebbles as they clattered out of the yard on flashing steel hooves.

The second time he met Mrs Dover-Davies in the flesh was when he returned home to find her talking to Hannah about James and that remarkable performance as young Oliver Twist. Mrs White must forgive her enthusiasm, she said, but she had always wanted to be an actress herself though her parents put a stop to that. She'd always kept in with the acting profession, though, and she knew there was a great demand these days for talented child actors. She wanted James to have an audition with another friend of hers, not the stage-manager but a real theatrical agent called Mr Olleranshaw who was coming down from London to interview young hopefuls.

'But James is only twelve,' protested Hannah.

'Just the right age,' said Mrs Dover-Davies, 'because nowadays you've got to be good at a lot of things, like dancing and singing and juggling. If Mr Olleranshaw saw fit, he could get James into a company where he'd learn all that and in years to come I'd be able to say I played a part in launching James White on his spectacular career.'

The real-life Mrs Dover-Davies did not quite match the woman of Charles's imagination. She was a bit smaller, she had narrow shoulders and she might even have been wearing a wig because when she turned her back on Charles to rummage in her handbag he could see, under her black straw hat, the auburn hair ending in a suspiciously straight line. But she had the same pale wedge of a face, big gingerbread eyes and the intense manner which could work itself up into a blaze of excitement and sweep them all, not only James, into the magic world of theatre.

'Oh, no,' said Hannah, 'We'd be crazy to think of letting him go for an actor. I'm told it is a very hard life.'

Which is what Charles would have said if Hannah hadn't said it first. 'I don't know about that,' he said. 'The boy's got something. Where is 'e, by the way?'

As though acting on a premonition, Charles began to insist on knowing just where James was when not in bed or at school. On the occasion when Mrs Dover-Davies was trying to arrange an audition for him with her friend Mr Olleranshaw, James was sitting unobtrusively in a corner drinking the conversation in. But at other times he was more elusive and Charles tracked him down, with a determination he was almost ashamed of, to the beach or a seat in the public gardens, the boy always by himself. He had few friends and for days at a time seemed to be mysteriously turned in on himself; or as though he had some invisible companion whose voice he alone could hear and to whom he paid the closest attention. Charles wondered whether it had anything to do with his having been baptized into the Roman Catholic church. Mrs Smorfitt had said Polly would come back and haunt them all if her son was not given a Roman upbringing. Charles regarded himself as above such superstitious nonsense, but it was not nonsense to suppose that one day Father Gillespie might make a dramatic reappearance to check on James's spiritual well-being and to make a fuss.

One Saturday afternoon Charles ate a couple of sandwiches at the yard and went off to the rugger match between Penarth and the South Wales Police. When he arrived back at 'The Lookout' for tea Hannah was distraught because James had gone out in the morning, not returned for the midday meal and now, here it was, 5 o'clock and no sign of him. She had been down on the beach and all round the Yacht clubhouse and then she had seen the Stringer boy – James sometimes played with him – but no, the Stringer boy had no information. He'd been fishing with his father.

'I'm just terrified something has happened to James.' Charles had never seen Hannah so upset. She was throwing her little pinafore up and grimacing as though ants were running over her face. 'You'll have to get the police.'

'Little sod,' said Charles. ''E knows. 'E knows what 'e's up to; 'e's playing us up, that's what, and 'e'll feel the weight of my 'and when I lay it on 'im, I tell you.'

'Don't talk like that, Charles. You don't know he might have come to harm, like his grandfather.'

''Is grandfather? Oh, yes. But if you think he got pissed and fell in the dock you can put that right out of your mind, girl. 'E'll turn up with some lie on 'is lips, you see.' Charles was so angry he shouted, 'I'll tan 'is arse.'

'You don't meant that, Charles. You're just as worried as I am, or you wouldn't use language like that. It's not nice, Charles. Oh, for God's sake, I'd give anything to see him come in through that door. Please God, I'd take a vow to I don't know

48

what. I'd give five pounds to that Catholic orphanage at St Briavel's.'

'It's where 'e ought to 'ave gone in the first place.' Charles was savagely serious about this. 'We've made a great mistake in our lives. The kid's always been against us, in spite of everything we've done. Do you think 'e's grateful? Do you think 'e understands?'

'He's never been told, Charles.'

'Makes it all the worse. Turning against 'is own mother, as 'e takes you to be.'

Hannah's face stopped twitching and she put her hands up to her breasts. 'Let's be clear what we're talking about. James is missing, that's all. And you've got to find him.'

Charles was silenced by her bearing. She was erect, wide-eyed and hostile in an impressive, even regal sort of way, as though (he thought) she was Marie Antoinette facing the mob during the French Revolution. 'So far as I am concerned,' she said, 'I am his mother in everything that matters and you've got to find him, Charles. Please!' The tears were running down her cheeks.

The police were no help at all. The station sergeant said that men going out on the beat would be alerted, but boys would be boys and the chances were the kid would turn up. By now it was getting dark and Charles, who had spoken to the Stringer boy to check that he had not lied to Hannah, returned to 'The Lookout' to sit at his desk with the idea of listing the possible explanations for James's disappearance: spirited away by Father Gillespie, possibly at the bidding of Mrs Smorfitt; or he could have taken up with a new gang of kids who had dared him to stay out until midnight by way of an initiation exercise (there had been press talk about youthful gangs and their rites); or he could have made his way into the Tiger Bay area of Cardiff where there were black men and Chinese and loose women and God knows what else of vice and violence. The *South Wales Argus* had run a series on the colourful world of Tiger Bay; Charles had read these with great interest and it now occurred to him that James might have done the same. It settled his mind to put the possibilities on paper.

But as he lifted two eyes from the notes he was making he realized that something odd had happened. He had been so agitated that he had sat down at the desk and begun writing almost in one movement when, he now realized, that should have been impossible to do. It was a roll-top desk he always kept locked with the key secured, with other keys, on a ring stowed in his right-hand waistcoat pocket. This

49

ring was attached by a fine silver chain which threaded the middle buttonhole of his waistcoat and was held there by a bar, from which buttonhole another fine silver chain led to the watch in his left-hand waistcoat pocket. These two chains hung in symmetrical loops and these loops – like the lower outlines of a woman's breasts (as Richard Burton, translator of the *Arabian Nights* which Charles was currently reading, might have said) – were not to be seen on the stomach of any other man in town. Charles looked down to verify that they were still in place. They were; the watch was there, the keys were there. But the roll-top had quite undeniably been up when he seated himself and that was impossible. He pulled the slatted and flexible top down and examined the lock. Just as he thought. It had been forced, and so clumsily the brass framing had been yanked off and the wood gouged. What is more, the drawer where he kept money was empty. The wash-leather bag, with anything up to ten sovereigns inside, had disappeared.

Charles's strangled shout brought Hannah into the room. 'Bloody burglary! Would you believe it? The sod's taken my money and not even left the bag.'

'Thank God!' said Hannah.

'What d'you mean, thank God! Look, 'e's smashed the lock of my desk. A carpenter's son and 'e does an unprofessional job like that! What's there to thank God for?'

'Because it means James has run away, which is bad enough, but at least he's not been murdered.'

'Not yet,' said Charles, as though he might relish the job himself. 'This is a police job.'

'You'll not go to the police?'

'Course I'm going to the police. They'll show more interest now they know it's robbery.'

The Station sergeant spoke as though boys were burgling their own homes every day of the week. An officer would call in due course, but not before Monday. 'We'd take a view of this, you see; it's more of a domestic affair. You wouldn't want to press a charge against an under-age boy, legally an infant, would you, sir? And your own son, to boot? But an officer will call. Ten sovereigns, you say. Or more? A boy could live well on that for some time. When he's spent it he'll come home, mark my words, if he hasn't joined the Army that is. Tomorrow is a Sunday and the day of rest. But Monday will be all right.'

'The Army?'

50

'Or, this being a seaport, run away to sea.'

Charles decided there was no more to be done that night, but the following morning he went down to the docks and boarded a Liverpool registered banana boat where he had a couple of men doing carpentry work. It was quite a big job – fitting bunks in the crew's quarters – and they had been working for at least two weeks. Charles remembered now that he had sent James along the previous Saturday morning to get the feel of that kind of work and the boy had come back saying it smelt good on that boat, he'd really liked it there, and a man had given him a mug of cocoa and a piece of biscuit. This man, he said, was nice. 'Come and be a sailor,' he had said, 'You're just the type.'

Being a Sunday there were no carpenters on board but the master, in a peaked cap and overalls, was making ready to sail and assumed Charles had come for his money. The work was finished. Everyone satisfied. A proper job. So when Charles said he'd be glad to take the money, hand to hand, though normally he would expect to pick it up from the agents, the skipper said yes, well, he'd give him a chit certifying the work had been carried out. Perhaps that would be more regular.

'I'm looking for my son. You've not got 'im aboard, eh?'

The captain looked surprised. 'Not so far as I know. Let's go and look.' They went everywhere but into the refrigeration plant and spoke to the first officer and the engineer. No, there was no stowaway, nobody had been signed on extra, not even a twelve-year-old boy.

'It was just an idea,' said Charles.

'He's missing? That happens. Was he in any sort of trouble?'

'He is now.' Back at 'The Lookout' he found Mrs Dover-Davies in a neat suit with white piping on the broad lapels, along the bottom of the jacket and on the cuffs; a marine effect which, together with the spell cast by those bold gingerbread eyes, had a pleasurable effect on him. Mrs Dover-Davies had been talking to Hannah with great animation, but as soon as Charles walked in she said with the kind of dramatic emphasis that must be due to her theatrical ambitions, 'Mr White, even without this knowledge I had slept scarcely a wink.'

'What knowledge?'

Hannah intervened. 'It seems James went to see Mrs Dover-Davies yesterday afternoon to ask for the London address of Mr Olleranshaw, the actors' agent, and she gave it to him.'

'I'm sorry, Mr White.' Real tears appeared and winked at him. 'I had no idea to what use he would put this confidential information.'

'Charles, send a telegram,' said Hannah, still in a high state of excitement at the realization that James had done nothing worse than run off to London. 'Say "Is James with you?" Send it to Mr Olleranshaw, reply paid to this address. Oh, dear!' Her face lengthened. 'What if that answer comes back "No".'

'It's Sunday. You can't send a telegram on Sunday.'

The time was well after 1 o'clock and the three of them stood in silence for some time as the powerful smell of meat roasting and cabbage boiling wafted through from the kitchen. Agnes came in and they all looked at her as though expecting her to say something important. She was a jolly-looking girl, about eleven years of age, with high, wide cheekbones like her father and a way of dipping her head as though to look at the ground but raising her eyes, as it might be over invisible spectacles, and so looking at whatever interested her with extra shrewdness. She gave them a merry sort of examination as though deciding which of her stock of riddles she would try on them. That morning she did not try one, and Hannah sent her into the kitchen to lift the lids on the vegetables.

'Well,' said Hannah, 'if you're not sending a telegram, what are you going to do?'

Charles turned to Mrs Dover-Davies. 'What time did James come to see you?'

'It must have been soon after 2 o'clock. I'm sorry, Mr White, it was in all innocence I acted.'

'And, 'Annah, you say 'e went out in the morning and didn't come back? Well, 'e must've forced the desk before 'e went. 'E took the money before he knew what 'e was going to do with it or where 'e was going, because it wasn't until past 2 'e came to you Mrs Dover-Davies.'

'What are you trying to prove?' asked Hannah.

'That what motivated 'im was a crime. 'E knew the money was there and 'e determined to take it. Only then did 'e start wondering what to do.' Charles spoke fiercely. When Agnes came back from the kitchen he asked, 'Now think carefully, Agnes, did your brother ever talk to you about running away to London?'

'No. Is that where he's gone?'

'Did he ever talk about running away?'

Agnes was in her Sunday best, a sergette sailor suit, complete with a naval flap at the back under her long hair, and bosun's whistle tied to a buttonhole. Perhaps it was this costume which emboldened her to say, 'Not by himself. He always said he would take me too, but I wouldn't have done that. I wouldn't have gone even if it was just on the steamer to Weston.'

Charles and Hannah both thought of the dairymen's outing all those years ago when he had said just that; 'Let's run away together and live in sin.' They would go to Bristol and set up an establishment where they would live like roses. From time to time, when in one of his jokey moods, Charles still liked to talk of running away. 'Let's run away together, 'Annah, and start a new life.' He was so absurd that Hannah had long ago ceased to rise to the bait. How could they run away together and leave the children? She sometimes thought that behind all his joking there was something serious and his secret wish was to run away from her. Was it any wonder that James, like his father, should think of running away too?

Mrs Dover-Davies said Mr Olleranshaw was a real gentleman and his wife was a lady who sang comic songs (that being her career before marrying Mr Olleranshaw). They had children of their own, and if James had presented himself the Whites could be sure he would be looked after – and a telegram sent at the first opportunity.

'I'm not waiting for a telegram,' said Charles. 'I'm taking the afternoon train from Cardiff General.'

'I'll come with you.' Hannah wanted to be on hand when father met son, but Charles asked who would look after Agnes. Hannah was so fearful of the thrashing the boy would get that she suggested Agnes should come along too, but Charles would have none of it. Think of the expense, for one thing. And what if the boy was still lurking about the town? He might turn up unexpectedly. There must be someone in the house, other than the daily domestic, to take him in.

Charles had not been to London before and he was not clear how to get from Paddington Station to the address in Islington that Mrs Dover-Davies had given him. He bought a London street map on Cardiff Station and settled down in the corner of his third-class carriage to study it. It was quite a trek – four or five miles by the look of it. True, there'd be the Underground railway and omnibuses, not to speak of hansom cabs, but the more Charles considered the alternatives the more nervous he became of trusting himself to any form of public transport. He would be swindled by cab-drivers or put down at the wrong place by the omnibus. Going on the Underground would be too great a gamble. Much safer to walk; that way there was less chance of being made a fool of by some smart cockney.

Olleranshaw lived in Drill Court off White Lion Street, and Charles intended to get there by walking out of Paddington Station and striking east along Praed Street. On the other side of the Edgware Road he would reach the Marleybone Road, when it would be plain sailing straight ahead into the Euston Road as far as King's Cross where he would take the Pentonville Road towards the Angel. Drill Court was a couple of minutes from there. Charles was able to work all this out because the map had a street index. He was as confident as anyone could be on a first visit to London, but what he had not reckoned with was the fog.

The huge vault of Paddington Station was made even huger by the fog. The steam locomotives coughed like lions and all Charles could see were sulphurous lights glaring through the limitless gloom. He followed the crowd up the platform, past the engine with its firebox open and blazing. He held a handkerchief to his nose and mouth to keep out the acrid mix of fog, steam and smoke and, with the other hand, held his Gladstone bag up in front of his stomach as protection against the something – a running passenger with a bigger bag, a horse, a truck, a barrier – he would certainly be colliding with. In the Gladstone bag were the sandwiches and overnight things Hannah had packed for him, together with a change of underclothes for James. Apart from the clothes he stood up in, the only extra garment the boy had taken with him was his tweed overcoat.

'No gloves!' Hannah had declared with dismay. 'No scarf! No cap!' And these too had been put in the bag.

Once he had reached what he deduced was Praed Street, Charles realized it was not only the fog he had to contend with. There was the night. Under one street-lamp he could only dimly make out the next. Because it was Sunday there were fewer people abroad. In any case, the fog blanketed sounds so there was little warning of traffic looming up out of the night. My God! he thought. This is terrible. I can't go on in this. But he did go on until he reached a point where he had stepped off the pavement without knowing how far away the other side of the street might be. Footsteps tapped, the grinding of wheels came from both sides. I'm lost! he thought. I shall be run down!

But he was not run down. He fell in with another walker who had been shouting at some invisible threat by man or horse and now seemed to sense Charles's fear. He took him by the arm and began to steer him.

'Where are you making for?' the stranger asked.

'A place in Islington.'

'Strewth! You'll never make it. You from Wales, then? I can tell. Look, Taffy, I'll see you to Edgware Road Station. My advice'd be to take the Underground to King's Cross.'

'I'm not a bloody Welshman.' Charles was unaware he had picked up a Welsh lilt; he thought he still spoke proper 'Gloster'. He was furious with the stranger, with the night, with the predicament he now found himself in and, above all, he was furious with James. What had he, Charles White, done to deserve this punishment – numb with cold, far from home, walking as it might be in one of the circles of hell, his eyes smarting in the sulphurous air?

''Ere you are, Taff. This is Edgware Road. Mark my words, take the Underground.'

Charles was so desperate he was prepared to risk even the Underground. It had not occurred to him to wonder what it would be like, shut in a tunnel with a puffing steam-engine. He soon knew. It was like Paddington Station all over again, but a Paddington Station compressed into a small space so that the air was that much thicker with steam, smoke and the smuts that settled on his face like flies. To keep all this muck out the carriage windows were firmly shut and the overheated passengers steamed pink under their Sunday best, bonnets, bowlers and buttoned-up overcoats, hot and still torpid from the evening service.

At King's Cross Charles, when asking the way of a ticket-collector, was told he ought to have stayed on the train and gone on to the Angel, but he was determined never to go on the Underground again. The fog was thicker than ever when he walked out into it, white and windless where lights played upon it. Each street-lamp was cocooned in fog so thick it would have to be scraped off with a knife. 'Pentonville Road,' Charles said to himself, as though the words could be used to conjure a passage through the fog as Moses had conjured a passage through the Red Sea. A policeman appeared, enormous in his helmet and glistening cape to hold up a lamp and invite pedestrians to follow him to the pavement opposite. There were other policemen out there with lamps calling to each other and to cab-drivers. The driver of an omnibus had dismounted to lead his horses. The few passengers peered out into the night with hands shading their eyes to see where they had got to.

With the swiftness of a dream Charles was alone again, feeling his way along some iron railings. A clock struck 8 o'clock, a time when in a proper world he would be sitting down after a supper of cold beef and pickle to play the harmonium. But this was not a proper world; it was a nightmare, and who had drawn him into it but James? The boy was out there, just beyond hand's reach, jeering at him but leading him on and on like a blindfolded prisoner. Charles's anger mounted. If only he could reach James he would drop the Gladstone bag, take off his gloves (the better to get a grip) and fasten his hands round the boy's throat to strangle him. Why had the boy been born to torment him? The boy was not a boy. It wasn't just the Irish blood; he was a devil from hell who had trapped Charles, against his will, into fathering him. And how had he done it? Through Hannah and her yearning for a child. Through that great yearning he had been ensnared and as Charles crept, inch by inch, along the Pentonville Road, swept by fear and anger, he hated Hannah too.

'God help me!' he said out loud after what seemed hours when he had bumped into a few swearing drunks and dodged crawling cabs only seen at the last minute. To his own amazement he heard himself say aloud, 'For the sake of your son, Jesus Christ, please help me.'

'Who is there?' A man wearing a tall hat and carrying a hurricane lamp suddenly appeared, as mysteriously and dramatically as a genie out of a bottle. In Charles's distraught state of mind it was fleetingly possible for him to believe that this, in answer to his prayer, was a divine manifestation.

'I am looking for Drill Court,' replied Charles.

'Who are you seeking in Drill Court?' the man asked, lifting his lamp the more clearly to see Charles's face.

'Are we that near?'

'Close at hand.'

Ordinarily Charles would have thought the man's questioning an impertinence and made no response. But his manner had something cheerful and reassuring about it so he said, 'I am looking for a Mr Olleranshaw.'

56

'That's my name,' declared the man with the lamp. 'There are not many of us about, especially in Drill Court. It wouldn't be me you're looking for, by any chance, would it?'

''Ave you got a wife who sings comic songs?' This crazy question was the only one Charles, on the spur of the moment, could think of to establish exactly which Mr Olleranshaw he was talking to.

'Yes, I married Meg Upcher. She had a great following on the halls, but she sacrificed her career when she married me. The children, you see. You've heard of Meg Upcher, of course, no? You must be an antipodean. I know from your utterance you are a Christian, as I am, but more than that sir, I know not. Who might you be, may I ask?'

'I'm James's father.'

'Well met, Mr White. I thought I was not mistaken. It's a foul night. We must be indoors.'

# 4

At the time Charles was too confused to marvel at the way Mr Olleranshaw and he had chanced on one another. Only when he was telling Hannah about it later did he realize how curious it was. Hannah was enthralled by his account of the fog, and the ride on the Underground railway. Thick sea mists she knew, but a London pea-souper was something she had only read about and her imagination was really aroused by the thought of Charles plunging into one. Like a hero in a fairy tale he had penetrated the ogre's smoke-filled domain to rescue poor little James, safe home now after his adventures. That he should even have found Mr Olleranshaw's house in such conditions was remarkable, but that Mr Olleranshaw should meet him by chance in the street was nothing short of miraculous. Charles was prepared to admit that providence had guided him to the immediate vicinity of Drill Place – providence plus his own skill in map-reading and good sense of direction – and, being arrived at that point, there was a not unreasonable possiblity that Mr Olleranshaw and he would meet, particularly when it was remembered that Mr Olleranshaw had fancied he might turn up on that one afternoon fast train on a Sunday from Cardiff and had ventured out into the fog to stretch his legs at what he calculated to be roughly the right time. Charles might have gone so far and then, like an explorer in the Amazon, gone round in circles. But when Hannah learned that Charles had actually offered up a prayer for God's help she was convinced that no matter-of-fact explanation would do. God had responded to his prayer, as God always did when called on by the true believer in his hour of need.

Mr Olleranshaw was unsurprised by the encounter. To him it was the most natural thing in the world to step out of doors on a devilish foggy night an hour after the arrival of the Cardiff train, turn a corner or two and come upon a man carrying a Gladstone bag, a complete stranger, who immediately claimed to be father of that boy who had arrived at his house the previous evening,

58

demanding an audition. Such was life. He was an optimist. Everything would turn out to be for the best. If one door did not open, try the next. Above all, smile and be confident, because the theatrical profession was fickle with its favours. Gifted men and women had been destroyed. Sometimes by mistaking their gifts. Sometimes by thinking they were cut out to be tragic actors when they'd have been perfectly good Lancashire clog-dancers. Some gambled. Some were destroyed by drink. Walter Olleranshaw had seen it all and believe the best way to command success was to give the impression it had already arrived. Above all, he was not afraid to enjoy himself.

Much of this philosophy he communicated within minutes of Charles entering his house. He was a big, fresh-complexioned man with sandy hair and sideburns who might have been up from the country, a farmer or auctioneer, but for the rings on three fingers of his left hand and two on his right – on his left a marriage ring, a signet ring, a ring bearing a little cameo; and on his right a ring like a coiled snake and a ring with a polished stone, garnet probably. As Charles sat in the little sitting room drinking hot tea brought by a pale girl, little more than a child, who wore a little white cap and frilly apron, he could hear the sounds of the house, rattle of plates from the back, footsteps upstairs and, more remotely, the tinkling of a piano. He wondered where James was.

Olleranshaw went back to talking about the profession. 'Your boy is a case in point. Did his little Oliver bit for me. All very well. But no good to me. I'm just preoccupied with this show at the Ally-Pally. Now, if your boy could whistle, I'd give him a try. But he can't. The Warblers are one short; they're whistling boys, you see, but your boy can't whistle and I can see his gifts are otherwise. I can see that in years to come he could play something dark. He's a dark sort of boy. I don't mean in looks, I mean in his manner. He's not even a good Oliver, let alone make one of the Warblers. When he's grown, that boy could play something dark. But he'd need training.'

'I'm not paying for any training.'

'Mr White, I'll be frank with you. In twenty years' time that boy could be playing Richard the Third.'

'I don't want to know about it. Where is 'e?'

'I expect you would like to see him alone. That wish will be respected. I gather he came here without permission. When there was a knock at the door and I opened it to find this boy

59

in the big brown coat standing there saying he'd come from Mrs Dover-Davies, d'you know what I thought? First of all that Mrs Dover-Davies is a sweet lady and I worship her. My imagination was aroused. I thought she might be there too. But she wasn't. I like that elfin woman. Not a word to Meg. It was real-life drama. Now, that's the sort of thing I respond to. Theatre is one thing but life is another. For all my professionalism, give me life. I just wanted to put my arms round that boy. Meg felt the same. *She* wanted to put her arms round that boy; she wanted to give him a cup of tea and one of her special home-made Cornish pasties. You know what? He insisted on doing Oliver first. Not a drop of drink nor a crumb of food would pass his lips until he'd done Oliver. And he did Oliver, right in this room, for Meg and myself, without taking the slightest sustenance. We had to admire him. But we could see he was too dark, even for Oliver. I'll have him sent in straight away. And then you'll join us for a bite of supper. No going out on a night like this. We've always a spare bed or two for the odd friend who drops in.' Mr Olleranshaw flashed his rings. 'But, Mr White, remember a boy is a boy and a boy with spirit is a rarity and to be applauded. You ought to be proud of him.'

Mr Olleranshaw retired and James was pushed into the sitting room by a hand on the end of an arm in a very full emerald sleeve. 'He won't eat you, James. He's your father.' The words might well have come from a comic song – they were delivered in a bouncy sort of way - and Charles half expected an orchestra to start up. He stood to greet Mrs Olleranshaw, but the lady chose not to appear. The large hand was waved in his direction and that was all, Charles's cue to play the stern father in what was becoming something of an Olleranshaw production. Charles sensed that the Olleranshaws were prepared for him to be very stern indeed, but to be warm and forgiving in the end. That was their scenario; they had no conception of his cold rage.

Yet the boy, as he then appeared, made a deep impression. He was in his grey Norfolk jacket, trousers to match which came down to just below his knees, worsted stockings and black boots. James looked unblinkingly at this father, alert as a monkey, not the slightest bit afraid. There was only one interpretation Charles could place on such defiance. That the boy had no concern for the trouble he had caused –exposing his father to the fearful fog, to the fearful danger of being run down and trampled on by fog-crazed cab-horses, and to the fearful Underground steam train. The boy cared for none of this. He had no remorse over the stolen sovereigns. And if he was told, if Charles had spelled out the hell he had been through, it was even likely that a soft grin would slide across that stiff little face. So Charles believed.

At the same time, he must have been responding to the boy on a profounder level. Into the depths of his nature, into his very soul, he must have received a spirit image of the boy which, when its time came, developed into what Charles came to regard as the true picture of James. That was not yet, not until the years had washed away the memory of an errant, dishonest and defiant boy. Charles loathed him and at the same time, so it seemed retrospectively, took him into his heart. When he had gone for ever James appeared in dreams to his father, still dressed in this Norfolk jacket as he was that foggy Islington night, a twelve-year-old, afraid in spite of his bearing and yearning, without knowing he was yearning, for his real mother, Polly, who had died soon after he was born. But Charles was never to tell Hannah of these dreams.

'Well, James.' At the time Charles thought his tone was ordinary enough, but in retrospect the words took on a vague yearning quality as though they had been uttered in a different acoustic. They echoed. He might have been in a church and that was where, in his dreams, he so often found himself, the boy shrinking into nothingness and the words coming back at Charles from the cold stone.

'Who are you?' James put the question as though he did not know the answer and Charles, at the time, was tense with anger. The boy went on looking at him enquiringly. Then the anger was touched with fear. What if the boy was not just being defiant and genuinely did not know he was looking at his father? Perhaps he was a bit touched in the head. James was ungettatable because all the time he had been nursing this touch of madness.

'I'm your dad. You know very well who I am, I'm your dad.'

'My name's Oliver Twist,' stated James. 'I've got no dad.' These words, too, echoed endlessly. To Charles the years that passed became a vista of free-standing stones, like tombstones, and it was from these stones that the words came echoing back even at the most unexpected moments – playing the harmonium or fishing from the groyne on a winter morning – but most strongly of all, in his dreams. The boy had stood there in his Norfolk jacket asserting rather flatly, certainly with no emotion, that he was not James White but Oliver Twist and Charles eventually, and after much torment, came to believe that the boy was not completely wrong but there

61

was *something* in what he said, something that fitted. In Charles's dreams, he popped up before the stones endlessly reiterating his claim, 'My name's Oliver Twist.'

Mr Olleranshaw now appeared, followed by his wife whom he introduced by much waving of his beringed hands and the words, 'This is Mrs Olleranshaw.' He presented Charles, 'And this is Mr White from South Wales. Had a terrible time of it in the fog. Not fit for a dog to be abroad.'

Mrs Olleranshaw had a transparent look about her, she was that delicate and fair and watery-eyed, her flesh all the more transparent because of the emerald dress she was wearing. 'It's worse than usual, the fog,' she said. 'The asthma sufferers and people with chest complaints are to be pitied.' Her robust soprano would have come more naturally from a bigger, firmer, more opaque woman. 'So I hope you're fit, Mr White.'

'You said I could see the boy by myself. Alone! Just me and the boy!' Charles stood up. He began shouting and waving his arms. 'But 'ere you are! Listening!'

Walter Olleranshaw and his wife took no offence at all at this outburst of rage. They smiled appreciatively, as though the drama was working out even better than expected. Olleranshaw explained that their intrusion was not out of vulgar curiosity. Mrs Olleranshaw had judged this the appropriate moment to serve some hot green ginger cordial – and there the steaming glasses were, brought in on a tray by that same pale girl in white cap and frilly apron.

Charles just wanted the house to collapse around them – for the Olleranshaws, their green ginger cordial and the pale girl to be snatched up. . . he did not know by what, though The Four Horsemen of the Apocalypse crossed his mind. But anyway, by some supernatural predators who would rid him of these tedious people so that he could be alone with James. If the boy was playing mad, he would thrash it out of him. With what? He could go out into the hall where he had seen walking-sticks in an umbrella stand. The other possibility was for Charles to pick up his Gladstone bag, grab James and march him off the premises. But he could not do that because of the fog; he was too frightened of it. So everyone sat down to drink the hot ginger cordial, all except James who stood with his legs apart, his hands clasped behind his back and a look on his face which dared the pale girl to offer him any cordial.

'You must be glad to see your father,' remarked Mr Olleranshaw, apparently to heighten the drama.

'He's not my dad. I'm Oliver Twist.'

''E's playing silly buggers,' said Charles.

Mr Olleranshaw spoke to his wife. 'Real Thespian.' He turned to Charles. 'Does happen. Certain Thespian types get taken over by the characters they portray. There was a man, friend of mine, who played Potts in *Love in the Mist*. Remember Potts? A self-sacrificing character. So this friend of mine, Algie Vivian – that was his stage name, his real name was Sparkes – became self-sacrificing too. For a while, that is. Long enough for his cronies to sponge on him. Cleaned him out. Algie slept on a park bench under newspapers.'

'You mean this boy thinks he really is Oliver Twist?'

Mrs Olleranshaw semed to think this was rather jolly. 'You don't really, do you, James? You know that you are little Jimmy White and your dad's come for you.'

'I've got no dad. Nor no mother neither. I'm Oliver. I'm an orphan and I've got my own way to make in the world.'

'Poor little darling.' Mrs Olleranshaw put on a show of mock motherliness. Her eyes shone, but the near-tears were of laughter rather than compassion. 'Do you know what happened to Oliver after he left the workhouse?' No, James did not. 'Then you can't be Oliver can you, or you would.'

'It'll wear off.' Seeing the tension in Charles's face, Mr Olleranshaw put a hand on his shoulder. 'It'll wear off when you get him back home. Then' – to James – 'we'll keep in touch, you and me. I'm down to Cardiff and Swansea from time to time, and that's how we'll keep in touch. You'll come and see me back-stage at the Empire. By then you'll have learned a new part. Not Oliver.'

''E'll learn no other parts. 'E can start in the workshop after Christmas. 'E's twelve and 'e can do as I did and start work.' Charles took a step towards the boy, only to find that Mr Olleranshaw had tightened the grip on his shoulder. 'Come and sit down, Mr White. We'll all have another round of hot ginger – and what's for supper, Meg?'

'Cold meat and mash. Can you sing, James? We'll have a bit of a sing-song after supper.'

Charles shook off Mr Olleranshaw's hand only to find that Mrs Olleranshaw had interposed herself between him and the boy.

''E's not only mad, 'e's bad. Broke into my desk and made off

63

with ten sovereigns. In a wash-leather bag. Where's that money then, James?'

But he was not so angry that Charles's own imagination could not kindle. He thought how some historian – Carlyle, say, writing about the French Revolution – would have reported this meeting in the fog-begirt home of the Olleranshaws in Islington. They had made their own little drama – runaway reclaimed by tyrannical father – but Carlyle would see the broader implications. The crazy boy standing there in his Norfolk jacket showed the same kind of truculent defiance which made the French Revolution possible. And he, Charles, was against revolution. The confrontation was not, as the Olleranshaws thought, domestic. It was a cosmic battle set against . . . well, a great bewildering, mind-numbing fog. Beyond the fog there must be stars, and Charles was determined to see them.

A lot of this was related to Hannah when he returned home to Penarth with James. Surprisingly, he rather enjoyed telling her all about the Olleranshaws, even trying to imitate Mr Olleranshaw's voice and manner. He said Mrs Olleranshaw made him think of one of those big tropical insects they had in the Natural History section of the Cardiff museum – waxy bodies and brilliant wings – and he even had a shot at the song, 'Everything in the Garden's Lovely', which Mrs O. launched into after supper. But Charles heavily censored his account. James's head had undoubtedly been turned by his appearance in the school play, but he did not report James's claim that he was not their child but Oliver Twist himself, a waif and an orphan. He was not indignant about the boy denying he was his son, because Charles knew full well that he was. But denying that Hannah was his mother was a different matter, and Charles hoped the boy would be shaken out of his fantasy before he upset her.

That night at the Olleranshaws, a wind sprang up and rattled the windows. Charles could hear the boy breathing in the other bed, undoubtedly asleep, but he himself could not sleep and he went and looked out of the window. Nothing was to be seen but a yellow street-lamp in the distance and the fog rippling over it like gauze. Charles found a piece of paper and stuffed it in the window jamb, but the window still went on rattling as though someone out there was trying to get in. He was more unnerved than he would have liked to confess. What happened now? Was James developing into a youth he and Hannah would be unable to handle? If so, why? Where did the fault lie? Certainly not in Hannah. As for Polly, what now nibbled at Charles was her being R.C. and James being christened R.C. Was there any possibility the Papists might have got at James? That was more likely (Charles was not superstitious) than that there was magic at the christening which was now working itself out. He was confused and a bit frightened. In the world there was right and wrong, a left hand and a right hand; over all, in spite of appearances, there was authority which would see justice done at the last. So he had always thought. But now, he simply did not know. If God had guided him through the fog to Drill Court, it was into a sinister trap where there was only more fog and confusion. He told Hannah nothing at all of his almost overpowering impulse to put his hands round the boy's throat and strangle him as he slept. He just spoke of the cold in the room and how he put his clothes on again, including his overcoat, just to keep warm while he stood at the window until the fog, with the wind behind it, rose like smoke and then thinned.

As Hannah had feared, there was an entry in the *Penarth Times* the following Friday. Half-way down the 'Town Talk' column was the query: 'Why was the gentleman (?) descending from the train at Penarth Station kicked on the shin by the boy he was accompanying; so that the gentleman (?) kicked back and found himself having words with the other passengers. What is the world coming to?'


Well, what? That is what Charles wondered too and whenever he met Mr Minsky these days they talked about the building trade, how long the new Scandinavian soft woods needed to season, fletton bricks as against the fancy red bricks coming down from the English Midlands, North Wales slate as against local tile, labourers' wages, carpenters' wages, the way workers were getting unionized – that was the sort of thing they started off with. But then they turned to speculation. Which would come first, war (with France or, more likely, Germany), or would it be revolution starting in the Welsh coalfields or in Liverpool (the Irish were behind it), where troops were being called out to face showers of stones from striking transport workers. They could spark a general revolution which would so cripple the country that 100,000 French troops in baggy blue trousers could land at Dover unopposed.

Mr Minsky played down the possibility of nation-wide revolution. British workers lacked what he called 'spite'. But war was another matter. Not with France – that country was decadent and the English King too popular there. Not even with Germany – in spite of the sabre-rattling and the naval build-up the Kaiser was, at heart, a man of peace. The real danger was Russia.

'Russia is a sleeping giant with bad dreams. She is having dreams of revolution and Tsars murdered. Russia is a land of stupid peasants and bomb-throwers.' Mr Minsky sawed backwards and forwards clapping his gloved hands gently together. 'What is happening in a big country with such dreams? The rulers will be going on foreign adventures. So they damp down internal troubles. How? They shall turn the attention of their people to a big external one. Aggressive war.'

'War with Russia? I mean, 'ow would we get at each other?'

Charles so discounted the French and the Germans as warlike nations that any future conflict with the Russians would, he thought, see them sitting on the sidelines. England would fight without allies. They only complicated matters. Look at the Crimean fiasco, when the French showed how unreliable they could be. He foresaw the British fleet bombarding St Petersburg and landing an expeditionary force for the march on Moscow. He saw white tents pitched in rows, dead horses with flies feasting on their entrails, howitzers firing into hilltop copses, regiments marching to cut off supplies to the enemy's van, the cavalry waiting for the order to charge.

'No,' said Mr Minsky. 'The war won't be in Europe. The Russians will invade India.'

Wherever the fighting was to be, Charles hoped the war would not come before James was old enough to join the Army. War was the tester of nations, as Ruskin said; victory would be to the strong, those who survived would be the fittest to survive. He himself was too old to go for a soldier and he had family responsibilities, but young James could be just the right age and it might be the making of him. He would have the dishonesty, the self-centredness and the play-acting knocked out of him. He would learn what it was to put the general interest above his own.

'India!' Charles was doubtful. 'The Russkis wouldn't stand the climate.' He still thought Europe the likelier place for James to be made a man of.

It bothered Mr Minsky to hear Charles speak so badly of his

son. He could not understand it – so unnatural and unfatherly. 'No. you are not meaning that, Charles,' he would say. 'It is all so bad, for both of you. And your dear wife and your dear daughter. You have a bitter way of laughing, and I tell you life has been kind to you.' He was appalled by Charles's account of the boy running off to London and having to be brought back. 'You've got to be understanding of the boy. He is flesh of your flesh, he is needing your help. Please, my dear.'

He pushed his spectacles up on to his forehead and revealed how the big lenses had shrunk his eyes. 'We exist and have our being, through God, with our children. We must love them without any hanging back, whatever they do.'

'A man should not be . . .' Charles hesitated. 'I just feel I'm victimized, in some sort of way.'

'But what sort of way? How can you say such things?'

'I just got this feeling there's a devil in the boy.'

Mr Minsky raised both his hands, palms outward, as though asking for mercy. 'I'm saying to you, with great seriousness and intensity, the boy is needing your help.'

'Help? What to do. I even let 'im keep one of the sovereigns. I 'aven't actually laid 'ands on 'im. My dad would've given 'm the buckle end of 'is belt. But I've not said I won't thrash 'im. Course, 'e's 'ad a shock and I won't thrash 'im when 'e's down. 'E's on probation. If 'is spirit's of a kind that 'as to be broken, so be it!'

'That is very hard and unloving.'

'The way I see it, Mr Minsky, a great deal of misery comes from too much indulgence.'

'Think about it, Charles. Remember that one day he'll stand at your graveside and inherit your business.'

Hannah was flatly opposed to taking James away from school and setting him to work in the carpenter's shop. For ever afterwards work and the idea of punishment would be linked in his mind, so he would hate work and end up as a waster. She said she was surprised that Charles, with all his book reading, had no greater ambition for his son. Clearly he was an intelligent and imaginative boy who needed all the book learning he could get. Going on the stage and becoming an actor wasn't the real issue – in a few months' time he might have forgotten all about it – but what would remain was the need for proper education. Leaving school at twelve might have been all right in years gone by, but they were living in a new century now.

''E's going into the carpenter's shop after Christmas,' declared Charles.

Hannah was surprised by what she then said, but once the words were out decided she intended to stick by them. 'If you try to do that I shall leave you.'

Charles snapped his head up and stared at her in astonishment. ''Annah, you don't mean that!'

Hannah was surprised not only by what she had said but by the calm and resolute way she now backed it up. 'I shall pack my things and take James and Agnes to my mother.' Mrs Jones was now a widow and lived alone in a rented four-bedroomed terrace house, railway property on the Cogan Road which the company had allowed her to keep on, so there was plenty of room for Hannah and the children.

Unexpectedly Charles found himself laughing. Hannah's relationship with her mother had not improved even after her father died. 'You'll scratch each other's eyes out!'

'I'm serious about this, Charles.' The amused expression on his face annoyed her, because now she could not be sure that Charles had meant what he said about putting James to work. It might turn out to have been one of his teases – like all the other teases, running away together, rearing chickens in Canada and so on. That would be particularly annoying because it had surprised her into blurting out a truth: that she would be prepared to leave Charles if he made life impossible. She did not like him knowing so much at so small a cost.

Charles looked delighted in a fiendish sort of way and did a little dance, lifting one foot and then the other. 'You'll scratch each other's eyes out and I'll 'ave to come round and prise you apart. And think of the row about money. I'd come round every Friday and push money through the letterbox. What would the old girl say to that? She'd want most of it. Life would be 'ell for you, 'Annah. But you could always come back. Everything would be 'ere as you left it. Except for a lot of dirty washing. Reckon I could cope with the dishes myself. Eh?' He was laughing so much that even Hannah had to smile.

'Then that's settled,' she said.

'What?'

'James stays at school.'

'What you said about education is dead right, girl.'

If Charles had really been teasing he would have kept the joke

68

going much longer, weaving even more fantasy. The speed with which he dropped the idea of taking James away from school showed he really had intended it, only to be frightened by Hannah's threat. She knew this for certain . . . and Charles knew that she knew. And he also now understood – what he had not understood before – that if things went badly she was capable of walking out. The information was absorbed with unconcern, even gaiety, but it confirmed Charles in the growing conviction that fate was dealing roughly with him, might go on dealing roughly with him, and he could not understand why. That night he dreamed he was in the Palace of Versailles, where all was brilliant but outside was dense fog. People out there in the fog pressed their faces against the windows; he ought to know those faces but he didn't. He was frustrated and made so much noise Hannah had to shake him by the shoulder to wake him.

'You kept shouting "Polly",' she said.

The first week back at school after Christmas, Agnes came home to say that James had been kept in. Olive was at 'The Lookout' to drink a cup of tea with Hannah (it was Thursday early closing and Olive kept shop hours even though she was training) when Agnes walked in with this news, and it was enough to cause Olive to say it was time James was spoken to by someone outside the family – not a teacher, but someone who nevertheless was in a position of respect. The Minister, for example. The Reverend Mr David Llewellyn had known James all his life, and although the Whites no longer went to the Tabernacle he would surely be ready to talk to the boy. The minister was such a good, cheerful man who could sing and play the flute; the sort that Olive would be quite ready to consider marrying herself. She recognized that she was not sufficiently educated to be a minister's wife but what she lacked in book learning she could, as the manageress of a Singer's Sewing Machine shop, make up for in common sense and business sense and . . . well, she was pretty, wasn't she? A young minister could marry for love. The Reverend Mr David Llewellyn was old. He himself was not in question; he was married already – for money, it was said – with three children, but Olive wanted her cousin to know she was thinking about prospective husbands.

'What's James being kept in for?' Hannah asked.

'He tried to stop Mr Rumble giving me the cane.'

'The cane? Whatever for?'

'Talking in class. Mr Rumble had me out in front and he'd got

69

his cane out from under the desk and he'd just said "Hold out your hand" and James, he came out, looking very funny and staring. He caught hold of the cane. Oh, it was awful. James didn't say anything but Mr Rumble did, he said "Go back to your seat, White."'

Hannah took Agnes's right hand and examined the palm. There were two red marks running across it. So she *had* been caned. Hannah was not all that put out. A caning now and again was neither here nor there, it was part of school life. She herself had been caned three times, once for copying, once for talking in class and once for trimming the hair of the girl sitting in front with her dressmaking scissors, but she bore no ill-will. Agnes did not seem to mind either. Cousin Olive kissed the palm of Agnes's hand and said Mr Rumble must be a brute.

'Did James go back to his seat?'

'Mr Rumble got the cane away from James and gave him a push. He said he was to go back to his seat and come to him after school. Everyone was looking and that. So I could see James might be getting in trouble. "Go to your seat," I said, but he stood there and I pushed him. "Everybody's got to have the cane," I said. He's had the cane, hasn't he, Mam? It's nothing to carry on about. Anyway, James said, "It's different. You're a girl," and d'you know what everyone began laughing and talking. Up to then nobody had said a word. I *wanted* James to go to his seat. Mr Rumble sometimes takes boys away and beats them on the behind. But not the girls.'

'He must be a brute,' said Olive. 'He likes it; that's the worst part.'

'I *made* Mr Rumble cane me. I held out my hand.'

'Does it still hurt?'

Agnes shrugged. 'It's all right.' Hannah had fetched some lard and was working it into Agnes's palm with the ball of her thumb. 'James cried.'

'Because Mr Rumble gave him the cane?'

'No, he didn't give him the cane. He was just that upset, and Mr Rumble clouted him across the ear and said he wasn't to be such a baby but he didn't cane him.'

'James cried?'

'Yes.'

When Charles heard of this later, he said that James was a softie. They had all been in the carpenter's shop the other day and a mouse ran out. Charles went straight away to borrow the cat, Roger, from the glass department to set him at this mouse, and James had become near hysterical. He said, 'No, no, no!' He couldn't bear the thought of a cat after a mouse.

'But you can't 'ave mice running about. What if it was a rat? Would 'e 'ave felt any difference? No. But rats are the bearers of bubonic plague. Would that 've registered with the young master? Not on your life!'

'We don't have plague any more.'

'We would 'ave if young James 'ad his way.'

'He frightens me,' said Hannah. 'Anyway, it wasn't a rat, it was a mouse.'

''E's a softie. Where is 'e now?'

James was up in his room making a picture by the light of a single candle. When his father walked in he took no notice but went on crayoning. There was no heating but, even so, the night outside was colder and the boy's breath had misted the window.

'What are you doing?'

'Painting.'

The colours on the white cardboard trembled in the candle-light. A brown ellipse floated on a blue scribble. Charles identified palm trees rooted in the ellipse, a house with four staring windows and a spider.

'What's 'e doing there?' Charles jabbed a finger at the spider.

'That's Robinson Crusoe.'

'It's too cold up 'ere. Why don't you come down and draw by the fire?'

'I'm Robinson Crusoe and I've got to be by myself.'

Charles felt the boy's hand: it was icy. The gesture moved air, the candle-flame flickered, and the shadows of father and son flapped in the chill against the glass cabinet where James kept his pebbles and fossils.

'Robinson Crusoe? What do you know about 'im?'

'Last lesson Friday afternoons we get a reading, and Mr Rumble has been reading Robinson Crusoe.'

'So you're not Oliver Twist any more?'

'No, I'm alone on a desert island.'

Charles put his arm round the boy. 'You're not alone, James. I'm your dad. Your mam's downstairs getting supper in the warm, and your sister Agnes is proud of you. I know all about Mr Rumble and the cane.' James said nothing. 'There's got to be order kept or none of you would learn anything. Agnes was talking in class, she admits it.' Still James said nothing. 'I expect Mr Rumble was as upset as you were 'e 'ad to give Agnes the cane.'

'I'll kill him.'

'What?'

'If I knew how to kill him, I'd kill him. But I don't know how. I'm not strong enough. One day I'll kill him. I'll get a gun or something and shoot him. Or I'll stab him with a knife.'

'You think Robinson Crusoe would do that?'

'No. Sometimes I'm just me and sometimes I'm Robinson Crusoe.'

'But you're not Oliver Twist?'

'Sometimes.'

Charles still had his arm round James's shoulder, but there was no response. The boy was as stiff and unyielding as ever, so Charles straightened up and moved away. What the hell was to be done with him? Here they were together in this chill, flickering room, but they might have been sitting on different islands for all the contact they made. Words were passing but they were just lights flashing in the dark, now on, now off, as the shutters in the lanterns rose and fell to send out the dots and dashes in some code he could not understand. The boy couldn't understand it either, Charles was sure of that. When he said he was Oliver Twist, or now Robinson Crusoe, deep down he was saying something else. Help me! Love me! Did he know that is what he was saying? The boy would never admit it even if he knew.

'What makes you so interested in Robinson Crusoe?' James did not answer, so Charles went on. 'We could read it together if you like. What d'you say? You'll find out Robinson Crusoe didn't stay alone. There was a black servant called Friday. And there were goats. The interesting thing about Robinson is the way he used 'is own resources to set 'imself up. Like me, you could say. I started up with nothing. I worked. Now we've got all this. You've got this telescope. I always wanted a telescope when I was a boy, but I never 'ad one. You've got one because I was like Robinson Crusoe and built everything up.'

'You're not like Robinson Crusoe,' said James. 'He was all by himself. Whichever way he looked there was nothing but sea. He was just alone.'

'Nobody is alone. There's always God. Robinson Crusoe thought about God all the time.'

'God?' said James. Charles was startled by the tone, which was almost mocking. He wanted to talk about Robinson Crusoe and God, but he could not. The boy was challenging him and the ordinary guff wouldn't do, the talk Hannah or the minister would have provided. If he wanted to reach James he would have to be honest. The kid, he now understood, would expect nothing less. Yet if he was totally honest, what would he say?

'Yes, God. He's always with us.'

'How do you know?'

'I just do, that's all.' He would have liked to say that the fact he'd done so well in business meant that God was with him, but James would only answer something doubting or mocking. In any case, Charles knew perfectly well that getting on in the world didn't mean God was with him. Half-understood fragments of old sermons and Bible readings came fluttering around him. Nothing he could do would win the sense of God's presence. Only God could confer that kind of grace. Faith was a God-given gift he didn't deserve and might not even ask for. There was nothing to do but wait. With one hand on the telescope and James turning in his chair to look at him in the candle-light, Charles felt he had already been waiting an eternity.

He wondered why they had always called the boy James. Lots of kids were christened James, only to be called Jim in the family. But not James. From the beginning there had been a formality in the relationship which, no doubt, Father Gillespie would have been able to explain.


That was the year of the storm. The Whites were lucky. Elsewhere in Penarth roofs were peeled off like the lids of sardine-tins, but the Whites lost only glass from the conservatory, and a silver birch was blown over to turn up a great heel of root and earth. A French ship ended up on Penarth beach in front of the Yacht Club; everybody in town went to inspect the stranded vessel, many of them thinking that was just the sort of harm the French would come to, not being natural sea-going people like the British.

The town went out and had their photographs taken with the French boat in the background. Charles took Hannah, James and Agnes down to the beach so that they could be photographed by Mr Pym of Cogan under his black hood. He thought the photograph would be a historical document. In years to come, children and grandchildren would hold up this photograph and say, 'This was the year the French ship was driven up on to Penarth beach.'

The storm was good for business. Charles sent men into Cardiff to buy as much tarpaulin as they could lay hands on; there was a great run on tarpaulin – everybody wanted it to cover shattered roofs until proper repairs could be made. Charles himself spent a lot of time at the docks buying timber and German glass. He also took on more labour, including a couple of pit workers from the Sirhowy Valley, relatives of Hannah's relations at Abercarn. They specialized in pit-props, maintenance work usually, not skilled carpenters by any means, but they were on another lock-out and needed the money. Charles was glad to have them, labour was that scarce in the building trade. He was out of the house all hours, away before daylight these short winter days and back for supper sometimes as late as 9 or 10 o'clock. For days he did not see James or Agnes at all, and the only news he had of them was from Hannah.

Mrs Dover-Davies had been to tea and given James a friendly talking-to. Just what was said Hannah could not be sure, because Mrs Dover-Davies had insisted on inspecting James's room with him alone and the talking-to was up there. When they came down, she enthused about the fossils and the telescope. She also said that James now quite accepted the need for corporal punishment, even of girls like Agnes. It was approved by all the leading educationalists and nowhere more vigorously practised than in the leading boys' public schools, such as Eton and Harrow – no doubt Cheltenham Ladies' College too.

Hannah continued with her report. 'Oh, and another thing Mrs Dover-Davies said. Mr Olleranshaw has been in communication and he is still interested in James.'

'Water under the bridge.' Charles had nothing to say about Mr Olleranshaw. He was sorry to have missed Mrs Dover-Davies, though; in his imagination he saw himself basking in her admiration, the little pinched face lighting up as he told her how business was expanding. 'Is there a Mr Dover-Davies?'

'Paralysed from the neck down. It came out in conversation. She works to support him.'

'Poor sod! She can't 'ave much fun.' Charles was really taken with Mrs Dover-Davies and for days he went about fantasizing over the way she admired him. Without the slightest sense of disloyalty to Hannah he thought of Mrs Dover-Davies's slim figure, so slim he could have slipped an arm right round her and given her the most almighty squeeze. Hannah took to referring to Mrs Dover-Davies as, 'That friend of yours'. Later, she spoke of 'That lady friend of yours', but with no suggestion of criticism. They were both well aware the relationship was all in the mind. Charles worked all the harder, driven by his dream of taking Mrs Dover-Davies in his arms and shocking her with his passion.

Olive finally graduated from her training course and was told she would be taking over the Singer Sewing Machine shop in Glebe Street, which amazed and impressed everyone in the family. It was almost as good as being made a bank manager or a station-master. Those were jobs for men, but the appointment Olive had secured was one of the few managerial jobs (as Hannah saw it) open to women; and, what was all the more amazing, there was living accommodation behind the shop. Singer's were obviously an advanced company. When Olive took over after Easter she would be her own mistress. Quite the independent lady. In the meantime she drew her trainee pay but did not work at all, which Hannah thought very grand.

Olive was present when the Reverend David Llewellyn had his little talk with James – which was just as well because Hannah became so upset. James said he did not believe in God.

The minister wore what Hannah considered very fine clothes. His suit was carbon grey, his winged collar as white as a daisy, his knitted and slackly knotted violet tie lolling like a tongue. White hair stood out in wings over his ears and he smelled of aniseed drops (which he took because he fancied they gave his voice more resonance). When not preaching in chapel where he was all passion and *hwyl*, he was a creaking, deliberate sort of man who proceeded cautiously.

'What do you want to be when you grow up, James?'

James did not answer. He shut his eyes and compressed his lips.

'Your father has a prosperous business, so no doubt you will follow in his footsteps. But wealth is not everything. Are you happy, James?'

'No.'

'You have a loving father and mother. You have a sister. You are gifted by God—'

'I don't believe in God.'

Hannah was upset but the Reverend David Llewellyn was not.

75

'I understand what you say, James. I hear you and wish you had spoken differently. You know what the Bible says? "The fool has said in his heart there is no God."'

'I'm not a fool.'

'Of course you're not a fool, James, and I'm not going to argue with you here and now. But consider some questions. Who made us? How did we come to be here?'

'The sun warmed the mud. Little creatures came out of the warm mud.'

'I don't think that is quite right, scientifically. But who made the sun? Who made the warmth?'

'I don't believe there's a God or Mr Rumble would never have been allowed to give Agnes the cane.'

'Was that so terrible? We all have to be punished when we do wrong. Listen, James. I'm sure you are a good boy and I have to admit there are many things we don't understand. Thank God we don't have to live by our understanding; we live by something that happens in our hearts, not in our heads. It is love and innocence. I see that you love your sister, Agnes, and that is good. But we have to love everyone, even Mr Rumble.'

Hannah was horrified by James's defiance and was disappointed that the Reverend David Llewellyn had not reacted more dramatically. Was that all there was to say to a silly boy who said he didn't believe in God. She thought of the time when Charles had frightened her by laughing at the idea that God was an old man in the sky with a white beard. Hannah had no taste for abstract ideas about religion; she wanted the voice from the burning bush. At the beginning of the family Bible was a steel engraving of clouds parting to reveal a huge hand pointing an accusing finger at a wicked world. That was the sort of divinity she understood. The minister couldn't take James to the window and invite him to look to the heavens for some supernatural manifestation, but he really ought to have done better than he had.

Afterwards Olive tried to comfort her by saying that in spite of James's bad manners she thought the minister's words really had an effect. You could not expect an immediate result. James would now be up in his room, chewing the words over and, who knew, this time next year he might be a changed boy.

Everyone agreed that James cheered up a lot when the snow came, particularly when the hard frost followed and he could slide with the other boys down the steep lane behind the Yacht

Club. His snowballing was a bit frenzied. Because of the frost the snow had slivers of ice and a well-aimed ball could do damage; James threw one that cut Fred Stringer's cheek. He was excited because he had never known such snow and frost. South Glamorgan was normally mild. It was unusual for rugger to be stopped by the weather – not that year, though. The ground was a rigid white blanket and a couple of games were cancelled in succession. Gulls walked about pecking at the snow in what looked like disbelief.

The turning point came when James developed itching in the palms of his hands and the soles of his feet. There was no rash and Dr Brownlow made a joke about itchy feet indicating that James would be a great traveller, and itchy palms meant he would be rich as a result of his travels. He prescribed zinc ointment, which gave no relief at all. At night James writhed in his bed, scratching himself until the blood came. Hannah washed the itchy skin with dilute hydrogen peroxide, as suggested by Cousin Olive who had known it to be effective in the treatment of impetigo; but it did nothing for James.

Dr Brownlow hit on the idea that acute itching could be caused by lack of calcium in the diet (calcium being important to the nerve endings in the skin), and prescribed accordingly, but still the itching went on and James slept for scarcely a few minutes at a time. Hannah's mother brought round a bag of ice which she had bought at the ice factory. When applied this gave considerable relief, but it did not last. Mrs Jones thought it was an affliction of the blood. Was James constipated? Well, yes and no. He was given spoonfuls of Californian Syrup of Figs. Olive said the itching was brought on by the snow and would disappear when the thaw came but James could not wait for that, he was so desperate. But he *had* to wait. There was nothing else to be done and, true enough, when the wind turned to the south-west and the thaw came, when there was running water everywhere and floods in the Vale of Powys, the itching faded and eventually died away.

James said he had been tormented – not by God because there was no God, but by things which had come to him out of the air after the Reverend David Llewellyn had spoken to him. That was all he would say, all he ever said, because within the week he walked out and successfully hanged himself.

*

77

What struck officialdom was the efficiency with which the operation had been carried out. The boy was precocious. First of all the police surgeon, then the police superintendent, then the Coroner himself, Mr Illtyd Carpenter, said it was unprecedented. For a boy of thirteen to pile boxes on a table, tie a rope treble-knotted to a beam, put his head in a noose and then kick the boxes away was very shocking, certainly, but it was also astonishing. That this crude and rather ignorant model of a gallows actually worked passed belief. Indeed they did not believe it. Mr Carpenter made an inspection *in situ*, tugging his black beard in a distraught sort of way; he took the view that more was involved than appeared on the surface. James died because his neck was broken, not because he was strangled and that, if self-inflicted, was too professional to be believed. Had somebody helped? He came to change this view.

Even though it was Sunday, Charles was down at the docks when the catastrophe took place. Ewart Paul went into the carpenters' shop to saw joists he was behind with and came across James with a blue face, hanging from the beam and slowly rotating. His first thought was to run away; then he took a saw and severed the rope so that James fell on him awkwardly. Even then Ewart could not believe what had happened. What he did he did mechanically, instinctively, without thought. He laid James on the floor still with the noose round his neck. He could see that the neck was at a peculiar angle, but even then thought James might be up to some game. He knew the boy was interested in theatricals.

'James,' he said. 'Stop fooling.'

James made no response whatsoever. Ewart tried to slacken the rope round his neck, but it was tight as a tourniquet. Only then did Ewart, looking at the tumbled boxes and the treble-knotted rope round the beam, really understand that something real had happened which could not be blinked at or ignored. He could not run away. As he said later, 'It looked peculiar.'

Because Ewart was confused and delayed doing what was necessary, it was an hour before Dr Brownlow arrived on the scene. Arriving at 'The Lookout', he was badly thrown to discover Charles was not there and he had Hannah staring at him.

'When'll he be back, then?'

'What's the matter?'

'I must see Mr White, ma'am.'

'What's happened?'

'There's been a terrible accident in the shop.' To Ewart's shame and horror he began to sob and Hannah, now thoroughly alarmed, said, 'You've got to talk sense. What's happened?' Ewart was crying, rubbing his eyes with the backs of his hands.

'I'm sorry but it's James.'

'Oh, my God!' Hannah blanched so suddenly her heart might have stopped beating, but she was not so shocked that when Agnes appeared asking what was the matter she could not collect herself to reply, 'Go to your room and read from that new book of yours, the one Grandma gave you. We'll talk about it later. Go on now.'

Agnes looked curiously at Ewart and did as she was told.

Hannah broke the silence that followed by saying she must go down to the shop.

'No.' Ewart was clear that was not what Mr White would have wanted. 'I must go back by myself. Dr Brownlow is with him.'

Hannah took no notice. After she had put on her black straw hat and coat they set off together, not talking, taking the short cut through the Windsor Gardens, past the bandstand and the water-tanks sunk in the ground and winking blackly under the sullen sky. The Channel away to their right ran brown, grey and silver in the wind.

'He's dead, isn't he?' Hannah asked this in a matter-of-fact sort of way as they passed the town library. She gave the impression she had always known that this (whatever this was) would happen. Ewart said he did not know.

Dr Brownlow was there with a policeman when they arrived and so were Tom Williams and Edgar Thomas, the two pit-prop men turned carpenters who slept in a loft over the timber store. It was they who had called in the policeman at Dr Brownlow's suggestion.

James was covered with a blanket from one of the men's make-shift beds and Hannah went on her knees to lift it so that she could see James's face. What she saw made her cry out in pain.

'What happened?'

'I'm grieved to say his neck is broken and—'

'But how?'

Dr Brownlow indicated the noose that was lying on the floor and the other end of the rope that was still tied to the beam. 'It will be for the Coroner to say.'

The police found out where Charles was and brought him back to Penarth in a cab. When he walked into the carpenters' shop to encounter Hannah, Dr Brownlow and the rest (more and more police were involved), he was prepared for what he was about to see. He looked at James's face, kneeled and kissed him on the brow. Hannah came over and stood by his side. Still kneeling, he held one of her hands, pressing it gently. It was all too much for any man to bear, or woman either. Hannah cried silently and he was holding her hand tightly now because he was dizzy and thought he might faint. One of the policemen helped him to his feet.

'Who did this? How did it happen?'

Mr Illtyd Carpenter was sitting on a bench, wood-shavings clinging to the bottom of his trousers. The sweet smell of sawdust hung in the air; for Charles it was for ever afterwards the very smell of death.

'You are this boy's father? You are Charles White?'

'Yes.'

'My most profound sympathies. The death of a child is peculiarly shocking. It makes one feel guilty that one ought to have been able to say to the Almighty, "Take me instead." But that is not how we are permitted to exist. I promise there will be the most thorough investigation of the facts.'

Charles turned to Hannah. 'Where's Agnes?'

'She's at the house.'

He looked at Mr Carpenter, 'So, what 'appens now?'

The Coroner shrugged. 'I suppose you should instruct an undertaker, Mr White. But it must clearly be understood that what I have in mind is the usual preparation for burial – nothing more than that preparation. I may wish to view the body and this building with my experts. You understand, Mr White, all I am permitting is an arrangement that will preserve the decencies. The burial must not be proceeded with.' Mr Carpenter corrected himself. 'The burial must wait on my inquest. That won't be until Wednesday. No need for a jury, I'll take this myself.' He turned to the police superintendent. '11 a.m. Wednesday. That all right?'

During the following two days Charles and Hannah were interviewed several times by the police, both together and separately. An Inspector Routledge, who had not been present at the original session in the carpenters' shop, took charge of the enquiry – a foxy, quick-moving man who always looked the person he was talking to squarely in the eyes. He had been to the school and interviewed Mrs Dover-Davies, so he knew all about Oliver Twist and James's running away to London. He talked with Ewart Paul about the rope James had used. 'It's a very ordinary piece of hemp rope,' said Ewart. 'There's lots of it about.' But the Inspector was not satisfied until Ewart showed him coils of the stuff and explained how it was used in scaffolding.

The Coroner had his own special police-sergeant (his name was Rix) making enquiries too, often – on separate occasions – putting the same questions as Inspector Routledge, though he seemed more interested in James's acting. Sergeant Rix stood talking to Fred Stringer at the corner of the street while other boys stood round, listening. He visited the Reverend David Llewellyn at the manse to have confirmation of what Hannah had said, that James had declared to the minister he did not believe in God.

On Wednesday morning in the Coroner's Court Charles was astonished to see the theatrical agent Olleranshaw, wearing yellow gloves and a light brown overcoat with an astrakhan collar, sitting next to Mrs Dover-Davies. It later appeared he had come down on the early train at the Coroner's request. As time passed, and interview followed interview, Charles formed the impression that opinion was, in some way, hardening against him personally. Just what was the relationship he had with James? He was under scrutiny. As he understood it, Coroners did not conduct a trial; they were there merely to establish the facts. So Mr Carpenter was conducting an enquiry. What purpose, then, was served by the presence of Olleranshaw, who was in London at the time and whose opinion on how James met his death would be valueless? And why Mrs Dover-Davies? Charles fought against the idea that he was under judgement. Shortly before the Coroner took his seat the door of the Court opened and Charles turned – half-expecting to see Polly's sister, Mrs Smorfitt, accompanied by Father Gillespie – but it was only Ewart Paul, red-faced and breathless from running.

It was his evidence which Mr Carpenter called for first, and what he had to say merely confirmed what everyone knew already. Medical evidence was given by Dr Brownlow and confirmed by the police-surgeon. A policeman who had been called to the shop that Sunday morning reported how he had found James lying on the floor, three wooden boxes lying there too and a severed rope dangling from a beam. He confirmed that the noose was still around the boy's neck. Mr Carpenter was conducting his enquiry in such a relaxed and informal way that Charles thought it was a charade. Something more official and decisive was being planned, such as Inspector Routledge (who said nothing throughout the whole proceedings) coming up to arrest him. For what? For being James's father? Charles's anger built up.

The Coroner's police-sergeant revealed that he had experimented with those boxes.

'When piled on top of one another, what height would they attain?'

'Nearly eight feet if piled in one way. Five feet if another.'

'They could have been piled erratically, of course, but I think we can take it the height at the maximum was eight feet and at the minimum five feet. Do you agree?'

'Yes, sir.'

Mr Olleranshaw was now called to give evidence. What sort of a boy had James been? Charles was aghast when Olleranshaw was called.

Olleranshaw stood on the witness stand and gave a restrained performance. 'James was an engaging little chap with real gifts. On the dark side, you understand me, sir? His character had sombre elements in it. Later, he could have been . . . a, well, it is not too much to say an Irving.'

'As promising as that? He was imaginative?'

'Yes.'

'And adventurous?'

'It was adventurous to come up to London by himself to see someone like me he didn't know.'

'No doubt it would be something of a drama to him? A drama he was creating himself? A play?'

'Very likely. He thought he was Oliver Twist.'

Nothing seemed to happen in the court for quite a while. Mr Carpenter scribbled away, Inspector Routledge walked out, Mrs Dover-Davies whispered in Mr Olleranshaw's ear and a young man who had been making notes throughout, probably a journalist, appeared to fall asleep.

Finally Mr Carpenter looked up and slapped his desk with the flat of his hand. 'This is a sad case. I have considered all the evidence, not least that taken both here and elsewhere as to the facts and to character. My finding and verdict is that this attractive and inventive, also experimental, child was carried away by a kind of zeal for enquiry. He might have been Edison. Nothing I have heard persuades me he was suicidal. No letter which would usually be found in such a case exists, and there is no jot of evidence that any other person was involved. It was a matter for James White alone.' Mr Carpenter fell silent and started to write once more.

A clerk whispered up to him, hoarsely, 'What is the verdict, sir?'

'Eh? Oh, misadventure.'

Charles knew this was a lie and he could not understand why the Coroner brought it in. Perhaps there was some Coroner's rule about the suicide of infants? One thing was clear. He had been wrong to think the police might have his own role under any sort of scrutiny; he had been wrong to think some miscreant from outside had come in to hang James. There was no enemy but James himself. That was the truth of the matter, but he knew enough about James to realize the boy would not have seen it that way. His last act had been a continuation of the war against him, his own father, and as Charles walked out into the winter sunshine he could see no end to that war. He was so dizzy he had to put a hand against a wall for support.

The Baptist burial service, presided over by the Reverend David Llewellyn, took place next day in the municipal cemetery on the Lavernock Road. Hannah did not attend, just as she had not attended the inquest. Women, traditionally, did not go to funerals. Uncle Ted and his two sons from Abercarn were there in their Sunday overcoats and suits. Mr Olleranshaw had postponed his return to London so that he could be present. Ewart Paul, in navy blue serge, highly polished boots and a flat grey cap looked particularly grim, as grim as the day itself. A stiffish breeze sprang up from nowhere and the Reverend David Llewellyn's hat went spinning. Mr Minsky clutched at his glossy black top-hat with both hands. Charles was sorry the burial had to be in this low-lying desert of gravel paths and marble gravestones. He would have liked it to be up at St Augustine's, a place where there was a view of the Channel, its shipping and the Somerset coast. As the earth he cast crackled on the coffin, he had another dizzy spell and Mr Olleranshaw supported him. Mr Minsky pressed his right hand, but was too distressed to say anything coherent.

Everyone was invited back to 'The Lookout' for light refreshments, but Mr Olleranshaw excused himself, saying he had to catch an early train from Cardiff.

'Mrs Olleranshaw would, I am sure, like to join me in offering our condolences. We thought him a sweet boy. Choirs of angels sing him to his rest. Remember, it is we who grieve and suffer. Not

James, who is free and at rest. Death comes suddenly. Alex Findlay, you've heard of him? Bookings manager at the Ally-Pally here. We had a drink and, poor fellow, he walked out and dropped dead. No advance warning whatsoever. Very sad. Could be me. Could be you. What is life? 'Tis not hereafter. Coroner, very human, I thought. He'd given James some thought and I agreed with his merciful verdict.' Mr Olleranshaw had a cab waiting. 'You all right now, Mr White?'

'I'm all right.'

Presumptuous bastard! Charles watched Mr Olleranshaw's receding back with hostility. *Agreed* with the Coroner's verdict. Well, Olleranshaw could keep his opinions to himself. Charles did not, in fact, feel all right. The minister slipped an arm through his and they walked slowly towards the main cemetery gate.

There, surely, they would find Father Gillespie in his priest's cap and cassock. After all these years it would have been absurdly unlikely. Indeed, there was no sign of the priest, he was not there. But that did not stop Charles from seeing him, waiting for them with a book in his hand and a sly look in those small eyes.

Had Father Gillespie really been there, Charles could imagine how the encounter would go. To begin with he would challenge him. Are you that priest? Then he would ask how he knew about James, the place and time of his burial. These were questions to which there were simple answers. And then Father Gillespie would raise the book so that Charles could see it clearly, saying, 'This, Mr White, is my service-book.'

'What have you been doing with it?'

'Saying the Catholic service for the burial of the dead.'

'In Latin?'

'Keeping my distance, I read the service in time with yours. After the appropriate period has elapsed I shall say a Requiem Mass.'

After that Charles could not imagine how the conversation would go. He stumbled and the Reverend David Llewellyn suggested they sat on a seat for a while but Charles said no, he was all right. The wind was too cold for sitting. Charles then knew what Father Gillespie would have done. He would not have the same horror of alcohol as the Baptists, and from somewhere inside his tunic he would have produced a leather-covered flask, saying, 'Drink this, Mr White. It will set you up.'

Charles turned to look back at the plot where James was lying. The grave had been filled in and the low mound was covered with wreaths. Gulls fluttered their wings and soared brilliantly against the grey sky. It seemed strange that after such a death creatures like himself, the Reverend David Llewellyn and those gulls could persist in living. Yet Charles could not fully accept that there had been a death. The war between James and himself still seemed that real.

# 5

Ewart Paul was called Ewart because that was Gladstone's second name and the Pauls were Liberals, not from any clear idea of what Gladstone stood for in politics but because the gentry were Conservative in Somerset and the Pauls were against the gentry. Ewart's father and mother were not surprised when the gentry (Sir James Budden, who owned their property), the miller and the yeast merchant got together to enforce their bankruptcy. What else could you expect? In Penarth the gentry were not so much in evidence. Most people voted Liberal and Ewart's political allegiance, such as it was, remained untroubled. But he had no strong party loyalties, Liberal or Conservative. Both parties were fighting to serve their own interests and he thought of neither of them as his own. He was hostile to Labour because that was a new party his father and mother did not understand. Ewart thought the Labour lot were demagogues who wanted power. Power for what? They would grind chaps like himself (without a union, just chaps on their own) into the ground. He wanted to obey no kind of boss, employer boss or union boss. Politically, he did not know what he was and didn't much care.

He wanted to get away from Penarth. Because of James White, the place horrified him. Dead, dangling limbs fell about him in dreams and in waking. He would never again go into that carpenters' shop. Emigration was something he thought about from time to time. Canada was too cold, so it was either the States or Australia. There were two reasons why he did not emigrate. He could not bear the thought of separating himself so enormously from his mother, now a widow. The other reason was that he had fallen in love – desperately and, it seemed, hopelessly – with Olive.

Olive was like champagne, so far as a Singer Sewing Machine representative could be effervescent. She was aware of Ewart's admiration and thought it a giggle. She had a number of admirers (*beaux* she called them), all of them more eligible than Ewart,

86

who after all was just a common labourer in spite of his robust good looks and undoubted sincerity. Olive was not at all sure she valued sincerity highly; what she wanted was a bit of fun and devilry. Her mother, Hannah's aunt, had died some years ago and her father married again to a widow who owned a market garden just outside Cowbridge. Olive felt there was no family home she owed any loyalty to. She just wanted to be on her own and independent. Even to Hannah that had seemed puzzling. To others it was a scandal and there was a correspondence in the *Penarth Times* about suffragettes, the female's place in society and the New Woman, in which an oblique reference was made (without naming her) to Olive herself. The writer said that if ever the day came when women were regarded as the equal of men it would be against nature and with what consequences no one could foretell.

Olive responded to public opinion by looking around for some respectable female to share her accommodation. The search was harder than she expected. Advertising was out of the question. Who knew what undesirable approaches that would lead to? Contact was eventually made with the right woman through Hannah and Charles. They learned that the wife of a sea captain needed a shore base while her husband was shuttling to and from the West Indies in the banana trade; the very same captain, master of the Liverpool registered *Gower Prince*, whom Charles had sought out when poor James first went missing. For year Captain Peacock's wife had accompanied her husband on these voyages, but now she had had enough. She did not rule out the possibility of taking the occasional voyage with her husband at some time in the future, but for the time being she wanted a more settled life. She was a small, dark woman in her thirties who laughed nervously when she talked, even when there was nothing to laugh about, and hopped rather than walked. Olive rather took to her, partly because of her passion for embroidery which Olive shared. So Mrs Peacock moved in, bringing two wicker hampers full of clothes, on the clear understanding that when the *Gower Prince* was in port Mrs Peacock would join her husband on board. There could be no question of Captain Peacock paying anything but short visits to Glebe Street, to take a cup of tea perhaps. Overnight stays were out of the question.

Ewart Paul did not attach importance to the arrival of Mrs Peacock on the scene until he realized Olive was much freer to associate and flirt with men now that she had such a readily available *chaperone*. On Sunday mornings he would see her being attended along the front by some fellow in a straw hat or bowler while the birdlike Mrs Peacock hopped at her side. When the weather improved, Ewart too sported a straw hat so that he could have the pleasure of raising it whenever he passed Olive's shop and saw her in the window treadling away at her sewing-machine. These occasions were not frequent because he was usually at some building site digging foundation trenches, or carrying mortar for the brickies, when Olive was giving her sewing demonstrations in the window. But he took the odd half-day off. And there were other occasions when he made an excuse to slip out of his working clothes and go into town wearing his straw hat.

Whenever Olive saw him she waved her hand and smiled sweetly, because Ewart was undeniably attractive and she liked the sense of power that came from having so many men in tow. She had a romantic fantasy that the day would come when two of them would fight over her.

Ewart just had to get on. There were no openings in the baking trade (not in Penarth; plenty of jobs up in the valleys but he did not fancy that), and the building trade would employ him only as an unskilled labourer. He was too old to serve an apprenticeship. He had a good school-leaving certificate which said he shone in arithmetic and geography, but what use was that? Perhaps the Gas Company would employ him as a meter reader, but that would not be good enough for Olive who currently had a bank clerk and one of the keepers from the Mumbles lighthouse in tow. Ewart thought well of the lighthouse-keeper because he was away in his lighthouse for weeks on end and his existence divided Olive's affections. Where division existed there was always a chance of disillusionment, and that would be Ewart's opportunity; if only he had a decent job and prospects.

He lodged with a tobacconist's family. The tobacconist maintained a morbid interest in the White family and from time to time asked Ewart to describe again how he had found James.

'And what about Mr White himself?' The tragedy had been reported not only in the *South Wales Echo* and the *Argus* but in the London papers too. What interested Mr Walsh – who was a newsagent as well as a tobacconist and read all the papers – was how Mr White was withstanding so much publicity. Critical comments had been printed. A letter in the *Morning Post* had argued for a more extended service of social welfare to monitor the conditions in which children lived.

Ewart refused to talk about the Whites to the pot-bellied and heavily moustachioed Mr Walsh, but the truth was he did not like what was going on. He was more open in the letters he sent to his mother because she was lonely and needed diverting. Mr White, he wrote, had the wind quite taken out of his sails and was neglecting his business. There were days when he did not come to the office or any of the sites his men were working on. Ewart understood he was either reading or taking long bicycle rides in the Vale of Glamorgan. As for Mrs White, what kept her going was Agnes. The child was enchanting, full of fun in spite of the death of her brother and the profound melancholy that descended on 'The Lookout'. Hannah lavishly spent money on her – clothes, parties, treats of all kinds, including pantomimes at the Cardiff Empire and boat trips, in the season, to Weston-super-Mare where they sat in the Winter Gardens listening to the band and eating ice cream.

Ewart liked a modest bet on the horses and his way of interpreting Hannah's attitude (he always called her Mrs White) towards Agnes was that she was laying money on her daughter. He also reported to Mrs Sarah Jane Paul, in her almshouse just off the main street of her Quantocks village, that Mr and Mrs White had quite broken with the Baptist Chapel. He had this from Mr White himself who said, 'We British 'ave mistakenly identified ourselves with a slave religion and we must now stand up in the sun for what we are.' Ewart's mother wrote back that he must be working for a man whose mind had been turned by his misfortunes; why did he not try to get away and seek employment with the Co-operative Wholesale Society, who recognized the Bakers' Union and paid good wages?

A crisis arose in the White business when the goods yard at Penarth Station reported the arrival of two trucks of engineering bricks which Charles White swore he had never ordered. He had no call for them; he wasn't building any bridges and they cost too much to use as footings. No other builder in the Penarth area would want them either. They would be dead stock if he accepted them. He wrote to the brick company rejecting what they had delivered, and they replied saying that if he did not accept the delivery, value £250, they would take him to court. This exposed a weakness in the White organization. Charles employed a foreman and storekeeper, but he did the book-keeping himself; when the shock of James's death hit him he had wandered off in other directions and the various record journals were neglected.

There was no reason why Charles should have confided in Ewart, but he did. He had increasingly used Ewart as a checker on supplies and they were down at the docks watching timber being unloaded.

Charles looked at it unseeingly. 'Sometimes a man feels just everything is 'ostile. What 'appens is so painful you just can't believe it's an accident. Per'aps it is though. And now comes this bugger-up with two trucks of industrial bricks. Could be just chance. The wrong bit of paper sticking to some clerking twit's finger.'

'It's your fault,' said Ewart.

Charles was staggered. He switched his attention from the timber to Ewart's face, bewildered by this attack from someone he had thought a friend.

'From what you say,' Ewart went on, 'you don't keep proper records. You got to keep tight journals and file copies of your orders and payments.' Ewart's father had done just this. 'Then if the brick company take you to court you can just show up your journals and they'd accept that. But the magistrate won't just take your word, specially if the brick company hand up your order, properly signed. They'd have got you.'

Charles was impressed. 'It's not as bad as all that. I run a proper office. This order for industrial bricks wasn't a mistake, it was a bloody try-on. Massey Kilns 'ad a glut, so they thought they'd palm some off on a poor, ignorant customer, like me.' Charles went on being impressed not only by Ewart's understanding of office work but by his bearing, which was confident, outgoing and manly.

'It's not as bad as all that. I've got this lad from the accountant's to go through the paper stuff two days a week. But you're right in a way, Mr Paul. I'm groping, I'm trying to find my way. Can you know what it is, Mr Paul, to be stunned by somebody you can't get back at? That is my situation. I'm low. Now you are a young man who might be doing better for 'imself than just labouring. What do you know about keeping the books?'

'I used to help my dad.'

'So that's why 'e went bankrupt!' It was the first time Ewart had seen Charles laugh for weeks. 'D'you know that more builders go bankrupt than any other tradesman? I sometime feel that's what I'd really like, to go bust. If it wasn't for Mrs White and Miss

Agnes, that is what I'd really like, come to think of it – go bust and wallow in muck. I've 'ad my life.'

'You don't mean that, Mr White.'

"ow do you know what I mean? You've not been where I've been. In the valley of the shadow.'

The unloading finished, Charles and Ewart went into the office of the shipping agent to sign forms and when they emerged into the spring sunshine Ewart was emboldened to say, 'You've been hit, Mr White, and I'm more sorry that I can say.'

'Thank you.'

'But I don't know what you mean when you say you've been stunned by somebody you can't get back at.'

Charles caught Ewart by the arm and turned so that they were facing one another. 'You found James, Mr Paul. Did you not see an expression on his face that said "I defy". No? He left no note but he left that expression on his face. I saw it. *I defy*. And who does he defy? Me, 'is father Why? Answer me that?'

'How can I answer? You are wrong. James died because of a terrible mistake. That's what the Coroner said and he'd studied it all.'

'James wanted to strike at me.'

'Mr White, I've got to say that doesn't make any kind of sense.'

They were intimate, man to man, in a way that surprised and pleased Ewart. Deep down he was not moved by Charles's irrational response to James's death, nor his muddle over the paper-work in the office. Ewart's real interest was with Olive and how he could get her. She so took charge of his imagination that the whole coastline of South Glamorgan, Penarth included, seemed irradiated by her presence, and what previously he had thought a boring place of countryside in comparison with his native Somerset took on the aura of an earthly paradise.

To improve his chances, to make himself more eligible, he borrowed from the town library Mr L. R. Dicksee's *ABC of Book-keeping*, in the hope that Charles White would at some time see fit to employ him as a proper clerical assistant. Ewart worked at his book-keeping and Charles, who had come to think of him in precisely this role, continued to take his lonely bicycle rides, trying to make sense of the incomprehensible disaster which had befallen him.

And befallen Hannah. Hannah and Charles could not think of

anything sensible to say to each other. In bed Hannah's eloquence came out only in tears, while Charles fought back his. They were both afraid that Agnes might hear them and be upset. Hannah wore black for months and never went without a black veil and black gloves. The dress meant nothing at all. It would do nothing for James; it did not help to answer the question: where had she and Charles gone wrong? But in some strange way the costume made their loss seem that little bit more bearable and she wore it until one afternoon in early summer, when the palm trees in Alexandra Park glistened as though they had been oiled and she herself, in her black, seemed as insubstantial in the brightness as one of those black 'strangers' that hung on bars of the fire-grate in winter. Here she met a woman on a park bench who had a thin face, wore pince-nez and seemed authoritative on every subject under the sun. What she said led to a relationship which brought Hannah out of mourning.

Not that every subject under the sun came up for discussion. It was the woman's manner and actions which conveyed the impression that she knew everything. She drew little trenches in the gravel with the ferrule of her umbrella; she flashed her pince-nez in the sun in a way that implied scorn of ignorance; the unusually large handbag on her knee was gripped so tightly her knuckles whitened. So she was a determined woman as well as a knowledgeable one. Rich too, judging by the quality of her clothes, her shoes and the musky perfume that was so strong it made Hannah's eyes water.

'I see you're in mourning. I'm a widow too.'

'I'm not a widow. It's for my son.'

'My dear! I'm really distressed for you, believe me. How awful! Have you other children?' The woman said her name was Trevor. She'd been a widow for five years, and as there were no children of the marriage she was alone in the world.

'Alone in this world, that is to say, Mrs White. In the larger creation, of which this is only a part, I have the never-failing companionship of God or, as we prefer to call him, Jehovah. I take it you, too, enjoy the comforts of religion?'

'No. I used to go to chapel, but I don't go any more. It seems such a mockery.'

'That is because the chapels and the churches do not teach the truth.' Mrs Trevor went on to explain, working away at the gravel with the tip of her umbrella as she did so, that true religion was not a mockery. Everything would become plain once the errors of conventional belief were swept away. 'Tell me, even when you went to chapel regularly did you, in your heart of hearts, believe in a God who was all-loving and at the same time all-powerful? It's nonsense. Would such a God permit the premature death of my husband and the even more untimely death of your son? It is not like that. Tell me now, Mrs White, is it?'

Hannah was bewildered. 'Is what?'

'Why, we just know in our bones that God is good but he is not all-powerful. He is fighting a battle. We are on his side in this battle and it is against evil. Is that knowledge not more in accord with our sense of the world as it is?'

Mrs Trevor opened her handbag with a snap and a pamphlet shot out. 'The invisible ruler of *this* world is not God but Satan. In the larger universe it is of course another matter. There Jehovah is supreme. This pamphlet will explain how we can join Jehovah in the fight against Satan in this lower world.' Mrs Trevor produced a pencil and notebook to record Hannah's name and address. 'I shall write to you. We must meet again. I shall hope you will become a Millenial Dawnist like me. Good day, my dear.' She rose and walked away, using her umbrella as though to test the ground ahead for pitfalls and then swinging the handle round ceremoniously at the extent of her arm. The musky perfume lingered behind her in the still air.

Mrs Trevor lived in one of the big Plymouth Road houses with her cook-housekeeper and a couple of servants. Having informed Charles of her new friendship, Hannah took to visiting her every Thursday afternoon for tea and general instruction in the beliefs of the Millenial Dawnists (which, to begin with, she did not tell Charles about). The furniture in the house was enormous; huge sideboards, bookcases, desks and, in the sitting room where tea was taken, a life-size portrait of the late Mr Trevor – a porky man with blue eyes, who had been a mining engineer. And everywhere the pungent odour of Mrs Trevor's perfume.

Hannah was really drawn to the idea that the world was ruled by Satan. She had always suspected something of the sort, but it was not until Mrs Trevor explained that this gave reason for hope rather than despair that she realized she had been a Millenial Dawnist all her life without knowing it. A great battle would soon take place, it was called Armageddon, and there the forces of Satan would be confronted by the forces of Jehovah himself, led by his son

Jesus the Christ. Of the outcome of that battle there could be no
doubt. Satan and his minions would be utterly destroyed and life
thereafter would be ideal. Armageddon was so imminent that many
Millenial Dawnists now living would never die but go straight to
heaven. Mrs Trevor could even put a figure on their numbers:
144,000. There they would rule with the Christ over the earth.

To Hannah it became clear that the misfortunes of her life had
been the work of Satan. First of all there had been the protracted
battle for pregnancy, then there had been the death of Polly and
now, most agonizing of all, the death of James. Mrs Trevor learned
all this in the course of the weeks that followed and was able to
confess griefs of her own.

'So you see, Mrs White, we know the cause of our distress.
The fault is not in us. We are the innocent victims. Even when
we sin it is Satan working through us. So do you not agree you
should become a Millenial Dawnist too, go about doing good and
distributing pamphlets so that the armies of righteousness will be
gathered for the last and greatest battle of all?'

When Hannah broke the news to Charles, he read one of the
pamphlets. 'It's all nonsense, of course, and American nonsense
at that. But I can see your mind's made up and I'll not stand in
your way.'

Hannah attended many meetings of the Millenial Dawnists
before making up her mind to join them. There were no more
than twenty or so of the sect in the town, mostly women, and
Hannah was impressed by the simplicity of their proceedings;
these took place in a large upstairs room, and were led by a
Mr Jennings who was known as the Elder. He read passages
from the Bible and commented on them, then members of the
group put questions. It was very like a Bible study session, but
unlike some Bible students they took it for granted that every
word was literally the word of God. This was one of the things
about the Millenial Dawnists which Hannah liked. They believed
in real things: they were practical and took it for granted that all
Jehovah's creation was solid and practical too, with real marble
floors in heaven, and that the Second Coming would involve the
use of carriages and horses. Money must be raised to provide
them. Yes, Mr Jennings believed that signs would be seen in the
sky. One might even take the form of a huge hand with downward
pointing finger.

Like the Baptists, the Millenial Dawnists had an initiation

ceremony that involved total immersion; unlike the Baptists they had no concealed tank under the floor-boards – how could they, being in an upstairs room? The Town Council refused them the use of the Municipal Baths for such a purpose. Mrs Trevor, one of the few members of the group to have a bathroom in her house, said immersion there was out of the question as the bath was too small. She could not understand why immersion could not take place in the sea, from a bathing cabin, which was the way she had been initiated. Mr Jennings was against this, because he claimed the privilege of ducking Hannah's head under the water for himself and a man could not possible approach a lady's bathing cabin. it was the kind of discussion they had had many times before.

Mrs Trevor hated to presume on an old acquaintance of her husband's but there seemed no alternative. In the gardens of Mr Illtyd Hughes at Dinas Powys was a large lily-pond, said to be a one-time fish-pond of the ruined religious house nearby. So to Dinas Powys the Millenial Dawnists went in four crowded cabs and Hannah, concealed from head to foot in cotton sheeting, was thrust down among the goldfish and water-lillies. In a suitcase she had brought a change of clothing: a dark blue cotton dress with white collar and cuffs, a blue and white straw hat to match. She dressed in a bedroom and put her mourning clothes in the suitcase. She felt lifted up, purified, at peace for the first time since Ewart came with that awful expression on his face. The sweet face of James came vividly to her mind and she saw that he was happy with her conversion. Mr and Mrs Hughes entertained them all to tea and, when thanked by Mr Jennings for the use of their pond, he said they were welcome any time. It had been such fun to watch.


In the town library you could not go wandering around the stacks trying to find the book you wanted. You had to queue until you reached a window, rather like the ticket-office window at the railway station, and then make your request to the librarian sitting on the other side. It could be made in the most general terms. At various times Charles had heard women asking for 'real life stories with a happy ending' or 'a historical novel without fighting'. Men he had heard asking for travel books. The librarian would go off and return with three or four books from which the borrower would select one. No catalogues were available for consultation. Not wishing to be fobbed off with any old book that pleased the librarian's fancy, Charles tried to make his request as specific as possible. But this time he could not be specific.

'Is there a book called *Philosophy and Religion*, or something like that?'

'We're strong on that kind of book.' The librarian was waiting with his pencil poised.

'I don't want a pious book. I want something that cuts into religion.'

'It's Mr White, isn't it?' The librarian pushed up his glasses to see Charles the better. 'It's not customary, but as you can see I'm short-handed today. No assistance. If you like to go through that door there, you will find yourself in the library proper. The case of religious and philosophical works is in the far corner, on the left as you go in.'

Being at close quarters with so many books gave Charles a thrill. Most of the authors meant nothing to him and he rejected some works simply because the title looked boring. He did not want pap. He was after the kind of ruthless, rationalistic work on religion which the library probably would not want to possess anyway. A desk and a chair were handily placed and Charles took down volume after volume to sit and leaf them through. Martineau, T. H. Green, W. R. Sorley and others were examined and rejected. Two authors seemed to be in the area he wanted, Feuerbach with his *Philosophy and Christianity*, and the one author who on superficial examination most caught his fancy had an unpronounceable name. It was Nietzsche.

Charles turned the pages and certain phrases sprang out like grasshoppers. For example, ' . . . the Christian belief . . . that God is truth, that the truth is divine . . . what if nothing any longer proves itself divine, except it be error, blindness and falsehood; what if God himself turns out to be our most persistent lie?'

Charles was a quick reader. Some novels he could gut in an hour. His eyes danced over the pages, picking up the dialogue and missing the descriptions. Nietzsche could not be treated like that, but Charles could take samples here and there; enough to tell him the whole must be good. Even electrifying. The titles of some of the volumes (the library had the complete works) were enough to excite him by themselves. *Beyond Good and Evil*. What

96

did that mean? That there was some unimaginable height from which human beings could be seen scurrying about like ants; and that their behaviour was meaningless?

Meaningless! The word was like the deep, bull-like roaring of a foghorn heard from out in the Channel. It signalled something special. And here, sure enough, was a sentence that roared even louder: 'Through Nihilism is the conviction that life is absurd.' Life was absurd, certainly, but what was Nihilism? Then Charles turned pages and fell on the words, 'God is dead.'

He remembered, from years back, hearing the story from the time of the Emperor Tiberius, when a voice from the shore hailed a passing ship, saying, 'The Great God Pan is dead.' The preacher said that was an acknowledgement by the pagan world of the great victory that Jesus had won in his crucifixion. The Christian God had supplanted the pagan gods. Now came this German philosopher to say the Christian God who had lasted for nearly two millennia was dead too; and Nietzsche wasn't shouting from some island. He was standing up, in full view (shining, it seemed to Charles), to tell the world that not only was there no God – not even pagan gods – but life itself was absurd. That is to say, meaningless.

Surprisingly, Charles was elated rather than depressed by this. If that was the way it was, well, fine! Even exciting.

'I'll take these two,' he said to the librarian.

'You're entitled to three non-fiction, Mr White.'

Charles went back and picked up the Feuerbach. He walked out into the sunshine and saw how the chestnut trees put their candles up to the sun. Men and women were walking about as though nothing had happened. How could they be so stupid? He wanted to run; he wanted to express himself physically. But how? He walked home, deposited his three books on the table in the hall, collected his swimming costume from the wardrobe on the first-floor landing and took himself off to the Public Saline Baths, where he tried to control his excitement by swimming two, three, four lengths without stopping and then stretching himself on the matting in the sun room. In the radiant heat, he could almost hear the salt water crystallizing on his skin.

He used to bring James here. He taught James to swim by putting him in harness and attaching this to a line at the end of a cane road, and then held him rather as an angler held a fish. James splashed about in the water and Charles kept him from going under with his rod and line. He thought of the boy's sinewy legs and arms thrashing at the water and the way he cried out in excitement. 'I pressed against the water. I'm sure I can swim soon.'

Charles remembered saying, 'You've got to trust the water. Let it buoy you up. It's salt water. That means it's buoyant. Just trust it. Face into it with your legs up. *Lean* against it. It's all a matter of confidence. Go on! Push your arms out. Wider. Now shove the water behind you. Yes, that's right. Keep your legs going. Good! Good! Good!'


Ewart was shrewd enough to know the advantage which, in Olive's eyes, he had over her other admirers. He was not vain, but he knew he was handsomer. He was big, over six feet, with broad shoulders and a freshness of complexion which could look radiant. There were young men like him on advertisement hoardings advertising brown bread. Added to that, Olive thought he was a bit wild.

He liked a bet, and the tobacconist he lodged with had some arrangement with an on-course bookmaker. Sometimes he won but usually he lost. Back home in Somerset he used to go to Taunton Races, which was far and away the greatest time in the year for him. He loved the big white marquees and the way toffs in their carriages or motor cars came with luncheon baskets. He made a point of pressing as near to the saddling enclosure as possible, then hared off to make his bet on the horse he had seen there and fancied. During the race he would stiffen up with excitement until, as they came up to the finishing post, there were times when he thought he might faint out of sheer excitement.

He used to meet Olive at the Whites' house and when he talked she thought he was more interested in racing and betting than in her. It was outrageous. But deep down, she thought it crazy in a nice sort of way and possibly dangerous. Hannah used to say that no good would come of horse-racing and, as for betting, that was an evil second only to drink. Olive took Ewart's side. 'Times are changing, Hannah. All things are good in moderation. I'm sure I wouldn't say no to a glass of champagne. Men have all the fun. They just go off, racing and gambling and, I've no doubt, chasing women. The world thinks none the worse of them. But women! What sort of a life do *they* have?'

Hannah would have liked to smack her. 'That's no way to talk.'

Placards went up at the railway station advertising an excursion to Chepstow Races. Ewart determined to go and take Olive with him. He called at her shop, not so much to invite her but to tell her that she was coming because when racing was in prospect nothing he felt could be denied him. So confident was he that her abrupt refusal was taken calmly.

The more he thought about having Olive with him at Chepstow Races, the more masterful he became. 'Think about it, Olive. It's a Bank Holiday Monday, so there's no work. The sun will shine. You know, it'll be really hot. You'll need a sunshade. I'll just show you everything that goes on. When you see the jockeys and their colours! And the crowds! Can't you imagine it?' He was even masterly confident about the weather.

It was his enthusiasm and blazing blue eyes which carried the day. Hannah would be against it and, for Olive, that was another attraction. The *Gower Prince* was in port and Mrs Peacock would be spending a week or more on board so there was no need to take her into account. Yes, said Olive. All right, she'd go. She'd even run up a special dress for the occasion and buy a hat. Going racing? That was perfectly respectable, wasn't it? Royalty went racing.

Ewart was right about the weather and they had the most glorious day. The sun shone. He would let her pay for nothing: seats in the crowded third-class carriage, admission to the course, programmes, ice-cream in wafers, lemonade, ham-and-lettuce sandwiches and bets, a shilling each way (Ewart having marked her card) on every race. Olive Scion had two shillings on him to win. Nearly all the horses were named to make them irresistible: Quantock Laird was another. They all lost but, in a way that quite amazed Olive, this caused Ewart no concern whatsoever.

'You're paying for pleasure. What's money? Let's go and get next to the rail.' Clods of turf from the flying hooves shot around them. Olive was stunned by the drumming of hooves and deliciously terrified. 'Smell it,' said Ewart. 'You can smell the grass.'

'This is just beautiful.'

Over there was the River Wye, running along the race course, and above were the riverine cliffs crowned with trees in their trembling spring foliage. Patches of wild daffodils were sere and already faded, but the hawthorn hedges stretched out like white billowing steam vapour from unseen expresses. 'We must come here again, Ewart. Oh, my God!'

At the hurdle nearest to them a horse took a tumble and the

jockey rolled over on the ground with his arms clapped over his head.

'He'll be all right. Look, the horse is up again.'

'Oh, Ewart,' she said, gripping his arm. 'It *is* dangerous. I couldn't bear it if anyone got hurt.'

She looked entrancing in the green and yellow dress she had made for herself and in the wide-brimmed hat she bought in Cardiff. It left the upper part of her face in shadow. She wore white gloves and one of those gloved hands was gripping Ewart's arm.

'I love you, Olive,' he said. 'You know that.' He was amazed to find himself talking in this way; it had been brought on by the horse-racing.

'Don't spoil this lovely day. Can we go and have a cup of tea?'

Ewart was making notes on his card. 'Why Dolly Kop should have let us down I just don't know. She was out of Spion Kop and Dolly Varden, and you can't say much better than that. Oh, well! Tea. Let's go and have some tea. *And cream buns*, Olive,' he said with particular relish.

'Is it important? I mean, the breed. Of horses?'

'It's everything. If you ask me, horses are better off than human beings in that respect. If we bred humans as we bred horses, we'd have a race of supermen and superwomen.'

'What are they?'

'They're what Mr White tells me about, the race that are going to take over the world. You know what he's like. Deep in German books now.'

There were no cream buns, only scones with cream and strawberry jam. The found a table where they could sit and eat them with their tea. Ewart took the opportunity to tell Olive once more that he loved her. She replied tartly that he must not read too much into her accepting his invitation to come to the races; she had just been curious. Now he was annoying her.

'Will you marry me?'

'Certainly not.' She struck him playfully with her rolled-up parasol. But inwardly she was saying yes. She would tease him; she would tease the cheek out of him; she would really punish him, for weeks, perhaps for months. How delightful it would be to torment him. She would be strong, she would make him crawl. At the same time she was so practical she wondered about the Singer people. Would they have a view? It was one thing to have

100

a spinster living over the shop and quite another to have a married couple.

'If you don't marry me, Olive, I don't know what I'll do.' He was delivering her back in Glebe Street in the still hot evening. Shadows stretched half-way across the road. 'Join the Foreign Legion, could be. It's a job in the sun.'

'You're a silly boy. Thank you for everything. I did enjoy it. Really!' Before putting her key in the lock and completely indifferent to the passers-by, she kissed him on the lips. 'Good night, Ewart. It's been heavenly.'

During the summer Mr Minsky and his wife (not Ruth; she was in London doing social work in the East End) went off to Russian Poland to visit relations, and they both came back with coughs and what he called 'squitters'. Mrs Minsky's trouble soon cleared up, but his went on and on and it coloured his outlook; he became gloomy. Mrs Minsky tried to rally him but it was no good. One of the qualities Charles admired in him was the way he quoted literature, and on this occasion Mr Minsky did not disappoint. He said that coming from eastern Europe to Britain was like coming from one of the circles of Dante's Hell to Aristophanes' Cloud Cuckoo Land. Everybody in Russian Poland knew bad things were happening and that worse would follow. But here, in Britain, in South Wales, people were thinking of what? Nothing! They were such credulous fools. 'Regardless of their doom the little victims play' – that was his quote. Money, clothes, food, fun – that's all they thought of. The Cardiff Empire was a good example. Women showing their legs and making lewd jokes. Not that he'd been, but he knew from the placards and advertisements. And all the time, out there in Russia and Austria and Germany the twentieth century was being monstrously born. He actually used the word 'monstrously', making it sound like another quote. That madman Nietzsche Charles had been reading was right about one thing at least: the Europeans were in for wars and revolutions.

'And this,' he said to Charles, 'is the moment you are choosing to become an atheist! A trivial response.' He did not say what to, but Charles knew well enough.

Mr Minsky's 'squitters' turned out to be dysentery. He became so enfeebled that he had to go into hospital where Charles visited him from time to time. He put Mr Minsky's apocalyptic mutterings down to his illness. He could not see why his atheism should be linked with what was going on in Russian Poland. The fact was that Mr Minsky had showed he was too low physically to think clearly. What was more he was, as Nietzsche explained, an inheritor of that Jewish tradition – which had become the Christian tradition – of being passive, of turning the other cheek, of suffering patiently, of saying not 'Yea' but 'Nay' to life. In other words always expecting the worst. Had Charles gone to Russia with Mr Minsky, he would have come back with a different story.

Mr Minsky wore his hair long and now, in hospital, allowed his beard to grow. He was all hair, bone and parchment, his voice hoarse and raised scarcely above a whisper. He could still smile, though.

'When I come out I know what to do. I buy one of those motor-cars and am driven round the country like a lord. Oh, it shall be so good, just riding along everywhere, free, up the valleys and into the mountains.' His laugh was gruesome, but Charles admired the spirit.

He thought Mr Minsky's talk was bravado. Next time he saw him Minsky was in slippers and a dressing-gown sitting in the sun. His hair had been cut, his beard trimmed and there was colour in his still sunken cheeks. Obviously he was on the mend. Strangely, though, he still wanted to talk about motor-cars. He had a copy of *The Autocar* on his knees. 'This is the future, Mr White.' He tapped it for emphasis.

Charles still thought it was bravado, but with a difference. The first time Minsky enthused about motor-cars he was a sick man and wanted to show he was going to survive. When it was evident that he was recovering, motor-cars came to represent something else; they gave a respite from talking and thinking about his relatives in Russian Poland. Charles understood this because, in the course of that summer, he too found that by thinking about motor-cars he could now and again stop thinking of James.

When Minsky had recovered and was back at work he made no move to buy a motor-car, but he still passed on copies of *The Autocar* to Charles, who read them attentively and came to the conclusion that the German Opel Dolly was the most desirable of all cars and certainly the one, if he was serious, for Minsky to buy.

It was so dainty. In the advertisement it looked like a real lady. Charles could imagine himself sitting behind that face-high steering-wheel and swivelled windscreen, looking along the bonnet to the knobbly little radiator cap and the open road beyond. He worked out it would cost him a year's income. Even more exciting was the 'Prince Henry' Vauxhall but that was a sports car and, at £500, beyond his means. What he might be able to afford was a two-seater Riley with a dickey seat at the back for Agnes. Charles gently slid into the idea that he might, just possibly, become the owner of a motor-car in which he could transport Hannah and Agnes to picnics on the Gower peninsula where he had not been. From what he'd been told it was Paradise. It would be one way of saying 'Yea' to life. But not just yet. While Ewart worked at his book-keeping and at courting Olive, both Charles and Minsky took to motor-cars as other men took to drink. So the summer passed.

Ewart was proving himself as a book-keeper and accountant, even making a fair go of providing estimates. Charles was amazed at the clever way he managed the books. Asked for an estimate for sewerage work at some hours' notice (while Charles was in Court fighting that industrial bricks claim), Ewart took one of the foremen over to the site and with his help analysed the job – materials, time, labour – and went back to his little office in the corner of the yard to work out an estimate for Charles's scrutiny. Charles was pleased, but a tiny bit unsettled. The fellow might turn out to be a real cuckoo in the nest. He had drive and ambition. Who knew where they would take him, even in Charles White's own business? But Charles did not care, not really. He had a real liking for the boy. When the time came to think of a successor, he could do worse than think of Ewart. He looked wholesome, had a good nature and was clever. How could he, a baker by training, come into the building trade and in a short time acquire such an understanding that he was able (using little reference books) to quote for connecting a house to the gas-main and even building a two-storey extension to a house in Sully Terrace? Charles marvelled and warmed even more to the boy.

He knew all about Ewart's infatuation with Olive and wondered whether his rapid progress in the business was due to biology. Charles never forgot Darwin. There was not only a financial imperative, there was a biological imperative too. Ewart's efforts were fired by the thought of Olive's trim little figure, her small waist, those bright eyes and the way she moved her legs. Love of power and the love of women – these were what drove men; so

103

he decided and, remembering Nietzsche, particularly the love of power. He gave Ewart another pay rise and was so pleased to do it he might have been giving the money to his own son.

Business was brisk. Charles had the contract to build six villas at Barry intended for managers and supervisors at Barry Dock; villas with detached brick garages. The garages really brought home to Charles the idea that lots of people were going to have cars, not just the well-off. The men who bought these villas would drive into Barry every morning and drive home every evening. It was a social revolution; not only the horse but the bicycle would be superseded. This had been going on for years and Charles had known it, but only now did he see the light. He was angry with himself for having been so blind to the march of progress, and placed his order for the Riley two-seater with a local garage. He was distraught when informed that delivery would take at least two months. In his now over-excited mind, it seemed he might be too late to catch up with history.

'I've bought a motor-car,' he told Hannah. 'Everyone's getting them. I'll use it for business and Ewart will work out 'ow to put it into the accounts as legitimate capital acquisition. But we'll go out on trips. The Gower is country and sea too.'

'A motor-car!' Hannah put her hands up to her cheeks, which had reddened. 'But who's going to drive it?'

'I am.'

'Charles, you don't know how to! You'll have to take lessons. What colour is it?'

'Colour? The motor-car? Black, of course, but with red lines round the panels like real coachwork.'

During the weeks before the Riley was delivered Charles had bought and studied carefully an illustrated work on the internal combustion engine; he believed in mastering essentials before proceeding to the Riley manual which Mr David Tew (the garage proprietor) lent him. Mr Tew took him out for a spin in his own Riley and then encouraged Charles to drive back into town which Charles did at a steady ten miles an hour, keeping as near to the centre of the road as the other traffic allowed. The next day Charles did all the driving and Mr Tew just watched. The result was that the very day Charles took delivery of the car he was able to drive solo down to Barry, where he gave the workers time off to inspect the machine, drove it up and down, reversed and manoeuvred with all the pride of a horseman exhibiting the qualities of a thoroughbred. For a few minutes he was happy and ashamed of it – so ashamed he decided he had not been happy, even for those few minutes. He had anaesthetized the pain. How? With a motor-car! This was behaving so absurdly that Nietzsche would have approved of it.

On the way home he drove into Minsky's yard and found the boss sitting in his office.

'There she is, Mr Minsky.' Charles felt no pride. He was raw all over.

Still sitting, Minsky looked at him through the open door but made no move. Charles thought this strange. A workman went by pulling a truck and from the carpenters' shop came the sound of sawing and hammering, but Minsky seemed oblivious to everything. He was wearing a wide-brimmed black hat and, in spite of the warm weather, an overcoat. He looked at Charles so bleakly he might even have been on the point of tears.

'Mr Minsky, are you all right? I thought you'd like to see my purchase.'

Perhaps he'd had some bad news from Russian Poland. 'Your purchase, Mr White?'

At last he'd come out of his office and walked over to the Riley. 'It is a smart car. I wish you well of it. I wish you happiness in what you have acquired.'

'I expect you've got a car of your own by now.'

Minsky shook his head. 'I shall never have a motor-car.'

"ave you 'ad some bad news?'

'I don't want to talk about it, Mr White. Just a private family matter.'

Charles had never thought of him as an old man, but that is what he looked as he straightened his shoulders and, with no more to say, made off across the yard towards the workman with the truck. Charles was deflated. He had expected smiles and congratulations. Instead, only the most perfunctory acknowledgement of his rise into the ranks of the motor-car owning fraternity. Undoubtedly there had been bad news from Russia and it had taken the heart out of Minsky. Charles felt for him, though it could not be worse than what had happened to him. Nothing could.

He owed a lot to Minsky. Without his encouragement and financial support he would never have been able to set himself up. He did not know why he had been favoured in this way; Minsky did not make a practice of helping lame ducks. Charles could only think that he looked on him as a decent sort of English peasant who, by kindness, could be inveigled into regarding the Minsky family like any other family and not as foreigners. Only slowly had he come to understand, intuitively, that Minsky might feel uncertain of his place in this Anglo-Welsh community and need reassurance. Why was he a builder in the first place? Charles knew of no other foreign builder. Perhaps there were lots of Jewish builders in Russian Poland, but he doubted it. Being a builder and a Jew into the bargain, perhaps he wanted a Gentile friend in this Gentile line of business.

He did not buy a daily newspaper, only the *News of the World* on Sunday, so he went into the periodicals room at the library to see whether there were press reports of disturbances in Russian Poland. There were not.

That something was going on in Russian Poland Charles did not doubt for a moment, however, and he could not understand why the papers were so unaware of it. He asked for back copies of the papers but no, even over a period of some weeks there was nothing about the parts of the world Minsky was interested in. Plenty about Serbia and Bulgaria, with Austria looking on in a threatening way, but they were always at each other's throats in the Balkans. Nothing new there. Charles wondered about this inadequate coverage of foreign news. The real world seemed to be unreported. He was prepared to believe that whatever had been said in that letter to Minsky (he was now quite convinced of its existence) was the truth, and the world should know about it. Charles would suggest that Minsky wrote to the newspapers himself. To *The Times* in particular.

When he told Hannah what he had been doing and why, she said it was likelier Mr Minsky was concerned about more domestic matters. Mrs Minsky might have been taken ill, or his daughter might be ill. She could not believe Mr Minsky would worry about what was going on the other side of Europe, even if his own relatives were involved. It was all politics out there, wasn't it? She knew somebody who knew somebody who worked in the Minsky household, and there might be ways of getting some information. Charles was really angry with her for being so parochial. What did she mean, it was just politics? For all they knew there might be a pogrom going on.

'When I say politics, I mean conflicts of an entirely worldly nature, Charles. That is of no importance. The actual struggle is on a spiritual level. It will develop into real fighting between the Satanic and Heavenly forces all right, but that is still to come. Worldly affairs are nothing in comparison. I'd be very sorry to think Mr Minsky's relatives were in trouble, of course.'

Charles no more argued with Hannah about her Millenial Dawnists than she did with him over atheism. They thought they owed as much to the memory of James, yet both knew exactly where the other stood.

The summer was maturing all around them. They saw what was happening but felt no part of it; they were numb. Apples were swelling on 'The Lookout' trees, grapes turned from green to boot-polish black in the conservatory and cherries ripened on the south-facing wall. Agnes, in her wide-eyed, pink and creamy way, was putting on puppy fat. Yachts in the annual regatta performed a ceremonial middle-aged dance out in the Roads. The Welch Fusiliers' band played Grieg and Souza in the park, their music rising and falling as the breeze came and went, like the deep breathings, the quiets and silences of a man contentedly slumbering. The hot afternoons put a swoon on the town. The smell of summer came from powdery-blue, vanilla-scented floss flowers and the pungency of geranium leaves rubbed between finger and thumb.

For Hannah it was also the parched smell of new cotton clothes. For Charles it was now the inky, oily odour of the two-seater Riley with the sun on it, so hot he could not have placed his hand flat on the bonnet. Yet they saw without seeing, heard without hearing and smelt the warm air without responding to its scents. They were too stunned. The natural world had no meaning. That was to be found only in what went on inside their heads: ideas, imaginings, longings, defiance. Neither of them wanted consolation, in their different ways they wanted to strike back.

Charles was never ready to talk about James, but Hannah was. Now and again she claimed to have seen him walking in the street, but even this could not make Charles talk.

Agnes loved picnics. Hannah tied a rope round her waist and held one end of it so that, without looking back, she could see Agnes safe in the dickey seat. Hannah had a veil over her face because of the dust, and Charles wore goggles. It took longer to get to the Gower peninsula and back than he had bargained for, because there were always punctures. They picnicked in a field overlooking a sea that was blue like the sea on comic

107

postcards, and they went down to the beach. Agnes wanted to play ball.

Or paddle. Or collect shells. Well, why not? Life had to go on. Charles thought it might not mean anything, but it had to go on and be endured. When he was at work these thoughts could be kept at bay but out on the beach, with the sun shining and Hannah unpacking the Etna heater to boil a kettle, they came leaping at him like hounds. Hot weather and blue seas were not to be trusted. When the sun shone, that was when life was most meaningless. You were misled into expecting the good but the dazzle was false. He was mocked by the beauty of that radiant afternoon

'Charles, remember that picnic we had at Llantwit Major, the one when there was that trouble with the gypsy?'

''e tried to make off with James's racquet.'

They said nothing for some time. 'James so enjoyed himself. He wanted the gypsy to keep the racquet, he was that sorry for him. Charles, I do so miss James.' Hannah tried to control herself but could not.

Charles felt a pulse of anger. He was haunted by the belief that James had acted with hostile intent. Against whom? Against him, Charles White – his father who, God knows! had done no wrong except to provide his sterile wife with a child. If he deserved anybody's hostility, it was Polly's. Hannah sobbed bitterly and he went and put his arm around her.

''Annah, think of Agnes.' She was building a sandcastle and unaware of what was going on.

He wondered if Hannah too supposed that James had acted out of hatred for his father and, as a result, held him responsible for what had happened. Responsible? Why was he responsible? What had he done or not done? Where had he gone wrong? Even in a godless, abandoned, absurd world there must be natural justice. Otherwise there was no law but that of the jungle.


For all his good intentions Charles realized he had not suggested to Mr Minsky that he should write to *The Times* about the treatment of Jews in Russian Poland. When he did so, Minsky turned on him.

'*The Times* is an idiot newspaper. What is it doing? It is stirring up trouble between Germany and Russia so that they will destroy

108

each other. Why? To save India for England and the King. It's making me sick to the stomach. What good will that do for ordinary human beings who just want to live in peace? France will be destroyed too. And England? England will stand back and plunder the corpses. That is what *The Times* wants. Anyway, they would not print my letter. It would mean nothing to them.'

Charles had given Minsky a tour of his yard and up to that moment they had just talked business and played a bit of a game, Minsky dropping in a few complimentary remarks about the way Charles had got on. The little game was this. Because of Ewart, Charles knew to the nearest five pounds the value of his stock (bricks, slates, tiles, chimney-pots, pipes, sand, cement, timber, lavatory pans and tanks, the lot) and he had challenged Minsky to put his own figure on it too. Minsky went round making notes on his starched cuff and eventually came up with a figure within spitting distance of the real one. What fun! After congratulating each other – the one on the wealth this stock represented, the other on his acumen – Charles raised the matter of writing to *The Times* and all playfulness just went out of the air. Minsky said he did not go in for empty gestures; he was too tired for that sort of thing. Indeed, he now looked it, and so sad that Charles had an impulse to put his arms round those thin shoulders and give them a hug. This is when he delivered his diatribe against the British Empire.

'It's his daughter,' Hannah was able to explain some time later. The friend of a friend who worked for Mrs Minsky had produced this information on firm guarantee that it was confidential and not to be passed on: 'Cross my throat and hope to die.' But the friend thought that Hannah could not possibly be included in this total ban and so the secret came out. Hannah thought her husband could not be included in the ban, either.

'What's the matter with his daughter?'

'She's got married in London, that's all, and the Minskys don't approve of the man because he's not Jewish. They've taken it really bad. The photographs of her have been taken down and her room has been locked up. Nobody is allowed to mention Ruth; the name is forbidden. They've completely washed their hands of her, poor girl. That's worse than death, it's treating her as though she'd never been born. Can you understand that sort of behaviour, Charles?'

'There must be something else. It isn't just marrying a Gentile.'

'It seems it is.'

'Mr Minsky isn't like that, nor Mrs Minsky for that matter. They're both of them good, gentle people.'

'You've got to look at it from their point of view. What would we think if Agnes married one of those blacks from Barry?'

'That's quite different.'

'At least we'd not turn our backs on her. At least, I wouldn't.'

Charles reflected. 'If this is true, it must have been something terrible for the Minskys to be'ave like that. And I can't ask. 'E'd shut me up.'

If Minsky was having trouble with his daughter, he was probably too upset to think clearly and that (together with the state of his health) might explain why he had this absurd idea of casting England as the European villain manipulating the guileless Germans and Russians. He was not himself. He was not the wise counsellor he had once been, recommending Tolstoy and Theodore Herzel. Embittered by the state of his bowels and the defection of Ruth, he showed spirit only in the denunciation of that evil genius Nietzsche and, by implication, Charles who had become his disciple; and in denouncing England.

But was there anything in Minsky's views on the game the British government was playing? Charles gave up his usual reading in favour of Seeley's *The Expansion of England*, which he thought good patriotic stuff. He also read the *Daily Mail* and *John Bull*, both of them violently anti-German. Charles tried to balance this with *Reynolds Newspaper*. Out of all this reading he emerged with the conviction that England was not the villain of the piece at all, but Kaiser Wilhelm of Germany who suffered from a morbid resentment of the British Empire. Germany and Russia going to war was just wild theorizing. It was on England that the Kaiser had fixed his sights.

'Mr Jennings thinks there will be a war and we'll be in it,' said Hannah. This was the view the Millenial Dawnists had come round to in their study meetings, though they were still uncertain whether it would be Armageddon itself. If the end of the world was indeed at hand they needed a supernatural sign, restricted to the Dawnists themselves, and the latest news from headquarters in California was that no such sign had been detected.

# 6

For some time the town took no great notice of the war, and then the owners of horses fourteen hands and over were summoned to parade them on the Rugby football pitch for inspection by Army officers. Charles took two horses and they were bought for £25 apiece. They were going to France to draw gun-carriages and Charles wished he was going with them. Soon after (but it couldn't be, could it? Time had telescoped) miners were coming down from the valleys with £5 notes stuck in their hats. They bought peaches at £1 each and walked the streets of Cardiff eating them and throwing stones at each other. They were living high and rejoicing in it. Peaches now, you bourgeois bastards! It'll be your daughters next! Because miners' wages did not rocket for some time, memory must have played him false; £5 notes and peaches really came quite a while later.

Ewart would have joined up straight away, but then decided to wait until after Christmas when he planned to take Olive over to Somerset to meet his mother. Charles thought he might be too late. Modern wars were over in a jiffy. The Hundred Years' War, the Thirty Years' War, the Seven Years' war were no longer possible in an industrial age. The duration of wars was coming down. Modern weaponry was so effective that a protracted struggle was out of the question. Victories would be won by heavy bombardment and ruthless cavalry charges, followed by waves of infantry. No slackness. Everyone would be determined to bring the war to a rapid conclusion. It could well be over before the bad weather set in and Ewart would miss the fun.

Charles was glad that Minsky had been proved wrong. England went in from the start – not standing on the sidelines as he had predicted – and her role would be decisive, the French being the second-raters they were and the Russians such peasants. In a British triumph, the Kaiser would be marched in chains through the streets of London. Charles relished the thought. He drained the radiator of the Riley and put it on blocks for the duration. Two

111

of the workers joined up, a carpenter and a plasterer. Charles said he was proud of them, presented them with £5 each and said he would do the like for anyone else who volunteered. War would give the nation the jolt it needed. Men would step out more sharply and, as Ruskin had prophesied long ago, society itself would be reinvigorated. A pity Nietzsche was a German, but a prophet could not answer for his origins.

Ewart took Olive to see his mother at Christmas, but the visit was not a success. Because of the war there was no cross-Channel shipping, so they took the train from Cardiff through the Severn Tunnel to Bristol where they changed for Bridgewater. They were not even engaged, so Olive thought herself very much the New Woman to be travelling alone with her *beau*. If challenged, she would say the war was doing away with stuffy old ideas. From Bridgewater there was no other transport but the carrier's van – the very same van Ewart's father had driven – the night was black, the horse seemed sluggish, the rain lashed down and when they arrived they were both chilled and tired. Mrs Paul obviously thought Olive was a loose woman. Ewart, she directed, was to sleep on the sofa in the sitting room and Miss Jones would sleep in the tiny room, no more than a cubicle, next to hers so that any nocturnal movement would immediately be detected.

'She doesn't like me,' Olive said when, the weather clearing the next day, they went for a walk and climbed the hill behind the village, where they could see across the Channel to Penarth and Cardiff. 'I never thought you could look at Wales like that. Being there, I mean, you don't think of people watching you across such a distance.'

'Of course she likes you, Olive. You know what mothers are.'

'Anyway, she doesn't want you to join up.'

'As I say, you know what mothers are.'

Ewart showed her his father's old shop. 'Dad did a lot for the village. That town clock, he paid for having that put right. And there it is, still going.'

Mrs Paul served a roast capon given by a village charity, followed by plum pudding which Olive looked at and then added to her unpopularity by saying she could not eat it because of her figure.

'It's got threepenny bits in it, Miss Jones.'

'Give me a threepenny bit and I'll suck it. That'll give me the flavour of the pudding.'

Ewart ate her helping as well and when they took the carrier back to Bridgewater on Boxing Day he said, 'She never got over my father going bankrupt and being driven out of the choir.'

Olive had not heard this story, and when Ewart explained she said, 'How silly! Did he drink?'

'Of course not.'

Ewart was so infatuated he left it at that. 'Some people brush off misfortunes. Others don't: my mother, for one. Or the Whites. I don't reckon the Whites will ever get over young James going the way he did.'

'Ewart, you know the boy was not Hannah's son, don't you?'

No, Ewart did not know this. He was amazed. They had been talking quietly because there were other people in the van, and he shut up altogether now because he had become aware of the interest taken in their conversation.

Olive did not seem to care who listened. 'The boy was actually –'

'Sh!' He took her hand and squeezed it.

'Little pitchers,' he whispered.

'What?'

'They've got big ears.'

Olive giggled and did not withdraw her hand, so he held it all the way into Bridgewater.

As they walked up and down the platform waiting for the Bristol train, Olive told him that James had been Charles's son all right. 'The mother was an Irish servant-girl. Cousin Hannah seemed to have taken it all in her stride. She didn't appear to hold it against Charles at all.'

'What happened to the girl?'

'She died and the Whites formally adopted the kid. It's well known, though nobody ever talks about it. You didn't know?'

Ewart shook his head. 'Mr White doing that sort of thing, well, it's unbelievable. Was it before they were married or after?'

'After. I don't know how Cousin Hannah stood for it. Cousin Charles always ruled the roost. He'd just tell her that's the way it was, and she'd accept what he said. I'm sure I wouldn't have stood for it. Cousin Charles is a funny sort. I never liked him, really.'

The train was crowded and they could not talk. Soldiers with kitbags stood in the corridor and Ewart was lucky to get a seat for Olive. He stood holding on to the luggage

113

rack, swaying with the train, digesting the news she had given him.

He never really knew James, had just seen him now and again and remembered the alert, questioning way he looked about him; as though he was up to some mischief and did not want to be caught out. A squirrel of a boy. He had an idea the Whites had trouble with him, but didn't quite know why. If only he had reached the workshop five minutes earlier, the boy might still be alive. He was drawn to him even more by what Olive had said.

Between Bristol and Cardiff there were fewer passengers and they had seats next to each other. He asked whether James had known that Mrs White was not his mother.

'Oh, no. If he'd known there'd have been trouble.'

'But there *was* trouble.'

'You shouldn't ask me these questions. I'm sorry I mentioned it at all. Ewart Paul, will you stop talking and let me close my eyes? I'm that tired. The kid was impossible. What can you expect with Irish blood in his veins? Charles White, though, he's not my kind of man. One day he's all right, but the next he can be that rude! It's his conscience that troubles him. I don't wonder. if ever there was a case of a man being punished for his sins! He fancies himself as a lady's man, too. You know what? Just because he's got on and has money in his pocket, he lets his eyes wander. I've seen it. There's that Mrs Dover-Davies. Do you know her? She was young James's teacher and brought him on as an actor. Ever seen her? She's got a crippled husband. She looks like a ferret but they've been seen talking. Cousin Hannah is a saint to put up with him. It's her I'm sorry for.'

'They seem happy together; I mean as happy as they can be in the circumstances. And that Agnes is really enchanting.'

'Agnes? Yes, she's sweet. A pretty girl. Takes after her mother. Do you know what I think? Divorce should be easier. It stands to sense a man and a woman will fall out.'

'But mostly they don't fall out.'

'They usually do.'

All the signs were there for Ewart to read, but he shut his eyes and ears to them. Even though he was put out by Olive's views on divorce (it was a disgrace much worse than bankruptcy in his opinion), they just made her seem more provocative and desirable. He asked her to marry him at least once a week. She always said no, and it was this regular refusal that prevented Ewart from joining

114

up. He could not bear the thought of leaving Penarth and setting Olive loose on the market; and yet the war with Germany had clearly come to a turning point. The German advance had been stopped, the French and the British were digging trenches in preparation for the counter-attack. That would come in the spring and drive the Hun back over the Rhine.Ewart wanted to be in that counter-attack, but how could he when Olive would not marry him? Thinking in the military terms he had picked up from the newspapers, he saw marriage as a way of securing his base and he turned to Hannah for advice on how to win Olive over.

For Hannah, Olive was not so much a cousin as a younger sister. Poor girl! She had lost her own mother; her stepmother was jealous, and seemed to regard Olive as a rival for her husband's affection. The girl had been badly treated and Hannah, though she knew Olive was flighty, felt she had a duty to help. She hesitated. Olive and Ewart might not be a good match. He was straight, a tidy sort of man who dressed respectably and held himself well. It was obvious why Olive encouraged him. No, Hannah was sure now it would not work, this relationship, not because of Ewart but because of Olive. But she dared not say this to Ewart. He had such charm she weakly decided to talk to Olive on his behalf, not doubting it would all end in tears.

Olive listened patiently. 'Hannah, I'm fond of Ewart but marriage is a big step. I sometimes think there ought to be trial marriages.'

'What do you mean?'

'A couple should live together for a year. If they got on, fine. They marry. If it went sour, they just part and no harm done.'

'But if there was a baby?'

'They'd have taken precautions. Don't mistake me, Hannah. It's because I think marriage is serious. If the couple don't match, it's hell. So there ought to be a try-out.'

'You mean you'd live with Ewart on trial?'

'If it was London, yes. Nobody would know who we were. But we're where we are. So, in Penarth, no. Anyway, what's so new about living in sin? Isn't that what you and Charles once thought of doing? Running away to Bristol! My, what a young rip you were!'

'That was all a joke. You know Charles's jokes.' Hannah had conventional ideas, but recognized that times were changing, particularly now there was a war. She felt on the edge of an abyss, just as when Charles told her God was not an old bearded man in the sky. Now she knew better, he really was an old bearded man in the sky. What Olive said brought on the same vertigo and reminded her of her past blindness to the truth.

'Oh, Olive, he does so love you and it doesn't bear thinking of that he should go away to the Army without you supporting him – as a wife, I mean.'

'I'd consider it if I knew we could divorce without a lot of trouble.' Olive tapped Hannah on the shoulder. 'Everyone isn't so lucky as you and Charles.' The two women looked at each other, Hannah not knowing how to take this and Olive's eyes sparkling because she was being cheeky.

'If that's what you feel, you ought to stop seeing him.'

'I couldn't do that.'

'Divorce? You're not serious. It would be such a scandal. You wouldn't marry Ewart with the idea of getting a divorce?'

Olive gave a little gurgling laugh. 'I believe in being realistic. Has Ewart put you up to talking to me? Leave it to me. I'll talk to Mr Ewart Paul, that I will, Cousin Hannah!' This was said with a show of anger she did not in fact feel. Both women knew this. Olive was quite an actress.

So the next time Ewart proposed, Olive said she was interested only in a probationary marriage which, if unsuccessful within a period of, say, two years (one, she conceded, might be too short a time) would end in an amicable divorce which he would finance and provide whatever evidence was necessary to establish her as the innocent party. As to who would decide whether the marriage was a success or a failure, that could not be decided by common agreement. It would be her decision alone. Did he accept these conditions?

Ewart stood very stiff, staring at her in disbelief. No, she was not joking; her lips were set too firm for that. She returned his look unblinkingly. He was so angry that he raised his hands and seemed quite ready to take her by the throat. First of all she was frightened, then she was excited and looked back at him defiantly. Ewart dropped his hands, walked away and, still in his workman's clothes – without going back to the yard or to his digs, his fists all the time clenched except when he was fishing money for the fare out of his trouser pocket – he went straight into Cardiff and joined up. He asked to be sent to France immediately.

The recruiting sergeant had a red band across his chest scarcely more vivid than his plump and crumbling face. 'Steady now,' he said in a North Country accent, 'We don't know as we're going to take you yet. We weed 'em out you know, at least one outa three. For one thing, you've got to see the Officer. Then there's the Medical. Flat feet and you're out. There are other reasons why we might take agin you. Personality, for example. How do you think you'd stand up to a Uhlan cavalry charge, eh? Have you had any experience of cavalry charges, Uhlan or otherwise? No? Well, don't pitch your ambition too high, sonny. It's trained men that face the enemy. However, Private Paul (provisionally I've admitted you on an experimental basis until the Officer and the M.O. have had a look at you), I would be wrong to discourage you in the belief you might at some time in the future find yourself confronting the King's enemies. Because you might be doing just that. All right?'

Ewart saw that the sergeant was a man who enjoyed his joke and was in bouncing good humour this afternoon. Perhaps he'd had some good news. Perhaps he'd just heard he was being sent to the front.

'Now, if you'll go along that corridor and knock at the first door on the right, that will be the Officer. Go in and stand to attention. he'll pass you on to the M.O. – unless he takes against you, that is.'

Ewart's basic infantry training was done at Catterick and, because he admitted to knowing how to bake bread, he was posted to a Service Corps unit – not even to bake bread but to collect it in a van and distribute it to units all over Salisbury Plain. After a year he volunteered for an infantry lot and underwent further training before embarking with his unit at Southampton to sail not – as everyone took for granted – to France, but round the Isle of Wight and back to Southampton again where the unit disembarked. Apparently a high-up had made a mistake. Most of the men celebrated by getting drunk, because by now the casualty figures made it clear what kind of bloody slog-out was going on in Flanders. Ewart stayed sober because he was a teetotaller and he came to believe that abstinence was one of the reasons the officers thought well of him. They got tight themselves, of course, but it was good to have a sober N.C.O. around. Ewart was a corporal by now. He had a good parade-ground manner. Without warning or consultation he was transferred to the Corps of Military police, where they made him a sergeant.

Here he was taught to ride and loved it. One of the exercises was to ride bareback with no stirrups or reins, the idea being to sit

117

there with folded arms while the horse jumped low obstacles. He fell off every other ride, but it gave him a new insight into racing over the sticks and even the wild idea that when the war was over he might have a go as a jockey; over the sticks you didn't have to be all that small, and Ewart was twelve stone and five feet eleven. If he could not be a National Hunt jockey he might stay on in the Forces as a regular because he liked the life. He had a black stallion called The Cat because of the delicate way he placed his feet, like a cat in longish grass. Ewart rode him all the way from Bulford Camp in Wiltshire down to Wareham in Dorset, a distance of fifty miles or so. There were half a dozen of them in the party, all well-mounted, and because it was a map reading and pathfinder exercise they were directed to avoid towns, villages and main roads as much as possible. It was a dry, hard, chilly November and Ewart rode along, very pleased with himself, enjoying the huge open fields, the cawing crows and the leafless lines of trees with the pale sky behind.

When he went on leave it was to stay with his mother in Somerset. Penarth he saw only from a distance, across the Channel. He kept in touch because Hannah White and he regularly wrote to each other.

The war had changed everything and it changed nothing. Olive was still running her Singer Sewing Machine shop, but also running a working party of women who made uniforms for nurses. Charles was not building villas because he was building huts for soldiers and doing very well out of it. His problem was labour. There were just not enough skilled tradesmen available. He could have used all the carpenters he could lay his hands on just to work on ships in the docks. Interesting, but what Ewart waited for was some news that Olive had taken up with somebody; this news never came, and he did not know whether or not Hannah was being discreet. He would not put the question direct. Then Olive herself wrote to say she had been deeply upset by the way he had joined up without saying goodbye to her but she forgave him and hoped he was all right. It did not occur to him to wonder why, after all this time, she chose to write just then.

The temptation to see her again was irresistible, and the opportunity came when he and a corporal were detailed to escort a prisoner from Tidworth to the military prison outside Worcester. He was a private in the Worcesters who had stabbed another soldier in a drunken brawl, but he looked harmless enough as he sat smoking cigarettes in the locked railway compartment, handcuffed to the corporal. It was a Friday and Ewart had put in for a weekend pass, so when they had delivered the prisoner the corporal went his way and Ewart caught a train to South Wales. By the time he reached Penarth the Singer Sewing Machine shop was locked for the night. He rapped at the side door and, when there was no reply, rapped again. An upstairs window opened and Olive looked out.

'What do you want?'

She had no idea who it was. Looking down she could see, foreshortened, a soldier in breeches and leggings and wearing a peaked cap with a red top to it. A Military Policeman usually meant trouble of some sort and although she knew perfectly well that Ewart had become one she did not connect that fact with the Redcap taking a couple of paces back on the pavement the better to look up and see her. She expected him to accuse her of something horrid, like harbouring a deserter. Or he might be bringing her bad news.

'What do you want?'

'It's me. Ewart.'

'What?'

'Ewart'

'No!' It was not a cry of delight or even amazement. It sounded more like a denial. She did not want to believe he was standing there. To Ewart it was like a blow in the face.

'Well!' More softly now, warm even, as warm as the May evening. She hadn't been cold, just utterly taken aback. 'You are one for surprises, Ewart. Why didn't you let me know? Wait! I'll come down and let you in.' Olive began whispering. 'Mrs Peacock's had a bit of bad news. I mean just a few days ago. Her youngest brother's been killed in France, so we're a bit quiet. Seeing you standing there, I thought you might be bringing more bad news.'

'Would you rather I just went away? I could come round in the morning.'

'Stay where you are for a few minutes. I'm just changing and then I'll be down.'

When she opened the door she was just the same Olive – more mature, a bit plumper and her lips were bright; so she used lipstick and had been putting it on while she kept him waiting. She had the same smooth skin and big eyes and when she stood hesitantly before him she seemed – after the years of barrack and camp – just impossibly beautiful. The last time they had been together he had been tempted to put his hands round her throat and she had defied him. Now it was immediately clear to him, if perhaps not to Olive, that all had changed and nothing could stop their coming together. He wanted to grab her.

'Mrs Peacock and I were just going to have supper.'

'I'll go away. I ought to have let you know I was coming.'

Mrs Peacock, dressed in black, was sitting in the kitchen when they came in. She presented to Ewart a much eroded face. In comparison Ewart was so huge and healthy, radiating energy that was too great for the small room. He held his cap at his chest and Mrs Peacock kept her eyes on it while they talked. Yes, she remembered him. Times had sadly changed, though.

Ewart refused to share their supper – rationing would have made it unfair – so he sat in a corner while the women ate. He was tongue-tied. The meeting was so different from what he had expected and, to be honest, he wished Mrs Peacock to the devil. She was hostile and he could not imagine why.

Olive looked at him from time to time, still not absolutely sure he was who he claimed to be and, if he was, that he actually sat there. 'You've changed, Ewart. You're bigger. They must feed you up in the Army. Or is it the Police? And you look quite . . .' she hesitated, 'well, hard. I don't mean that in a bad way. Like a rugger player.'

'I like the life, Olive.'

Mrs Peacock turned on him. 'I remember you well and I'm a bit surprised you take it on yourself to turn up like this.'

Olive shushed her down.

'But wasn't there something awful he was mixed up in?'

'No.' Olive was firm. 'It was not like that at all.'

Mrs Peacock seemed to hold Ewart responsible for all her family misfortunes just because he was a soldier and apparently thriving. 'Three days ago I learned that my youngest brother, Walter, had been killed.' She put down her knife and fork and cried with her mouth open, the tears running down her cheeks. 'Walter! What had the poor kid done to deserve that? He was sick in hospital and the Germans shelled it. Can you imagine that, killing sick men in hospital? And what were you doing about it?'

'I'm sorry.' In fact he was unmoved. So many Walters had been killed that news of another had no real sting. He was bothered by her tears though, and was glad when she mopped them up, still whimpering.

Olive handed him a piece of cheese, a pickled onion and a slice of bread on a plate and, in spite of his protestations, he began eating.

'I hope your husband's all right.'

'Captain Peacock was torpedoed. He was on a raft for three days before he was picked up. He was given another ship. Thank God he's all right so far as I know. But he suffers, you know. Nerves.'

Just to be near Olive and to smell her perfume, whatever it was, stirred Ewart but did not totally undermine his common sense. Why should she wear lipstick, which most people still thought common, and why should she have this perfume?

He spent the night in his old digs with his tobacconist friend, who pretended to be frightened of him because he was a Military Policeman. The following morning, a Saturday, he went round to Olive's shop, assuming she would be shutting at 1 o'clock and he could take her out somewhere to eat.

'You've got to make allowances for Mrs Peacock. She's a good sort really, but she's under a lot of strain – as most people are, I suppose. There's this brother who's been killed, and then the Captain being away at sea all the time.'

They were in the Kardomah where they served omelettes and salad. There Ewart proposed for the umpteenth time and Olive accepted without any mention of probationary marriage. They went out into Alexandra Park where they embraced and sat on a bench up against the bandstand with a view over the Channel. Olive was giggly and very pink, while Ewart was in a daze. He knew people were looking at them and smiling but that is what he wanted. He wanted everyone to wave at them, to come up and congratulate them.

'For God's sake, Olive. Whatever went wrong between us?'

They found a jeweller's shop and Ewart bought a silver ring set with a single small artificial diamond because he was not carrying enough money to buy anything better; it was just for the time being. Next time they met, he'd buy her a proper ring. This one he was able to place on her finger in the shop; the manager congratulated them and offered sherry which they declined.

'Now we must go and tell the Whites.'

Their arrival took Charles and Hannah by surprise and when they

121

learned that Ewart and Olive were engaged they were so excited that Charles kissed Olive and Ewart kissed Hannah. A sergeant in the Military Police commanded something approaching awe in the White household, and after the congratulatory embraces it was some time before Charles could say anything coherent. His hair was flecked with white just above his ears now, and he wore glasses, but otherwise he had lasted well. Hannah was at ease with herself, bright-eyed and thinner, looking not a great deal older than Olive.

'It's funny, isn't it? said Charles. 'You not getting a crack at Jerry? I mean the War Cabinet, or whoever it is 'as the last word, must 'ave put a special value on you.'

'Oh, pull the other one. You're always kidding. I don't know why they keep me back. I used to worry about it, but I don't now. I reckon it's because I don't drink.'

'It can't be that, sergeant. They're too clever for that. Stupid the generals may be in several respects, but they know deep down the Army depends on its leaders. You are a leader.'

'You can't be a leader in the Military Police.'

'I accept that, but there's something in the system that requires men of your particular qualities to be held in reserve. That's what Napoleon did. 'E kept the Old Guard in reserve at 'is big battles. But, seriously, you're well out of it. What's going on isn't war; it's men being slaughtered like cattle. Stay out of it as long as you can.'

Agnes came in from her piano lesson and they all turned to look at her. She was seventeen, but seemed older because her eyebrows were almost continuous and this helped to give her a severe expression when she was not smiling. She flushed to be under so much scutiny.

'Agnes, you remember Mr Paul? Cousin Olive and Mr Paul – I should say Sergeant Paul, shouldn't I? – have just become engaged to be married. Isn't that nice? Come and give Cousin Olive a kiss. Give Sergeant Paul a kiss too! That's right.' Hannah turned to Ewart. 'Oh, you do so bring back the past, though.' She was sad and silent for some time.

For the Whites the picnic was the only meal they could regard as a celebration. The following day, being a Sunday and a fine one too, Charles took them all out to Lavernock with a hamper; there Olive sat extending her hand to show her engagement ring and Ewart put his arm round her so that Charles could take a

122

photograph with his big tripod camera, hiding his head from the sun under a black cloth the better to see through the focus and lens. Ewart and Olive were in the centre, naturally. On Olive's left was Hannah with her chin up, challengingly, and on Ewart's right Agnes. They were all so happy. 'To think that Olive and Ewart are going to be married!' That is what Charles said, and he looked around as though expecting heads to pop up from behind the hedges to echo his cry.

Charles had arranged for a cab to pick them up at 3 because Ewart had to catch a train at 6 o'clock. Back at 'The Lookout' there was time only for another cup of tea and, at Hannah's suggestion, the performance by Agnes of a little piece by Grieg on the piano (which had replaced the harmonium). Then she sang 'Blow the Wind Southerly' to her own accompaniment and everyone was rapt. She had such a pure, unaffected little voice which had not yet made up its mind whether she would be contralto or soprano. Sitting at the piano, she looked – with her brown hair gathered and pinned at the back, and her straight nose almost in line with her brow – not of the twentieth century at all but from some remoter, classical period. She had lost all her shyness and when Ewart eventually went off, with Olive on his arm, she stood with her parents at the door to wave them goodbye and blow kisses.

When they said goodbye on Cardiff Station, Olive clung to him.

He kissed her again. 'This weekend my life's been turned round.' The guard was blowing his whistle and Ewart thought she would never let him go. He leaned out of the carriage window waving goodbye until her white dress became a dot and then was not to be seen at all.

During that summer Charles heard that three men who had once worked for him had been killed and a fourth, Sam Whitley the plasterer, had lost a leg and was in hospital in Llandough. Charles went to visit and found Sam surprisingly cheerful. He had been with the 32nd Division on the Somme. So far as he knew most of his mates had been killed but he did not want to talk about the fighting, he was just glad to be out of it. There was talk of fitting him up with an artificial leg – then he would be as good as new, just as good a plasterer as he'd ever been. He hoped he'd be working for Mr White again, one of these days. Charles's mother wrote from time to time from Northleach to say which of the local boys had been killed or wounded; her distress touched Charles deeply, more deeply than the casualty lists published in the papers and the reports of the war correspondents. He suggested she came and stayed with them in Penarth for a while, but she would not come. Where she was, she could go through the old routines; if she hadn't the usual chores to do and the grammar school work, she'd be thinking of the fighting. Work kept her mind off it. Oh, she was all right, she assured Charles. She just felt like a rat which had been chased and hit with a club. She was a determined rat and wanted to stay in her own nest, defiantly. The high-ups told such lies – particularly that Lloyd George, who was no gentleman.

Charles had met Mrs Dover-Davies several times quite by chance in the street and the encounter always cheered him up. They had little to say to each other. She looked so slim, so perky, and her eyelashes were so long, the old urge to hug her tight came back to remind him that there were other ways of living than being obsessed with the casualty lists. Her natural expression was so cold, then, when she caught sight of him, it would change – it would become warm, the lines on her face would soften and her eyes shine.

One day, on impulse, he took her into a teashop and she told him how she'd received a letter from guess who? Mr Olleranshaw! He was now an Army major in Egypt and hated the country. Olleranshaw made them both think of James and she was able to say, without mentioning his name, 'At least he's not going through it like other kids of his age,' and Charles knew who she was talking about.

He found he could talk to Mrs Dover-Davies about James in a way he could not talk to Hannah. Mrs D-D was so unsentimental and matter-of-fact whereas Hannah – well, not that she was emotional but there was nothing new for Hannah or him to say to each other.

'I sometimes think . . .' Charles hesitated.

'Go on.'

Charles shook his head. 'I've got a way of letting my mind race. When I was younger it used to run away with me. Well, now it's beginning to run away with me again and it began a while back when I said to 'Annah that it's easier to think of 'im as one of the war dead.' He spoke slowly, pausing so long between words that Mrs D-D would open her mouth to speak and Charles would hold his hand up. Eventually he did stop.

'James?'

'One of the war dead. Yes. Mad, isn't it? Just mad, because of course 'e isn't one of the war dead. The old mind races, though, and that's where it races to. In my mind's eye, I even see the name James White inscribed on a memorial. Now, Mrs Dover-Davies, does that seem bad?'

'I wish you would call me Gladys.'

'Eh?' He looked across the table at her, knowing what this would lead to. She would be wanting to call him Charles and nobody called him that but Hannah, his mother and some of Hannah's relations. Even Olive did not call him plain Charles, but always Cousin Charles. He decided to ignore what Mrs D-D had said.

'Tell me, honest, does that seem bad, letting the mind race and thinking James was a war casualty?'

'Yes, Mr White, I do think that would be bad. It would be self-deception and fantasy.' She had made him aware she had noticed his rebuff.

So he called her 'My dear'.

'My dear, I don't believe in God any more, but I swear that the boy – you know what 'e did – the Coroner said "Death by misadventure" but that doesn't take away from the fact 'e 'anged himself.' He was whispering so as not to be overheard. 'I don't believe in God any more, but I swear that 'is death was no more meaningless and, yes, inexplicable, than the way these tens of thousands are dying in the trenches. All these deaths, James included, are without meaning or significance. They are absurd.'

But soldiers don't set out with the idea of committing suicide.'

'In effect, my dear, that is what it is and I think they should be stopped. The war should be stopped.'

When he began talking about James as one of the war dead Charles had no idea he would finish up by saying the war should be stopped, but now that the words had popped out he reflected and agreed with them. When Ruskin had said what a good thing war was, he was not thinking of a war like this one. Charles had gone off Nietzsche too. Neither of these men had sons, so what did they know? Deep down, what did they really know? What did anyone know who was childless?

The next time Charles met Minsky was soon after some particularly bad casualty figures. Minsky drove about in a trap these days, drawn by a neat little fawn pony. He stood in the yard holding her by the head. It had been raining but the sun was out to give the pebbles a shine. Charles had a big fuchsia in a pot and Minsky said something admiring. He tied the reins to a post and followed where Charles led.

Minsky said he was planning to build bungalows when the war came to an end. Charles could not understand why; he associated bungalows with India and felt that something more substantial was needed in Britain. Minsky explained that they did away with the need for going upstairs. Land there was in plenty, so spread the houses out and spare the elderly the labour of climbing stairs. He himself was getting on. His ideal house was a number of ground-floor rooms, each leading into the other so that the children of the house and in due course the children of those children could be members of a community. He would like to play a part in setting up family communities of this kind.

'After the war?'

'You've got to think ahead.'

'And 'ow d'you think it's all going to end?'

Minsky shrugged. 'Out of exhaustion. There won't be enough men left to carry on.'

'I never thought it would come to conscription.' They were out in the open and light rain was falling again, but they took no notice.

'You can't fight the Germans with volunteers.'

'We've never 'ad conscription. Press-ganged for the Navy was the nearest we got, but if you take away a man's right to volunteer or not to volunteer as he thinks fit that's bad.'

The rain became heavier but still they didn't move. Minsky's bowler glistened and Charles, who was hatless, took out a handkerchief to wipe his face. For up to a minute they looked each other in the eye. Then Minsky patted Charles on the shoulder. 'You're a changed man, Mr White.'

'Who isn't? D'you mean to tell me you've not changed?'

'Not as much as you. But I was never being so optimistic.'

'You got this idea of building bungalows to . . . what was it?'

'Make communities.'

'That's optimism.'

Minsky walked over to his pony and untied the reins. 'You must remember that deep down I was always taking a more desperate view of the world than you. And when you're that desperate you make plans. And you make jokes, too.' He climbed up into the trap

126

and prepared to drive off. 'Because if the plans come to nothing, what have you lost? Only the plans on paper. But the jokes go on.' With a sharp, wristy movement he slapped the pony's rump with the reins, raised one of his yellow-gloved hands to the brim of his bowler and drove away, dripping. What jokes? Charles thought. Here was a man who had turned his back on his only child, a daughter, and he talked of building family communities. Was that his idea of a joke, to build up communities for others but not for himself? Perhaps Minsky was as mad as Charles suspected he was himself, or as Hannah was when now and again she came home and claimed to have seen James in the street.

How could he know if he was going potty? How could he know anything? He had read a book which made an impression, *Problems of Philosophy*; its author was Bertrand Russell. The librarian, Mr Swift, pushed the book his way, saying 'This looks up your street, Mr White.' He read the book up in James's old room, the telescope looking over his shoulder out to sea and the night, and with the fossil collection in its case behind him, the butterflies and moths to the right. He read by the popping gaslight. The lighthouse on Flat Holme flashed against him regularly, as regularly as the beat of his heart, twenty heartbeats to a flash. Nobody thought of going up to James's room to find him, and he could concentrate as he could nowhere else. Russell's was only the latest of many books he had tackled in the hope that some truth, some certainty would emerge to prop him up, and it came as something of a shock to discover there was no general agreement about basics. There could be no certainty that the real world was what he, Charles White, perceived. It might be illusion. Bertrand Russell did not think it was illusion, but Charles thought he might be wrong about that.

Russell's book said nothing about politics, so Charles was intrigued to learn that he was now going about the country making political speeches. There had been a meeting in Merthyr, another in Swansea (Charles read in the *Western Mail*) was in the open air, on a common; so was the meeting at Port Talbot. And now Russell was to speak in Cardiff, in a hall this time, and Charles decided that he would go in the hope that seeing the philosopher in the flesh he might better understand the puzzle about meaning, whether life really was an illusion and, as a consequence, know whether he was going out of his mind.

By the time Charles arrived the hall was nearly full, men mostly aged forty and over; dock and railway workers, clerks

127

and tradesmen like himself. Nobody was in uniform. Some of the men might be miners doing well out of the war, being in a reserved occupation, not personally affected by conscription and spending their wages on the black market. Still, they cared, otherwise they would not have come. There was a scattering of women. Charles sat next to a man with a notebook on his knee whom Charles took to be a journalist. Men loosened their collars because of the heat, women fanned themselves and cries went up for windows to be opened. Most of the audience smoked and Charles, who never had, found the atmosphere intolerable to the point where he thought of leaving.

And then – with the slightly dishevelled appearance of having been shot up through a trap-door – here was this little man with a big head and thin face above a winged collar suddenly on the platform with a lectern in front of him, though he appeared to speak without notes. Charles looked at him incredulously. He had expected a more sage-like figure, but this man gave the impression of being too peremptory, too cunning and . . . yes, too mischievous to be a philosopher. He had no aura. As he talked, Charles found that although Russell was saying a lot he agreed with, he more and more disliked the man and resented his self-assured, even self-satisfied manner. Russell dealt with interruptions firmly.

'Anti-British,' shouted somebody up front, 'and pro-German.'

Russell turned on him. 'I'm ready to believe, sir, that the Germans are every bit as bad as they are painted, but that is no reason why men should go on dying in their tens of thousands.'

From all sides came murmurs of assent. There was no doubt Russell had the meeting behind him, though what appealed to them was not his tirade against conscription and what he described as the brutal treatment of conscientious objectors; it was the anti-war talk they liked, particularly the bit about men of goodwill sitting round a table and ending the slaughter in a matter of weeks. The journalist was taking all this down in shorthand and it occurred to Charles that he might not be a journalist at all but in the pay of the police. Even this suspicion did not put Charles on Russell's side though, because the little man seemed to relish the misery he was crusading against.

At the end questions were invited and Charles stood up and asked, 'What about the dead?'

Russell plainly thought he had a crank to deal with and so did the rest of the audience, who laughed and jeered.

128

'What about the dead?' Russell rapped back. 'My concern is to ensure that their number is not prematurely added to.'

'I mean, 'ow do you come to terms with the death of boys, because that's what they are mostly.' In spite of having heard a political talk, Charles still yearned for any guidance which the author of *Problems of Philosophy* might provide. Here was a professional lover of wisdom and he might never meet another; he just had to prise some sense out of him.

'That's a religious question and I'm not a religious man.'

'Neither am I but –'

Russell turned to another questioner and Charles had missed his chance. He knew he had made a fool of himself, he knew also that he would never have put his naïve question had he not taken such a dislike to Russell and wanted to knock him off his perch. He had chosen the crudest missile that came to hand, wanting to surprise Russell into being human. When, some time later, he told Minsky he had been to a pacifist talk by Bertrand Russell and had been disappointed, Minsky was amused and Charles could not understand why.

'Today philosophers are not interested in wisdom. It is too vulgar for them.'

'He said nothing we 'adn't talked about between ourselves. But what notice would they 'ave taken of me if I'd got up and talked like that? Run me in for sedition, I expect. They cheered 'im. They thought 'e was great and 'e went off with 'is tail up, I can tell you.'

'What you heard was not from a philosopher. He was more important than that. He was a man. Did you ask a question?' Charles told him what it was and said Russell had ducked it. Minsky dropped his amused expression and patted Charles on the shoulder. 'You and I are too much alike. We go on trying to solve problems that don't need solving any more because they're in the past.'

'I don't know what you mean.'

'You have lost a son and I have lost a daughter.'

'Look!' Charles was furious. 'If you mean you've turned your back on your daughter because –'

'It is not a question of turning our backs. Ruth left us, it was of her own making.'

'It's a bloody shame. The cases are different. I'm angry you put them in the same bracket.'

But Charles was more taken up with his reflections on the fact that Russell had said nothing he had not thought of himself, and weeks ago at that. That could be no mere coincidence. It showed that quite different minds, Russell's and his, could arrive at the same conclusions, the one quite unprompted by the other. Therefore, they were responding to a real world and real problems, not to illusions. Russell was undoubtedly sane. Charles had not liked him, but there was no doubting the man's sanity and that could only mean Charles too was not in the least bit potty.

On and off Charles thought about Russell for days, not what he had said but his appearance and manner. What did they remind him of? A conjurer? No, that was not the sort of performance at all. A minister having a go at sinners? No, that was not it either. Then it came to him. For all the difference in their appearance and message, the person Russell conjured up in Charles's mind was Father Gillespie. They were the only two men by whom Charles had felt intimidated.

Agnes said that in normal times she would never have got into University College, Cardiff, because she was not clever enough. The College led a ghostlike existence in wartime. The students were mostly young men who had failed their medicals for the Army, a few conchies, men who had been invalided out and women. To her father's satisfaction she decided to read history (not music which was her real interest), with literature and philosophy as subsidiaries. Just what Charles would have elected to do himself. Agnes could have lived at home (what Hannah wanted) but she said all that travel to-ing and fro-ing would be tiring, especially in the winter. Besides, there would be students' societies which met in the evenings and she would not want to miss them. The College put her in one of their Edwardian houses where her room had a view of Roath Park. Hannah went to inspect it and said she was well pleased. Yes, it was more sensible to live in a College house in Cardiff, though Hannah did not know that the real reason Agnes wanted to be there was her need to get away from 'The Lookout'.

Her father walked about with a preoccupied expression on his face and her mother was religious in a silly sort of way. Agnes had no time for the Dawnists, whose meetings she had attended at her mother's insistence; she was just repelled by their beliefs.

It was childish to think that Jesus Christ would appear and expect a wheeled carriage to be put at his disposal. As for her father, she thought he had been knocked out by James's death and that was something she no longer wanted to think about.

What was she aiming at? Not teaching. Something with more teeth to it. At eighteen she did not know where she was going, but she loved history. It absorbed her; it was bliss to be up in her room reading and writing with a view over the park, trying to imagine what her lot would have been 100, 200, 300 years before. Once a month, no more frequently than that, she went home for the weekend, sometimes taking a fellow student with her, usually a girl from the valleys. She played the piano and sang for her guest; music-making was what she missed more than anything in College. When the weather was fine they went for walks, sometimes taking Olive along because she liked talking about the forthcoming marriage where Agnes was to be bridesmaid. She was more interested in the marriage than Olive herself appeared to be. When would it be? Some time in the summer, said Olive. But it all depended on the war and when Ewart could get leave. He might be sent to France at any time. This time there were just the two of them walking, Cousin Olive and Agnes.

'Then he'd have embarkation leave. You could get married then.'

'It's to be a real church wedding, Ewart being C. of E., with proper banns. His mother will be coming over from Somerset. You can't do all this on embarkation leave. It comes unexpected. Besides, I want a proper honeymoon. Do you know what, Agnes, when I told my dad I was engaged to be married he didn't seem all that interested, so I've half a mind to ask Cousin Charles to give me away.'

'My father? But he's not responsible for you, so he can't give away what was not his in the first place.'

'Is that right?' Olive gave Agnes an affectionate hug. 'You ought to be a lawyer. Anyway, I think the idea of a man giving a woman away is disgusting. What do they think we are? Pieces of furniture?'

This made an impression on Agnes. Yes, why should women be given away?

When they arrived back in Glebe Street they found Mrs Peacock drinking tea with a soldier whom Olive greeted with a surprised laugh.

'Hallo, Tom! What luck! Where have you been all this time?'

Olive introduced him to Agnes. 'This is Tom Barr, Mrs Peacock's brother who sometimes' – said coquettishly – 'honours us with his presence. My cousin, Agnes White.'

He was a pale, stocky man with a moustache, about the same age as Olive, in the uniform of an artillery captain. Everything was spotless, his M. C. ribbon, his Sam Browne, breeches and highly polished brown boots, so spotless he might have been got up for a play. He had actorish good looks, too, and was aware of the fact, so that when he spoke his voice was all the more of a surprise. It was not a voice; it was a hoarse crow-like croak, a strain to listen to and, by the gulping that went on, a strain to emit.

'Tom was gassed,' said Mrs Peacock. 'It affected his vocal chords.'

'Not a nice noise, eh? But it's the best I can do. Keeps me to desk work.' He gasped the words out. 'Ought to be in a rookery, eh?' Looking at Agnes. 'By God, you're a pretty girl. I tell you straight.'

Agnes was disturbed by his voice and manner. She ought to have been sympathetic and admiring (he was a war casualty and decorated hero), but the frog utterance appeared to invite an intimacy she had to resist. It was horrid. But Olive seemed to like the sound and stood beaming at him. Agnes not only disliked the noise the captain made, she disliked his compliments and she disliked the way he stared at her. It was rude.

Her face felt so hot she was sure she had gone scarlet and she'd made a fool of herself. And still he stared! She made an excuse and went upstairs, where she pressed the backs of her hands to her cheeks and looked at herself in a mirror. If she had not been able to escape she might have burst into tears, but now she was angry. Did he think she was a slut that he could behave in this way?

'Are you all right, Agnes?' Olive had crept silently through the open door. 'You've been a long time.'

'I hate him.'

'Who? Tom? Whatever for? He's had a rough time, you know, and he was only admiring you. Oh yes, I saw what he was up to. You're not a girl any more. You're a young woman, and you've got to learn how to deal with a man who's making eyes at you. He's harmless really. One day you'll know how to put men like Tom in their place. Come on down now and act as though nothing has happened.'

Mrs Peacock and her brother were deep in conversation and did not even look up. Captain Barr was smoking a cigarette. Agnes refused a cup of tea and said she must leave; her parents were expecting to see her before she went back to Cardiff. To her horror, Captain Barr stood up and said he would see her home – it was a dark, nasty evening, not one for a lady to be out walking alone: there might be drunken soldiers and sailors about.

'I think not. It's too early for that.'

'I would never forgive myself if you came to any harm.'

He picked up his cap and cane, and as Agnes was still in her walking clothes there was no reason why they should not leave immediately. She looked pleadingly at Olive, but Olive pretended not to understand the message; she was that amused by the emotions stirred up and would be glad of whatever further amusement Agnes's meeting with Captain Barr might provide.

'Take care, Agnes dear,' she said with a wide smile.

Agnes could see no way of stopping Captain Barr from walking with her and she comforted herself with the thought that it was only ten minutes to 'The Lookout'. The park gates were shut at sunset, so they had to go down the hill and along the front. The sea was banging and roaring at the beach pebbles, which every now and again could be heard snarling back. The wind was strong enough to justify taking his arm. He offered it and was refused.

'I can see I've upset you, Miss White. For that I apologize, but honestly I was so surprised. You suddenly appeared and I was unprepared. It was like a vision. You're so gorgeous. And I'd just climbed out of hell. I couldn't believe my eyes.'

'I didn't want you to bring me home.'

'But on a night like this?'

'I'll never forgive Olive for . . . for, well, the way she allowed it all to come about. Anyway, here we are. This is where I live.' They had climbed the drive and been spattered with water from the overhanging bushes. She put her key into the lock, opening the door. 'Good night.'

'Good night, Miss White. You're a real smasher and I could just gobble you up.'

Before she could stop him he had pulled her towards him and would have kissed her on the mouth if she had not turned her face away. But he kissed her cheek. He reeked of tobacco. What made it all the nastier were the inhuman croaks that came from those tobacco-y lips and from under that scraping moustache.

133

She might have screamed, but she did not. The moment he let her go she stood there, gasping and incredulous. But if she screamed and her father came out, there was no knowing what might happen. So, acting in the way she had read about in novels – which made her a heroine – she slapped Captain Barr's face so hard that it hurt her hand, and he walked back down the drive, rubbing his cheek and making a noise like sandpaper on wood in her father's workshop. It was laughter.

Now that he had gone she stood listening to her heartbeats until they steadied and she felt sufficiently collected to go in and meet her parents. Captain Barr was a beast. Olive must have known how he would behave and yet she had done nothing to prevent it. No doubt back in Glebe Street they would all – Captain Barr, Mrs Peacock and Cousin Olive – be having a good laugh at her. She hated Olive more than anybody, even more than Captain Barr, who was just a man who had been turned into a savage by the war.

She was never going to like men, ever; she would never marry. When she left College she would strike back at men. If that meant she would spend the rest of her life wiping from her memory what Captain Barr had done to her, so be it! Amen! She would be another Mrs Pankhurst and, once the war was over, campaign for women's rights. Votes for Women, that for a beginning! Then she would stand for the local council, and after that Parliament itself!

She said nothing to her parents but later that evening, just before taking her down to the station, her father – normally he did not make personal remarks like this – looked at her and said, 'You seem pleased with yourself.'

'It's Mam's cooking, after what they give us in College.'

Not true. She had seen her future. She would devote her life to putting a stop to the persecution of women. Like Joan of Arc she had heard voices, was sure she would hear the voices again and go on hearing them.


The friend of Hannah who had a friend who worked for the Minskys passed on the information that their daughter Ruth was back home again. There must be some terrible reason for this. Rumour had it that when she married this Cockney Gentile the Minskys were so upset they had the Jewish burial service read for her by a rabbi, but Charles said this was nonsense. He had

134

been borrowing books on Jewish history from the library and had come across nothing like that. The Minskys, in particular, would have been incapable of such behaviour; it was too extreme. But they had certainly shut up her room and, apparently, cut her out of their lives. And now she was back, all apparently forgiven, and Charles saw signs of the reconciliation in Minsky's more cheerful manner. He walked more briskly, wore a bright brown bowler hat with his heavy, double-breasted overcoat, and swished about him with a cane so flexible he could put no weight on it, so swish it was all he could do. Ruth had even been seen walking in the park with her father, a slim figure in a long grey coat, chin up, her large eyes peeping this way and that under the wide brim of her hat. If you stare at me I shall stare at you, she seemed to be saying. I've as much right here as you. So if there was some terrible reason for her return, she gave no sign of it. Charles came on them unexpectedly.

'You remember Ruth, Mr White? Her husband is a prisoner-of-war. So we know he is safe. For a long, long time all Ruth was knowing was that he was reported missing. Imagine her suffering.'

'I've had a card from him, through Switzerland.' Ruth looked Charles in the eyes as she spoke and then turned away with a sudden sadness in her face, a frown and a trembling lip. She's a real thoroughbred, Charles thought. Behind her stretched a pedigree as long as your arm – no, much longer – a culturally controlled lineage which ran through the centuries; and what was he? He scarcely knew who his great-grandparents were. For all his atheism Charles was touched with awe at the realization that Ruth was a blossom on a very ancient tree indeed, and its roots were the kind of beliefs he had turned his back on.

'How the war is changing everything,' said Mr Minsky. 'I am coming out of it a different man from what I was. I have been a fool. Now you, Mr White, you have a daughter too. And what is the news of her, may I ask?'

As they talked they walked round the bandstand. In the thin sunshine patches of white, blue and yellow crocuses were brighter than the sky. Ruth broke away, saying she had to meet someone off a train, and the two men stood watching her go.

'Your daughter. Agnes, isn't it?'

'She's all right.'

But was she? Now that she was at College, Agnes was changed. For a while she had come home at weekends, but now Hannah

135

and he rarely saw her and when they did she seemed to be sulking. Hannah said it was her age and she probably had a crush on one of the lecturers who was not responding. Charles was surprised Hannah had allowed her imagination to riot in this way, but he did not think she was right. There was a hardness about Agnes he had not seen before, even (and perhaps he was now allowing *his* imagination to riot) hostility to her mother but more particularly to him.

'She's at College in Cardiff,' Charles now went on. 'Doing well. End up making a career for 'erself.'

Minsky looked at him sharply, as though he knew Charles was not telling the truth. Soldiers in hospital blue got up lazily from a seat and made off, presumably back to their convalescent centre for a meal, and Minsky and Charles took their places. On the grass under the palm trees where the sun could not reach patches of frost still lingered, but the day was mild enough; the sea was an emptiness beyond the turrets of the Yacht Club, with no horizon, but they could smell it – or imagined they could smell it.

'A daughter is closer to her mother than to her father.' Minsky hesitated. 'Of course, I never had a son, but I would have expected him to be nearer to me. Strange how one is thinking of these things, but Ruth comes home and it is to her mother she is really come. I feel out of it. I was nearer to her when she was not here and I was grieving because she was so unhappy. Have you noticed, Mr White, how hard it is to bear the unhappiness of other people? It's harder to put up with than one's own personal miseries. Don't you think?'

Charles didn't understand what he was driving at, but he didn't like Minsky's line of talk anyway and stood up to go.

'I'm glad your daughter's 'eard from 'er 'usband. Mrs Minsky must be tickled.'

'Tickled?'

'Well, 'aving Ruth 'ome. Times like this, families want to draw together.'

He raised his hand, made off and Minsky waved his cane after him in a friendly sort of way. There was work to do. He should not have seen idling in the park, but something Minsky had said now struck home. Whatever Agnes was moping about, she could have no justification like young Ruth's there. But it was thinking about her which had led him impulsively to put on his overcoat and walk out of the office for a breath of fresh air. It would be too

136

much to say that he agonized more over Agnes's state of mind than over his own misfortunes but, no mistake about it, he was bothered. He would have to talk to her, he decided, even if it meant going into Cardiff and looking her up in her lodgings.

When, later that day, he arrived back at 'The Lookout' Hannah said, 'Olives's been here. She's in a state; she says Agnes has sent her a note saying she won't be her bridesmaid at the wedding. No reason given. You should have seen Olive's face, she was that angry. But what's the good of being angry with me? I don't know why Agnes has turned against her.'

'She's turned against all of us, Agnes 'as, if you ask me, and I want to know why. I'll go to Cardiff and see 'er.'

'Oh, don't do that, Charles. Not without warning.'

Charles considered this. 'All right. I'll send 'er a note and ask 'er to 'ave a bite o' something with me in a restaurant on Saturday.'

'I'd better come too, Charles. It would be a day out.'

# 7

'Talk of the Town' had been suspended for the duration, no doubt because its archness would have seemed smug in time of war. Otherwise the column might have carried some reference to the quarrel between Olive and Agnes. 'Why did the two young ladies taking tea in the Kardomah Café part on such bad terms that neither remembered to pay the bill? Could it be they are related and had been discussing family history?'

Such an item would probably have been impossible. For one thing, it broke the rule that really serious matters were not to be touched on. For another, only Agnes and Olive were sufficiently in the know to submit such an entry, and it would be out of the question for either of them to make mischief in this way. Out of the question for Agnes, certainly. But come to think of it, now the possibility was raised, could Olive be ruled out with quite such firmness? Judging by her subsequent behaviour it might even be said this was just the kind of defiance of the proprieties she would have been capable of. You could even say that, since her mischief-making was responsible for the quarrel, placing an item like that would give her special satisfaction.

The quarrel had been some time ago. Olive had known for weeks that Agnes was not to be her bridesmaid, so the note could not have come as a surprise. Then why such an outburst now? Hannah had been taken aback by her rage; after all, not having Agnes as a bridesmaid might be a disappointment, but it was of no importance as seen against the cosmic events that were now to be unfolded – the Second Coming and the Final Rout of Satan. She would have been even more taken aback if she had realized that Olive had worked up her rage like an actress, with flushed cheeks, tears that dropped on to her bodice and clenched fists that were laid across it.

'There's no need to be so upset, Olive.' Hannah thought for a moment. 'You can always ask Florrie Townsend.' She was a girl of about Agnes's age who went bathing with Olive.

'I'd set my heart on Agnes. It's a real insult to be rejected like this. After all the talk about the dress she was going to wear; white satin with coral trimmings and little coral bows all down the arms to match my own dress. Of course, I'm having coral tassels as well. She throws all this in my face, the bitch.'

'Don't use that language to me, Olive. Why won't Agnes be your bridesmaid?'

'She was upset by the way Mrs Peacock's brother paid attention to her, and she blames it all on me. She ought to have been flattered. Captain Barr was gassed and had the M.C. From what I hear, Agnes just spat in his face.'

Hannah was shocked. 'I know nothing about this.'

'She went at me like a wild cat. What's it got to do with me, I ask you?'

'It just doesn't sound like Agnes.'

'She said I was disgusting because all I thought of was pleasing men.'

'She's certainly got a mind of her own. It's the war, Olive. We must understand that we live at a time when great changes will take place in all our lives, even before your wedding day perhaps.'

Olive knew all about Hannah's Millenial Dawnists and went off, throwing Agnes's note to the ground in a genuine, not assumed, huff. It was too bad that her annoyance with Agnes should be side-tracked in this way. Her theatrical behaviour had been put on to anticipate the trouble she had probably stirred up by telling Agnes that James was not her proper brother, that he was just a half-brother and illegitimate at that. She had given Agnes this information the moment she realized, much to her surprise, that Agnes was ignorant of it.

At the beginning of the row in the Kardomah Café Olive had taken the line that whatever Captain Barr had done was natural. Men were like that, it was in their nature. Agnes said she was more interested in female suffrage than in the nasty way men behaved. Olive ought to be ashamed of herself encouraging one of them – she meant Captain Barr – to be such a beast.

'You've got to take human nature as it is.'

'I want to change it.'

Not wanting to be overheard, Olive began hissing at Agnes. 'Who the hell d'you think you are? Change human nature! What about your own father? He's done much worse than anything Captain Barr may have been up to.'

139

'What do you mean?' Agnes looked at her with such round-eyed innocence that Olive realized she knew nothing of her scandalous family history. She decided that what Agnes needed at this stage in her life was the shattering of girlish illusion, and she set about doing just that with relish. She wanted to shock Agnes. When the tale of Hannah's sterility, Polly's obliging nature, her death in childbirth and the adoption of James had been told, Agnes's face was white. In these circumstances the two women left the café, Agnes a good two minutes before Olive and without paying her share of the bill, and Olive forgot the bill too.

Charles and Hannah stepped out of the train at Cardiff as a hospital train was discharging its patients in the goods yard on the other side of the station, and they went over to join the crowd of onlookers. These men had not come straight from France; they had been hospitalized in Brighton and Oxford (Charles learned from one of the orderlies), so the walking wounded were in the now familiar hospital blue tunic and trousers, crutches and sticks rattling on the cobbles as they made their way to the waiting ambulances. Others walked, some joked noisily, supported by medical orderlies. The stretcher cases were less boisterous. Some of the onlookers were lighting cigarettes between their own lips and transferring them to the men on the stretchers. Snow was falling, just a shower, out of the bright sky and melting on the cobbles. Feeling he had to do something, Charles held his umbrella to keep the snow off the men's faces. Everyone was so good-humoured. The patients had labels tied to the lapels of their jackets or pyjama tops and these labels had to be read – name, number, rank, regiment, religion, diagnosis – as the men went into the ambulances and the odd funny man shouted out a bogus identity (Kaiser Bill, Charlie Chaplin, Colonel von Kluck) for the orderlies to check against their lists.

One of the stretcher cases raised a hand and smiled a sick smile at Charles. 'Where've they brought us to now?'

'This is Cardiff.'

'Is my missis 'ere? Name of Wilson. She 'asn't been to see me yet, but she said she would. 'Ave a scout round, will yer mate? Can't miss 'er. Big, strong woman in a brown coat, is Mrs Wilson.'

Charles looked round the crowded, bustling yard. The first ambulances were moving off through the mob of people that had now gathered. There might have been a big, strong woman in a brown coat by the name of Wilson out there, but if she was Charles could not see her. When he turned to speak to the man who asked for her he had gone, taken off by a couple of stretcher-bearers. The snow now fell in great flakes, settling on caps, capes and shoulders, muting the noise, so it seemed, enhancing the brilliant red of the Military Policemen's cap-bands and the crosses on the sides of the ambulances.

By some minor miracle Hannah had found Agnes in all this crowd, or rather Agnes found her because she had come to meet their train, failed to find them and wandered over to the ambulances. She looked peaky and cold. For one thing she was not properly dressed for this weather; a little straw hat and a thin coat with no gloves. The snow tinged her face blue. Charles was glad Hannah was enfolding her in her arms; the hug ought to give warmth, but Agnes was still thin-lipped and withdrawn.

'There are over three 'undred men on this train,' Charles told her, as though the statistic ought to put her own troubles, whatever they were, in perspective. 'We'll go and see what they can do for us in the Angel. 'Eard tell they got some black-market venison.'

'I don't want to go to the Angel, not in these clothes. It's too posh.'

'But I booked a table.'

'It's too posh,' Agnes insisted. 'Let's go to one of those places in the market.'

Hannah thought respectable people should not go the market to eat, and would have settled for one of the restaurants in Queen Street where they served a good bowl of soup and a pork chop with chips; but Agnes was in a funny mood and just where they went and what they ate seemed not worth arguing about.

In the covered market there was a man with an open biscuit tin at his feet, a few coins in it, singing a song about being away and coming home again. 'When the fields are white with daisies,' he sang in a plaintive tenor, hand cupped to his ear the better to hear the sound he was making, 'I'll return.' Because of rationing the butchers had a poor display of meet on their stalls, no poultry hanging up as there had been before the war, and there was only one wet-fish stall where once there had been four.

'There must be some reason you've come to see me.'

They had found seats in a booth where faggots and pease pudding were served on wooden platters, not the kind of fare Charles had in mind, and he was annoyed. Sensing his annoyance, Hannah laid a hand on his arm.

'It's so long since we saw you, Agnes dear. We thought we'd give ourselves a day out.'

'If we've got to eat this muck,' said Charles, 'at least let's order it.'

What he did not order was tea, but this came first as an appetizer in a big brown pot served by a gaunt man, all eyes and cheekbones. Charles tried not to generalize about the Welsh. Most of them round here were English or Irish under the skin anyway, but they had acquired a Welsh lilt and a widening of vowels; they were more chauvinistic than the genuine Welsh. Charles wanted to be part of all this, the acquired Welshness of the immigrant and the real Welshness of the ancients (provided he didn't have to learn the lingo). But for all his cultural flexibility he could not be brought to accept that tea was an aperitif. He had supposed this tricky meeting with Agnes would be eased by a proper meal in a proper restaurant; tomato soup followed by a meat course (venison was hoped for), then baked jam roll or syrup tart. Tea would settle the stomach and Charles would not have been against it at the end of the meal. But *before* the meal! It was disgusting! He would have nothing to do with the tea, and was sorry to see Hannah and Agnes sipping it gratefully out of the thick cups.

They all ate without saying much, as though an imprudent word might release an outburst. When Hannah caught Charles's eye he was amazed to see she was smiling. She had been talking to Agnes quietly and he had not heard what she said.

'I reckon they're clearing out the front line 'ospitals. They're getting ready for the Big Push,' he said. 'That's why they're sending these cases down 'ere.'

The faggots had been crisped on top; they had a lid of savoury crispness like the outside stuffing of a Christmas capon fresh from the oven. They were delicious. He crunched up the faggots and plunged his bread – sliced from the top of a cottage loaf – into the peas with real relish, so to transfer them to his mouth. The cold had made him hungry. But still he, Hannah and Agnes held off what they had really met to talk about and in spite of Charles's acceptance of the faggots (how crisped? There must have been a gas grill) the talk languished for lack of – well, courage. Charles knew this without knowing quite what they were afraid of.

'Olive tells me you've decided not to be her bridesmaid.' Hannah was conciliatory, as though this decision of Agnes's was perfectly understandable.

'I don't believe in that sort of thing,' said Agnes.

'What sort of things?'

'You know.'

'I don't know.'

'I think the present kind of marriage is degrading to women.'

Charles had been hoping to keep out of this, but Agnes had shocked him. ''Ow else can the species be perpetuated?'

'I see no reason why it should be. This war. This killing. Mankind is killing itself off. We're just like a lot of prehistoric animals.'

Just having the opportunity to use the word 'species' had given Charles satisfaction, and Agnes's talk of prehistoric animals gave another nudge to the autodidact in him. 'I know what you mean. We're almost an extinct species.'

'If that's the way you want it. The real reason I'm not going to Olive's wedding is that I don't like her.'

Charles ignored this and went on to say she was wrong in thinking that what happened to a lot of Europeans was necessarily of critical importance to the rest of the world. 'Think of the untold millions of China,' he said. 'This war may mean the end of Europe. But other parts of the world will take over.' He would have liked to say more, but realized that neither Hannah nor Agnes was listening.

'She's your cousin, once removed,' said Hannah, 'and that still counts for something. What's she done to upset you?'

'I don't want to go into it.'

Hannah opened her handbag to produce a handkerchief with which she now dabbed at her eyes. 'We don't see so much of you these days, Agnes. You've changed towards your father and me. You're not like you used to be. What is wrong?'

The gaunt man produced bakestone cakes, margarine and raspberry jam. He also brought a jug of hot water to replenish the teapot.

'I know about James,' Agnes said after a long pause.

Both Charles and Hannah looked at her, quite startled, and saw that she was smiling. This was confusing; they had no idea why she had brought James up, still less why she should smile. But she looked back at them with this strange smile on her face. There was no merriment in it – her eyes were too hard for that and her lips too set – but a smile it was, with the lips turned up at

143

the corners, a smile to keep her parents cool, controlled and at a distance. As they were silent, she said, 'I know why he hanged himself. Why didn't you tell me?'

She went on smiling, like someone in authority (a teacher, say, or a lawyer) explaining a complicated argument which was not in the least bit funny, but pleased by its very complexity. A smile that said, 'All right, this is what we've got to put up with. All bearable life is a kind of smiling.'

To Charles it was incongruous that they should be talking about James in a market booth, the rough taste of faggots and stewed tea in their mouths and plaintive singing in the background about returning when the fields were white with daisies. He did not want to talk about James anywhere. If talk were forced on him it would be out in the open air, with fields and woods all around, the sea in front and the open sky above. The sun would stare at him. He would have needed that kind of support. Even then he would be deeply reluctant to talk, except about James as a war casualty. He was not so deranged as to believe that James *was* a war casualty, but as he had watched the ambulance train being unloaded he had toyed with the idea, as he had toyed with it in conversation with Mrs Dover-Davies. He fancied that James might be lifted out on a stretcher. He would have taken the boy's hand and said how proud he was to be his father; and how ashamed not to be doing *something* to stop the killing. He ought to have fallen in behind Bertrand Russell. He ought to be in prison. 'Sorry, James,' he would have said and then kissed him.

'James dying that way was an accident; that's what the Coroner said, so it's official. I've never quarrelled with what he said. Do you think you know any better? You're daft. You 'aving trouble with your work, or something? Your mother thinks you fancy somebody and it's 'aving a bad effect. Well, there's got to be some explanation for the way you're be'aving. Out with it. I'm just sick of this 'orrible bloody atmosphere. D'you want to give up College, is that it?'

'No.'

'Then what is it? There's this feeling I've got you're 'ostile.'

For a while Agnes looked at her father steadily and then, as though dismissing him, turned to speak to her mother. Hannah had been blowing her nose, making an astonishing trumpeting noise, while Charles talked, and she went on trumpeting in a way that deceived nobody. She knew what Agnes was going

144

to say and she was sending out trumpet calls of defiance and despair.

'Is it true James was not your son?' This to Hannah.

Charles saw Hannah's distress and he reached out, took her hand and patted it, making reassuring, chuckling noises as though he had thought of a joke. But they might have been suppressed sobs. What had he and Hannah done to deserve this? To be called over the coals by their own daughter!

'Don't upset your mother.' He wanted the present conversation forgotten. What could he say or do that would wipe it all out? 'James was my son just as you're my daughter. Who's been talking to you? Olive, is it? I can see why you don't want to be bridesmaid.'

Hannah stopped blowing her nose and, as though to show her defiance and despair was now under control, tucked her handkerchief up her sleeve. 'Listen, Agnes. Your father loves you and I love you. Why should there by any need to say this? You know we love you.'

Agnes still managed her bright, wintry smile. 'Don't you understand? I can't tell you how I've been humiliated, to be told what I've been told and not to have been told by you.'

Hannah said she was shocked to hear Agnes talking like that and could not think who she had inherited such bitterness from. On her side of the family they'd been all chapel people, all good and gentle. She knew enough of Agnes's grandmother on her father's side to know there was no malice there. 'Of course, I didn't know your father, Charles.'

''E never made any trouble.' Charles leaned forward. 'Agnes, you're not yourself and I think we should knock off. Go into the air.'

Agnes ignored him. 'You haven't answered my question,' she said to her mother. 'Was James your son?'

Hannah thought, calmly to outward appearance. 'I don't know.'

'You don't know!'

'That's right, Agnes. When you've been through what your father and I have been through, you don't know how it all came about. You don't remember the details.'

'You must remember or not remember giving birth.'

'What I most remember is not giving birth. I just wanted a child. We even tried eating snails.'

145

'But you remember me?' The two women, motionless as if their photograph were being taken, looked at each other steadily.

'Yes, I remember you. You're my daughter.'

Agnes had kept her blue leather handbag on the table. Now in one movement she snatched it and stood up. 'I've been thinking about this. James hanged himself because somebody told him he had no real mother. Gossip. Well, I understand that. Some kid heard it from some nasty-minded parent. There are two things I can't forgive. The first is that you didn't tell James and you didn't tell me, tell us out of your own mouths. That's what hurts. But the main thing is that a child should be got in this way, by some . . . ' she hesitated '. . . some male and that you, my mother as you say you are, married to this male, should tolerate it.'

All this, still ignoring Charles, she had thrown at Hannah who now saw that if anyone needed protection it was Charles. 'Don't you think you're exaggerating?'

Charles saw that Hannah did not know what she was saying and that Agnes was hysterical. He, a male?

'What we're really talking about,' said Agnes, 'is why a boy hanged himself.'

At this Charles stood up. 'That's a priggish thing to say. You've got your mother's milk still on your lips and you think you can talk to me about morality. Let's go out of this place.'

But where to? They might have gone to Agnes's digs, they might have taken a train back to Penarth, but they were so stirred up they could only stand on the pavement in the now steady fall of snow. They all felt the talking had to go on; they did not want to part. A horse-drawn cab came by and Charles put up his hand. He thought Agnes might refuse to get in but get in she did, following her mother, so he thought all was not lost.

'Where to?' The driver, in his old-fashioned greatcoat and bowler hat, leaned down from his high seat and shouted as though they were at the other end of the street.

'Show us the sights. Take us for a drive around.'

The driver climbed laboriously down to the pavement so that he could look more closely at his passengers. 'That's a funny sort of order. Most people want to go somewhere. You're all sober, eh?'

'Get on with it, cabby. Sober? Some ways I wish we wasn't.'

The cabby blew on a red handkerchief and wiped his heavy moustache. 'You've been meeting one of the lads, I can see that. Your boy, eh? I could run you out to the 'ospital. Comfort yourself,

146

my friends. He's got a Blighty and I won't say no more. You're lucky. I'll take you up the Llandaff Road.'

'Your son?'

'He was a brave boy, just nineteen, Welch Regiment. The lad died that we might all be free – if you believe that rubbish.' The cabby returned to his seat, cracked his whip and off they went, Hannah and Agnes side by side on the wide seat, Cardiff outside rocking by. The tide was in so the River Taff was glutted with muddy water. On the other side of the bridge substantial houses sprang up, boxed in by hedges of hawthorn just bursting into leaf.

The cabby opened a shutter and called down. 'Feel like going as far as the Cathedral? I would join you in a prayer. It's a very ancient foundation, you know, older than Canterbury.'

'I want to go home.' Hannah had been trying to hold Agnes's hand, but Agnes would have none of it. 'Come home with us, Agnes.'

Charles shouted up to the cabby, 'Take us to the station, the General.'

'Come home with us, Agnes. We can't part like this.'

'No, I'm not coming home. I'll leave you here.' At her insistence the cabby let her out and she walked off without looking back.

At the station another ambulance train was unloading and Charles insisted that Hannah and he went over. He did not want to use a handkerchief, so he tried shutting his eyes firmly; the tears still came. The waste! The waste of young men, just boys they were, was more than he could bear. Hannah thought he was upset because of Agnes. She hardened and took control, seeing Charles back to the platforms where the Penarth trains left.


Olive and Ewart were married in the summer when the news from the front was of heavy bombardments and limited advances. Casualties, it was agreed, were heavy, heavier for the enemy. There was real hope of victory.

Olive was anxious. 'I don't want to be a war widow, Ewart. For God's sake, take care. Don't go. If they want you to go, don't go, unless you have to. I love you. If you were killed I would shrivel and die.'

'We've got to take our chances. It was something that we even met.'

147

'What do you mean?'

'Of all the people in the world, just you and me, we met. It's miraculous.'

Yet for Ewart it was not the rapturous experience he had looked forward to. Perhaps he had expected too much – the thought of Olive in his arms, her body against his, was erotic to the point of frenzy – so that the reality was, well, disappointing. It was as though he had been through it all before; the wedding, Olive's flushed face and shining eyes, the drinks, the laughter, the confetti – all lacked surprise or novelty. The ceremony and the rowdy breakfast and toasts that followed were almost a routine. Olive seemed not to notice. Ewart thought he might be tired. Everybody was tired. Too many men were being killed and real jollification was impossible. It did not fit into the general understanding of what the world was like and what meaning, if any, life had.

Olive was determined that her wedding would be really festive. She wanted to push the war and all that horror as far away as she could, dance in the bright lights, drink champagne and be kissed by way of congratulation by as many men as possible. One of them was Captain Barr, very dashing in fawn breeches and highly-polished leggings, with a fair-haired fattish young woman in tow whom nobody knew. He wiped his hand across his moustache before kissing Olive on the lips. Olive's father had finally decided to behave, given her away and agreed to foot the bills. He was a silly man, cheeks like pouches with white sideburns, who shouted his remarks above the din like a town crier; for all his noise he was plainly under the thumb of his wife, Olive's stepmother who was dressed in pink satin. She was all pink, flesh as well as dress; even the rims and handle of her lorgnette were pink. Ewart floated through all this without making contact. Olive's father stood on a chair to shout a speech. 'To be honest I thought Olive was too much the choosy sort to get married, but I was wrong and I am glad to be wrong because she's been choosy to the end, I mean choosing Sergeant Paul, there.' And so on. Ewart's best man was a fellow sergeant, but he was too shy to say anything and a bit drunk into the bargain. Holding Olive's hand, Ewart made a little speech saying it was the happiest day of his life.

As a young man his thoughts had been chaste. There were chaste men in the Army, and those who weren't made no impression on Ewart. They were the odd men out, they were stupid and carnal. He was neither but he wondered now, at his wedding, whether he

148

had been coarsened by the Army and that was why the day seemed so stale. He was not behaving with the freedom and the candour he would have liked. He had been regimented – disciplined to the point where his natural feelings and desires were muted so that even Olive's touch, her softness and warmth, her perfume could not rouse them.

He saw his mother sitting alone with an empty wineglass in her hand and went over. 'I've been hoping to meet Mr and Mrs White, but they don't seem to be here,' she said. 'Surely they were invited?'

Invitations would have gone out from Olive's father and step-mother, and Ewart had not seen the list. He vaguely remembered there had been some disappointment over Agnes. Now was not the time to make enquiries, so he patted his mother's hand and asked if he could fill her glass. She said, 'No, thank you,' then added dutifully, 'Olive makes a lovely bride, I'll say that for her. Pray God she's good to you and is a loving and faithful wife.'

Olive had imagined herself sailing away on one of the cross-Channel steamers to a honeymoon in Ilfracombe, but the steamers were laid up for the war and she didn't fancy the long journey by rail. For Ewart the ideal place would have been Chepstow if only there were races, but the course there was one big tented Army camp. The only races worth going to were at Newmarket where the Derby and the Oaks, usually run at Epsom, were staged that year; Ewart was very tempted, but Olive said that if Ilfracombe was too far Newmarket was worse and, in any case, she didn't want to go to the races on her honeymoon. Ewart had a special reason, which he did not reveal, for wanting to go to Newmarket; but if Olive was against the idea that was an end of the matter. They went to Crickhowell up in the Black Mountains because one of Olive's grandfather's (no longer alive) had come from there and, as a child, she had a holiday there. He had taken her fly-fishing in the River Usk, Grandpa Powell had, and picking whinberries up on the mountainside too. She had been there only that once and fancied the idea of going back. It did not occur to either of them to write ahead and book accommodation, so they were much put out to discover that The Bear, the main hotel, was full of Army officers. There were soldiers everywhere and a big hutted camp just outside the town. Ewart, still in uniform because he had no civvy suit to fit, carried the two suitcases down the main street, Olive following behind and peering in shop windows.

'This place is much smaller than I remember,' she said.

They found a bed-and-breakfast cottage near the bridge. They were a couple to be taken note of, he in his uniform and red-topped cap, Olive in her grey-green going-away outfit, light jacket and wide-brimmed hat with a grey-green feather in it. The landlady certainly took note of them, to the point of saying she wasn't sure whether she had a spare room. Olive stared at her aggressively and said they had been married that morning and come up to Abergavenny from Cardiff on the Birmingham train.

'It's a honeymoon, is it?' said the woman. 'There'll be a shilling extra to pay for the linen.' But in spite of her reserve she cooked them a special supper of grilled trout with game chips and a salad with real home-made mayonnaise. For wartime this was luxury indeed. All the landlady would say – 'The name is Mrs Ferris' – was that her two brothers were both farmers.

Ewart's special reason for going to Newmarket arose out of a conversation he had had with one of the officers, Captain Bliss, who followed what racing there was in wartime with more attention than he gave to reports of the fighting. Ewart admired him greatly because he studied form and could tell Ewart which horses had won the big races right back into the last century with details of their breeding; not only that, he placed bets by telephoning a bookmaker in London. Whenever Ewart felt like it, Captain Bliss would put a bet on for him too.

The conversation had gone something like this.

'Can you think of a filly that's ever won the Derby, Sergeant Paul?'

'No, sir. It's a race for colts, sir.'

'That's where you're wrong, sergeant. Fillies can be entered too. And they *are* entered. But even when they're entered they don't always run. Now listen to this. Eight years ago a filly won the Derby at 100 to one and went on to win the Oaks two days later. Amazing! The filly was called Signorinetta, bred by some Wop. My father had a tip-off and made a bucketful. Now it's my turn to get a tip-off. There's a filly called Fifinella running in the Derby and the Oaks, so I'm putting a month's pay on the double. I believe history repeats itself now and again. I'm rather taken with the Italian flavour. What about you?'

'What's the odds in the Derby?'

Captain Bliss told him and Ewart said he'd put one pound on Fifenalla to do the double. '*One* pound!' The captain smacked his hands together and laughed. 'You're a real plunger, aren't you, sergeant?'

'I'm getting married, sir, and I can't afford to lose the money.'

'Getting married? Tell you what. I'll double your stake for you as a wedding present. If you win, you'll pick up a cool three hundred.'

Ewart would have liked to have been on hand when Fifinella was running in the Derby and the Oaks at Newmarket but there he was, far away in Wales, and no way of knowing the winners except in the morning paper the day after. But as a Redcap he had some standing. The Derby was being run the very next day and Ewart was determined to pal up with some other Redcap in the town in the hope that the Army was quicker with the racing results. He might even be able to telephone Captain Bliss from the local Military Police headquarters on the pretext of official business, say soon after tea, by which time the Captain would certainly have had the news.

On the morning of the race Olive and he climbed half-way up a flat-topped hill and sat there, holding hands, looking west along the valley. When the sun broke through the cloud, patches of bright green slid across the mountains, brighter over the patches of young bracken, and then blue up to the rocky summits. Married! They had not a lot to say to each other, almost as though they had only just realized the significance of the step they had taken. To be married was - well, to be together and enjoy yourself. But now they were alone with each other, thinking what the future might hold and how much of it, because of the war, would be theirs to decide.

'I'm hungry,' said Olive and Ewart pushed her back until her head was on the grass and he could kiss her hard. He was putting his stamp on her and making her his own. 'Hungry for love,' she went on and put both arms around him.

She pushed her thigh against him and he thought God! She can't be expecting me to make love to her in the open air? Because of inexperience they'd had a clumsy night and he'd been shocked by the blood on the sheet. Olive had calmly washed it away by dipping that part of the sheet in a bowl she had filled with cold water from a jug. She said she had found the experience painful but now here she was, teasing him, arousing him, smelling of crushed bracken. At any moment someone might appear on the path, so he tried to distract her by saying the Derby was being run

151

that very afternoon and he had put money on a horse – well! a filly
– hoping to win enough money to pay for the honeymoon.

'And if you don't win?'

'Oh, I've got money.

'When will you know if you've won?'

'In Cardiff it'd be in the *Argus*. But here I dunno what happens.
You can bet all the officers will know.'

'I love you, Ewart.' They kissed again. Ewart was worried
because he was not responding as he should; rather the flesh
was not responding. To hell with anybody coming up the path!
That is how he should have felt. He was a soldier, there was a war
on and here he was with his bride. If you don't like what we're
doing, that's just too bad! The sun was hot. Surprisingly he had
not until that moment removed his cap. He was on leave, wasn't
he? So he took if off, his jacket too, and he lay there with Olive
pressed against him.

'Funny the Whites weren't at the wedding.'

'Does that really bother you?'

'I can't understand why they weren't there. Perhaps one of them
was ill. But they'd have sent a message. Was there a present?'

'They weren't ill and there wasn't any present. Oh, isn't there
something else we can talk about? No? Well, my dear Ewart, I'm
as sorry as you but I was that upset Agnes wasn't my bridesmaid.
I'll never forgive her! Never! Never!'

'But that's no reason Mr and Mrs White didn't come to the
wedding, Agnes not being your bridesmaid. Why wasn't she
anyway?'

'You wouldn't go back working for Charles after the war, would
you, Ewart?'

'Why not? There are other things I could do, I suppose. National
Hunt jockey, for example. I really like riding.'

'A jockey!'

'National Hunt is over the sticks. I'm not too old; I'm not too
heavy. But why shouldn't I work for Charles White?

'I hate him and what he did to that poor kid.'

'James?'

'I gave Agnes a real piece of my mind. I can't stand the way
things are hushed up. Perhaps I should have had it out with
Charles and Hannah direct but there she was, Agnes, sitting
in front of me with that innocent expression on her face, and I
just couldn't resist giving her a real shock. Hannah and Charles

152

should have told the kid right from the beginning that Hannah wasn't his real mother. Would he have loved her any the less? Of course not. So instead of getting the truth from Hannah and Charles, somebody had to whisper the nasty little secret into his ear. Couldn't they have seen it was bound to happen? They're stupid. God! Can't I just feel for that kid! Who could he turn to? Nobody! Nobody on this earth.'

'Is this what you told Agnes?'

'I can't stand hypocrisy and pretending things are not what they really are, just to be respectable. Respectable! The word makes me want to spit. What hanged James was respectability!'

So that was why the Whites had not come to the wedding. Agnes had told them what Olive had said. Olive said she hated Charles. No doubt Charles (and Hannah?) hated her too. If Ewart said anything which even slightly questioned whether Olive had acted for the best, he knew she would turn on him. She had become stiff in his arms. So he let it pass, not wanting a row on their honeymoon.

'Poor bastard.' He was thinking of the way James lay in his arms at the last.

'That's just what he was,' said Olive.

It turned out that Ewart was wrong to think Crickhowell was so remote that the Derby winner would not be known until the next day. That evening, as Olive and he were coming back from a walk by the river, they met a boy with a bundle of newspapers under his arm, shouting, 'Big push in France. All the winners.' The *Evening Argus* had no doubt come by train to Abergavenny where the Stop Press news caught up and was stamped in locally. The winner of the Derby was Fifinella.

'Oh Ewart, you darling. You've done it. We're rich.'

'No, steady on. We've won nothing at all yet. The way Captain Bliss laid the bet, it was for the double. All or nothing. If Fifinella wins the Oaks, we'll get three hundred quid. If she doesn't, we'll get nothing.'

'Who's Captain Bliss? Well, he ought to be ashamed of himself tricking you like that. Reckon he's pocketed your winnings.'

'He wouldn't risk it. If Fifinella came up in the Oaks as well, he'd have to fork out three hundred quid out of his own pocket. No, he put the money on for the double all right. It all depends on the Oaks.'

What with the heat and the excitement Ewart had come out in

153

a sweat. He agonized over what would happen. Please God, let Fifinella win the Oaks and make me rich. He wanted the sensual pleasure of taking the sixty crisp £5 notes and stuffing them down the front of Olive's dress

So when Fifinella did indeed win the Oaks two days later, Ewart was lifted on to a higher plane of existence. Once he had led an ordinary life but now he was exalted, he was a success, even a great man, possibly, a potent lover and certainly above all married. The big win consummated his marriage. He heard the news from Captain Bliss himself by telephone in the Assistant Deputy Provost Marshal's office, which was in a hut off the Brecon Road. Captain Bliss congratulated him and said Ewart had scooped a good £350 at least. He hadn't done too badly himself either, but what he was most concerned about now was to keep quiet. It was not every year a filly won the Derby or the Oaks, but for the same filly to win both was a startler. It would lead to a lot of talk about who'd battered the bookies. So not a word to anyone. Officers had been court-martialled for doing less than he had, laying bets on behalf of one of the lower ranks, and there ought to be a reward for the risk he had run; say a commission of 10 per cent. Would that be all right? 'Still leave you with three hundred and fifteen smackers, Sergeant! Wedding go all right?'

'Yes,' said Ewart. And he wanted to add, 'I'm really married now, sir, what with all this money.' But he didn't.

That hot evening Ewart and Olive walked to the bridge where they stood and peered into the rushing water trying to see the trout, then on, hand in hand, into the beech woods of Gilwern. The smooth, clean trunks rose forty feet or so before breaking out into their canopy of branches and leaves, quite motionless in the still air. Underneath was a cool and comforting darkness. There was little grass. For the most part the ground was just brown earth and the sere beech mast accumulated over the years lying there. Out of the hot day, they were now so far into the wood that trunks rose on all sides like the columns of a fantastic temple. Shafts of sunlight gimleted down here and there. Ewart was still quivering with the knowledge that they were rich and he took Olive to a mossy bank where they caressed as they had caressed on the mountain two days before, before the Derby and the Oaks had been run, and before Ewart knew his own strength. So this time he took his cap off straight away, laid his jacket on the ground for Olive to lie on and made love in the way she longed for.

154

Some weeks later Ewart, back on duty, received her letter to say she was pregnant. It was not too early to be thinking about names, she said, and Gilwern seemed in every way appropriate. It would do for a boy or a girl. Gil was what it would be shortened to: Gil Paul or, in the case of a girl, Gilly; but she was sure it would be a boy. Gil! Pronounced with a hard 'g'. What an unusual and what a happy name, happy because of the woods where he had been conceived.

Charles wrote a letter to Agnes.

Dear Agnes

It was nice seeing you the other day but at the same time it was not nice because it was cold, snow falling, and you looked frozen. Now Agnes, what you said about James is not the case, as the Coroner's verdict made clear. You may not remember this, but he acted young Oliver Twist and had a most lively imagination so that for all we know he imagined he was Bill Sikes in the same book who, as you will know from your reading, was accidentally hanged too.

You reproach your mother and me for not being more open. I expect you are right. But you're asking a lot, my girl, for how to be more open? Think what it would have meant. One day we would have had to say to you, 'Agnes, there's something serious you ought to know' and that's no way to talk to a child. You would have been bewildered and upset. So we let it all slide, I suppose. That's human, isn't it? Pray God when you marry you have a child quickly and not go through what your mother and I went through. If you don't, you would understand how James came to be born. His mother was Polly. She was an Irish girl, but she wasn't like the rest of the Irish because she was clean and good and full of fun, though R.C. with a priest who came and enquired about her when she was gone. That's just like the Roman Catholics, isn't it? Coming along at the right moment and asking for money.

The casualty lists are terrible. What's happening in Flanders is beyond what human beings can bear and yet remain human. Your mother detects light in the east, the chariots of Jesus with the sun coming up behind them in preparation for Armageddon which will do away with all this filth. That is her comfort, but I don't see it that way myself. It is no comfort

155

to me any more, I suppose, than it is a comfort to you. In these dark times we need one another. I must tell you, Agnes, that I am in the grip of Giant Despair. If I have done wrong, forgive me. Your mother is spotless and has done nothing that calls for forgiveness. But, as for me, I just don't know. No one else but you is in a position to forgive me for whatever it is I've done. Once I would have asked God to forgive me, but now there is only you I can turn to. You will not desert me. Your mother and I love you.

From your Father, C.W.

Some considerable time after this letter was sent it was Hannah's birthday and Charles gave her a string of pearls, long enough to go round her neck twice and still hang gracefully. Hannah was quite overwhelmed because she had never had such an expensive present before and she wasn't at all sure it was right to wear so much wealth round her neck. Of course, the pearls were lovely. They had a milky glow she fancied could be seen even in the dark. Certainly they lay in their black velvet-lined case in swirls of splendour which made her think of the clear night sky and the celestial bodies, stars and planets, swimming there. No, her pearls were not just stars and planets; they were more like the glorious seraphs who ranged in all their purity before the Heavenly Throne. She hoped that was not blasphemous.

'The clasp is real silver, Charles, with a hallmark.' She threw her arms around his neck and kissed him.

'Thought you might like them.' For that matter Charles liked the pearls himself. 'Saw them in that jeweller's in Queen Street. I just felt I 'ad to go in and 'andle them. They were like silk. They're second 'and, of course, as all the best things are.'

Hannah had a birthday card from Agnes with a design of red and yellow roses and the message 'To my dear Mother on her birthday'. Inside the card was a sheet of notepaper on which Agnes had written:

Dear Mam

As you will guess I am working hard for the first-year exam. I must really do well or they'll ask me to leave, but I am sure I shall do well. But what I wanted to tell you was that I've started working evenings and weekends at the military hospital in St Fagan's. I just scrub and carry bed-pans, but it's the least I can do. So it seems to me. I can work there full-time in the vac and still have time for study. Just so that you know what I'm up to.

Love, Agnes

'And that's all?' said Charles after she had shown him the card and the note.

'But I'd so *love* to show Agnes my pearls! Oh, why doesn't she come home at least once in a while?'

Hannah went to St Fagan's one Saturday afternoon without telling Charles – not all that difficult a journey by train, one change at Cardiff and then a walk. She went from one hutment to another and then ran into a Medical Corps sergeant who took her to Reception, where a woman consulted a book and said so far as she knew Miss White was in Ward G14. Acting on this information, Hannah found Agnes wearing a blue smock and cap pulling a trolley laden with baskets of soiled linen.

'You shouldn't have come,' Agnes told her. 'I'm just taking this lot to the laundry. Sit here and I'll be back.'

She looked better than when Hannah last saw her. She had more colour and her face seemed fatter, though that might have been because the cap hid all her hair. When she come back Agnes took her into the ward sister's office, saying they would be all right there for ten minutes or so because Sister was going the rounds with the M.O. Hannah was glad to sit down because her feet ached after the walk, which had been longer than expected.

'I wanted to be sure you're all right, Agnes. What you're doing here and your studies, I mean it may be too much.'

'I'm all right. Matter of fact I've never felt better.'

'Well, what time do you have off? I mean, we'd like to have you home once in a while. You're not abandoning us, are you?'

Agnes took off her cap and ran a hand through her hair. It was a real mess, Hannah thought, an untidy mop that could do with a shampoo, it was that dry and lustreless.

'You've come because I haven't answered Dad's letter, haven't you?

'What letter?'

'D'you mean you didn't know he wrote me a letter? Sly of him, wasn't it?'

The news that Charles had written without telling her came as

157

a shock; it was unlike Charles to keep something as important as this to himself. And now she was worried about what he might have said. All this she gave away by the expression on her face and Agnes read it easily.

'He's a good man, Agnes. You should see the pearls he gave me for my birthday.l I'd have brought them to show you, but the fact is I'd be afraid of losing them. So I just keep them locked up all the time.' She could see Agnes was not interested in the pearls, so she went back to that word 'sly'. 'No, your dad's never been a sly man. If he didn't tell me about the letter, there must be some good reason.'

'Would you like to see it?'

'Oh, no. I couldn't do that. He doesn't even know I've come to see you.'

'So you're sly as well. I'll go and get it.' Agnes replaced her cap, tucked in her hair and was off before her mother could say another word. Hannah was tempted to get up and run off too, she was that frightened of what the letter might say. An Army officer with a clerical collar instead of a tie came with an envelope which he placed on the ward sister's desk, smiled at Hannah and then went out again leaving a faint musty smell behind as though he was in need of a good airing.

He reappeared. 'Oh, would you mind telling Q.A. Goodenough the Padre left that envelope? I forgot to put in a covering note.'

So he was R.C., therefore not married. Without a wife a man would naturally smell musty after a while, and she tried to remember whether Father Gillespie, the only other R.C. priest she had known, smelled musty too. It was all too long ago. She wondered, as she had wondered many times before, whether Father Gillespie even knew what had happened to James. Probably not, otherwise he would have called. Would there be any point in asking this padre whether he knew Father Gillespie? But no, she would not want to do something that might bring on another visitation. She was not even sure whether musty was the right word for the mild aroma left by the padre, and there was no way of sniffing it again because it was quickly swamped by the hospital smells, iodine – or what she thought was iodine – mouthwash and steam, as though suet puddings were being boiled at the other end of the ward.

'There it is.' Agnes came in and handed the letter over, still in its envelope. It was not lost on Hannah that Agnes carried the letter about with her when it would have been more reasonable to leave it in her lodgings. So it *was* important to her. It had been read and re-read, Hannah could tell, from the way the paper was crumpled and the smudges that might even – Hannah could not be sure of this – have been caused by drops of - well, liquid of some kind. Couldn't be tea, because that would have left a more positive stain. Raindrops? Agnes might have been reading the letter in the open air and been caught in a shower. Whatever it was, it had caused the ink to run here and there. She knew all the time of course that the drops had come from Agnes's eyes, and she had to fight quite hard against this knowledge because it brought tears to her own eyes too. It seemed natural to sit in the Q.A.'s chair, smoothe the letter out on the Q.A.'s desk (on top of the padre's envelope), put on the gold-rimmed pince-nez spectacles she had bought by way of a birthday present to herself, and read with painful slowness the letter Charles had written with infinitely greater slowness and a heaviness of heart that was not just painful but a weight which pressed him down and down and down.

The letter was a single sheet, written on both sides. Hannah held it taut, then crumpled it into a ball which she squeezed tightly in her right hand while the two women – Agnes amazed and Hannah really (as she would have said) 'put out' – looked at each other fully in the eyes. The looking was both intimate and revealing. Hannah remembered how within minutes of Agnes being born she had stared into her eyes in the hope of exploring this other person, who had been part of her, before she receded into being just her own quite separate self. The eyes said everything. So, mother and daughter now looked into each other's eyes and Agnes knew her mother was disturbed and loved her for it while Hannah knew that Agnes, for all the defiance, was bewildered and lonely.

'Why did you do that?' Agnes touched Hannah's hand, the one that held the crumpled letter.

'He shouldn't have written that way. It's not like him; he owes more to himself than that.' Hannah vaguely remembered a sentence out of the Old Testament which she had never understood anyway but now took on a special meaning. 'Thou shalt not uncover thy father's nakedness.' She did not quote this to Agnes, but she wanted to say something like it. When a man let his guard down as Charles had, the decent thing was to avert one's eyes. Once a man lost his self-respect there was no knowing where he would end up. And who was this Giant Despair?

Agnes put out her hand. 'Please give it me.'

Hannah handed over the crumpled letter and watched as Agnes smoothed it out. 'Are you going to answer it?'

'I don't know what to say.'

Sister Goodenough of the Queen Alexandra's Imperial Military Nursing Service blew in, tremendous in her white uniform and scarlet cape which sported a couple of miniature medals. She looked from Agnes to Hannah in a surprise that, being a Liverpudlian, she heightened for comic effect.

'Well! Women in my office! Attractive women too. What will my poor love-starved boys be tempted to? And I try to run the ward as though temptation was impossible. Oh, Miss White, it's you! I didn't realize. Your mother, eh? How nice! But I'm kicking you both out all the same.'

Agnes walked as far as the main gate with her mother who kissed her, then gave her a hug. 'If you don't know what to write, just come and see your father. There may be no need to say anything at all. As for me, I just wish all this could be forgotten. It's all due to Olive. I'd never have believed she could be such a mischief-maker.'

Charles was not to be found when she arrived back at 'The Lookout', so Hannah took her cup of tea into the conservatory where she sat among the tomatoes and young chrysanthemums listening to the rain. It drummed on the roof and slid glassily down the sides; she was reminded of a little cabin her mother had made for the Christmas cake one year, all sugar but not the white kind sugar mice were made of. It was sugar clear as glass and Hannah had no idea how it was done. Perhaps her mother had bought panels of the stuff. Anyway, it was a delight and here she was, the rain falling so heavily that the glass of the conservatory seemed sugar too – and she sitting inside like the little Father Christmas her mother had placed in the cabin all those years ago.

When Charles arrived he was soaked and had to change all his clothes. Hannah lit a fire under the copper and hung the clothes on a rack to dry. He had been round talking to Mr Minsky, and been caught in the downpour on his way back. Minsky, he said, was upset because he'd had news from his relations in Polish Russia that Austrian troops were now in control there; they were living on Red Cross parcels and suffering hardships they couldn't go into because of the censorship. Minsky had also told him that

160

the British Government had stopped Bertrand Russell from going
to the States.

'Bertrand Russell?'

'He's that pacifist philosopher I told you about. Don't like the
man, but the Government shouldn't take his passport away. I
suppose they thought he'd run a stop-the-war campaign in the
States. Well, and why not? He's one man that'll feel clean when
the fighting's over. I want to feel clean too. But what can I do? Go
to meetings and pass resolutions. But we're getting out a pamphlet
for distribution.'

'Who's getting out a pamphlet?'

'It's a branch of the Anti-Conscription League called Peace
Now. Where've you been, anyway? I hung about waiting for you
to turn up.'

The rain had stopped, the sun had come out and Charles sat in
the conservatory in his underclothes; off-white wooly vest and
long pants in spite of the time of year. They too must have been at
least damp, because in the sun and warmth of the conservatory they
began to steam. Hannah had brought him a dry shirt and trousers,
but when she saw Charles's long pants giving off vapour she sent
him upstairs to change his underclothes too. 'Wet underclothes,
that's the way people get rheumaticky.'

'I went to see Agnes,' she said when Charles had returned and
was drinking a cup of team. 'You didn't tell me you'd written
to her.'

Charles's eyebrows went up and he gave her a sharp, enquiring
glance. 'You went to see Agnes? Where?'

'At the hospital. She was carting the dirty linen about.'

''Ow d'you find 'er? No, I don't mean 'ow did you track 'er
down. I mean, 'ow was she?'

'Quite well, really. Better than when we saw her.'

'Looked real peaky then, she did.'

'She showed me the letter. Why didn't you tell me you'd
written?'

Charles grinned. 'The fact is, 'Annah, I thought I'd told you.
More than, I thought I'd discussed it with you. I didn't? Well, that
just goes to show, doesn't it? What does it show? Well, we're that
close I just take it for granted you always know what I'm thinking
and doing.'

'I never know what you're thinking, not deep down.'

Charles judged the time had come to put on his dry shirt and

161

trousers. He walked round the tomato plants nipping out the axil shoots – pretending to be amazed, even hurt that she should find him difficult to understand. 'I've always 'ad an open character, 'Annah. Anyway, what did Agnes say?'

'She hadn't answered your letter because she didn't know what to say.'

Charles thought about this. 'I understand that. When somebody as close as your own dad puts all 'is cards on the table, it can be quite a shock to a wench.'

'If you meant all you said – all right, you did – you put too many cards on the table. You ought to have written a more dignified letter.'

'I don't care about dignity any more, 'Annah. I don't care about anything except, in a manner of speaking, being clean. I want to be clean about this war. I want to be clean about whatever it is Agnes is reproaching me for. So, yes, I put down all the cards. You and I are in this together, 'Annah, so *you* can't say I'm clean. I've got this notion Agnes can, though.'

'If you'd put your pride on one side and come with me to the Sabbath meeting, you'd remember just who it is can say you're clean.'

Pride? Yes, he had loads of it. He went on grinning and pinching the tomato plants savagely.

'And who's this Giant Despair?'

Charles stopped and turned a smiling face on her. 'That's what Carlyle might've said in a letter, and I'm like Carlyle. I get carried away with rhetoric. If I wrote a book it would all be purple patches. But one thing you can be sure of, 'Annah. You'll never find yourself in the grip of Giant Despair. Agnes is more like me. We've both 'eard the Giant's 'eavy tread.'

# 8

Hannah went without fail to the Sabbath meetings of the Dawn
Millenialists, and now she had taken to distributing their pamphlets
from door-to-door. To Charles their beliefs were just rubbish, but
they meant everything to Hannah; when she came home from a
meeting or one of her door-to-door proselytizing missions, her
complexion had a special, almost mischievous glow and her
eyes had a sparkle that was near coquettish. Charles could only
marvel. Hannah was aware he thought she was wandering in an
intellectual wilderness, but it made no difference. She had taken
her comfort, consolation and reassurance from where she could
find them – from God himself, she believed – and her respect for
Charles as a book reader and thinker had to take second place.
She was well aware he had no intention of arguing with her or
even discussing the D.M. That did not stop her from behaving
and talking as though he were D.M. himself, to the point where he
wondered from time to time whether she was laughing at him.

'A lady in Plymouth Road was most interested. She was really
nice. She said she'd lost two sons, one on the Somme and the
other in Mespot, but she wasn't the least bit down. She had spirit
messages all the time and they were at peace. And when I said
God was not all-powerful and that he was fighting another God
who was the evil force in the world, she just said that was the
last piece in the jigsaw. She gave me sixpence for the pamphlet
. . . and she gave a funny sort of laugh. "Now everything made
sense," she said.'

Charles wondered whether lunacy of this kind could be justified
if it made people happy. Perhaps every consolation was lunacy.
There were people who believed they were reincarnations of ancient
Egyptians. Other's, he'd read, claimed to be in communication with
a supreme spirit in Tibet. Well, what harm did it do? The Christian
belief that a certain man was God who sacrificed himself to wash
away the sins of the world was only a few degrees less dotty than
Hannah's expectation that Jesus could descend at any moment

163

from the clouds and step into the waiting motor-car the faithful had provided.

He asked Mr Minsky whether he thought some people needed some kind of illusion just to keep going.

'I don't know what you mean, Mr White.'

Mr Minsky looked neat and tidy that autumn day. He was wearing a silver-grey Homburg hat and a long, rough-looking overcoat which might have been made from cloth spun out of dog's hair; and, on his face, an expression which seemed to indicate he was looking to some remote horizon.

'This must be hell,' said Charles. 'The world has gone to pieces. People are just numb or running for funk-holes, really crazy funk-holes like my wife. She's in a funk-hole, I reckon.'

'Your wife is right in thinking great changes are coming.' Mr Minsky knew from Charles about Armageddon and the thousands now living who would never die. 'But the changes that will come are not apocalyptic; they are real. The soldiers everywhere are being pushed beyond all endurance, and what I am hearing is talk of mutiny in the armies. Particularly the French are mutinous. And who is blaming them? Not me. I would have no stomach for this slaughter. But what else am I hearing? In spite of censorship I am hearing bigger and stranger things.'

'Who says there are mutinies?'

'My daughter Ruth works in the hospital office at St Fagan's. She is hearing rumours among the men.'

'That's where Agnes works.'

'Then they must be seeing each other. Is Agnes talking of mutinies? We don't read about it in the newspapers, but there's talk. The word is getting round. Hospitals are the biggest breeding grounds – the gossip they hear wounded men bring back to England. Is it surprising there should be talk of mutinies?'

'No, there may be talk, but whether there are any mutinies is another matter. As like as not, yes, you can't drive men beyond a certain point. Then they crack. They refuse to go over the top and the officer shoots them. I understand that. Nobody likes to talk about it but it 'appens. Mutiny is different. That means men getting up on their 'ind legs and threatening their officers. Never 'eard of this French lot chucking it in, but then they're just Frogs, aren't they? British troops wouldn't mutiny. They're too – 'As Charles thought, a grin slid across his face. 'They're too stupid.'

'I am hearing of British mutinies. Ask your daughter if she is hearing about mutinies.'

'We're not on very good terms.' Charles wished he had not said that. 'I couldn't ask 'er about mutinies.'

Minsky and Charles were in the Minsky backyard where asters and dahlias exploded in brilliant reds and yellows. In a hutch against the pale blue, staring clematis on its trellis was a large white rabbit, called Disraeli, with a twitching pink nose. Mr Minsky broke off to talk to Disraeli. 'I know you are missing your mother, but these things are happening in a war. Do not be disturbing yourself. Not a rabbit war. A war between human beings. Rabbits are peaceable.' Mr Minsky explained that 'mother' was just a joke. Disraeli was Ruth's rabbit and he'd lived longer than expected. 'Why are you not on good terms with your daughter?'

They had met by chance in the vestibule of the Town Hall where Charles had been consulting the Municipal Engineer about connecting houses to the main drainage and Mr Minsky had been arguing with one of the borough's lawyers about some equally gritty matter, a disputed right of way. Mr Minsky wanted to go into a hotel for coffee. There was talk of the stuff being rationed out of existence; so grab some while it was still on offer. Charles said he'd never got into the foreign habit of sitting down for refreshment between meals; but why didn't they stroll up to the recreation ground? A couple of American troopships had come into the Queen Alexandra Dock. Up at the rec, they'd have a good view of what was going on.

So that's where they went – after calling at the Minsky house to deposit some papers and talk to Disraeli. There was no hurry. Gnats danced in the mild sunshine. The foliage of the lime trees in Albert Road were beginning to rust. Straight overhead the sky was deep blue, shading down to a sea-mist blue just over the roof-tops, and the two men took the slight uphill climb easily, saying nothing because Charles had still to answer that question about Agnes. It was the kind of silence which stopped Mr Minsky from saying anything until Charles had. It so happened that their route took them past the house in Arcot Street where the Whites had lived before moving to 'The Lookout' and Charles paused to look in, rather cheekily, at one of the windows. Nothing to see. Lace curtains from top to bottom. This was the house Father Gillespie had come to with the news about Polly.

'It's what I told you, Mr Minsky, that's why we're not on good

165

terms with Agnes. She got to know that I'd played the Abraham. It was a great shock, you can imagine that.'

'She did not know? You did not tell her?'

'That's what she's chiefly angry about.'

There were few other people in the recreation ground and they had a seat to themselves looking down over the bay to the docks, the white harbour buildings, the cranes and the shipping. Someone had said it was like Bombay, but Charles did not know whether a Hindu would have thought so. He guessed that Bombay did not have those mountains in the background as Cardiff did, so near and clear in this morning light that he fancied he could pick out a few white speckles which would have been sheep.

'Those must be the troopships.' Mr Minsky waved his yellow-gloved hand in the direction of a couple of single-stacked steamers painted all over with grey and blue camouflage. At this distance they'd have needed binoculars to see what was going on 'The first lot to put in here. Pray God the others come quickly before it is too late.' He turned to Charles. 'You talk to your daughter. Ask her about mutinies. You've got to talk to her, you understand? Mutinies are a good subject for conversation.'

It crossed Charles's mind that if Mr Minsky was so interested in picking up news about British mutinies, he might be a spy. In tumultuous times the unbelievable could happen, and Minsky with a good view of Cardiff docks and relations in Europe was well placed to be a spy. The possibility made him more interesting.

'Those are not troopships, they're much too small. They're Campbell paddle-steamers. I can see the round cage things the paddles are in. In fact there are no big passenger ships.'

'Your eyesight is better than mine. Well, I am just wondering how these rumours start. Perhaps it is the same with the mutinies.'

They both knew they should not be sitting there: they should be back on the job, but they made no move to go. From this high point they were looking east, in the mind's eye, over the green and smoke of England to the Channel. An elephant-grey stain stretched across Flanders and the north of France, slurping down to the white points that marked the Alps.

'It isn't just mutinies.' Mr Minsky was talking to himself rather than to Charles. 'There'll be revolution, and that is the way it will all be ending. France will have a revolution, there is no doubt, Mr White.'

'I wouldn't be surprised. They're a wobbly lot.'

'In Germany too there is starvation. There are bound to be risings.'

'That's propaganda. I don't believe it.'

Mr Minsky clapped his hands together and smiled at the prospect of European revolution. 'It is the only thing. Nothing can stop this madness but revolution. Then the world will be better and men will come together like brothers. It must be God's will, Mr White.'

'I should've thought anyone who believed in God would do nothing but curse the old fool.'

'Oh no. Let me tell you a Jewish story.'

Surprisingly Mr Minsky drew out a packet and extracted a thin, brown cigarette, then found it so difficult to light that Charles had to do it for him, striking the match in his cupped hands. He had never seen Mr Minsky smoke before; he had never seen a cigarette like that either. They must have been foreign and probably Minsky had a supply sent through Switzerland by his German, Austrian or Russian spy-masters. Who knew where Minsky's real loyalties lay? He offered Charles a cigarette but Charles shook his head.

'Mr White, you have to be imagining an old Jewish tailor talking to God. He shows God a book, and in this book the tailor has written all his sins. Then he takes out a much bigger book. He says to God, "These are all your sins, the wars, the massacres, the pogroms. Who is the bigger sinner, eh? You or me? But it is a feast and a time of reconciliation. So I'll let you off lightly. Master of the universe, I forgive you, and in return see to it you forgive my sins against you."'

Charles thought this a silly story and began to chuckle, though uneasily because he did not know what Mr Minsky was driving at.

Mr Minsky drew on his cigarette, exhaled the smoke through his mouth and, as rapidly, drew it into his nostrils – looking like an idol drawing up incense, Charles thought, with his wide cheekbones and deeply recessed eyes.

'This is a scandalous story, an ordinary man – just a tailor – talking to God about his sins and the great debt God owed mankind. Because God does owe us. It was brave to say so. We call it *chutzpah*: great impudence. You would have thought the Master of the universe would be tormenting the tailor like he tormented Job. But do you know what happened?'

'No.'

167

'God and all his angels came into that tailor's house and everyone rejoiced.'

Mr Minsky took the cigarette from his mouth and looked Charles in the eye. The muscles round his mouth quivered, his mouth quivered and then went up at the corners before the dark eyes sparkled and the laughter came. Charles began laughing too. Mr Minsky patted him on the shoulder and Charles patted him in return, both laughing, Mr Minsky actually guffawing, throwing his head back and showing his teeth. In some mysterious way he had secreted cigarette smoke, because now it puffed out of his mouth and up to his eyes which began watering so copiously he had to produce a handkerchief to wipe them so that Charles thought he wasn't laughing after all, but crying. A bit of both perhaps.

'I think 'Annah would like that story.'

Mr Minsky's mood changed rapidly. He glared at Charles out of his dark eyes. 'I'm a fool. I talk like a fool. I've probably given you quite the wrong idea. What were we talking about? Yes, revolution. You can feel the spirit of revolution coming out of Europe like a breeze of fire.'

'You were wrong about Russia invading India.'

'Russia? There is still time. That is not a real revolution they are having there. The people are too poor and the intellectuals can't make up their minds. Yes, the Tsar goes but the Tsar will come back. There is another story I can tell you. Not religious this time. A Russian intellectual, a landowner, always went to the railway station with his family to start on a holiday without having made up his mind where they were all going. Were they go south to the Crimea? Were they go west, go abroad to Baden, say? And the whole family argued as they went to the railway station. Now, thinking Russia is like that. Indecisive. There will be turmoil in France and Germany. Yes, I can see that. But the very fact the Russians can't make up their minds is probably their salvation. They can be mercilessly cruel. Yes. But they don't know what they are doing; they are just indecisive. Russia will last and turn out to be the knout for the rest of Europe.'

If Minsky turned out to be a spy, he could not be of much use to his masters if he relied on hospital gossip for his information and mistook Campbell paddle-steamers for American troopships. Charles did not really believe Minsky was a spy. From that time on, though, it pleased him to feed him with information invented

168

– largely for his own pleasure, and partly, if passed on – to confuse the enemy.


When Ewart appeared on a black and windy evening at 'The Look-out' Charles was not as surprised as Hannah was because, off and on, he and Ewart had been writing to each other. And Hannah did not know about this, any more than she had known about his writing to Agnes. The correspondence began with Ewart asking advice on what to do with his winnings. Charles's advice was not to put it in War Loan or even bank deposit, but into bricks and mortar. He had enough to buy one of those semi-detached villas on the Cogan Road and if Ewart wanted he, Charles, would do the negotiating. It didn't have to be the Cogan Road; there was attractive property in the Plassey Street area. But property, that was the thing. They'd had their revolution in Russia in spite of Mr Minsky's predictions; there'd been bread riots in Germany, the French were as volatile as ever and Charles did not rule out the possibility of social upheaval in Britain once the British got it into their thick skulls that this slaughter on the battlefields was pointless. The difficulty, Charles wrote, was that so many men had been killed, so many families had lost somebody, nobody liked to admit it was lunacy and that these men had died for nothing. Nothing! Charles reiterated. The remarkable thing about this correspondence was the way neither Charles nor Ewart mentioned Olive and her pregnancy. Later, Charles was miffed to learn that in spite of his good advice Ewart had put the money into War Loan.

'Who's there?' Charles shouted at the locked door when Ewart knocked.

Ewart came in and took off his cap and greatcoat. Charles looked at him in admiration. The Army life suited Ewart all right. He glowed; he stood upright, his face had a kind of goodness about it, a manliness. He was alert, he smiled, he was unfearing. Charles was so excited by Ewart's outgoing masculinity that he wanted to take him in his arms, but that of course was out of the question and when Hannah came into the room Charles could only say, 'This is quite a surprise, isn't it?'

'Ewart!' Hannah was apprehensive. 'Out in this night. Is anything the matter?'

Charles took him into the sitting room. Only then did he realize Ewart had a new insignia on his lapels, a curious squashed oblong.

169

'I'm sorry to call in this way.' Ewart had left his cap and greatcoat in the hall, but in his khaki tunic and puttees he was overdressed for 'The Lookout' and began to sweat in the heat from the fire burning in the grate.

Charles just loved him. A soldier and a hero. Not a war hero, by any means. Just a great and glorious example of what the human race was capable of. In spite of the slaughter there would be men like Ewart; a man who took pride in being what he was, human and defiant against the odds. What odds? Of time and chance and the bloody malice of things.

The last time the Whites had seen Ewart was the day when he and Olive got engaged. Then they all went out to Lavernock for a celebratory picnic and Charles took a photograph. They had not been at the wedding because they had not been invited, a fact that was uppermost in Hannah's mind. Ewart's visit was not so unexpected, and the pleasure of seeing him not so great that her resentment over the rebuff could be hidden. It was what Hannah wanted to talk about.

'We've still not given you the wedding present, Ewart. It's up in the attic still in its box. We weren't to know we were not going to be welcome.'

'I'm sorry about that, Mrs White. I was surprised not to see you. But the invitations went out from Olive's step-mother – it must've been she just didn't know. It was terrible. Next to my mother, you were who I most wanted to be there.'

'Ewart, you know it can't be true that Mrs Jones didn't know.'

He hesitated. 'Yes, Mrs White, it wasn't true and I'm very sorry. It's all the more difficult because the reason I've turned up like this is to ask you and Mr White a favour. I don't know what's going to happen to me. I've been transferred into the Tank Corps. So far as I can see' – Ewart grinned – 'they need tank crew more than they need policemen.'

'The Tank Corps? What's the favour?' Even Hannah had heard about tanks and thought they didn't sound natural. A tank was something you had in the roof to keep water in. The transformation of part of the plumbing into an instrument of war chilled her, and that Ewart should be mixed up in such a development was even more confusing. He had worked in Charles's yard, as good an employee as you could wish for, but now he was one of the men turning plumbing into warfare. The devilish ingenuity of mankind was out of control and the sooner the forces of light confronted the forces of darkness the better.

'Olive's your cousin, after all. You know she's expecting? Well, I'd like you to keep a sort of friendly eye on her. You see, she's got no one. She doesn't get on with her father and his wife. So she's all alone when I'm not there, except for that Mrs Peacock but she's not family.'

Charles was astonished that Ewart had given up his cushy job in the Military Police to be crewman in a tank. Everybody said the tanks were going to win the war for the Allies, but they hadn't achieved much so far. There had been a lot of casualties among the crewmen, and no doubt that was why Ewart had been shifted over.

'What's it like in a tank?'

'Hot and noisy. It's a real bone-shaker. I'm not a driver or a gunner. I'm just a gearsman in a female tank, so I ought to be pleased they let me keep my rank.'

Charles was even more astonished. 'What do you mean, a female tank? Are there male tanks?'

'It's like in life, male and female. The male carries the 6-pounders and the female has the machine guns. It's the machine guns that do the killing. They're supposed to work in pairs, the male and the female.'

'Like the Himalayan bears,' said Charles.

'Eh?'

'Of which it is said, the female of the species is more deadly than the male.'

'That's true. The 6-pounders knock out the defences, but with the Vickers machine guns the female tank can enfilade a trench. We've had training on Salisbury Plain, so I reckon we'll soon be off. But I don't see what this has got to do with bears.'

Hannah wanted to make some tea and produce Welsh cakes out of her storage tin. Ewart said the mood he was in he'd not be able to stomach anything, but Hannah had already gone to the kitchen. Charles, now that he'd had more time to look at Ewart, saw that the first impression of him as glowing with manly health and ready for anything was misleading; it must have been the effect of a warm room on a man who had been walking through a very cold night. In fact, he was worn and tired.

Coming back, Hannah said she had put the kettle on.

'I'm not staying,' Ewart said.

171

He sat for some time, looking into the fire. 'When I came out this evening I didn't know where I was going, honest. I could have walked into the sea. I reckon I was more surprised than you when I turned up here. Olive and I had an upper-and-downer. She just can't bear the thought of me in the Tank Corps – as if I was given any choice in the matter. But she said I could've got out of it; and I suppose I could but I mean, somebody's got to go, know what I mean? Olive said I was just not giving any thought to her and the baby. I was just being selfish. Selfish? I mean, going into the Tanks Corps selfish! I've never seen her in such a state. What set if off I don't know. After all, I've been in the Tanks Corps for a while but something just set her off this evening. She was hysterical. It might have been nothing more than the uniform. Not having the red top to my cap, and with this Tank Corps badge. I honestly thought she was going to claw me.'

'She may be worried about the baby,' said Hannah.

'What I say, she needs a real woman friend, not like that Mrs Peacock. She's your cousin, Mrs White; I know you're not on good terms but she's your cousin.'

'Does she ever talk about us?'

'No, to be honest, but I don't think that's any bearing. How's Agnes?'

'We don't see her. She's got her College work, and when she's not doing that she works at the hospital.'

'Olive was cut up she wouldn't be a bridesmaid.'

Charles went off to wedge a window that was rattling in the wind, and when he came back Hannah was telling Ewart he really ought to be going home to Olive. She would be wondering where he was.

Ewart, though, was in no hurry to go. He sat looking into the fire as though mesmerized. 'I suppose what I'm asking is for you to keep a friendly eye on Olive.'

'Yes, I'll do that. I'll go and see her.' Hannah was increasingly impatient. 'In fact, I'll come back back with you now, if you like.'

Charles was as surprised as Ewart was embarrassed by such an offer; if he had talked in a way that gave the impression it was not safe for him to go home to Olive unaccompanied, for fear of his reception, then plainly he'd overdone it. He would not hear of Hannah coming out on such a night, but still he made no move to go.

Charles belatedly realized the home life of the Pauls was under greater strain than he had thought. Since Hannah hated going out in the dark, her offer was all the more momentous.

'Olive is sitting there wondering where you are, Ewart. That's all.'

Charles had no objection to taking a stroll in the dark. On the contrary he would rather enjoy it. He'd love a breath of fresh air off the Channel, straight up from Lundy, smelling of salt and shrimps and cockles! But what happened when they reached the house in Glebe Street? If the row had been as violent as Ewart said, the chances were that Olive would have locked the door against him. Again, she might be upstairs ready to fling a jug of water over them. Or, thirdly, the door might indeed be locked, but Ewart had the key and Charles would feel obliged to follow him into what might turn out to be an ugly scene. When a married couple were having a row they should be left alone to enjoy it in peace, without witnesses. He wanted to do whatever he could to help Ewart; his fatherly feelings for the lad had been fired again by this news that he had transferred to the Tanks Corps, but he could not see that facing Olive at Ewart's side would be of any service to the lad at all.

He offered to go, though, and was relieved when Hannah dismissed the suggestion. 'You'd be no use. It needs a woman.'

Eventually Ewart went off by himself. The row with Olive had shaken him, that was clear, but more by accident than calculation he had Hannah's promise to go and see Olive so he cheered up. He climbed into his greatcoat and stood in the hall twisting his cap. Hannah and Charles knew what was in his mind. This might be no ordinary goodbye. He was rejoining his unit the next day. Then what? Hannah kissed him on the cheek and Charles grasped his left hand – not his right, that would have been too formal – and said he hoped Ewart had given up financing the bookmakers.

'No, Mr White, I wish I could say as much, but the fact is a bob on a horse seems about the last decent thing open to a chap. I just can't give it up. It's the only excitement I get. It's all chance and luck. What isn't? I win now and again. I sometimes think it's God's way of letting me know whether he's for me or against me.'

Hannah decided this was a matter on which she could speak with authority. 'You can't presume to test God. That's sinful. Keep your money in your pocket. God loves you.'

Then he was gone, out into the blackness, the collar of his

173

greatcoat up around his ears. The gaslight in the hall caught him as he spread his arms to make sure he did not walk into the bushes. He might have been a great golden bird preparing to take off.

'He was really upset.'

'That cousin of yours is a bitch. I'm sorry, but this coming on top of what she said to Agnes!'

'Her mother died,' said Hannah, 'and her father married again, that's what's at the bottom of it. That and this war, Ewart going off in a different regiment – and the baby coming. She just has to hit out at somebody.'

'A woman must've got a devil in 'er to make Ewart think of walking into the sea.'

'Is that what he said? Must have been when I was in the kitchen. You don't have to believe what people say. Ewart wouldn't have liked getting wet. I'll go and see Olive, as I said. I'll take her some of my calves' foot jelly. Agnes will understand.'


Some time that winter Minsky said to Charles that in spite of the news from the front nobody should think life was meaningless. Just conceivably, a half-educated or self-educated man or woman might, but they were a group to be pitied.

Charles assumed Minsky was putting him somewhere in this category but pretended not to understand.

Minsky went on to say that uneducated men and women,on the other hand, knew that life could be hard but, when they prayed, God listened and at the end would gather them to himself. That was wisdom.

'And as for the educated, even when they are atheists they are seeing that human beings are capable of heroism and dignity even in the most terrible conditions. It is amazing the sacrifices men are ready for. Where does that heroism and dignity come from, I am asking?'

'It only looks like 'eroism. Deep down men are doing what they want to do, and that's fight. We're still savages. Do you think that if we weren't savages the war wouldn't've been over long ago? The world is mad. Drunk on blood. And it'll go on and on. There's no meaning to it, and if that puts me in the 'alf-educated or self-educated bracket so be it! But I 'ad no idea of educating myself. What for? No, I read and I read the same way as I eat

174

because the 'unger is there. And what at the end comes of all this reading? Not education, not even semi-education. Just bitter wormwood.'

'I'm sorry, Mr White.'

'I tell you I can see as far in the dark as the best of them. Simple, ignorant people see more clearly – like children. It was a child told the Emperor 'e 'ad no clothes.'

'I am sorry for being so clumsy. Don't think I'm counting myself among the learned. My family from way back is in the tailoring, and I only went into building because of my weak chest. The more open-air life is more healthy for my chest. Learning, certainly not. But I am having a great respect for the learned. I know what they think and I am having to say it again. They do not think life is meaningless.'

Charles was short of a skin or two when it came to discussing his education or the lack of it, but he did not want to quarrel with Minsky. 'It isn't learning that counts, Mr Minsky. What counts is finding a way to live with despair. In a 'appy sort of way, I mean.' He was not sure whether this was original. He might have read this bit about despair somewhere, but he did not think so. The idea it conveyed was novel to him. He was impressed and not a little proud of himself.

Minsky seemed impressed too. 'That doesn't sound very Nietzschean. You must have moved on. Good. There is a Jewish saying that the time to be on the lookout for trouble is when you are not on the lookout for trouble. Perhaps we are lucky because we know we are troubled. So if you are feeling like that, Mr White, I am having to say that you, in a manner of speaking, are a Jew too. All peoples who look for a decent way of living with trouble are Jews of a kind. I have no news from Russian Poland since the Revolution in St Petersburg and look at me, Mr White. Or even before that for two years. My sister and her family are there. I am living with that. You, I imagine, live with lesser problems.'

Charles looked at him. His problems were lesser, that he conceded. But he thought that in spite of his professed anxiety about his relations in Russian Poland Minsky looked remarkably sleek and pleased with himself. His nose looked a bit longer than Charles had remembered, and his eyes were deeper set and more challenging. There was so much stubble on his chin that it appeared as though he was attempting a beard. He looked well enough, though. The information about the weak chest was interesting and Charles

175

wondered how much truth there was in it. Perhaps this was part of the invented role which masked the fact that he was not in fact ill but a secret agent. Minsky had always been brisk and energetic; he did not cough any more than anyone else. To be a spy you had to be adept at deceiving people and the fantasy Charles had invented, just to amuse himself, was extended to explain why Minsky should claim to have a weak chest when, quite plainly, he did not. As for Nietzsche, it was quite true he had moved on. What with all the slaughter in France, Charles thought that Neitzsche himself might have moved on too.

Him, a sort of Jew? Charles tried the idea on for size and yes, he could see it might fit. If he had been a real Jew instead of a Cotswold peasant, though, he would have had a richer ancestry – not of education, that was the wrong word, but of beliefs and practices. As it was, the best he could hope for was to be an honorary Jew and even then, Minsky had enrolled him not because of any cultural link but because he had said what he had said about living cheerfully in a bad time. No doubt Charles was romanticizing about the Jews. He knew nothing about them. Minsky was the first Jew he had ever met and even then he had not realized the fact until Hannah told him. All that seemed a long time ago.No Chapel (where they did not baptize infants), no Church. No Jews at a christening. No nothing.

'Your son,' said Minsky. 'You are not thinking he was absurd too?'

Charles was shocked. 'Absurd?'

'To use the word that Nietzsche taught you.'

Charles was so shocked he could have lied. Who was Minsky to probe him like this? Not even Nietzsche had the right. To agree that James's death was absurd, Charles would have to be a monster. Never a day went by without his thinking of James. And the dreams! The boy was repeatedly running away from him in a smoky tunnel which had branches leading off. This was the trip to London coming back in disguise. James might have taken any one of those exits, so there was no way of knowing where he had escaped to. The lie Charles had thought of telling was that Hannah and he did not brood about the past.

'What happened to James was just a mistake.'

A meeting of businessmen where they talked of fund-raising had just ended. The idea was comforts for the troops, and the proceedings had started with each of them putting an envelope

176

containing money into a black tin box. The back room in the Town Hall, still reeking of tobacco smoke, was lit by two spluttering gas-lamps, spluttering so much the room wobbled in the uncertain light. It was cold – one reason why the meeting had been short and had come to no decision about what to do next, other than to hold charity whist drives – and Minsky's breath and Charles's breath rose in vapour as they sat there. They were the only two left, sitting under an oil painting of a former mayor, a stern man seated with a black and white cat on his lap. Charles had wondered about this cat; it made Abednigo Clough more interesting. There must have been votes in it from cat-lovers.

'Mr White, I am thinking it is all very well to have large ideas about the world and all that, but when it comes down to thinking about one particular person one has loved and lost it is not making sense to be pessimistic. The heart knows it is not making sense to be pessimistic. The grim philosopher paints a black picture, but we are not grim philosophers. We are ordinary men with our natural feelings. And we don't deny them. We have to be positive and affirm things – just as we must believe that when this war is over the world will become better. Come now, Mr White, you don't think it would be possible for another war to take place, not ever? Everybody's eyes are opened. The men would not fight.'

'Why do you tell me this?'

'You are down in the dumps. You are unhappy about your daughter, yes? I have a surprise for you. She is a guest in my house.'

'Agnes? With you?'

Charles was incredulous. First of all Minsky had shocked him with that question about James, and now he was shooting this news about Agnes at him. Matters were being decided behind his back – that was how it struck Charles, because surely Agnes would not have gone to the Minskys without Hannah being consulted.

'You are perplexed, Mr White, but it is all simple. She is a friend of my daughter Ruth and Agnes was suffering –'

'What's the matter with 'er, then?'

'Influenza. It is going about. But the worst is over.'

''Ow long 'as she been with you?'

'Three days, four days. The crisis is past.'

If Charles had not been so perplexed by Minsky's behaviour he would have been angry. Minsky had started this conversation in

177

the most innocent way imaginable (by a discussion of the significance of human existence), called Nietzsche into question, complained about the cold, drawn his coat more closely around him and clapped his yellow-gloved hands together when all the time he had this information about Agnes up his sleeve. Why should he put that cruel question about James when all the time he was leading up to this astonishing revelation about Agnes? Who the hell did he think he was? Charles reflected. To begin with, Minsky was the benevolent friend who had helped him on his way, from employee to master-builder; he had looked after Charles as one of his own. Why? There was more behind Minsky's philanthropy than appeared on the surface. After all, the man was not English. Minsky might be not only a spy, sending misleading information about Campbell paddle-steamers back to his masters in Europe, but he might have more immediate ambitions such as taking control of a simple Englishman to serve some larger and unknowable Jewish purpose. But what? His friendliness seemed to have developed a cutting edge.

'Why didn't you tell me before?'

'The news would be upsetting to you and I wanted to approach it delicately. We have known each other so long now. May we not be calling each other by our first names? Mine is Mendel.'

Charles was not sure he would remember this name. 'Mendel? Mine is Charles.'

'I knew it. I have seen it on your bill-heads, but I wanted to hear it from your own lips. Then we understand each other. She is a sweet girl, your daughter, and I can assure you, Charles, she is better.'

'She should be in her own home.'

'Exactly what Ruth said! But Agnes would not come to you, just refused. I know it is upsetting, Charles, and I have been upset with Ruth too, so I know what it is to be upset by a daughter. It seems that Agnes was not seeing her way clear to coming home to you. In fact she said no. But she was so ill; she was in a high fever, there was no bed for her in a soldiers' hospital and she could not go to her College room alone. Who would look after her? Ruth thought she might have died. So Ruth invited her. It was a surprise! Such a great surprise! An ambulance with a great red cross on it outside our house, and two soldiers coming in with a stretcher case.'

'You should've told me straight away.'

'She would not allow it. If she was well enough to be angry,

178

I think she would be angry that I am telling you now. But I *am* telling you, Charles.'

'I'm going to get Hannah. We'll 'ave Brownlow around to see 'er.'

'I would not advise it. Dr Brownlow has already seen her and prescribed medicines which Ruth has obtained. Your Agnes is all right, Charles. Nothing to worry about. Dr Brownlow says the crisis has passed and she will soon be on her feet again. There is a lot of this influenza going about, not only in this country but in Europe.'

Charles wondered whether this information came through Minsky's international information spy network. He needed this fantasy now more than ever. 'It's unnatural. Why should she spit in our faces like this?'

'Children are children and parents are parents. There is no measuring the anguish between them. Leave her in peace for a few days and I will send Ruth to talk to you.'

The Town Hall caretaker was giving warning that he wanted to go home by coming into the room with a lighted candle and putting out the gas-lamps. Charles and Minsky stood up to go and Minsky – much to Charles's surprise – grasped his arm, steering him almost affectionately out of the room. Charles was touched and at the same time bothered. He did not like this kind of – as it seemed to him – intimate physical contact, and as they emerged into the night he quickly distanced himself. No doubt other people, particularly from hot countries, liked touching each other. He could understand that Minsky was making a gesture, but it was one he could have done without. Was he right? Was he responding as he should have done? Was he just the Cotswold yokel, in spite of the serious study he had given to Carlyle, to Darwin and to Nietzsche? This was something he often thought about. Sleet became visible like white scribble in the street-lighting and the two parted, Minsky making for his house near St Augustine's and Charles for 'The Lookout' where he knew Hannah would be distraught by the news he had to give her. Or perhaps not so distraught. Agnes was all right; that was the main thing, and Hannah being the woman she was she might even rejoice.

'Good night – ' Charles had forgotten the name already.

'Mendel. Good night, Charles.'

If someone (his mother, for example) had asked Charles whether he understood Hannah – *really* understood her – he would have

179

been puzzled. Certainly he understood her! Without question. He was married to her, wasn't he? And he knew her ways. If really challenged, he would have said he knew how she would react in any given situation, even the extraordinary one she looked forward to with such idiotic confidence. The Second Coming would amaze her, in spite of this confidence, and Charles was sure she would be hysterical if Jesus even so much as looked at her. He would have to calm her down. 'Well, it's what you wanted, isn't it?' he'd say as the great wings throbbed over the house and the golden Rolls moved down the Cogan Road towards Cardiff, transfiguring Tiger Bay with its light as it passed by . . . or however the Millenial Dawnists envisaged the possibilities. Having taken his speculation so far, Charles was honest enough to think he too should consider what his response would be. Of course it was all rubbish, this belief in the imminent arrival of Jesus. But what if it happened? It would make him feel a bit of a fool.

So, thinking he knew his Hannah, he was completely taken aback by her reaction to the news that Agnes was ill and being cared for by the Minskys. He had never seen her so angry. 'She can't do such a dreadful thing!' He had thought her first concern would be for Agnes's well-being, but not at all. The fact that Agnes was ill made her disloyalty all the more outrageous. When in her great need (she might even have been dying; people were dying from influenza and its complications these days) she ought naturally to turn to her parents, she had instead gone to strangers – not even family, not even English still less Welsh, just foreigners, and if Charles was at all right spies into the bargain. But she had never known when Charles was serious or joking.

She was behaving quite differently from the woman Charles had known. The way she shouted, the way she clenched her fists, made her a stranger. 'Why you didn't go straight back with that Minsky and get Agnes out of the place, I'll never know. Why have we deserved such a daughter? No, I don't want you to come with me. I'll sort this out myself. You can put a hot-water-bottle in her bed to air the sheets because she'll be right back here with me, I can tell you.'

For she had decided to go round to the Minskys straight away. In spite of Charles's attempts to dissuade her she changed into her dark blue dress with red piping, looked out her big hat with the cherries on it and, because it was snowing, fished out her grandmother's boots which Charles had to secure for her with a button-hook. Her dark winter coat was in the Cossack style, even to the epaulettes, and in spite of the incongruous hat, Charles envisaged her as a Cossack throwing open the front door to step into the snow and jump on to a waiting horse. Instead, when she opened the door and the snowflakes blew in she opened her umbrella; it was so much of a dome that when she held it straight over her head she could not see where she was going. She lowered it into the wind, but then knew even less where she was going.

'For God's sake, 'Annah, she's all right. Leave it till the morning.'

'Don't use such language. It isn't for God's sake you speak but your own.'

Then she was gone, after leaving the impression of a wild woman with a glow in her face as though a fire raged somewhere inside her head and irradiated her countenance. He would have said her eyes flashed if he had not known eyes could not flash, there was no inner light, but it really seemed as though in her rage Hannah's eyes gave out such flashes against reason and nature. He went and looked out a hurricane lamp, lit it and set out to follow her, but it was not until he reached the Minskys' house that he caught up with her.

'I was expecting you, Mrs White.' These were the first words spoken by Mrs Minsky as Hannah, followed by Charles, stepped into her hall. 'Ruth has taken with it now, the 'flu, and she's gone to bed too.' There was a strong smell of cooking – onion soup most likely, Charles decided – and when the kitchen door opened it was revealed that Mr Minsky himself, wearing a woman's white apron and without the usual gloves, was in charge. Like his wife he seemed quite unsurprised by the invasion and even went so far as to say their arrival was timely. The girls would have no appetite for solid food, which meant there would be two lamb-chops over and the Whites would be welcome to them.

'We can all have a cosy supper together,' said Minsky.

'I want to see Agnes.' Hannah implied that the thought of food at such a time of crisis was intolerable and, directed by Mrs Minsky, she went upstairs while Charles stayed behind to put out the hurricane lamp and try to remember Minsky's first name. He could hear Hannah upstairs, calling, 'Agnes, where are you? This is your mother. I've come to take you home.'

Minsky took him by the arm and steered him into the kitchen. 'Everything will be all right, Charles.'

Charles was not so sure. He expected screams from overhead and even the possibility of Agnes being frogmarched down the stairs. But it was not like that at all. The house fell silent but for the hiss and crackle from the lamb-chops Minsky had frying in a pan. Minsky shrugged and lifted his hands to show his palms. 'Women, they are having their own thoughts and their own way of behaving. It will be a tragedy if the suffragettes win and women are made into men. They can't be; men and women are different. Kindness to one another is civilization, and if women become men the kindness will go and civilization will go.'

Charles was not paying much attention. There was a limit to his interest in political philosophy; he was more interested in what was going on upstairs. 'I'd 've thought the way things are going civilization 'as gone already. It didn't need votes for women to give it the push.'

Minsky turned the chops over with a fork and they gave out blue smoke. 'I would not like to be a woman. Demands are made on a woman I might not be able to meet.' Charles thought this was rich. Who could think of Minsky as a woman anyway? 'Your Agnes is a good girl. Do you know what I am thinking? I have been talking to her. Deep down I am believing that because of James not being there she is having to be both son and daughter to you. And she is finding it hard.'

Charles considered these surprising remarks. Bothered as he already was by the way Minsky was showing so much interest in James, and by the way he had touched him and so on, Charles could only stiffen. Everyone seemed to understand him and his affairs better than he did himself. Well, not everyone, but Minsky appeared to, the old fraud! This theory about Agnes was just irritating. If she had any sense of filial duties she had chosen a damn funny way to show it. But there was no question of forcing her back to 'The Lookout' that night.

Years later Agnes had her own account to give of that night at the Minskys when her mother burst into her bedroom – first of all to make little cheering remarks about her influenza and then to unburden herself about the rotten way life had treated her, Hannah White, a true Believer, married to an atheist and now rejected by her only daughter. Then for her father to come in and say it was still snowing and if they tried to take her to

'The Lookout' that night (a possibility which had not occurred to Agnes) she might develop pneumonia.

There were three or four events in Agnes's life which regularly turned up in her dreams; one of them was receiving casualties into hospital when nothing would go right for her; she was late and had to face a wigging from the Ward Sister, or else the ambulance tyres were flat and she could not find the pump. Not that this was her responsibility anyway. Just typical anxiety dreams. But the other two events were different. One was the taking of that photograph at Lavernock on the day when Olive and Ewart announced their engagement. She, not her father as in real life, was always taking this photograph. There they all were in sepia – her father sprawled on the grass, her mother looking straight into the camera, unsmiling, and Ewart with one arm round Olive's waist and the other holding his cap. In her dream the figures in the photograph would come to life and Ewart would step towards her, a strange expression on his face, and she simply could not move to escape him; or, it might be, Olive would start to take her clothes off while everyone else tried to stop her. Sometimes Tom Barr was in the photograph, leering and coming closer all the time.

The other event was this visit she received from her parents while ill in bed at the Minskys; she had never felt so helpless as when her father had appeared and kissed her on the cheek so soon after the weeping session with her mother. Perhaps two or three times a year she had this dream, but in different versions. In real life her mother had certainly cried a little but in the dream she sometimes cried a lot, like Alice in Wonderland who cried a whole lake; or again, she did not cry at all but reproached Agnes for behaving so unnaturally. Yes, Agnes had to say in all these dreams, 'I understand, I *do* understand, Mam,' but always she was told, 'No, you don't, Agnes.'

The talk which actually took place between Agnes and her mother was subdued. Without being explicit Hannah gave the impression that she was throwing herself on Agnes's mercy and the girl – whether out of physical weakness or because she genuinely saw her mother in a new light, as a much put upon, long-suffering, unfailingly patient woman – held her hand and whispered that she wanted to come home. She repeated this for her father's benefit when he appeared. In the dreams the reconciliation was more dramatic than in real life, with her father kneeling on one side of the bed and her mother on the other; and then the journey home was frustrated in all sorts of ways. She could not find her clothes, the Minskys wedged the door to stop her going, the cab-driver lost his way in the snow and they went endlessly up and down the streets of the town. But dramatic or not dramatic, the reconciliation was real and Agnes went home to be nourished with beef tea and cod-liver oil – not that night, nor indeed for several nights, but to 'The Lookout' she eventually did go and tried to catch up with her College work in James's room, with its view over the Channel, the telescope and the geological and zoological specimens in their glass cases.

Ewart was posted to France with his unit and Hannah – who had been as good as her word about keeping an eye on Olive – went round to see her yet again. She was running up items for the layette in her Singer Sewing Machine shop. From Olive's point of view the gain was obvious, and at the same time it was good salesmanship for Singers'. Olive could say to customers 'This is the sort of thing you can do while pregnant. Getting ready for babies isn't only knitting, you know. Run up sheets for the cot. And nighties.'

Remembering the hysteria (as reported by Ewart) brought about by Ewart's switch to the Tank Corps, Hannah was surprised by the cheerfulness. Olive said she could not really believe she was going to be a mother; thinking of the trouble Hannah and Charles had, her own experience was easy. Having a baby put an end to pleasure for many women, but she was not going to be one of them. Marrying Ewart, she sometimes thought, might have been a mistake. What set Ewart off was gambling on horses and she was much more for social fun, dances – Ewart did not even know how to dance – and parties. Parties? You just invited people in and had a drink or two – sherry, or it might be port and lemon or shandy, nothing too strong – together with potted paste on toast. With a war on parties were a rarity, but Ewart gave the impression that he did not know what fun it was just to have a lot of people in the room cheering each other up. Hannah thought it quite extraordinary for Olive to talk in this way while Ewart was sitting in a tank in Flanders. How could she be so hard?

The birth, when it came, was difficult. Labour was protracted, nearly twelve hours, and although the baby was delivered safely the birth left Olive in a state of sullen despondency. She held him in her arms, just the once, looked at him dispassionately as though for flaws and handed him to the midwife with the unforgettable words, 'He's no beauty, is he? He's like a guy for the bonfire.' So it was in this name, Guy, and without consulting Ewart, that he was registered. If she had produced enough milk to feed him matters might have turned out differently, but the milk did not come and a wet-nurse, a Mrs Muldoon, arrived on her bicycle four times in the twenty-four hours; the very regularity of her visits did not seem to suit Guy and breast-feeding had to be supplemented with a bottle Olive seemed incapable of administering herself. Mrs Peacock was of no use either. What is more, she complained of the crying. Olive said she herself was at the end of her tether, not getting any sleep because of the crying, so the outcome was that Hannah – having got more involved than she had expected – took Guy off to 'The Lookout' – 'just for a few days, just so as you can catch up on your sleep, Olive' – but after weeks of this odd arrangement it might continue indefinitely.

In spite of her name Mrs Muldoon was not Irish but only married to an Irishman, an ambulance driver in Cardiff. She was a big, fair-skinned mare of a woman from the Forest of Dean with broad, purring vowels which warmed any conversation she took part in. 'Wurn't that a lovely boy,' she said, 'with eyes like voilets.' Not violets but voilets. 'But's Mam's took against 'im. It 'appens, Mrs White. I've never seen such a bouncer of a boy. Seven pounds at birth, I'm told, and back to birth-weight already. Well, I take a glass of stout now and again and I don't mind admitting it. I think it does 'un good an' tha'. I'm sorry for the poo-er woman, 'is mother. Gwaing to 'er day in, day out, I could just imagine 'er skinny dugs. It's the war. Some'at she said, she thinks 'er man's a gonner. Even afore 'e is. 'E's fated, that's what she thinks.'

Hannah was bewildered by Olive's behaviour but Guy kept her so busy she had no time to dwell on her feelings. For the second time in her life she was in a charge of a baby boy not her own; and, really, Guy was so like James had been that she felt there had been a divine intervention to ensure that she lived part of her earlier life all over again and, this time, not to allow the slightest possibility of any mistake. She was being given a second chance. She prayed for guidance with great earnestness soon after 6 o'clock every morning, before Charles was awake. She asked for Jehovah's mercy on Olive and for His protection of Ewart in France – and indeed of all soldiers – and for the ending of the war soon. Still in her nightgown, she

185

prayed among the potted plants in the conservatory (the sun was already up and warm) for some revelation about Guy. Why had his mother behaved so unnaturally? Had Jehovah cursed her? And did that curse extend to Ewart? And would it be Hannah's fate (Guy had been at 'The Lookout' for two months now) to rear Guy as she had reared James? For that was what it looked like. Olive was not only recovered from her post-natal trauma but she was taking swimming lessons at the Municipal Swimming Baths ('The crawl', she told Hannah, was a way of restoring the figure she had lost when Guy was born). Hannah heard that she was taking regular massage from a Belgian refugee, a woman with an unpronounceable name who had promised her not only a relaxed state of mind but more, a heightened awareness of herself as a woman. To be fair, Olive came round at least twice a week to see her son and even softened to the extent of saying how like his father he was and offering to pay Hannah for looking after him.

'Aren't you going to take him back?' Hannah was insulted by this talk of money.

'Just another month, Hannah, dear. My strength is coming back. But I'm not right, I'm not right at all. Look! Here's a £5 note – it's for Guy.' But she did not come back at all.

For Agnes the baby was a revelation. She had had little to do with babies before, just peeping at them in prams or, by way of a favour, being invited to hold them; but here was this little pink and white creature with the most perfect tiny hands complete with fingers and nails; and these hands were capable of taking hold of her little finger with the obvious determination of never letting go again, while the blue eyes looked searchingly at her and smiles came which Hannah told her were not real smiles but wind. She did not believe this. Guy was *really* smiling at her in a way which made her so happy she was even reconciled to the thought that men might after all have some justification. Accepting that they played a necessary part in the procreation of such a baby as Guy, she grudgingly conceded they would have to be put up with. She saw Ewart in Guy: the same eyebrows, she thought, the same width between the eyes. It was almost as though Olive had played no part in making him, that he had come straight and entire from Ewart alone.

'I'm sure he'll grow up a lovely boy, not like Olive at all.'

Hannah was sad. 'I don't understand Olive. I've heard talk about the New Woman. Perhaps she's a New Woman, hard and unloving.'

'The New Woman isn't like that at all. I'm a New Woman. I want my rights as a human being. Votes are only the beginning. Do you think there'd be this war if women had a say?'

'If Olive is not a New Woman, then she's something different from anything I've ever known.'

Mrs Muldoon was marvellous and Agnes was quite ready to believe that her daily glass of stout was having a beneficial effect on Guy; but she also realized that her mother was tired and that her father did not realize the strain being placed on her by looking after the baby. Charles thought it was the kind of temporary arrangement which was happening here, there and everywhere while the war went on. This was Ewart's boy, wasn't it? He was glad to play some part in supporting the boy while his mother recovered from the mental disorder which had followed Guy's birth. He read the subject up in the library; post-natal depression it was called, and some women even thought of suicide. You would have thought that the process of Natural Selection would have led to this disability dropping out of the chain of procreation. He did not know of suicidal women from earlier centuries, but he had heard of such in Penarth. With such thoughts in his mind, he did not seem to notice how Hannah was wilting.

She had a bout of 'flu and Agnes took over. Without Mrs Muldoon's help Agnes did not know how she would have been able to keep the household going, because her father was now so preoccupied with the way the war was developing that he had no time for domestic problems. He bought all the newspapers and discussed them with Mr Minsky. He came in to beam on Guy from time to time, but his mind was plainly elsewhere. Agnes decided that her mother, Hannah, was the one in need of protection and there was no other way out of the fix in which the Whites found themselves but for Olive to take her son back – distressing though this would be for Agnes – and look after him herself. But who was to see Olive and persuade her that the time had come for her to take Guy back?

Mrs Dover-Davies was a possibility. She had taken to coming every Friday afternoon after school for a cup of tea and a biscuit because, as she said, now that her husband had died she needed a pleasant break before facing the lonely weekend. Agnes noticed her father patting her hand reassuringly when she spoke in this vein, calling her Gladys, so she assumed that Mrs Dover-Davies had his respect and some measure of his confidence. Her mother

– to whom Gladys took little presents of a box of sugared almonds one week, a bunch of violets the next, a Spanish tortoiseshell comb in a box and so on – seemed always pleased to see her. And, naturally, Gladys doted on Guy and gave him presents too – knitted socks and caps, a rattle, a coverlet – until Hannah had to stop her. All this present-giving must stop, Hannah said, because she felt too unwell to give presents in return and it was a bit humiliating always to be on the receiving end. Gladys Dover-Davies seemed a possible go-between with Olive and one Friday Agnes put the idea to her.

Gladys had understood there was something wrong with Guy's mother. What other explanation could there be for the boy's presence? But she had not realized that Olive had now stopped coming to see her son. She hesitated and then said she would have liked to help, but it would lie on her conscience if she played any part in restoring the boy to an unloving mother who might possibly neglect him. Agnes had thought of this too, but she had tried to think what Ewart would want.

Ewart had written to thank the Whites for taking young Guy into their house – because that, so far as he could gather from Olive, was what had happened. Would they write and let him know what was going on? He knew Olive was under the weather, couldn't cope etc. The M.O. had told him women went this way sometimes, but it usually turned out all right. He hoped so anyway. He thought the name Guy was all right. It was a bleak letter that only cheered up when he wrote about the photographs of Guy which Olive had sent him. 'He looks cheeky, don't he? A lot of character in that mouth. Eleven pounds isn't bad, I'm told, for a two-month-old boy, so he's thriving all right thanks to you both and young Agnes, I gather. Looks like he'll be too big to be a jockey, but you never know. Amazing what they can do with dieting these days. Poor Olive. It seems a shame women've got to suffer so. I'm all right; not doing anything really, just messing about. Let's hope young Guy is back with his mother by now. Ta-ta, then. Drop us a line.' Ewart would have been horrified to learn that not only was Guy still with the Whites, but that Olive seemed to have abandoned him.

Agnes put on her heavy blue coat, her gloves and mock-astrakhan hat, pulling it down round her ears, and stepped out into the bright, numbing morning where daffodils seemed to be straining to get out of their window-boxes, away from the east wind. Gulls came screaming over the houses on their way to the town's rubbish-dumps. She was not frightened of Olive. Somebody had to tell Olive where her duty lay, and Agnes wanted the encounter to be one she could look back on with satisfaction. Painful though it might be (she could not bear the thought of surrendering Guy), she had to do the right thing.

'Well, this *is* an honour,' said Olive when she opened the door to find Agnes on her doorstep. 'I wouldn't have thought you'd have lowered yourself.'

'I want to talk to you, Olive. Aren't you going to ask me in?'


Charles knew he was neglecting Hannah, but the news from France made him feel helpless to do or say anything sensible. Like any other ordinary bloke, he was impotent to stop the madness. The great military grapple was working itself up into some apocalyptic orgasm. Charles gave up reading books from the library and walked on the beach or, once more, went on long bicycle rides into the country. It was as though he was looking for a sign. Surely there must be some good in the world?

He thought about this word 'good', turning it over in his mind as he might have turned over a pebble from the beach. He recognized there was a difference. Whoever handled the pebble would see the same pebble, but everybody turned over the work 'good' to suit himself. For some it would be self-interest. For others it would be another word for justice or fairness. To Charles, though, it had to be something bigger, something that underpinned all human and animal life. But what kind of a universal virtue would that be? Life was nothing but a conflict where the weak and the unlucky were brushed on one side. By what? By something people used to call the Life Force. The Life Force was something he could understand without admiring it in the least. The Life Force would see him and his like off the stage and replace them with ambitious and strong-minded brutes. No doubt they would think they were the chosen, the elect, the good. But to Charles they would not be good; he was sure of that without knowing what 'good' meant. He thought about it as he walked about the town and under the cliffs to a groyne where he stood and watched the gulls and the tide swilling the black rocks. Ships were anchored out in the rocks, a camouflaged Campbell paddle-steamer among them, waiting for the tide that would lift them into the docks. The paddle-steamer made him think of Minsky. He was a good man. The only other person Charles could think of as good was Hannah. One day, Agnes might be good too.

Once you started thinking about the 'good', you were taking a path that would probably end up with God, or Jehovah or some even cloudier idea of what – at the peril of your life and sanity – you would feel like committing yourself to. 'Peril of his sanity' were words that went through his mind. Too strong, though. He must not exaggerate. He wanted to be good, though, he wanted to strive for the good, to be clean, to have nothing to be ashamed of.

One night he was awakened by Guy's crying in the room next door. He got out of bed and reached for the matches to light a candle, only to find Guy's room bright already. Hannah was up, but before either of them could get to Guy he was being comforted by Agnes standing like an angel (he thought) in her long white night-dress only lacking the wings, looking down into the cot. The face of the crying child was a crumpled rosebud. Charles could see the love in the faces of Hannah and of Agnes, and wondered whether this was the 'good' he was grasping for.

'You go to bed, you two,' he said. 'I'll see to 'im.' With Guy in his arms, Charles walked up and down the room in his striped blue and white night-shirt, listening to the child's breathing, stopping now and again to put his head down to listen more closely. This was how he had once walked with James and later with Agnes, listening with an intentness he felt necessary to make sure the breathing went on. James breathed lightly, but Guy was different. He kept his eyes open, stared at Charles and sucked thoughtfully on his dummy as though deliberating whether to let him into some great secret.


They received a surprise visit from Mrs Paul, Ewart's mother, who had called on Olive first but not stayed when she discovered the baby was still being looked after by the Whites. She had an overnight bag, but made it clear she was not looking for hospitality. 'I don't need to be catered for, Mrs White. I can sleep standing up like a horse if need be. But it won't come to that.' She seemed a bit horsey – a bony, humorous sort of woman with a scarf tied over her head. She had a harsh, mannish voice, liked a laugh and was put out when there was little to laugh about. She had tried to make jokes about her daughter-in-law, but they did not come off. 'Anybody'd think she was waiting for the police to call and put her in handcuffs; that's the way she's taken with having this baby. I had a real go at her. She'd done nothing wrong, I said. It was more than natural for a married woman to give birth. It was actually legal! Why was she so silly? Where is he, then? My grandson, the darling.'

This was the woman so desperate for the bright lights of Bridgewater that she hoodwinked her husband into thinking she was going to the dentist there and had a perfectly sound tooth pulled out to prove it. It was hard to think of her as being dominated by any man, so her husband must have been a real tyrant and widowhood probably came as a great release.

She insisted on waking Guy up so that she could hold him in her arms. He lay there quietly studying his grandmother's face, looking first at one eye and then at another. 'He's just like Ewart at that age,' she said, 'so much the little master of himself. I'm taking him back to Somerset.'

By this time Agnes had come into the room to stand at her mother's side, both of them shocked by Mrs Paul's announcement. Guy had been entrusted to them by his mother and even a grandmother could not overrule her. But Mrs Paul announced her intentions with a smile as though what she proposed was not in any way surprising.

Agnes asked her whether Ewart had written to say his mother could take Guy away.

'Oh, no, my dear, whoever you are. It came to me on the spur of the moment.'

'I'm sorry, Mrs Paul. This is Agnes, my daughter. She couldn't have looked after Guy better than if he'd been her own.'

'Pleased to meet you, Agnes. I'm grateful, I'm sure. And so will Ewart be. With Guy's mam being such a straw woman, I'm sure it'll be for the best, me taking him.'

Agnes thought she had never hated anyone – not even Captain Barr, not even Olive – as she hated this smiling, bony old woman in her headscarf. 'Has Olive agreed you should take him'

'Oh, no. As I say, it came to me on the spur of the moment, but I'm sure young Olive won't stand in my way. If she doesn't even come to see the poor mite, why should she raise any objection? She's straw through and through. No flesh. No blood. Guy *is* my flesh and blood and you can't go on looking after him, can you now?'

191

'We won't let him go,' declared Agnes fiercely.

Mrs Paul was astonished. 'What are you saying?'

'You talk as though he's just property. He may be a baby but he knows us. He's a human being.'

'With a baby,' said Mrs Paul briskly, 'you've got to remember they are very adaptable, babies. As for Guy, he doesn't *really* know you, my dear. He'll soon settle down.'

'It would be the most terrible cruelty to take him over to Somerset. There's no knowing the damage. He could be crippled.'

'Crippled?'

'To be taken away from those he knows and loves and who know him and love him – yes, crippled in his mind. It would be so bewildering for him. Deep down, for the rest of his life he'd never be able to trust anyone. He would always have this sense of – of loss! He'd always feel abandoned.'

'He's too young to know what was happening.'

'I don't believe that. In my bones I don't believe that.'

Guy began to kick and scream as though to second Agnes's sudden outpouring and Mrs Paul, not knowing which to react to first, to the baby or to Agnes, almost dropped him in her confusion and Hannah had to make a grab for him.

'Go and see if you can find your father, Agnes. He's somewhere in the house. Then we can all have a cup of tea.'

The very mention of the word 'tea' brought them all back to earth. Mrs Paul could not possibly walk off with Guy if the Whites stood in her way; she was not capable of it physically. Now that they all, silently, considered the practicalities, Mrs Paul's impulsive declaration of intent was obviously absurd. Just how could she transport, feed and change the nappies of the poor child? At the end of the journey there was not even a cot but, for all she knew, a policeman at the door enquiring at the bequest of its mother about a missing child. It was all very well to say Olive would not stand in her way, but Olive was unpredictable. Charles came down – knowing nothing of Mrs Paul's bid to kidnap Guy – to talk to her while Agnes made the tea and Hannah put Guy into a wicker cradle she was able to rock while watching Mrs Paul's every move.

For her part Mrs Paul studied Agnes – obviously impressed, and favourably – by the way she had spoken her mind. She did not resent it in the slightest. It was good to know Guy was in such fiercely loving hands, but that did not mean he could stay there for ever. Olive, she was sure, was a hopeless case; the sort of woman who didn't like children and should never have had one. Mrs Paul was ready to draw in her horns and sit quietly confident that her time would come.

Agnes had Mrs Paul in mind when she put on her blue coat and mock-astrakhan hat to go round to Olive's. She tried to persuade herself that she was thinking only of Guy's well-being and which of the possibilities that lay ahead would be right for him. She had to assume that Ewart would last out the war and that he and Olive would start a normal married life together; that being so, there was no alternative to making Olive face up to her responsibilities so that Guy would have a family to grow up in. He needed that love and reassurance. She meant what she had said to Mrs Paul about the sense of loss a child might have and keep throughout a lifetime. In her own experience, it was losing James that made her feel she would never be satisfied. To see women with the vote, to be on the Council, even an M.P. – these would be fine things, to be sure, but whatever good things came her way she would still feel that she had been cheated, that James had come to represent what she had been cheated of, more particularly since she had learned he was not a full brother but only half a brother. It was a double loss that no one, no human or supernatural agency, could make good. Guy must be protected against emotional damage as she had *not* been protected.

'Mrs Paul called and it made me think I ought to come and talk to you.' Once admitted to the house, Agnes was taken through to the kitchen where Olive sat her down and said 'She doesn't like me, Ewart's Mam doesn't, never did.'

It was 11 o'clock in the morning and Olive seemed all dressed up, ready to go somewhere, very smart in light grey skirt and jacket. Agnes belatedly realized that the shop, where Olive was normally working at this time of day, was shut with a 'Closed' notice on the door. She had seen this notice, but it had not registered until that moment.

'Aren't you running the shop then?'

Olive was amused. 'Not for months. Just goes to show – since you gave me the cold shoulder, you don't notice anything beyond the end of your nose. Course it's shut. You can't expect me to run a shop, having Guy and then being as ill as I've been . . . and still am. The company can't find anybody to take over or they'd have turned me out on to the pavement. That's the way you get treated nowadays. How's Guy? Oh, don't tell me. He's all the better for not being with me. I know, I know, I know! But I can't help it. I'm just bad. It's horrible, having a baby. Wait till your turn comes.'

Agnes had not been encouraged to take her coat off. She sat there in her outdoor clothes looking at Olive angrily. 'You must have Guy back. Look, if you have Guy back I'll make it my business to come round regularly and give you a hand.'

Before Olive could reply the kitchen door opened and Captain Barr, Mrs Peacock's brother, appeared in shiny Sam Browne and shiny boots looking – in spite of his medal ribbons and spotless uniform – as though he had not worn well since Agnes last saw him. He was thinner in the face, almost gaunt, and when he spoke the strained, rasping voice seemed much what you'd expect from his appearance. Agnes had not realized he was in the house. Seeing him was an unpleasant shock, but she remained seated and hoped that, once he realized she and Olive were having a private conversation, he would go away.

This he did not do. 'It's the virgin! Excuse me, Miss –'

'Shut up, Tom! It's Agnes, you know that. But shut up!'

'Agnes, that's the name! How could I ever forget? But I always think of you as the virgin.'

'If this were my house,' said Agnes, 'I'd ask you to leave it, but as it isn't I can't. So I'd better go myself.'

Captain Tom Barr actually clicked his heels, just to show what a merry fellow he was. 'No, don't do that, dear virgin. Look, Captain Peacock's boat is in dock and we were all going down there, my sister and Olive to have a drink because it's his birthday. Now, why don't you come along too? If I know the Captain he'll have every kind of duty-free liquor he can get his hands on. Stuff you've never heard of. White rum. Now, have you ever tasted white rum? And Pernod. You'll love Pernod. It will bring all Paris before your eyes.'

Agnes stood up, putting on the gloves which had been lying in her lap. 'I do beg you, Olive, to think of your son. He is a lovely, sweet child most women would be ecstatic over.' She shoved deep into the back of her mind the thought that if her own parents had produced a son like Guy in the first year of their marriage, she would not be tormenting herself by urging Olive to take back the child she would hate to surrender. And Olive did not want.

194

'On the good ship *Bruton* the Captain is organizing quite a booze-up, Agnes, so I think Tom's is a good idea. You ought to come along; you're so sort of damped down.'

'Is Mrs Peacock here?'

'Oh, she's gone ahead,' said Captain Barr. 'But what's that got to do with it? Just come along and let your hair down for once.'

'I don't drink. Even if I did, I wouldn't come.'

Barr advanced towards her and Agnes thought of pulling out her long and dangerous hairpin to fend him off. 'You are quite irresistible because of all the virtues you possess. I worship you!'

'Stop it, Tom!'

'Jealous, eh?' It came out like the croak of an expiring toy balloon.

Agnes made for the door and neither Barr nor Olive said anything or made any move to stop her.


About the middle of May the SS *Bruton* sailed for an undisclosed destination and with an unknown cargo. Some short time later the Captain's wife, Mrs Peacock, came over to see the Whites looking nervy and anxious, her eyes never still as though she wanted the Whites to calm her down. A letter had been received from the Singer Sewing Machine Company to say they had appointed a new local representative and that Miss Jones was required to vacate the premises by June 1st.

'Miss Jones?' said Charles.

'As was. Mrs Paul as is.'

Charles was puzzled by this. So the letter was sent to Olive?'

'Yes, but she's not there, you see, so I opened it.'

'Not there?'

'She must have written to you. She hasn't been there for weeks, she went off to London with my brother. But I'm really worried about my accommodation. Do you think the Company will turn me out?'

Charles ran about the house shouting. "Annah, your cousin Olive 'as gone off with Mrs Peacock's brother.'

'I suppose it was what we expected.' When she was eventually located, Hannah was not at all put out. 'It will all blow over.'

Charles was amazed. Could it be Hannah who was talking like this? Blow over! What did she mean? Did she condone adultery?

"Annah, listen to me! Guy's mother 'as gone off with another man.'

'Hallo, Mrs Peacock. It was in the wind, wasn't it?'

'No, Mrs White, I was that surprised. The world has changed though, hasn't it? What I want to know is where I'm going to live.'

'Your brother, you say, Mrs Peacock?'

'Tom, yes. He and Olive went off and didn't write me for days. It all leaves me homeless.'

'Captain Peacock must have the means to give you a home.'

Mrs Peacock became very agitated. 'Mrs White, do you know what is at the back of my mind and has been these years? Why doesn't a sea-captain provide his wife with a proper home? I sometimes wonder if he's got another woman in one of these foreign ports he goes to, and she's the one who gets the being provided for. I've never so much as breathed this to a soul.'

'I'm sure Captain Peacock is a faithful, good husband – '

'You'd have said that about Tom a while back and I'd have agreed. But look what he's done now, and him a married man already with a wife and child in Wandsworth.'

Hannah remained so calm that Charles wondered whether she had properly taken in what Mrs Peacock was saying. The two women sat in basket chairs in the conservatory with the door open because the sun was shining and the big thermometer behind the lemon tree had shot up. As Charles had never, so far as he could remember, set eyes on Mrs Peacock's brother, he could only imagine he looked something like his sister – rather pinched and put upon – which made Olive's behaviour all the more inexplicable. He could not have been a handsome man. It was disgraceful, too, but Hannah did not seem to see it that way and as a result Charles felt he could not be sure of the firmness of the ground he was standing on. He might fall and fall and fall . . .

'I wonder if she's written to Ewart.' Hannah might have been talking to herself for all the reaction she had from Mrs Peacock, who could think of nothing but having a roof over her head. It just showed what Hannah thought of Olive that she could believe her capable of running off without a word to her husband or to his mother. No doubt about it, Hannah was more worldly-wise than he was. Some inner resource – he could not believe her composure came from the Millenial Dawnists – had stiffened her. Charles

196

wondered whether the disagreeable duty of writing to Ewart and to Ewart's mother would fall to him.

Hannah questioned Mrs Peacock gently. Did Olive and her brother really go off without any warning? And, in any case, was she sure there wasn't some innocent explanation for their disappearance? Her brother might have wanted to take Olive up to London to introduce her to his wife and child. Olive had never been to London, and she was the kind of vivacious girl who would seize any opportunity to go.

'She took her clothes. Olive wrote me a letter and said she was at her wit's end living in Penarth and she was going to start a new life with Tom.'

'Did your brother write?'

'No.'

'It's all very well for Olive to talk of starting a new life, but many a wiser woman than she is has had to eat those words. She could be back here in Penarth in a week or so's time, weeping salt tears. Another thing, there's Guy. Did she say anything about him in that letter? No?'

'She's a bitch!' Charles stabbed a finger at Hannah and then drew it back when she lifted her chin. She was not responsible for her cousin's behaviour. 'She's capable of anything. Going off without a word to us, looking after her kid as we are. It defies the imagination.'

'I'd like to smack her face too,' said Hannah, 'but having bad feelings won't help. Did she put an address on that letter, Mrs Peacock?' It was produced out of her handbag. The notepaper was a hotel's, The Maypole at Henley-on-Thames, and dated more than a week previously. 'You could write to her there, Charles, but I expect they've moved on. The letter might be forwarded.'

'I don't believe a woman would do this,' said Charles 'if it hadn't been for the war. We're all brutes now. So what can we do?'

4 Pineapple Gardens
Hounslow, Middx.

Aug 3, 1918

Dear Hannah and Charles,
    Oh, not to be pretending any more but to come out with it. I

197

am so happy to tell everyone that Tom and I have made up our minds to spend the rest of our lives together. Yes, we have come out of that old, cobwebby, chapel-going, small-town hypocrisy. All I can say is thank God. Now real life can begin. You will know about this from Mrs Peacock, but I thought it right to send word direct. I feel sorry for Ewart and I have written him a really nice letter, telling him to look after himself and make sure he doesn't get killed, but let's face it, Ewart, I said, Love conquers all. That's destiny. To be honest, Hannah, I thought of him as a dead man as soon as he went into the Tanks. I'm sure my letter will console him.

You know I've always called a spade a spade. If a few others had been realistic as I am, do you know, I believe that poor James would still be with us. Myself, I've never told lies or pretended that things are different from what they really are. It is difficult, though. I can see that. Even I did not see the truth about me and Tom until it was staring me in the face. Tom and I were made for each other. He is being discharged on medical grounds with a pension and is setting up as a wine merchant. He's got real style, a special man, the first gentleman I've ever know. The war can't go on, he says. I am so thankful about everything and so happy. Have you ever been happy, Hannah? I hadn't, not till now. As I write the tears just run down my face, I'm so happy. I know what you think of me but I don't care. I just hope you don't take it out on that poor Guy. Who knows, the day may come when he will want to see and recognize his mother, and we can meet as one free and independent human being seeing another without any false bonds of sentiment. Ewart bought Guy some War Savings and here they are, but our immediate plans are not clear-cut. We are in digs and will be moving on. Tom's wife is R.C. and says she won't divorce him, but something will have to be arranged. As for me, I am sure I've done the right thing, which means being true to oneself and one's nature.

Yours sincerely
Olive Barr (which is how I'm now to be known).

Please find enclosed money for Guy as well as the War Certificates. You think I'm hard. Yes, I'm hard. The world we live in, you've got to be.

*

First of all Charles read this letter aloud to Hannah, then she read it to herself, and finally she read it back to him before they sat side by side and went over it sentence by sentence.

'Divorce,' said Hannah. 'There's nobody in the family ever done that. It's terrible even to talk of it.'

'Not more terrible than the way she's be'aved.'

'But a divorce gets in the papers.' Hannah had feared the press ever since 'Talk of the Town' had compromised her all those years ago with its sly innuendoes. 'It will get in the papers and everybody will know. Oh dear, Charles, I do hope this Roman Catholic wife will stay firm.'

'That's a funny way of looking at it. Ewart won't see it that way.'

'You think it'll come to that? I mean, divorcing Olive? They'll patch it up somehow, I expect. Ewart wouldn't want to have his name in the papers.'

''E won't give a fig for the papers. When a man's pride and 'is 'onour 'ave been touched 'e'll do what 'e thinks is right, regardless. And I'm behind the lad.'

# 9

Soon after the Armistice Ewart wrote to say that he had been given compassionate leave, and Charles decided he would go up to London to meet him. Hannah pleaded with him not to go. The chances of meeting Ewart on some London station were remote, but Charles could imagine the boy's feelings as he approached Penarth and did not want him to be alone. He felt sure he would run into Ewart; most of the troop-trains came into Victoria and he would meet every one. Minsky had a telephone, so if he did not see any sign of Ewart for a couple of days he could call Minsky to see if Hannah had left any message. He was quite excited. He talked of having the telephone installed at 'The Lookout', of pushing the Riley out of the garage to crank it up and see whether, after all these years, it was in working order. They would go out to Lavernock, even as far as the Gower peninsula, once more to have picnics and paddle in the sea. Now that the war was over they must do their best to be happy. By God, they would try! He had read in the papers how maroons had been fired in London, people had danced in the streets. It was all noise and rejoicing up there but in France, he read, the silence made men nervous.

Charles knew he would meet Ewart at Victoria. It was fated. Life must mean something. He waited there for three days, living on tea and sandwiches from a stall and telephoning Minsky in the evening from the Grosvenor Hotel. He had no thought of taking a bed for the night. Ewart would certainly come, but there was no knowing at what hour. When the troop-trains came in Charles stood at the barrier with a big piece of cardboard held above his head bearing the words, 'Sergeant Ewart Paul'. He took to questioning some of the men. Had they seen anybody from the Tank Corps? There was often so much noise that even when the men tried to answer Charles could not make out what they were saying. A military band played marches, sometimes there was the Salvation Army singing hymns and coming round with their collecting-boxes. The great vault of the station reverberated with music, hymns and shouts from men and women who just wanted to shout. Charles made friends with the Military Police in the Movement Control office. They knew when trains were coming in, not only to Victoria but to Waterloo and Charing Cross too. Not that they could help Charles much, but he liked talking to them.

'These are just odds and sods,' one of them said. 'Blokes coming on leave and that. What it'll be like when they start demobbing troops, gawd knows. We'll be swamped.'

The Redcaps went into action to let a group of officers and nurses through a crowd of soldiers, some still in their steel hats. There were no high spirits. The expression on most of these faces was sober, even apprehensive, and Charles thought they just could not get used to the idea that the war was over. A lot of blank faces stared at him. It was a though these men had seen the end of most of the world and wondered about the ground they walked on.

He had just come out of a barber's shop where he had been given an early-morning shave when he felt a tap on the shoulder and turned to see one of the Movement Control Redcaps looking down at him. 'There's a sergeant in the office might be the one you're meeting.'

Charles went back with him and saw a soldier who might well be Ewart walking slowly towards him. In his greatcoat and peaked cap he walked with his hands at his sides. Charles thought, 'No, that's not Ewart. He doesn't even look friendly. Thank God it isn't Ewart. It wouldn't be good if Ewart looked like that.' It was Ewart, though, as he saw clearly enough when they were nearer, but a much older and tireder Ewart who did not smile until Charles clasped him in his arms.

'Didn't expect to see you, Mr White. Just went into Movement Control on the chance of meeting some old Redcap I knew. They said they'd been looking out for me. All Movement Control had, not just at Victoria. Reckon they must've thought you were my dad. Well, here I am, you see. What you want to come all this way for, Mr White? Think I'm that helpless?' He had not shaved for days and the very light, fair beard softened a face that was more angular than Charles remembered it.

Besides his pack Ewart had two kitbags, so Charles insisted they took a cab to Paddington. Ewart clammed up; Charles could not get him to talk; he sat forward on the seat so that he could keep his pack on, glum as a bucket. On the train journey west

Charles talked about Guy, what a fine, jolly kid he was with a lot of golden hair already. Hard to realize Ewart had yet to see him for the first time. It would be different from the experience Ewart was entitled to expect – the soldier returning, arms outstretched towards the wife holding the child in her arms; the first sight of his son and heir.

'Mr White, do you know where they are?'

After the first exchange of letters there had been silence. The Whites learned at second-hand that a removal van had cleared out Olive's house. Mrs Peacock had moved into a bed-sitter in Plymouth Road, so Hannah was well-informed about her movements because she was close to her friend, Mrs Trevor, the Millenial Dawnist. Charles was annoyed to learn that Mrs Trevor was also holding spiritualist séances which Hannah was invited to. In fact, she attended one or two out of curiosity but gave it up because Charles ordered her to. No, he did not know where Olive and Barr were. He had even sent reply-paid telegrams to their most recent address, but what came back was a 'Not known' message. The scent was quite cold. Charles thought this was of no importance. Get a solicitor and institute divorce proceedings: that would soon smoke them out. But Ewart didn't seem interested in divorce, what he called that filthy rigmarole.

Some days later – after Ewart had taken a room with his old friend, Walsh the newsagent and tobacconist (the Whites offered to put him up at 'The Lookout' but he refused) and after he had bought some civvy clothes – Charles asked, 'Well, what are you going to do?'

Ewart did not answer directly and went over to Somerset to see his mother. When he brought her back and found her a room with a friend of Mr Walsh, the Whites assumed he was setting up a family conference to take decisions. He did not say how long his compassionate leave was for, and behaved as though he had no thought of going back to the Army at all. The war was over, they didn't need him. Yes, he recognized that even after an Armistice he could still be arrested as a deserter, but he did not think this would happen, particularly if he put up a fight as he would. The Army authorities would turn a blind eye, as no doubt they turned a blind eye to the defection of other men let down by their wives, now the Armistice was signed. There were lots of faithless wives and Ewart said there were probably generals sitting down in the War Office at that very minute to decide policy towards cuckolded soldiers who went missing. Ewart was sure he was clear of the Army.

What he had not expected was the first sight of his son (in Agnes's arms, as it happened) when he saw the fair curls like his own and realized the child was watching him out of blue eyes and laughing, yes, really laughing as his father took him from Agnes and felt the weight and the innocence and the vulnerability of young Guy. The experience shook him and he loved the child, even though he had thought he might reject him. That would have made two of them, wouldn't it? His mother and his father rejecting the soul they had created. The child, though, was too beautiful. Rejection was impossible. The blood and tortured flesh of Flanders were flatly contradicted by this bubble-blowing infant he held in his arms. He did not, as he had feared, see Olive in him at all. Ewart brushed aside the suggestion that Guy looked like him. The kid was just himself, and whatever Ewart had intended to do he must now ensure this angelic child would be safe and happy.

He noticed that it was Agnes who took Guy away to give him his bottle-feed and followed her to find she was changing a nappy.

'It's hard to believe the war's over,' he said.

'Thank God! And you've a son to bring up and love.'

'I've got this fear they'll come and take him.'

'Oh, no.'

'The court might decide a baby is best with its mother.'

'Not in your case, Ewart. Olive is the guilty party. The past is the past. Divorce her and marry someone who will give you and Guy the love you both deserve.'

Ewart was amazed. 'Deserve?' He had not heard such kindness ever.

'I suppose we're all a bit overcome and happy because the war is over. The feelings I have, I'm just drunk. I don't know whether I'm talking sense or not.'

Ewart looked at her in astonishment. He remembered her as a plumpish girl who walked very erect as though to balance her big hat, very sure of herself, not to say 'ikey' (his word for stuck-up, but now she stood before him like one of those young women he had seen in bicycle advertisements – not (as in the advertisements) in bloomers, but with the same curly-haired, wide-eyed, challenging air. And peachy! Yes, pink and white like a peach. After her 'flu Agnes was flourishing again.

'Me, marry again? Not likely. I've no time for women now.'

Ewart looked at her curiously. Her freckles reminded him of flecks of nutmeg floating on a milk pudding. Peach, nutmeg, milk pudding, whatever it might be that put him in mind of eating, she just looked edible. No doubt it was an illusion brought on by months of Army rations.


Even as late as this Hannah still hoped the marriage could be patched up and Charles thought she was capable, once Olive and Barr were tracked down, of paying them a visit to explain that divorce was unthinkable. Hannah's persistence was one of the reasons why Charles was pleased that in spite of their endeavours Olive and her *inamorato* could not be traced. Hannah must not be exposed to insult. The couple might have assumed false names and set up on London somewhere, who could say? Charles found out Barr's regiment from his sister Flo, but the depot in Aldershot did not reply when he wrote to them; he took it they were too busy winding the war down. Ewart actually paid Mrs Barr a visit in Croydon, but she had no idea where Tom was. The Army cheque was still being paid into her account and, to make both ends meet, she was working as a doctor's receptionist while her sister looked after the daughter. She was a decent woman, bearing no marks of resentment, and that made Ewart all the angrier. She was R.C. and no doubt some priest had said her husband would come back to her.

Charles took the Riley off its blocks and Ewart helped him push it out into the street where, not being able to get it to start, they set to work with the manual trying to fathom why it did not respond to the cranking they did by turns. Ewart's tank training came in useful. He explained the engine was all damped up from standing idle for so long and one thing they could do was clean the spark plugs. When that brought no result, Charles drained the fuel tank and put in a couple of gallons of fresh petrol he bought on the black market. Still the engine gave no sign of life. Charles thought Ewart's mind was not properly on the job, so he took him over to the yard and got one of the men to brew up some tea.

'I don't know why you're so intent on catching up with those two. It won't do you any good, you're just torturing yourself. Get a solicitor.'

'You don't understand.'

204

'Then what are you going to do?'

'Kill them. I'm used to killing. I got a pistol and a round of ammunition from this Boche officer: a Mauser.'

'Now, look 'ere – '

'My mind is made up.'

'The important person isn't you or Olive or that bastard Barr, it's your kid.'

'He's in good hands, I can see that. I'll kill those two fuckers and swing for it. Gladly, Mr White. So far as the kid's concerned, it'll be as though his mam and me never existed.'

'You're daft. Don't talk like that, Ewart. Nobody forgets, not even kids – specially not even kids. More than most, young kids don't forget. What 'appens sticks early in the mind.'

'Oh, how d'you know? Guy's only five months old. What does a kid of five months know?'

'I think babies suffer in the womb.'

Charles poured the tea into two tin mugs, added a shot of tinned milk and passed one of them over. 'You've only got to look at 'im.' They drank in silence. 'That gun. I'd like you to give it me for safe keeping.'

'No, Mr White.' He gave a barking laugh. 'It's just about the only real friend I've got.'

'You don't count me?'

Ewart hesitated. 'Sorry, you and Mrs White and Agnes, you've all been real friends to me. I wish I hadn't mentioned that gun.'

Over the years Charles had quite a bit to do with the police. His stock had been pilfered, there had been a frustrated burglary at 'The Lookout' and from time to time senior coppers had been invited to address the group of businessmen Charles belonged to. In this way he had got to know Inspector Deering and it was to Deering, quite shocked by what Ewart had told him, that Charles made his way. The information he provided was accompanied by so many nods, winks and shrugs of the shoulders that it was some time before the Inspector understood what Charles was talking about.

'You mean you know somebody who is threatening a homicide?'

'That's about it, Inspector.'

'What are you going to do about it?' This question surprised Charles, because without thinking too precisely on the matter he had assumed it was for the Inspector, not him, to do something.

Not that he wanted Ewart charged. It was all so confusing and worrying. 'I'm telling you, Inspector, aren't I? I can't take this gun from the boy. 'E's back from the front and 'e says 'e's going to kill 'is wife and the man she's run off with.'

'It's like that, is it? You may be mistaken, you know. Some men do talk in this excited sort of way, but it comes to nothing nine times out of ten.'

'So?'

'No magistrate is going to give me a warrant to enter a man's domicile and search his kitbag on the kind of evidence you've laid, Mr White. He's a soldier, you say. Fine homecoming for a hero, isn't it, Mr White, to have the police drop on him? What sort of a gun did you say it was?'

'I don't know about guns. I think 'e said it was a "mouser".'

'Mauser. That's a pistol. Loot, I don't doubt. A lot of that going on. Only natural. Even if I knew who this chap was, I couldn't take him up for wrongful gun possession at a time like this. Public opinion would not stand for it. We are not at war and yet we are not at peace. The Tommy who has confiscated a German Mauser commands sympathy and I wouldn't like to pick him up just on that account. The homicidal threats are a bit different, but only the people threatened could lay a charge. I take it he hasn't threatened you?'

'Of course not.'

'In any case, it's my experience that men talk wild without meaning a word of it. Who is this chap?'

'I don't feel at liberty to tell you, Inspector.'

'Then you're wasting my time, aren't you, Mr White?'

Charles had heard this sort of talk before. At some time he had talked to the police who, like Inspector Deering, had reassured him by saying that a lot of the problems and misdemeanours reported turned out to be baseless; the sensible attitude was to be sceptical and do nothing in the reasonable expectation that all would come right in the end. A policeman was not wise to be over-zealous in keeping people out of trouble, otherwise there would be no time for his real work which, at best, was apprehending villains in the act, and if that was not possible soon afterwards. The policeman was an officer of the law, not a nursemaid. A threat may or may not have been uttered. A Mauser pistol may be secreted somewhere in the town, or on the other hand it may not. Inspector Deering did not express himself quite like this, but that was the drift and

206

Charles formed the impression he was being advised to look on the bright side. Why the Inspector was playing the fool in this way he could not understand.

'I'd like you to make a note of this conversation, Inspector, so that we've got it on record what I said and what you said.'

'I'll make a special note of the fact that you made allegations against a person you refused to name. It won't look good, Mr White.'

Charles paused on the steps of the police station to put up his umbrella. He walked out into the rain trying to remember that other time when he had gone to the police only to be fobbed off, but he could not. His mind refused the memory, as a horse can refuse a fence no matter how often the rider brings it back to the challenge. It shied away again and again. The rain came down so heavily that the bottoms of his trousers were soaked and he took shelter in a shop doorway, closing his eyes to think more intently about the past, but nothing of any consequence came to the surface. He thought he might be losing his wits and then, quite unexpectedly, Polly was there with him – a warm presence ready for the tickling. Polly! He was amazed. Out of the past it was only Polly he could summon up. What did it mean? He ought to be thinking about Ewart, but it was much easier to think about Polly as the cold rain sheeted down and his boots let in water.

Mrs Paul, Ewart's mother, a regular visitor at 'The Lookout', was the only person who took any satisfaction in her son's misfortune; as she had a way of pointing out from time to time, she had never liked Olive and thought her flighty, not to say fleshly. By some magic, though – or more probably the blessing of Almighty God – the fruit of her son's unfortunate marriage was a child who most remarkably resembled her late husband, the bankrupt storekeeper turned carrier. Guy had the same widely spaced eyes and a smile in which the corners of his mouth turned up markedly. If you turned the new moon on its back, that would be his mouth perfectly. A typical Paul face. So far as she could detect it behind the beard, it had been her father-in-law's face too. Guy did not have the pointed chin yet, but he would. It was the Somerset face, as they called it in the family, and going about the county you'd often see it, so there was nothing of Olive and for that Mrs Paul was thankful. Just as much as Hannah, she was shocked by the idea of divorce. The war, however, had changed so much and she now had no doubt Ewart should rid himself of the woman.

She herself would bring up the child in Somerset, among his own people.

After a lot of thought about Ewart's homicidal intentions and even consulting Minsky (who said a heavy responsibility lay on Charles and he must talk day and night to Ewart), Charles decided he must tell Ewart's mother and then they could both, if necessary, talk to Ewart non-stop day and night.

'Thank God he doesn't know where they are,' was her reaction. 'Pray God he never does.'

Charles would have preferred to talk to Mrs Paul alone in the first place, but whenever she was in the house Hannah was there too. Time might be running out. So Hannah was privy to the calamity that threatened and, as she walked into the room just as Charles was giving a censored account of his conversation with Ewart, so too was Agnes. Four o'clock in the afternoon was an unusual time for Agnes to put in an appearance, but there was no time for explanations. She was dressed for bad weather, in a knitted cap and heavy coat, and gave the impression she was on her way to somewhere else. Of the four of them, she was the least perturbed.

'He would say that, wouldn't he?' She sounded slightly contemptuous. Agnes had made her mother gasp, so she went on, 'It's the way men talk. Injured vanity at bottom. If you like, I'll walk round and tell him he's a fool. Where is he anyway? What does he do with his time?'

Mrs Paul was distressed by what Charles had told her, or perhaps she would not have spoken so incautiously. 'There are some things young girls don't understand, no matter how clever they are.'

'I'm not a young girl. I'm twenty-one and I understand, all right. I can tell you something else. If I thought Ewart could shoot that precious pair and get away with it, I'd tell him to go ahead. That's what I think of them. But of course he won't get away with it; he's got to be stopped.'

'That's all very well. But 'ow?'

'If there was a button I could press and kill those two, I wouldn't hesitate.'

Agnes's ferocity set even Mrs Paul aback. She might have the same idea, but she would never have put it into words; nor would she have been able to press that lethal button. But Agnes would; she really meant what she said. Of more immediate importance, though, was the question as to how Ewart was spending his time. He spent some of it sitting in the yard office reading the papers and drinking tea. Now and again he worked on the Riley, and Charles understood he went swimming at the Baths. Swimming could not take up all his time, and Charles imagined him walking the streets of Cardiff or looking up addresses in the library. He was surely exploring ways of tracking down Olive and Barr and, for all Charles knew, practising with the Mauser. Ewart, he knew, had been in touch with his father-in-law, but he did not know where Olive was either.

Charles wondered whether money would help. Financially he had never been better off, and when holes of unhappiness opened up he had taken to stuffing them with money. He was uneasy about Hannah, so he had taken to buying her jewellery again. He gave Agnes a spectacularly large cheque for Christmas. And now he wondered whether, as he had once stuffed cotton-wool soaked in oil of cloves into a hollow, raging tooth, he could stuff banknotes into Ewart's aching void. He could talk to him about the future. If Ewart wanted his old job back, it was his for the asking. More than that, he would be thinking long-term. The time would come when Charles would want to spend more of his time just reading, perhaps even writing – yes, why not? – writing his own honest and unpretentious thoughts about life, and then he would wish to hand over the business to someone and why not Ewart?

The man was touchy though, and gripped by an obsession with Olive. He had loved her deeply. Now he hated her just as deeply, and might react angrily to any suggestion that he might eventually take over the White business if it implied he was not to enjoy the satisfaction of killing her and Barr first. So Charles kept off the subject of money and work.

Agnes was dressed in her knitted hat and winter overcoat because she had dropped into 'The Lookout' to pick up a book before going on to a college friend in Plymouth Road who wanted to form a Marxist feminist group. Now that votes for women had been won, the new challenge was what they intended to do with them. Were they to support the Labour Party, or were they to campaign for some new socialist party which would have more revolutionary ambitions? That sort of thing. This friend was also a poet and, having an indulgent father, her poems were in print and she now wanted to sell copies. The immediate issue at the Plymouth Road meeting was whether members of the new feminist group would undertake hawking them around. Adelinda (that was her name) was a disciple of Walt Whitman and when she realized Agnes had not even heard of him she took down a volume and began reading. A civilized society, she said, would be one 'where women walk in public processions in the streets in the same way as the men. Where they enter the public assemblies and take places the same as the men,' and Agnes entirely agreed. If that was Whitman, he was her kind of poet too. However, Adelinda was carried away and began reading from other poems which Agnes did not like so much because they seemed so hairily masculine, but she really responded to the poems about animals. She too thought that, like Whitman, she could turn and live with animals because they were so placid and self-contained. As Adelinda read she listened intently and the words stamped themselves on her mind.

She walked out of the overheated house, overheated both physically and emotionally, and walked through the mild black winter evening to the station on the way back to Cardiff, quite sure that a dew of social optimism, a dew of hope about the better world they were all about to enter now that the war was over, was settling on all men and women. At the station Ewart was waiting for her.

He said it was no accident; he had been observing her movements and knew that she had visited her parents that very afternoon. He had to watch her in this way because he wanted to speak to her alone. It was a matter of life and death, and he apologized if his sudden appearance had shocked or embarrassed her, but there were times when a man was tested beyond endurance and he had detected in Agnes – by the way she had handled Guy – that she might be his salvation. He was hatless, but his hair had caught the rain and little beads of it winked in the station gaslight.

Agnes thought he looked beside himself, like a man who might be dangerous, and she was frightened. 'What do you mean, bobbing up like this?'

'I'm sorry.'

'Look, my train is leaving.'

'There'll be another one in twenty minutes. Agnes, I want to entrust Guy to you. You see, I don't count any more but I want Guy to be yours. I don't want my mother to take him back to Somerset. You've got to understand, I've had shocks.'

The words of that Whitman poem about animals came back to her. He could stand and look at them long and long, Whitman could, because they do not sweat and whine about their condition. So why did Ewart sweat and whine? He had said it was a matter of life and death, but it was nothing of the sort. Why did he have to exaggerate?

'I don't know why you go on in this way.' He was ten years older than she was, but the state he was now in just reduced him to a drivelling boy and she attacked him fiercely. 'You haven't been drinking, have you? No? Then you should pull yourself together. If you're sober you still ought to be ashamed of yourself.' He had put a hand on her arm, but she shook it off and tried to get past him. There were not many other people about, just the station staff and a man buying a ticket before dashing to catch the train. She could hear the guard's whistle. The engine belched steam that was caught by the wind, whirled sideways and down so that Ewart and Agnes were momentarily caught in it and Agnes put her gloved hand to her nose and mouth to keep out the fumes. Her clothes would reek of sulphur for days and it was all Ewart's fault! The train pulled away and she did not believe there would be another in twenty minutes.

'I can do nothing for you,' she told him. 'It's rubbish to talk of me accepting responsibility for Guy.'

Ewart had not expected this attack and he fell back a pace or two. He had looked for sympathy and understanding, he had wanted to do something for Guy's future, but instead of the generous response he had expected he had met only anger and contempt. It had been a mistake to accost Agnes in this way, but God knows! He had been in a daze ever since he saw this blasted town again, saw the old Sewing Machine Shop, walked where he had walked with Olive. He could well understand Agnes thinking he might be drunk. If he had been, Agnes's response to his plea would have sobered him; as he was not drunk, his dazed mind began to clear, as if by the same wind as blew the smoke and steam away, and he started to wonder whether Agnes was right when she said he was making a fool of himself.

'Why are you so blasted unfair? Why? Tell me that. Isn't there anybody on my side?'

She wanted to quote Whitman and tell him not to whine, but decided against it. Instead, after looking round to make sure she would not be overheard, she said, 'My dad says you've got a gun. Is that right? Well, you're not safe with it. You talk about Guy. If there's one thing you can do for your son, especially if I'm

211

involved, it's handing that gun over to the police or the Army. I'll tell you something. My dad's in much a state over this gun he's of a mind to wash his hands of you and young Guy.'

'What do you mean?'

'I mean he wouldn't want the boy in the house. Where is this gun?'

'In my digs.'

'I'll come straight round with you and we'll pitch it over the cliff.'

He was shaken by the information that Mr White might turn against him. It was a lie, but Agnes thought it a fair sort of lie in the circumstances. Where he was doubtful she was certain, where he was wavering she was confident; the very stiffness of her figure, the very challenge of that upturned face persuaded him he had no alternative but to do just as she said, and with this realization came a release from his desperation. He breathed the night air; he was alive and hungry again. The streets, the houses, the Baths and the Public Library of that January town no longer mocked him. They hid no imaginary presences, and he was very ready to walk round to his digs and pick up that gun. He was afraid he might cry.

'You sure you want to do this, Agnes? You'll miss the next train too.'

'They run up until ten.'

What impressed Ewart was that she was doing this for him, and as they walked to his digs he said he felt he had been in prison and then an angel had come with a key and let him out. She was that angel. When he was in France, he just wanted to get home and make Olive come back to him. He was just miserable. He was not really angry until he realized the Army regarded his misfortune as a justification for compassionate leave. He was angry because he did not want anybody, least of all his sergeant-major, feeling sorry for him. But was he telling the truth? He had taken the pistol from the dead German with something more than collecting souvenirs in mind. He supposed, even then, he had wanted to hit back.

'Don't talk to me about me being an angel. I'm not. I'm just telling you what you ought to do. You're sloppy.'

'Sloppy? But pretty well worked up too. Very angry. Black anger. It drives out devils. If I'd not been angry I'd have gone mad. But my advice to you is don't fall in love, don't marry, because you're just surrendering yourself to the power of somebody or something you think you understand, but you don't, because nobody understands anybody else.'

He left her on the pavement while he went into his digs but he was back within minutes, a canvas satchel in his hands.

'That's it.'

They changed their minds about walking to the cliff and went down to the docks instead, where normally there would have been a guard on the gate but the war being over nobody seemed to care about security any more, and they walked past the sentry-box without being challenged. Gas flares were unsteady and the hawsers, the ships, the cranes wobbled and fluttered in their light.

'Well?' She knew Ewart was as wobbly as the light and she did not want him to start moaning about life again. To be honest, she had been impressed by the eloquence with which he had expressed his rubbishy ideas, but now she wanted to get this part of the encounter over as quickly as possible. She had even begun to understand why Olive found it so easy to make off.

A man in uniform about a hundred yards or so away began shouting. They turned to look at him and he walked in their direction.

'Here it is.' Ewart handed the canvas bag over to her. So even now he hadn't the guts to do the job for himself. She did not believe there had been the slightest danger of Ewart going out and shooting Olive and Barr; he might roar and gesticulate, but at heart he was too weak. The bag was heavy. The absurd thought occurred to her of hanging on to it and using the pistol and its ammunition in the revolution she and her fellow socialists hoped to engineer – yes, with real women walking with men (or even without them) in the streets and entering the public assemblies, with all the strife that would follow. Agnes was not afraid of strife.

'You two,' said the man in uniform who looked extraordinarily like Lord Kitchener, moustache and all, who had now arrived. 'You got passes, eh?' He turned to Ewart. 'You off one of these boats?'

'No.'

'Thought so. Didn't see you check in. You can't just walk into a dockyard, boyo. The war might be over, but there's still Customs and Excise. How do I know you're not a smuggler? It's gold they go in for these days. And jewels.'

Agnes turned with the heavy canvas bag in her hands and walked to the edge of the dock. With all her strength she hurled it out as far as she could manage and Ewart, 'Lord Kitchener' and she listened to the splash as though they might be expected to give an accurate account of what had happened when they were eventually – as Agnes guessed, Ewart wondered and Lord Kitchener relished – questioned by the authorities.

'You threw something into the dock,' said 'Lord Kitchener'. 'You understand I've got to check on everyone entering this dock. What was it?'

Agnes decided to be icy. 'A gun and ammunition. My friend here was thinking about shooting his wife and her lover and then he changed his mind. Obviously he had no further need of the weapon.' She made it sound like a question, as much as to say, 'Anything else you want to know?'

'Shoot his wife, eh?' 'Lord Kitchener' sounded as though he had suffered too. 'Pass, friend,' he said and waved them on their way. He ought to have taken their names and addresses, but plainly he thought life was too difficult for empty formalities. He would gamble on no disagreeable consequences.

After the rejoicing came a general numbness. The war had been won, but what did that mean? At least Kaiser Bill would not ride at the head of his troops down Whitehall and the Champs Elysées, but even hanging the swine would not bring back dead husbands, sons and lovers. There was anger, certainly in South Wales, that the war might continue in some other guise. Rumours abounded that troops were being kitted out to go to Russia and fight the Bolsheviks. Agnes was particularly incensed, and went up to London to join in the demonstrations in Hyde Park. Ewart had rejoined his unit and confirmed the rumours by writing to say he had been issued with a fur hat and been told he was bound for Murmansk. He wrote first of all from Amiens and then from Cambrai, feeling free to say where he was now the fighting had stopped and the censorship was not so strict. They had heard the German civilians were starving; that just about served them right.

Gladys Dover-Davies was insensitive to the gloomier response to the Armistice and, now that her husband was dead, took it upon herself to rejoice. She gave a party to which the Whites were invited. One of the games involved sitting the largest male guest on a chair and then inviting four ladies to insert a couple of

214

fingers under his knees and armpits. Another gentleman, Charles, was invited to put both his hands on the large gentleman's head and press down firmly, after which the four ladies were invited to lift and lo! the large gentleman rose into the air as though by magic. Mrs Dover-Davies said it was based on the best scientific principles, and there was no reason why all over the world large men could not be elevated by four women in the way they had just witnessed. Charles was puzzled; he had pressed down hard, but not so hard as to cause Idris Potter, the large gentleman, to rebound. But he could think of no other explanation and resolved to read the subject up.

Mrs Paul was there and enjoyed herself hugely even, if Hannah could believe her eyes, flirting with Idris Potter. The Reverend David Llewellyn, accompanied by his wife on the piano, sang, 'Trumpeter, what are you sounding now?' so dramatically that Hannah wished he had chosen something lighter. Mrs Dover-Davies served potted meat sandwiches and Welsh cakes. Her helpers, two other teachers, poured tea out of a huge brown pot and then she began to play the piano, little dance tunes, a polka and then a waltz which Mrs Paul could not resist. She and Idris Potter danced a miniature waltz because the floor space was so limited, particularly when the two teachers joined in, and Hannah thought the party was getting out of hand. Idris Potter was so fat and Mrs Paul so gawky that they looked ridiculous. But if that was their way of thanking God for the end of the war, so be it! Hannah still thought the real Armageddon was yet to come and refused to join the dance even though Charles, becoming sprightly, wanted her to. So Charles put his arm around Mrs Dover-Davies's waist, squeezed her hard and made her scream.

Hannah had kept in touch with the Abercarn relations, though not because they needed food baskets during the war. The men earned good money down the pit, spent some of it on the black market and threw the rest of it about as if there was no tomorrow. Saving was out. They bought second-hand beds with spring mattresses, they bought watches and they bought whippets. Some bought up sovereigns and buried them secretly in tin boxes. One of Reg's friends had set up as a bookie, and he made money out of the whippet races on the waste land adjacent to a tip that burned deep down and gave out gentle drifts of sulphurous vapour.

Hannah's cousin Reg had a curious attitude towards the war. He would not have wanted to join up – being a miner he did not have to – but during the holidays he would have liked to pop over to France and just watch. He had a theory that it was not so awful as people pretended. Otherwise, why would the men put up with it? Hannah thought it was because not many men from the valleys had been killed, so the awfulness of the war had not been brought back home to him, but Reg said no, one day the war would be over and he would have missed first-hand experience of it. All he knew was what he read in the lying papers. History would have passed him by. The only break in his routine had been the strike of 1917, when he and the rest of the miners were pilloried for lack of patriotism. Patriotism? It wasn't lack of patriotism, it was lack of a fair wage. The war did not rob a man of his political rights, and now the war was over he was joining the Labour Party to be with the lads he respected. There would have been no war if German workers and British workers had been asked to talk to each other.

Hannah was less interested in this than the fact that Reg's daughter Milly was no longer needed for filling cartridges in the little factory in the corner of the tin-works and was now looking for a job. She was fat, rather plain, but tender-hearted, so Hannah invited her back to 'The Lookout' on full board and fifteen shillings a week to help in looking after young Guy. As Hannah already had a cook-housekeeper who came in at 7 o'clock every morning, she felt she was set up respectably and could now devote more time to religious matters, distributing tracts and trying to interest people at their front doors in the Millenial Dawnists.

Charles looked on Milly and Mrs Lavender, the housekeeper, with approval. They cost money and the dispensing of money had now become the antidote to what he clearly realized was his developing meanness of spirit. He could not help it; the war had drained him. He ought to have been more loving to Hannah; instead, by opening the till, he could try to deceive himself into believing he was achieving some of the 'good' he yearned for and never thought about without remembering the spot under the cliffs where he had looked at the water swilling round the rocks and had tried to understand what the 'good' might be. Money, he saw, had nothing to do with that kind of 'good'. At fifty-two – or was it fifty-three? – he was brooding too much, thinking about himself too much when he ought to have been campaigning for a land fit for the returned war heroes to live in. Something was wrong, but he did not know what.

216

The Riley was bullied into life and Charles drove Mrs Dover-Davies out to the cemetery where he helped her pluck weeds from her husband's grave and plant lilies of the valley which, she said, he was fond of even though the strong perfume gave him a headache. Such an outing would have been impossible before the war without provoking gossip, not to say scandal, but the war had changed all that and nobody seemed to care what people did. It was a big cemetery. Hundreds of gravestones, some of them granite and winking like glass in the afternoon sun, stretched in rows, with paths of gravel laid down in orange-coloured bands that made Charles think of tigers. To him it seemed that Mrs Dover-Davies and he were making an ineffective gesture in the face of death. Her husband had been very ill anyway, quite ready to go, and there was only one of him – whereas there were millions of graves holding men who had not been ready to go. For them no mourning was profound enough, nor wide enough, not even if there were room round their graves for everyone in the land of the living to stand there. All the buglers in the world, standing upright on all the mountain-tops and sounding 'The Last Post', even they would not signify much.

Charles wanted to say something about the oddity of human life, but he could not think what. 'When God died he must 'ave 'ad quite a funeral.'

Mrs Dover-Davies did not understand. She looked at him in puzzlement, so Charles went on, 'It's just a way of talking. When lots of people stop believing in God, you can put it another way and say God is dead.'

'I didn't know you were an atheist, Charles.'

'I'm not sure that I'm up to it.'

'Well, are you? Don't you believe in anything?'

'A man's got to believe in something, 'asn't 'e?'

'Well, what do you believe in?'

Charles hesitated because he wanted to be truthful. 'I don't know, and that's a fact.'

'I do wish you'd call me Gladys, Charles.'

'Tell you what, I'll call you Deedee. 'Ow d'you like that?' She did not like it at all.

James's grave was a long way away and as they walked towards it the gravestones, the crosses, the occasional angel and broken columns opened up line after diminishing line like an exercise in perspective. There was a sea mist. Overhead were big-bellied pink clouds because a red sun was slipping down the sky. As they crunched along the orange gravel Mrs Dover-Davies (or Deedee as he now thought of her) took Charles's arm and Charles, who had tried in vain to say something about the oddity of human life after his glum meditation on mortality, was now tempted to repeat what he had done at her party, hug her fiercely and this time actually kiss her; but there were too many people about and it was not the place for such skittishness. Odd, though, that he could not bring himself to call her Gladys. Deedee seemed just about right.

Charles paid to have the grave maintained and it was impeccable, simple headstone, marble chippings and a laurel wreath which was replaced every six months. 'It still seems like yesterday.' Charles stood to attention, thumbs to the seams of his trousers. 'I can't really believe 'e'd 'ave done all that well in the theatre, though.'

'Oh, Charles, he was so gifted. A natural. I suppose we can comfort ourselves. How terrible it would have been if he'd had some splendid début and then been killed in the trenches.'

'We clutch at these comforts. But it's all cock, really.'

Charles wondered whether there had ever been a time when animal appetites and social decorum were in such balance that adulterous impulses such as the one which had just taken possession of him would have been out of the question. Probably not. Perhaps the real answer was polygamy which, if the man could afford it, seemed to have a lot to recommend it. All those years ago he ought to have thought about emigrating not to Canada but to some Moslem country, and turning Turk where a man's carnal nature could be harnessed within accepted conventions. Hard on women, no doubt, and he wondered what Agnes with her feminist crusading zeal would make of such an idea if (his imagination raced) he casually raised the subject over the supper table. I'm thinking of turning Turk, or becoming a Mormon, and taking Deedee as a second wife, your mother retaining precedence. The idea was so absurd he laughed and Deedee, not knowing what to make of the laughter, looked around to see what had caused it. Nothing! Perhaps he was not sufficiently carnal. A really carnal man (and casting about to know who that man might be, Charles settled on Captain Barr) would not have seen the joke.

As they walked back to the Riley Charles still spurted with laughter now and again and they were eyed curiously. Why was it wrong to laugh? They weren't fighting any more, were they? So

218

it was in order to laugh, even if he gave the impression to those people who looked at him that he was a bit crazy. Everybody was crazy, some because of all those dead and some because there was no more fighting – at least not much of it, and they felt a bit lost without those casualty lists.

'It's been on my mind to tell you this, Charles. I ought to have told you long ago. It's about James and Oliver Twist.'

'What of it?'

'It's nonsense of course, but he insisted that in the book Oliver Twist hanged himself.'

'Did what?'

'It was Bill Sikes who was hanged, but James wouldn't have it and said it was Oliver.'

''Ow would 'e even know about Bill Sikes? 'E wasn't in the play.'

'I didn't want the children thinking that Oliver Twist in the workhouse was all there was in the book, so I took them through it. I skipped a lot and paraphrased a lot and really played down the nasty bits, I promise you. But somehow that hanging of Bill Sikes came through. James was very sharp and he spotted I'd been taking a lot of liberties with the text.'

As she spoke Deedee began to realize there was an enormity about what she was saying. She understood now why this secret information about James had been a burden all these years, and had to open her handbag to pull out a handkerchief. She was flustered, became tearful, wished she had not started on this confession; the suppression of anything that might have some bearing on James's death – and then to blurt it out just because of a visit to the boy's grave amounted to a confession.

'He just said I'd got the story wrong; he said it wasn't Bill Sikes who was hanged, it was Oliver. He understood the book much better than I did, he said. I remember opening the book and showing him the page with Bill Sikes's name on it, but James was so stubborn and he just turned his face away. I went at him, I can tell you. I told him not to be so silly. One day he would read the book for himself and then he would know I'd been telling the truth, but he just said he knew best. He was – I don't know how to say this – a bit beside himself.'

They sat on a seat while Charles watched the red sun go down and the sea mist creep about them. Deedee held her handkerchief to her eyes, weeping. When the weeping stopped and Deedee had

219

apologized for her behaviour, Charles led the way to the Riley. Was she apologizing for the crying? Or was she apologizing for not keeping her mouth shut? Charles did not know. He was so confused he thought she might even have been apologizing for being so attractive that he wanted to hug her. No, it must have been just for her crying because that might be infectious. She might start him off too. Yes, she might, she really might. He really might begin to cry and real salt tears would slide down his face.

He opened the door for her to climb in, even in his distress noting how pretty her ankles looked in those fawn cotton stockings, before walking round to get into the driver's seat. He drove her home and went through the courtesies in reverse order so that he might have the pleasure of looking at those ankles once more. But he did not utter a word.

'I'm sorry, Charles.' She sounded quite desperate, but Charles stayed silent and drove off without so much as a wave.

Charles did not tell Hannah what Deedee had said because it was too painful. It rang true. It was just the sort of batty idea James would get into his head, but he would not have acted on it. He might have experimented, but he was not so crazy he'd set out coldly and deliberately to hang himself. That's what the Coroner had decided, using common sense and all the evidence available. Would his verdict have been the same if Deedee had given evidence? No knowing. Charles's not really knowing what had happened to James and why was always at the back of his mind. For months at a time the stress was quiescent but there were times, like now, when it came to life and was beyond bearing. Did it matter? It did matter to him, Charles White, because the unknowability was a kind of dark mirror in which he could see himself obscurely reflected. Who was scrutinizing him? Only he himself. There was nobody else.

To Hannah's pleasure, and a little alarm, 'Talk of the Town' started up again and she read the column eagerly, quite sure that she would find herself referred to in one of those little quizzes. She did not think the Millenial Dawnists made her vulnerable because the column did not touch on religion, at least not in the old days. As the weeks went by, though, she realized that the new 'Talk of the Town' was more waspish than the old one. 'Why did the gentleman fishing from a groyne the other day fall into the water? Did his foot slip or did the lady at his side push him?'

An idea occurred to her of such audacity that she could scarcely believe she had thought of it herself. She sat perfectly still with her eyes wide open, half believing the idea had come from some invisible presence, someone or something which had breathed words into her ear. Why not be a contributor to 'Talk of the Town'? Why not submit a teasing question? Questions had been popped in about her, so was it not about time she – well, not exactly got her own back, but certainly hit at somebody else. It was the destiny of women to be put upon, but she had been put upon enough and now wanted to put upon somebody else. She would have to think of an observation that could not be traced back to her. So it would have to be one which lots of other people might have made, and the more she thought about it the more it seemed evident that the quiz would have to be about Charles and Mrs Dover-Davies. They had made themselves conspicuous.

But what? She sat with pencil and paper, but the words did not come. She thought of Mrs Dover-Davies's party when Idris Potter had been elevated, but could not see how to bring that in even though Charles had followed it up by giving Mrs Dover-Davies a sly hug. The difficulty was to be saucy and yet say something in good taste. The merry widow? No, she did not want to be too personal. What she eventually looked at, after much crossing out and rewriting was 'Who is the lady in mourning who nevertheless wears fawn stockings? Can it be anything to do with the rides she takes in her friend's motor-car?'

That would not do either. Charles never read the column but somebody was sure to draw his attention to it, Mrs Dover-Davies herself quite possibly, and he would immediately guess who was behind it. Hannah was not jealous and did not want Charles to think she was. That was why she was considering this anonymous tease rather than speaking to Charles directly. She wanted to alert him to the possibility that he might be making a fool of himself.

However, speak to him directly was what she eventually did. Charles took her in the Riley down to Lavernock, where he showed her a field running down to the very cliff-edge which he said Mr Minsky and he were planning to buy with the idea of building a lot of bungalows there. Minsky was the one who had thought of bungalows. Charles's ambitions had always run to terraced houses and the occasional villa in a choice position, but Minsky had convinced him bungalows would be important in the future of the building trade. Stair-climbing might be all right for monkeys; it was not natural for human beings, particularly when they grew older. Minsky and he had really talked about this. They would employ an architect, set up a company called Lavernock Developments Ltd to get backing from the bank, and build not just a lot of bungalows but a community. Yes, of course they hoped to make money out of it, but they were idealists too. Now the war was over they were thinking positively. They could not hope to emulate the Garden City idea which had created Welwyn and Letchworth in England; they did not have what it took, but what they could do they would do. Lavernock Heights Ltd might even build a hall free, gratis and for nothing, where the bungalow dwellers could have discussions, lectures and whist drives. Give them time. He thought of the bungalow community as a trial which, if successful, would allow Minsky and him to establish a public company and finance a Garden City in South Glamorgan. Now that the war was over anything was possible. Charles was really enthusiastic. Hannah's mind went back to the time when they thought of emigrating to Canada, or chicken farming, or breeding dogs – wherever his imagination led him and she would have been prepared to follow. This project seemed disagreeably possible, though.

'A pity to build here,' she said. 'The way you and Mr Minsky go on, there'd be no natural country left. '

'Whenever I go to London I look out of the carriage window and it's very striking the amount of land there is. Field after field. There's plenty of land.' A thought struck him. 'You've never been to London, 'Annah. That's strange, isn't it? Now we've got Milly we could take a few days off and go up. See the sights. What do you say?'

'I wouldn't be easy in my mind. Milly's young to be left in sole charge of Guy.'

'We could take 'er and 'im with us. Stay in a 'otel. Be posh.'

'I'm sure you'd rather take Mrs Dover-Davies.'

They were still sitting in the Riley, so he had to skew round to look her in the face. He moved so abruptly and he was grinning so idiotically that she was momentarily alarmed. 'Deedee can go to 'ell for all I care, 'Annah, and that's the truth.'

'Deedee?'

'That's what I call her.'

For Charles to speak so violently seemed to show he had been more emotionally involved than she had suspected. She was pleased nevertheless to hear such hostility, and was able to calm herself while she waited for him to say what had caused it.

'You know I gave 'er a lift to the cemetery to plant some bulbs on Mr Deedee's grave? Well, it's not on a bus route and I've got to give the car a regular run. So I took 'er. What do I find? All she wants to talk about is James. She seems to enjoy talking about James and, straight, I can't stand it so I don't want 'er round 'ome. She upsets me.'

Hannah did not think he was lying, but she was sure there was more to tell than Charles seemed ready to admit. She was satisfied though. The rest of the story would come out some time or other. Of more immediate importance was the way Charles had been put on the defensive, and she decided to take advantage of it. 'I'm glad to hear what you say. Not about Mrs Dover-Davies' – 'Deedee,' he interrupted and they both giggled – 'talking about James, not that at all. What I'm glad about is you've clearly seen through that woman at last. She's been making a fool of you. Mind you, I've said nothing because I'm sure you'd see it for yourself. Now that 'Talk of the Town' is back I've been dreading some silly question appearing about an elderly gentleman taking a widow for rides in his motor-car. Everybody would have known then. I just can't bear the thought of you making a fool of yourself.'

'I don't count myself elderly, 'Annah.'

'The sort of thing I'd been afraid of in 'Talk of the Town' was, "Who is the lady in mourning who nevertheless wears fawn stockings? Can it be anything to do with the rides she takes in her friend's motor-car".'

'She'll take no more rides, 'Annah.' He brought a hand firmly down on hers. 'There'll be no more such jaunts, I promise you.'

Soon after Easter another letter came from Olive, and Hannah read it standing up near the kitchen window with Charles peering over her shoulder.

c/o Lloyds Bank<br>
113 Streatham High Street<br>
London

Dear Hannah and Charles,
　　You will wonder why I am writing after all this time and when so

much has been happening in the world, what with the Armistice. It seems too good to be true. Tom is disgusted the way things are going. He thinks the Allies should have insisted on the Kaiser being handed over. He is sure the Peace when it comes will be soft, just when we ought to be crippling Germany's strength for ever. We are so happy and quite convinced Tom and I did the right thing, though I don't suppose you will see it that way.

I find I am thinking about Guy more than ever. This is something I had not expected. I won't say who, but there is a source of information I have in Penarth so I know he is well and looked after. That is good but is not enough. After all the shocks I have been through I am in a better frame of mind, which is why I think of him so much and dread the thought he will grow up and believe I'm a bad woman. I can see now I should have brought him away with me. Well, who knows what will happen? I suppose Ewart will be serving papers on me some time, and when it comes up before the judge it will be for him to decide who has the custody of Guy. I know the chances are against me, but a baby should be with his mother. I will write no more now except to ask please for a photograph of dear Guy and a lock of his hair. That is not too much to ask, is it? I implore you to think more kindly of me and let me have what I ask.

We are negotiating the premises 'somewhere in the south of England' for Tom's wine business, and if that comes to nothing he has other plans which I don't think I ought to say anything about for the time being. Dear Guy! All I want is a photograph and a lock of hair. I am sorry I did not send him a present on his birthday.

Yours sincerely<br>Olive Barr

The letter was so unexpected and what it said so surprising that Hannah was dazzled by it. She could not be sure of what she had read, so she handed the letter over to Charles who had recently taken to glasses for reading; they were steel-rimmed and whenever he put them on he felt a bit steely too, that much more critical of what he was examining. Nietzsche had steel-rimmed glasses, so had Rudyard Kipling; he couldn't be sure about Darwin, or Carlyle for that matter.

'It's from Olive, is it? What's *she* want?'

'No, you read it. I scarcely know what she's saying. But what comes out of it is that she wants a photo of Guy and a lock of his hair.'

'The 'ell she does!'

'I'm not all that surprised. In fact it's what I expected.'

The two eggs boiling in the kitchen were forgotten, as was the kettle. Charles went into the sitting room and Hannah followed.

'And the source of information?' Once he had read it he offered the letter back. 'Some'at's changed 'er all right. Bloody woman! Why can't she be consistent? But I don't think she's really changed. Barr put 'er up to it.'

Hannah would not take the letter, she waved it away. 'Mrs Peacock.'

'Eh?'

'Mrs Peacock, she's the source of information.'

Guy screamed a lot those days. That morning he had one of his bouts and they could hear Milly's footsteps overhead. Mrs Lavender was down with 'flu, like a lot of other people, which was why Hannah was boiling her own eggs and making her own tea and toast. She was out of practice; this – apart from the disturbing nature of Olive's letter – was why the eggs not only boiled dry but went on being roasted over the gas-ring to a point when the shell went dark brown, cracked and gave off smoke while the kettle belched steam. Hannah had become a little deaf but she could smell and rushed off. Ever after she associated the scorched, sulphurous smell of burnt eggs with Olive's letter and the first hint that she was having a change of heart about Guy.

Charles stood with the letter in his hand. A photograph! If Barr had not put her up to it for some legal advantage it showed that deep down Olive might have a bit of humanity after all, and it was not for him to stand in the way of her being less of a bitch. But he suspected trickery. The hellish stink from the kitchen seemed to indicate something for him too; it became the very smell of that damned woman. All they could do, though, was to pass the letter to Mrs Paul so that she could send a copy on to Ewart.

When she saw the letter, Mrs Paul's view was that Ewart would not oblige Olive with a photograph and a lock of hair. He was too bitter. Surprisingly, she went on to say they must not even forward the letter to Ewart because it would upset him so. She would have taken Guy back to Somerset long ago if Ewart had

225

not made it plain he wanted his son to stay with the Whites, understandably because they could provide him with comforts beyond her means. She could not deny she had been hurt by Ewart's attitude. He had gone through so much, and now that he was off to fight the Bolsheviks there was no knowing what the future would hold, so she did not hold it against him. What particularly hurt was making Agnes the child's guardian if he did not come back from Russia.

'Agnes, Guy's guardian? First we've heard of it.'

In her annoyance Mrs Paul had already crumpled Olive's letter between her two hands. Charles insisted she gave it back. It was their letter, not hers, and as they looked at each other angrily the tension rose until Mrs Paul sighed and threw the ball of paper at him. 'I suppose you're right. It comes strange to a woman that her own son should deny her the care of her own flesh and blood. Why? Tell me that.'

The Whites were amazed that Ewart should be prepared to entrust Guy to Agnes and not to his mother. Agnes was young and Mrs Paul was not – that was the only reason they could think of. Any other explanation they would not want to put into words. Mrs Paul went on, 'If Ewart didn't come back I can't see the courts handing Guy over to your Agnes whatever he says in his will. They'll say his place is with his natural mother, and that's what really frightens me.'

Agnes still worked at the hospital and had started an M.A. thesis on various fighters for women's rights from Mary Wollstonecraft on, but now that Guy was at 'The Lookout' she spent more time there than ever, coming not only at the weekends but in the week too, whenever she could get time off from the hospital. When she saw Olive's letter she was unsurprised and even, it seemed, a bit pleased. 'You'll have to send it on to Ewart. I suspect this is the beginning of something quite dreadful.'

Mrs Paul was there too – she had been waiting for Agnes – and they all sat in the conservatory with the door wide open because it was so hot; the strongly coloured flowers which Hannah now favoured – fuchsias and amaryllis in purple, scarlet and peach – looking less strident in the intense sunlight. Outside the spring was under way, blue, white and yellow crocuses frayed and faded in the sharp winds and the daffodils very bright against the holly hedge, but here in the conservatory it was more than high summer, it was tropical. So much colour and heat was incongruous, making for

226

frivolity just when nobody felt frivolous – not to begin with, but as time went by and the sun took greater hold they relaxed and looked less hard round the edges.

Charles fiddled with the blinds, but it was impossible to cut out all the sun. In the shade Agnes's face looked petunia blue but Hannah had been looking into the sun too long, and too gratefully, to see normal colours. Even Charles's white hat looked green and the shadows under the wide brim were purple.

'What do you mean, something dreadful?' he asked Agnes.

'I think what this letter shows is that Olive and that man Barr are prepared to operate the law quite cynically. Olive doesn't really want Guy back, but she's all out to exact as big a price as she can for leaving him with Ewart. It wouldn't surprise me if they tried to kidnap him. Guy would be something to bargain with.'

They were all astonished. 'Kidnap?'

'One day he'll be out with Milly in his pram and before you know what has happened he's been snatched.'

'But what would she be bargaining for?'

'Pride. Even before this letter turned up I knew Ewart was worried about a kidnap.'

''Ow do you know that?'

'He wrote to me at the College. I wrote back and he's written twice since then. He can't get over the way I made him throw that pistol into the dock.'

This was the first the Whites and Mrs Paul had heard of Ewart being dispossessed of his pistol, and Charles for one was so pleased that he stood up and would have embraced Agnes but she pushed him off. 'He started right off in the first letter saying he thought Olive was up to snatching Guy, just out of malice, not out of any belated maternal feelings, and the words she uses in this letter – Agnes was holding it in her right hand and using it as a fan – 'makes me feel he's dead right. I like the word "please" in that sentence where she asks for the photograph and a lock of hair. Olive never used the word "please" in her life.' Agnes took another look at the letter. '"I implore you to think more kindly of me." Does that sound like Olive: *Implore!* I ask you! More likely she's been prompted by some solicitor she's turned to. Show yourself conciliatory and repentant, he'd say. And all for what? To hurt Ewart more!'

Charles was miffed by the way Agnes had fended him off – that was the old Agnes – but the tough young lady who had persuaded Ewart to get rid of his gun and now dismissed Olive's letter with such contempt was new to him. He knew about her political ambitions. For the first time he realized they might well be fulfilled and it would be God help whoever she got into a shouting match with across the floor of the House of Commons.

'What are we going to do?' Yes, she intimidated *him*.

'I don't think you need be afraid the court would hand Guy over to Olive if Ewart died.' Agnes was doing what she was happiest at, sorting out other people's confusions and being blunt. 'She could never marry Barr because his Roman Catholic wife won't divorce him. No court would hand over a baby to an unmarried couple. If Olive wants Guy for some reason, she'll either have to kidnap him or pay somebody to kidnap him for her.'

Charles pooh-poohed the idea of kidnap, but Agnes insisted Olive and that man Barr were capable of anything. Until Ewart was demobbed and came home to take charge of Guy himself, they had to be alert. When Milly took him out in the pram she should never be alone and should always carry a police whistle to blow in an emergency. For Mrs Paul's benefit, she added that Guy would be particularly vulnerable in a small Somerset village with only his grandmother to guard him. Here, counting Mrs Paul herself there were five of them. As for the letter, that would certainly have to be sent on to Ewart. What he did was up to him; she knew what a ditherer he was, but there came a time when a man had to make up his mind even on so small a matter as sending a photograph and a lock of hair.


Minsky had reasonably good news of his relations and friends in Russian Poland. The Poles, it seemed, were fighting everybody – Russians both White and Red, Germans, Rumanians, Ukrainians, Austrians – bent on setting up the old historic, independent Poland. Their houses had been plundered and then set on fire by Ukrainians, but nobody in the family had been killed. They put whatever belongings they could salvage into carts, went a long way south and stayed with friends. How the letter got through, Minsky could not imagine; the envelope had an Austrian stamp and a Vienna postmark; he could only think that in all the confusion someone had managed to get to Vienna. He shrugged. 'Trains are running, you know. It is not all chaos.' He was permitted only a short time for rejoicing because he soon went down with influenza.

During the winter the 'flu epidemic had accounted for a lot of lives. Cardiff was badly hit. Penarth was let off lightly due, Charles maintained, to its healthy position on its high headland constantly scoured by salty westerlies. There was not so much real poverty either, so sickness could be warded off by what food money could buy, some of it on the black market. Charles was a great believer in the health-giving properties of bananas and although consignments were rare indeed, ships under the command of such men as Captain Peacock turned up with green bunches of them which somehow defeated the checking system in the bonded warehouses and ended up – together with coffee beans, tea, butter, lard, sugar, sacks of flour, corned beef, pecan nuts and raisins – in the richer reaches of Plymouth Road and the meaner glories of the eastern part of the town. In spite of all this there were casualties. Charles's work-force, such as it was, fell to half strength one fortnight and Minsky did no better. Patching up, repairing, replacing tiles and gutters, that was the sort of work they were reduced to in early 1919, but they kept up their spirits by thinking and talking of what they planned to do at Lavernock. Charles thought that Penarth was luckier than in fact it turned out to be; the epidemic just struck later. First to go down in their immediate circle was Mrs Paul, then Minsky and Mrs Minsky took to their beds and were so ill they were too weak to prevent Hannah coming round to kneel in the sick room, pray for them and talk of the Four Horsemen of the Apocalypse. As an ex-prisoner of war, their son-in-law was back in England before the end of January and Ruth, who had gone up to London to join him, now returned to nurse her parents who gave instructions that visits by Mrs White were to be discouraged. 'She means well but make excuses. Say we are not wanting her to catch our germs.'

Talking to Minsky had become one of Charles's more pleasurable activities. Casting him as a spy and investing dodges he might have got up to gave even greater pleasure – he still had to chuckle when he thought of Minsky mistaking the Campbell pleasure-boats for troop transports – but even now that the war was over Charles was not emboldened to tell his friend what colourful adventures he had imagined for him. Minsky did not have an English sense of humour and Charles could see he might well be offended. The relief he showed when the letter from Vienna arrived was instructive: he talked in a way that showed where his loyalties lay, not to this country or to that country but to his own people.

England and the States were all right because, Charles gathered, those were countries where his friends and relations would love to escape to; to that extent England and the States commanded their loyalty, but it was not like Charles's loyalty. He was English and Minsky's relatives would be as welcome as Minsky himself to live in England, but they could never be English. Charles did not know about America. Over there they were such a mixture that, yes, he could see they would become American in the way they could not become English. British, yes, but not English. Minsky did not even seem interested in what the Allies should do to Germany, he was much more interested in what the Communists had achieved in Russia. In the Russian Revolution he saw some hope that anti-semitism would die out and pogroms be just horrors in the past.

They argued about the terms the Allies should demand in the peace treaty. Minsky was never in the 'Hang the Kaiser' camp – he thought the hard men in Vienna were much more to blame – but he certainly wanted Germany to 'Pay', as the *Daily Mail* put it. And he wanted Poland re-established as an independent state in spite of the well-known Polish anti-semitism. Minsky read the *Daily Mail*, and although he would have denied it strongly was influenced by its punitive tone. Charles, on the other hand, was against punishing the Hun overmuch because that would only stoke up resentments which would lead to more trouble.

'If the Germans turn the peace terms down, what then?'

'They are not in a position to reject,' said Minsky dismissively.

Charles thought of what Barr had been reported by Olive as saying, about crippling Germany for ever, and was convinced that was something the Allies could not afford. 'If they turn us down, you've got to think in terms of any army of occupation staying there for years. Where are the men to come from? Who's going to pay? And if we keep up the blockade, who's going to justify starving out the women and children? And Germany would go bolshie.'

'That would not be a bad thing. What the people are needing is more democracy and socialism.'

'We'd 'ave a Red Army crossing the Rhine before you could say Lloyd George.'

'He's not a socialist.'

''E's anything that will serve 'is turn.'

Minsky's influenza put an end to such conversations and nearly put at end to Minsky himself, so Charles found himself increasingly occupied with what Minsky would be doing; negotiating with the bank, getting the land at Lavernock properly surveyed, putting in planning applications, taking on labour and shedding labour as the prospects for the development waxed and waned and waxed again. Setting up Lavernock Developments as a limited company with Minsky, his wife, Charles and Hannah as directors – that involved a lot of talk and argument with D'Eath, the solicitor. There was a great deal of book work. Charles yearned to have Ewart back where he had once been, in the office. He had heard that individual soldiers could be demobbed if it was to do work of national importance and the employer gave the firm offer of a job. What could be of greater national importance than the building trade? Charles resolved to make immediate application to the authorities for the release, as a matter of priority, of his old yard manager and audit clerk, Sergeant Ewart Paul of the Tank Corps, who would certainly be more usefully employed back home than on some harebrained adventure in Russia. Charles kept this last sally to himself but he fired off a couple of letters, one to Ewart himself to say what he was doing and another to the Officer Commanding the IV Army, General Henry Rawlinson who, under Haig, was Ewart's boss. Charles believed in going to the top. He wrote on headed notepaper – Lavernock Developments Ltd – because he thought this might carry weight with the High Command.

Whenever Charles saw his daughter these days he went on the defensive – Hannah too, he suspected. Too strong to say that she actually despised them, but she certainly had a way of talking and behaving as though critical, particularly of their ability to look after Guy. The supposed kidnapping threat was a case in point. Agnes took his scepticism as evidence of his and of Hannah's irresponsibility. Charles supposed that she would never marry. Once upon a time, in the dark ages, she would have become a nun, then an abbess, then an agitator in the Roman Catholic church for fundamental reform which would make it possible for a woman to become Pope. And why not? He could imagine a medieval Agnes saying there was no more blessed human being than the Virgin Mary herself, and by that very fact women should not only be priests but the chief priest to boot. It amused Charles to think of Agnes as a church dignitary, just as it had amused him to think of Minsky as spy. In reality he knew nothing of Agnes's religious beliefs. He assumed she hadn't any, which brought him to the point where he wondered what she might have become in a more secular age. Florence Nightingale! Why not? After all Agnes had worked in a hospital and they were both spinsters. If the Lady of the Lamp had been his daughter, Charles suspected she would have looked down her nose at him too.

It was still a bit of a shock to discover that in answer to Hannah's letter to Ewart forwarding Olive's plea, the reply should come not to Hannah or to him but to Agnes herself. She did not produce Ewart's letter and gave the impression she had no intention of doing so; they would have to depend on what she told them. Ewart had been down with 'flu too and in hospital, but he was better now and wrote to say he had no objection to sending Olive a photograph of Guy and a lock of his hair. The Whites were incredulous.

When Mrs Paul heard this, she said she would believe it only when she saw it in Ewart's writing. Like the Whites, she could not understand why Agnes was the line of communication; nor why she did not produce the letter.

'He seems a bit confused, as though he hadn't really got over the 'flu, but what came through was his wish to be generous and understanding. I ask you, one minute he's ready to shoot her, the next he throws his hands in the air like this. He's so feeble! He wants to play the wronged husband who turns all forgiving and understanding. Doesn't that make you sick? He is so weak. Where will it end?'

Hannah asked Agnes why she was so angry.

'I like things to be clear-cut. We've got his son here and that gives us not only responsibilities but certain rights. We've got to know where we stand. Do you intend to do what he says?'

Hannah said she thought the decision was for Mrs Paul to take, Mrs Paul said she wanted nothing to do with the matter and Charles watched Agnes's face attentively until she looked at him directly, their eyes met and he realized she was very cross indeed.

'My belief is he isn't thinking. He's just there, sitting relaxed and pleased that he's not going to Russia – '

'Not going to Russia?'

'It's been called off. He sits there, a prey to his emotions, the sun comes out and he says to himself, "Why not? Give Olive what she wants". Next thing is we get a letter in which he says he's changed his mind.' Agnes dropped her voice. 'I suppose there's no need to do anything, really.'

Hannah said he would want to know what had been done.

'The state of mind he's in, he'll probably have forgotten all about it. He's war-shocked. I've seen soldiers looking the way he is; they can still hear the guns. We've got to face it. Ewart is demoralized and when he comes home he'll need all the help he can get.'

'I'd like him to bring Guy back home to Somerset.' Mrs Paul used knitting-needles like foreigners used worry beads, and she had clicked her way through all the talk. 'With his bounty he could start up a little business and be away from this town where he's had so much unhappiness.'


Guy had been a healthy and fairly trouble-free baby, thanks in part to the start given him by Mrs Muldoon who had long since faded into the background though she did pop in now and again to see how 'my lad' was getting on. 'What, look at that, Mrs White, actually sitting up! Ask me 'e'll be walking before 'is time. Look 'ow 'e 'olds 'is 'ead up. That's right, my boy! Don't let them laugh at you. Oh, 'e's so *sweet!*' Milly and Hannah bottle-fed him and he gnawed rusks and did all the things a child turned twelve months should do. One evening, though, Milly came down and said that Guy was very hot. She thought he might have a temperature because he was not only hot but moist as well; he kept putting his fingers in his mouth and gnawing at them. Hannah said this was just teething, but she went upstairs with her clinical thermometer and tucked it under Guy's arm. He resisted frantically and it took time and trouble to establish just what his temperature was. Milly had to hold him quite tight with his arm clasped to his side, but he struggled so much that she had difficulty in keeping him still. Eventually, Hannah put it up his rectum.

'He's a real rugger player,' Milly gasped. 'Play for Wales, 'e will.'

When Hannah read the thermometer it showed 104F, but she still thought it was a teething temperature.

After a wretched night when nobody in the house had much sleep, Hannah sent Milly for the District Nurse who arrived on her bicycle an hour later, unstrapped her black bag from its carrier and marched up to Guy's room where she demanded, 'What's all this noise I hear, young man? Let's have a look at you then.'

Nurse Howells was a wiry, efficient woman in her sixties who immediately ordered Charles out of the room, his presence being unnecessary, and then put the back of her hand against Guy's cheek while he yelled, wept copious tears, went surprisingly red and white in turns and then lay still as though now he had been able to take a good look at Nurse Howells he found her face hypnotic. 'Quite a sweat you're in, young man.' She tried to clean up his face with a moist flannel. 'And all bunged up.'

'He won't take his bottle,' said Hannah.

'Oh, won't he?' Nurse Howells inspected the bottle, removed the teat to fill a spoon with the warm milk it contained and amazed Hannah by the rapidity with which she had it in Guy's mouth. She did not actually hold his nose, but some special kind of District Nurse magic was performed and Guy received his first liquid for something like twelve hours. Nurse Howells had also seen down his throat and pronounced it 'very inflamed'. In short, Guy's trouble was not teething, it was influenza. 'He's got to have his drink.' She showed Hannah how to do. She put the edge of one hand on his little chin and then gently squeezed his cheeks with the fingers of her other hand. Guy was so exhausted by now that his mouth came open. 'Now you won't have the knack of using the spoon as well, so this young lady can tip him a spoonful. Keep him wrapped up and I'll be back.' Then Nurse Howells was away with her black bag, brushing past Charles in the hall to take off down the drive on her bicycle, her blue-capped head boring into the wind.

This was the beginning of Guy's fight for life and the time when Charles stepped down into the pit. The descent was so real he experienced it physically – down, down, with the ordinary light of day dimming as he went down. Not only was it dark, it was quiet enough for him to hear the beating of his heart; and so cold. Nobody noticed Charles was in the pit because so far as Hannah was concerned – and Milly, and Agnes when she came home because Hannah had sent for her – they all saw him looking as he always did and making a bit of a nuisance of himself by repeatedly bending over Guy to examine him more closely. Nurse Howells spoke sharply to him on her second visit, which she might not have done if she had known he was in the pit. But she did not know, neither did Hannah or Agnes or Milly, only Charles knew he was in the pit.

On the third day of Guy's illness Dr Brownlow appeared, the doctor Hannah had consulted over her infertility all those years ago, now brought out of retirement because so many doctors were in the Forces. He wore the same kind of black frock-coat (it might have been the very same one) with two buttons at the back just over the vent, but now he had carefully clipped white whiskers with the point of his chin shaved. Guy, who had cried so much, excreted so much and taken little in return, was exhausted. Dr Brownlow was able to sound his chest with his stethoscope after warming the ends in a cup of hot water, even to look down his throat.

'He's got a temperature of 105,' said Hannah.

'Those clinical thermometers are more trouble than they are worth. I've known people die from an inaccurately taken high temperature reading when they'd have survived if it had been kept from them. A little knowledge is dangerous.' However, he took Guy's temperature himself and agreed it was high without saying just *how* high. 'By some means or other you've got to get tepid water into him . . . all the time. If he won't take his bottle, squirt it in. Get one of those little syringes from the chemist and squirt it in. And look, here's a prescription for a bottle of medicine. Get that into him too. It's got tincture of quinine in it.'

The next day Dr Brownlow was back again for another examination and to give instructions for a fire to be lit in Guy's room and a kettle to be kept boiling on it. 'It is important he breathes warm moist air. Good for his lungs.'

When Charles heard this he was not only in the pit but the ground had closed over him. He knew that if Guy had not developed pneumonia already, there was a possibility that he might. He followed Dr Brownlow to the front door with the idea of asking whether a specialist ought to be brought in, but before he could say anything Brownlow patted him comfortingly on his shoulder. 'The little lad's your grandson, I take it?'

'No, he's nearer to me than that. I love him as I would love my own son.'

Brownlow was no fool. He knew what was going on and who Guy really was, just as he knew who Charles was talking about when he spoke of his son.

'Keep that kettle boiling.'

'There must be something more we can do.'

'No, there are three women here and the District Nurse to look in. Couldn't do more even if I sent him to hospital, which I don't propose. I'll look in tomorrow.'

Charles wanted to dodge Brownlow's next visit and went up to St Augustine's, where he drew the line at entering the church but found a seat in the churchyard and looked out over the Channel. On that calm, mild and sunless day, there was no one about. He was alone with the sky and the sea, knowing it was illusion – that he was not in the open air at all but in a pit. He was plunged deep in the pit and dreaming of the world he had once known and lacked the wit to enjoy for its own sake.

There were birds in the churchyard and their calls and twitterings penetrated even down into the pit. Gulls manoeuvred and dangled in the still air. James must not die! He said the words out loud and for some time did not realize what he had said. The pit was an echo chamber. More likely, though, that the words came back from the real echoing chambers which were the grottoes, the cirques and recesses of his own mind. Guy had become James, or James had become Guy. He was helpless in the pit and could do nothing but mouth words, gibberish from the most profound depths of his being asking for help, offering himself as a sacrifice instead of the boy James. He was ready to atone for all his sins – real ones, imagined ones, sins he had forgotten, sins he could not even imagine – by offering himself as a substitute if only James could live and they could be reconciled at the last.

'Well?' he asked when he reached 'The Lookout'. 'What did Brownlow say?'

'Just the one lung affected, he thinks.'

Agnes had observed her father curiously. 'He's just gone to pieces,' she said to Hannah. 'I noticed it in the hospital; it's the men who go to pieces.'

Not until the fifth day of Guy's illness when Dr Brownlow had decided the second lung was infected did Charles think of sending a telegram to Ewart, if a telegram could now be sent to a soldier. It could. 'Guy critical please come White.' There was much debate at 'The Lookout' as to whether a telegram should be sent to Olive too. Charles was in favour and so was Hannah, but Mrs Paul and Agnes were against on the grounds that Olive, undoubtedly accompanied by Barr, might be in the house at the same time as Ewart and there might be trouble.

Hannah said this possibility was of less importance than the redemptive experience, for Olive, of seeing her son in his sickness. It might be the means of her salvation and giving up her sinful way of life. Hannah was accustomed to nobody taking any notice of her

236

when she spoke as a Millenial Dawnist; but really, would she have spoken any differently if she had been an ordinary Christian?

Agnes thought about what her mother had said. 'If you mean there might be a death-bed reconciliation between Ewart and Olive, I think you're unrealistic. That's not how it will be at all.'

'Death-bed? What are you talking about, Agnes?'

'Let's face it, Guy is desperately ill.'

Charles insisted it was his turn to sit up all night, but Hannah was doubtful because there was more to it than just keeping the kettle on the boil. Feeding, or an attempted feeding, of a sugar solution should take place every half an hour. He would also have to be alert to the possibility that Guy might be uncovered. Hannah said it was important that Guy should not have any exertion at all; the ideal was for him to lie there motionless while, as a result of her prayers and Guy's good constitution, his fever was stabilized and then went down. Charles insisted again that he could cope and Hannah thought it was worth a try. The others had been up for most of the previous two nights and were whacked.

As bad luck would have it, Guy's coughing was worse than ever when Charles started his vigil. He took to steadying the boy's head. He must have dozed off, because he woke with a start to hear the clock downstairs in the hall chiming three. Guy, he confusedly realized, was making no sound at all – not coughing, not choking, not crying.

Charles turned up the gas-mantle and bent down to see whether Guy was still breathing. He could not tell. He put his ear down to Guy's face and was overjoyed to hear not only breathing but after some moments a gurgling snore. So far as he could tell Guy was calmly asleep. Then he was not asleep; his eyes were wide open, looking up at Charles as much as to say 'Who are you?' Those dark eyes were fixed unwinkingly upon him. Charles looked back, as much as to say, 'James, I see you.'

Hannah walked in and Charles said, 'He's been looking at me.'

'Go to bed.'

Charles did as he was told and found himself dreaming vividly of walking with Deedee on wet mud their feet sank into, and they had to keep hauling each other out. When he awoke, fully dressed and stretched out on the bed, it was daylight and so still he could hear the low, slow breathing of the waves as they broke on the pebbles. For a while he did not know where he was, he was still

237

trapped in his dream. Nobody about in the house – no voices, not the creaking of a board. He struggled to his feet, poured water from a jug into the bowl, washed his hands and face. He had not shaved for days. He liked the feel of his incipient beard and massaged it thoughtfully, only breaking off to go and sit quietly on the lavatory where he wondered about that vivid dream and whether it meant his annoyance with Deedee had been overdone.

When he walked into Guy's room he found Milly with a finger to her lips. Guy was asleep, his head on one side and a lot of mucus on his face and bedclothes which she did not deal with for fear of waking him. He had been sweating like a horse but had a better colour – still flushed but not angrily flushed, just as though he had been touched by the rising sun. Hannah came in with two cups of tea and they spoke in whispers, scarcely daring to put into words what they thought.

'Pray God, but I think he's taken a turn for the better.'

All the strength went out of Charles and he almost dropped his cup. He felt drained.

'What's the matter with you?' Hannah whispered.

Charles tried to remember what he had been doing at St Augustine's the day before; he remembered the gulls and the Channel glinting under the mist. A strange vision for a man who was not in the open air at all but down in the dark pit.

'Man is an animal.' He was surprised by the words he had whispered and even more surprised by what followed. 'But he is an animal who is ready to be sacrificed. I didn't know a man could pray to be sacrificed. I'd forgotten what it was to pray.'

Guy stirred and whimpered. Hannah went into action with a face-cloth, but she still found time to say to Charles, 'You didn't need to read all those books to know about praying. I could have told you, but you've too much pride to listen to anyone but yourself.'

She crooned over Guy and sent Milly off to get some boiled water in his feeding-cup. 'Look, his eyes are open like – like daisies. Look, Charles, he's even trying to smile.' Charles look down at Guy with his daisy eyes and thought confusedly that it was just as though the strength he had lost had gone into the child.

After Nurse Howells had arrived and snapped out a few words of satisfaction about Guy, Charles took something to eat for the first time in days, a bacon sandwich, and went up to James's

238

room where he sat with the telescope and the specimen cases as the sun moved round, flushing out the shadows. There he fell asleep in his chair. When he woke he knew that – by whatever strategem he could not imagine – he had climbed out of the pit and the sun was shining on him, a real sun and not an imagined one, as it might shine on and warm some naked creature in the rocks. An adder was what came into his mind. As a boy he had seen an adder in a sun-splashed ditch sloughing its dead outer covering, the grey head writhing out of its envelope, then quicker than he had believed possible the whole creature glistened naked in the sun and the slough, turned inside out, was lying entire on the grass like a ghost of the adder itself.

When Guy's crisis had really passed Hannah asked Charles what he meant by saying that man was an animal that sometimes prayed. He said he could not remember saying any such thing.

Hannah looked at him strangely. 'You said something like it.'

''Annah, I've 'ad an experience. I really went down into the depths and I came up again when' – he hesitated because the right words did not come – 'when I was at the ends of . . . well, despair. It was as though I could feel James coming to life again.'

'Thank God.' They were both tremulous with relief, but Hannah was more in command of herself than he was.

'I don't know 'ow I managed.'

'You? You didn't manage at all. It was Jehovah in his grace managing it for you. In your heart you know that perfectly well, otherwise you wouldn't have said what you did say about praying.'

'I feel drunk and clean.'

Hannah was not a demonstrative woman but now she put her arms around him, kissed him and cried until Charles's face was wet too. 'You've suffered enough, Charles. We've both suffered enough.'

Charles began laughing a bit wildly. ''Annah, I swear something's gone out of me. I've come out of a great hole and something 'as come away from me in the sun. And now it's all over I'm calm.'

They clung to each other. 'You're not calm, you're crazy.'

'I'm calm. I'm at peace. I've been able to make my peace.'

'For God's sake be more humble. You talked of sacrifice. Jesus atoned for all of us upon the cross, and it is by his grace I believe you are forgiven for James if you ever felt in the need of forgiveness.'

'Eyes like daisies. Yes, 'Annah, I saw those eyes.'

The kettle still had to be kept on the boil. Charles knew an old game to amuse Guy while he lay there and inhaled the water vapour. From the top of one end of his cot he set up two strings in parallel to half-way down the other end of the cot; but not quite parallel, because the strings were wider apart at the lower end of the track. A tennis ball placed where the strings were highest ran down until the strings were just sufficiently wide apart to allow the ball to drop through, not tamely on to Guy's counterpane but on to another string track which delivered the ball safely against Guy's left cheek. He was amazed and delighted; so Charles elaborated the system and devised not just two string tracks but four, the top trap delivering the ball to a lower track running down and in the opposite direction; and so on, down to tracks three and four. Guy never tired of this rolling ball game.

The last time Charles had set it up had been for James when, older than Guy was now, he had scarlet fever. It was as though James was having scarlet fever all over again, but this time Charles had no anxiety at all.


Charles went round to see Minsky in such exaltation that he did not notice how ill he was and talked to him about matters he did not want to hear. Minsky roused himself sufficiently to say 'You are being out of yourself. You are just being so happy the baby is better even though it is not your baby.'

''E's a cousin of my wife, once removed.'

Minsky lay with his eyes closed. His forehead glistened, his unshaven cheeks were sunk and because his top dentures had been removed he had no upper lip at all and the tip of his nose made vain attempts to make contact with his chin.

'Charles White.'

'Yes.'

'I am wanting to rejoice with you, but I am not well. Charles!'

'Yes.'

'You are still not believing? Yet you think you've made a peace with the past and you are reconciled. But who are you thanking and who are you reconciled with? It is not making any kind of sense.'

'If only I could tell you 'ow I felt.'

'It isn't a matter of feeling. It is a matter of believing. And what

240

do you believe? Nothing! You don't know what you are talking about. You are in a dream.'

Minsky had a fever or he would never have spoken like this. 'Would you please excuse me now, because I think I am going to die.'

# 10

When Ewart was demobbed he and his mother took Guy back to their Somerset village and Ewart started work in the Bridgewater Co-op bakery. Charles was angered by this; he had made it clear that Ewart was not only welcome to have his old job back but that he was actually needed. He had offered Ewart five quid a week, which was more than he could get in any bakery, and when Ewart turned it down Charles raised his voice. 'What do'you want to do, then? I'm in Lavernock up to my elbows. You want to drive me out of business?' He turned to Agnes. 'You talk to 'im.'

'It's not our affair.'

Hannah was upset at the thought of losing Guy. 'Not our affair? One way and another, we've made it our affair.'

'I'm grateful to you, Mrs White. But somehow I've got to re-establish myself, and this town is not the place where I think I can do that.'

Ewart was having a rough time with his solicitor, a yellow-haired man by the name of D'Eath who wore pince-nez secured by a black ribbon. He seemed to be entirely on Olive's side in this matter of divorce. Had Ewart ever ill-used her? What quarrels took place? As a soldier in France, had Ewart been faithful? French women were notorious. And could he put his hand on his heart and say that when he had married her his intentions had been entirely honourable? His situation was modest whereas Miss Jones, as she then was, managed a branch shop of the Singer Sewing Machine Company and might have expected advancement to the Cardiff shop and even to managerial status. Great changes were taking place in society. Women were usurping the roles played by men and no doubt this was a development that would gain momentum as a result of the war. There were not enough men to do the work. Mrs Paul, as she became, might have looked for success as a professional sewing machine woman. Was not Mr Paul aware of all these possibilities when he married her, and could she not reasonably claim that it was a misalliance and that she had been deceived in the disinterested nature of his proposal of marriage and was now sadly learning from experience? Had he married her not out of love but for her career prospects?

No, said Ewart. He had not expected the war to go on so long and so many men to be killed, so he could not have foreseen there might be career prospects for women which did not exist before. He had married Olive because he loved her and, as for himself, he had ambitions. He could have been an over-the-sticks jockey and made a lot of money that way. That ambition had now died on him.

'Very good.' Mr D'Eath tapped a document that lay on the desk in front of him and smiled. 'Well answered, Mr Paul. Your wife is in a certain difficulty, so no doubt her solicitor will do everything in his power to blacken your character.'

'Why?'

'My understanding is that she will now seek to gain custody of your son.'

'But she abandoned him.'

'She's a changed woman. And her solicitor will argue that you, a man on his own, can't bring up the child.'

'I'm not on my own. My mother will look after him.'

'The age, health and standing of your mother will be factors of which the court will take account. But don't let me cause you undue anxiety. I don't think the court will give custody to your wife, the admitted guilty party in this affair who is living promiscuously with another man. We shall get the decree nisi without any difficulty. What really counts is the interval before the decree is made absolute.'

'I don't understand.'

'The decree nisi is a kind of conditional divorce. A legal officer, the King's Proctor, will be alert to discover whether you are living blamelessly. If, for example, you were living with a woman, that would be relevant. Are you? Of course not. But I am exploring the possibilities your wife's solicitor might seek to exploit. You have no attachments of an amatory nature?'

Ewart hesitated and D'Eath was quick to notice the hesitation. 'Is there anything you wish to say?'

'No.'

'Mr Paul, you must be circumspect, you really must. Do you know what I mean?'

Ewart had been introduced to D'Eath by Charles, therefore it

243

was only natural that he should tell him how much he hated the man. 'I suppose he's only doing his job, but it's the way he smiles when he goes through all the difficulties. How does a man get a name like Death anyway! It's not comfortable dealing with a man who's got such a weird name.'

'It's not Death, Ewart. It's Dee-Ath, and I suppose it's a posh name.'

'After what she's done I can't believe Olive really wants Guy.'

'She won't get 'im. But as to why! Well, she's a trouble-maker and always 'as been.' Charles sighed. 'But for 'er, I think before we were married Mrs White and I might have gone off together all those years ago and all our lives might have been different. I was frisky as a young stallion. Time and chance 'appen to us all.'

'How do you mean?'

'We all went to Weston on a trip, Olive and 'Annah Jones as she then was. I 'ad the brave idea of eloping with 'Annah off to Bristol, but we didn't know what to do with young Olive.'

'The Lookout' seemed empty without Guy, and quiet after all the activity that had centred on him – Nurse Howells popping in, Mrs Muldoon coming to see how he was getting on, Hannah fussing about his weight and how much nourishment he was taking, not to speak of the occasional bad nights when either Hannah or Charles paced the room with Guy, crooning and trying to rock him back to sleep. Even Agnes had stopped coming. Although he was on the other side of the Channel, Guy remained a real presence in the house. Charles sometimes woke in the night thinking he had heard Guy's cry. Unable to sleep again, he would go up to James's room where he looked out in the direction of Somerset. He could see the flash of the Flat Holme Lighthouse and lights from shipping. Beyond the lights was the living and breathing child.

Charles still had this outrageous idea that he had pulled Guy through his pneumonia by the intensity of the agony he had gone through himself. Not only outrageous but conceited too. Charles would have conceded all that and then said you had to go through the James experience to understand his feelings. Purgatory was a word that came into his mind. When he looked it up in the dictionary, he learned it was spiritual cleansing.

'What have you been doing?' Hannah would ask him when he came back to bed.

'I thought I 'eard . . .' He never completed the sentence and Hannah never pressed him.

244

One night she said, 'I still think it's strange that Ewart should take Guy back to Somerset for his grandmother to look after him.' They lay in the darkness listening to the wind and the waves, holding hands. 'He was so set on his mother not bringing up Guy; he was all for making Agnes his guardian.'

'That's if 'e'd died. Now 'e's survived, things are different.'

'I think there's something between Ewart and Agnes.'

Charles was amazed. 'Then why would 'e run off to Somerset?'

'My guess would be that Agnes treated him rough.'

He was silent for a long time. 'I don't think anything bad can 'appen, 'Annah. When you've been where I've been and then come back and come through, you think there's a special light or glow settled about everybody and everything. When I turn my 'ead, like that, and look at you it's as though I can see you in the dark.'

'I can't see you. I can only make out the shape of the window.'

'Oh, but I *can* see you, 'Annah. You're like a saint, so naturally you give off light to be seen by those who've got eyes to see. I can see light everywhere. The night is full of fireflies. I don't think anything bad can 'appen now, 'Annah, 'owever rough Agnes's been.'

As soon as it became possible after the war Charles had the telephone installed, not only in the office but in 'The Lookout' as well. The very first conversation he had on the telephone was with Hannah, who was cool about this intrusion (as she saw it) into the privacy of her home. A telephone at the office was understandable, but to have one in the home was like leaving the front door open for anybody to walk in.

'Yes, I can hear you. But it is you, is it? I mean you sound different.'

'It's the electricity in the voice, 'Annah.'

'You sound, sort of . . . well, bigger.'

The news about Guy was all the more dramatic and disturbing because it came by telephone. Agnes telephoned from a Cardiff hotel to say that Mrs Paul had been pushing Guy out in his pram when they had been stopped by a man and a woman who had a motor-car. Yes, it was Olive all right and Mrs Paul assumed the man must be Barr – a nasty, sneering man with a harsh croaking voice whom she vaguely remembered being at the wedding. Olive just said something about having come for her son; she seemed angry with Barr for laughing and not taking the matter seriously.

She just snatched Guy up, took all the covers from the pram, and then they made off in the motor-car without another word. As soon as he got home that night Ewart reported the abduction to the police. Agnes knew all this because he had written her a letter enclosing a note from his mother. She said it was extraordinary that Mrs Paul had not gone to the police immediately instead of waiting for Ewart to come home; or she could have telephoned him at the bakery.

Charles tried to reassure Hannah. 'It'll be all right. The Court will order Olive to send Guy back to the custody of his father.'

'That's not the point. The proceedings won't come up for months. Think of Guy. The only real home he knows is with us in this house. Then he goes to Somerset with his father and grandmother. Now he's in a strange house being looked after by strangers. He'll be in all sorts of distress. What a way to serve Ewart after obliging her with that photo and lock of hair.'

When Agnes came home she had more news. Mrs Paul had been so upset that she had taken to her bed. Ewart was told by the police that a mother taking possession of her child was not committing an offence even though a divorce was pending. All they could do was advise him to consult his solicitor.

When Ewart arrived without an appointment, D'Eath was short with him. He seemed to think Olive was behaving quite naturally. Mothers were like that, weren't they? But he reassured Ewart: it would not affect the final outcome.

Ewart came round to 'The Lookout' and, although Charles and Hannah were both in the room, it was to Agnes he addressed himself. She looked quite blooming, bright-eyed, pink-cheeked, tightly enclosed in a grey costume that accentuated her figure. Hannah knew these were expensive clothes and suspected Agnes was not the complete, austere Labourite she pretended to be.

'So D'Eath wants the law to take its course,' Charles said when Ewart described the reception the solicitor had given him. 'It'll all come right in the end. I'd just like to know what goes on in that woman's mind, though. She rejects the child, then she grabs 'im back.'

Truth to tell they were all a bit stunned by Guy's abduction; even Charles's voice had a wobble in it. Agnes's voice did not wobble though; her tone, the expression on her face, the way she held herself all expressed her no-nonsense approach to the crisis. 'Just greed, that's uppermost in Olive's mind. Once she'd got over the

246

birth shock, Guy became just a piece of property she'd been done out of. Nothing maternal about it. Sheer possessiveness. So I'm not surprised. What does surprise me, though, is the way Barr has been so cooperative. Olive must have a real hold on him. I suppose Mrs Peacock made it her business to tell her brother what was going on. So knowing Guy was being looked after only by his grandmother, the precious pair pounced. How did Mrs Peacock know of Guy's movements?' She shrugged. 'This is a small town.'

Ewart now made what everybody present came to regard as a speech. It was mainly about taking the rough with the smooth, and that he had had as much of the rough as was tolerable. In the war he'd been lucky. Not a war hero by any means; just the usual service medals; there were better men than him lying dead in Flanders. But he had done his bit – and now, how did he find himself? He deserved a better deal of the cards, that's all.

Charles had been watching Agnes, remembering what Hannah had said about 'something going on'. He could see she was impatient with Ewart. He was talking too much, whining too. Any moment now she would say something sharp and deal Ewart another bad card; so Charles tried to say something emollient.

'Look at it in the long-term, Ewart. Guy will grow up in a better world. You'll be a grandfather one day – think of that.'

'A grandfather?'

'Guy will 'ave lots of kids, I reckon.'

Charles had wanted to throw Ewart out of his stride, but Ewart was having none of it. He looked about him. 'Mr White, Mrs White, Agnes, I know I'm just a baker with a wife who's run off, but I'm going to make sense of my life. You know what I mean?'

Agnes had a way of setting her mouth just as her mother did when she was angry. 'Stop it!'

'Mr White, Mrs White, you've been so wonderful to me. I've got a life to live without waiting to be a grandfather. If I've any reason not to regard this world as a dung-heap, you've given me that reason. But I'm greedy. As soon as this divorce is over I want Agnes to marry me so we can bring up Guy together and, God willing, have children of our own.

'The only man I would marry,' said Agnes, who was furious, 'is one I propose to myself. Not the other way round.'

Charles stopped inspecting Agnes and turned his attention to Ewart. 'So that's why you went off to Somerset?'

Ewart hesitated. 'Yes.'

'I'm glad to know that. I didn't like the thought of rejecting me as an employer in such an out of 'and way. My offer is still open.'

'There's the King's Proctor to think of. If he heard me saying what I've just said, when the decree nisi is made, he'd put a spanner in and there'd be no absolute decree. So, quite apart from Agnes having such a poor opinion, that's why I'm going back to Somerset in the hope of earning her better respect as time goes by.' This was uttered with such dignity that even Agnes could meet his words only with silence.

Charles could see that Agnes was too clever for Ewart and too 'ikey', but he had to admit he liked the idea of their marrying and making Guy his step-grandson. He imagined glorious possibilities. Agnes would go on with her academic work, she'd become a City Councillor and – who knows – put up for Parliament; then Ewart would come in as his office manager with a particular responsibility for the Lavernock development while he, Charles, gradually relinquished his business interests and embarked on a considered course of reading. He had already come to the conclusion that Greek philosophy was what he should have a stab at, particularly Plato who kept on cropping up in Nietzsche and Russell in the most intriguing way. He suspected that Plato and he had a lot in common, but would really like to examine his ideas to see whether they came up to scratch. Agnes marrying Ewart was by no means a necessary preliminary to such a study, but it would help in establishing the domestic calm he now hoped to enjoy in his declining years, now that the war to end wars was over. More important than anything else was the well-being of Guy. Agnes as Mrs Paul would be the best guarantee of that, and Charles saw Guy's political interests being fostered by her to the point where in 1960 or thereabouts Guy, after a colourful back-bencher performance, moved into Government and became a Liberal Prime Minister. Dear Guy! Once recovered from his grasping and amoral mother, he had a brilliant future before him!

In the late summer Charles and Hannah took the Paddington train, crossed London by motorbus and caught another train from Victoria down to Brighton, where Olive and Barr were now living. The bank address in Streatham had been misleading. Barr had his account there for years no matter where he happened to be – in Croydon with his wife, in the Army or in the various London

248

addresses he took Olive to. Olive had revealed the Brighton address when writing to thank Hannah for the photograph and the lock of hair.

A week before the abduction, Olive had written to Ewart from Brighton begging for Guy. She had come to her senses, she wished their marriage had turned out differently, but 'love could not be denied' (her words) and please, she was suffering, she saw Guy's face all the time and she wanted him. She had been a sick woman but now she was well. Love had made her sane. Love was the greatest of all doctors. The only bitterness in all her new-found happiness was not having her child. As for Ewart, he was a good man she respected but love was something different. He had nothing but her good wishes for the future. She hoped she had not hurt him and hoped too that he would marry again – someone who would love him as she loved Tom. And so on, and so on.

With Ewart's approval the Whites were making the journey to persuade Olive to face reality. It was most unlikely that the court would give her custody of the child, so why prolong the agony? Reality, said Charles, was difficult to endure. They all preferred self-comforting illusions and shadows to the real thing, like the prisoners in the cave he read about in Plato; they sat with their backs to a fire and saw on the wall of the cave their own shadows and the shadows of other objects passed between them and the flames, thinking that what they were looking at was the real world.

Hannah was not paying attention. 'I seriously wonder, Charles, whether it is a waste of time talking to Olive about the rights and wrongs of what has happened. How much money would you be prepared to hand over for Guy?'

'Money?' Charles had never thought of Guy in money terms and he did not want to start now.

'The only way we'd make any impression on Olive is with money.'

'But we can't buy Guy.'

Hannah was insistent. 'How much?'

'No, it's impossible. It's wrong. It's immoral. 'Ow can you be so cynical?'

'Don't forget you paid money for James.'

He was shocked by this blunt reminder. He had indeed paid money – £25.14s.6d., handed to that Smorfitt woman! Well, money was for use.

They had not said they were coming, so for Olive their arrival

249

was a complete surprise. She and Barr had a top-floor flat in one of the narrow streets leading off Marine Parade. When Charles opened the unlocked house door they found a pram, a bicycle and fishing gear in the hall. Hannah examined the pram, presumably Guy's, carefully and shook her head. Plainly, it had housed a whole succession of babies and in her opinion needed a good scrub and disinfecting. The Whites knew from the bell-pushes at the front door that Olive was two flights up, but they elected not to press the appropriate button. Their unexpected appearance when she opened the door of the flat was enough to make her scream, and behind her they could hear Guy screaming too.

Hannah pushed in front of Charles. 'I do hope you'll let us come in, Olive. Please!'

Olive looked well, but a bit wild-eyed and ready for a row with anybody who turned up. In spite of the warm weather she was wearing a green velveteen jacket that looked expensive to Hannah and not the sort of attire suitable for a caring mother; her lipstick was shiny and she wore lots of pearls – artificial, Hannah assumed – in a great treble rope knotted loosely half-way down the exposed blouse, plus earrings that were a cluster of pearls. Her defiant air seemed to indicate that she expected an intrusion. The police, perhaps. Ewart? Anyway, trouble. 'I've been legally advised I am within my rights in taking possession of my son.'

'Please let us in, Olive.'

'All right, but you might've let me know you were coming. Tom's in London on business.'

Charles was relieved that Barr was not there. What he and Hannah wanted most was to see Guy. And there he was, in a matter of seconds, lying in a cot with no clothes but his napkin, weeping pearly tears and throwing himself about.

'He's got a colic.' Olive stuffed a dummy into his mouth in the hope that it would stop him crying, but he threw it out of his cot and would have started screaming again but for catching sight of Hannah's face. She had removed her hat and was bending over him enraptured.

'He knows me. Look, he knows me! He's stopped crying. He's looking at me. He's smiling. Oh, the darling!' She picked Guy up and rocked him in her arms. If he did have a colic, it was certainly not troubling him then. He could switch a smile on and off like a light, and he did this several times while he looked from Hannah to Olive and then to Charles. Olive was not best pleased by this

250

demonstration, particularly when Guy started crying again as she took him from Hannah and tried to settle him back in the cot.

'It's only natural it'll take a bit of time to get used to me.' She looked first at Hannah, then at Charles. 'What do you want?'

Hannah did the talking. 'They'll never let you keep Guy – can't you just see it all, Olive? Be sensible. There'll be a court order and a policeman will turn up to deliver it. He'll have one of those big strong police nurses with him, and they'll just take Guy away. You wouldn't want that experience, would you?'

Olive sat rigid, cold with rage. 'I'd never let them take him.'

'I'm sure your solicitor doesn't encourage you to think you can keep Guy.'

'He's a right sod, that solicitor. Trust Tom to pick the right one. I don't care what solicitors say. Guy's my son and you can't go against nature whatever the law says; no woman in her right mind would see it any other way. I tell you what, Tom and I'd just barricade ourselves in. We'd create a great public scandal. It'll be in the papers. They'll never take Guy. Never, never, *never*, on my oath, Hannah.'

Guy held Hannah's little finger tightly and looked at her enquiringly as though to say, why is she making so much noise? Why is she shouting? Then he began once more to cry and throw himself about. Olive picked him up and would have walked up and down the room if only it had been big enough. She joggled him clumsily, but still the baby cried and Hannah took him once more.

'Don't put yourself more in the wrong, Olive. The law can get very rough.'

'They won't find us.'

Through all this Charles had remained standing, looking out of the window at other roof-tops, at bits and pieces of laundry pegged out on rickety-looking verandahs, at a large black cat with a white shirt-front and paws sitting on one of them, and at a small patch of winking sea wedged between a flat-topped building and an advertisement hoarding. He was amazed by Olive's stand. The boy meant nothing to her really; it was all an act. She could not even imagine what Guy meant to him, Charles White; he was a poor creature who had died and then been brought back to life. He turned.

'If you will let us take Guy, I am prepared to give you a thousand pounds.'

Olive stared at him incredulously. 'How dare you! How dare you! It's like spitting in my face. To think I'd take money for my child. What do you think I am?'

'Just think about it. 'Annah and I will come back in the morning when you've slept on it. Believe me, it would save a lot of misery all round. The money is nothing. I realize you wouldn't take money for Guy, don't think of it that way. Think of it as a present that has nothing to do with Guy . . . and let him go.'

Just how airless the little room was they only realized when they stepped out into the street and walked down to the front, Charles carrying the brown Gladstone bag that held their overnight things. They stood looking down at the beach – like birds released, flickeringly happy though they had no reason to be so.

'I didn't understand what you said.'

'What do'you mean, 'Annah?'

'About it being a present.'

'No more do I know what I meant. I 'ad to say something she could cling to, so that in years to come she could say she didn't take money for Guy. Yes, it's a bloody charade.'

They found a bed-and-breakfast establishment and left the bag there. Then walking slowly, they went as far as the Palace Pier. Crowds of people were about, a lot of men still in khaki including some Australians who sat on a bench drinking beer out of bottles and inviting passers-by to join them. The sea was not as blue as Charles would have liked, but it was certainly bluer than the Bristol Channel and there was an unmistakable seaweed tang in the air which he said was ozone.

'Real sea,' Charles pronounced. 'See 'ow those big waves come rolling in.'

'Are we really going back to Olive's tomorrow?'

'Not before the banks open. I want to take this money in fivers and wave them under 'er nose. Then see what she says.'

It was still light when they went to bed in a hot and stuffy attic right under the roof. Charles lowered the sash window to let in some of the cool evening air and stood in his shirt-sleeves looking down into a public garden where people were still strolling about. Hannah was already in her nightgown, sitting at a dressing-table to put cream on her face. Its perfume made him think of marshmallow or nougat and he went and stood behind her to rub the back of her neck with his thumbs in the way she liked. Sometimes he was able to rub so skilfully that she gave little moans of pleasure. So it was that evening. She released her nightdress at the front so that it slid down over her shoulders and he could mould and manipulate the flesh as far as her waist, saying, 'There, there, now. How is that? Does that make it better?' The 'it' was nothing in particular, not just her neck and back. It was anything you could put a mind to. The heat of the evening. Life.

The bed was broken. Something had given way in the middle, so they were rolled together whether they wanted to be or not. Charles laughed and Hannah laughed. Their love-making was not as fierce, not as desperate, as in the years when they had fought to conceive. The passion was gentler now: the struggle was to extend that passion as long as possible, to go on loving for ever if only that were possible.

'For ever and ever,' Charles said. 'Eternity. That's a long time and it scarcely bears thinking about but with you in my arms, 'Annah, I feel we're touched by it.'

It was not as easy as all that to draw a thousand pounds out of a bank where he was unknown. The manager himself was called, who said it was a large amount to hand over the counter even to someone who had an account at one of the sister branches: Mr White would have to pay for a telephone call to Penarth. The upshot was that they did not arrive at Olive's until gone twelve and Tom Barr himself was there, in shirt-sleeves, standing with legs planted wide apart, his hands behind his back as though he was warming himself at an invisible fire. Olive was in the little kitchen and Guy was rolling and stretching himself at Barr's feet. It was evident that Barr and Olive had been having an argument; there was that special chill in the atmosphere, to which Olive added a particular nip by rattling cutlery noisily in a washing-up bowl. She was still wearing the velveteen jacket and the pearls by way of demonstrating that domestic chores were not for her and once she had got them out of the way she'd be off. Where? Oh, somewhere bright, with music and dancing and clinking glasses. Tom could look after the baby. That was the impression she gave.

After a few preliminaries in which the reason for the Whites' visit was not referred to, and certainly no mention made of Guy, Barr launched into a long complaint about the Army authorities who, he said, were buggering up his gratuity and disability pension and, what was more, refusing to give him a reference. It was essential if he was to set up as a licensed victualler, but the Army said it wasn't their practice to give references. 'It wasn't just an ordinary pub I was thinking of, not a bloody ale-house. Something superior with an emphasis on wine, really nice snacks, asparagus, *pâté de fois*, French cheese when you can get it again – know what I mean? Found an ideal dive but, you know what? The magistrate won't give me a licence. I tried to get a brewer involved, but they're only interested if you sell their beer and frankly I hate the smell of the stuff. Anyway, that's all behind us. I've had enough. Olive and I've had enough.'

He hissed, wheezed, strained to get the words out in a way that made him sound more aggressive than he probably was. Charles thought that if a really big lizard could talk, that was what he would sound like. It was sad. Barr was not a lizard, he was a war hero, but if you sounded like a lizard it was as a lizard that people treated you. Charles was so carried away by this line of thought that he was not listening as closely as he should have done to what Barr was saying. He could have sworn the chap had said something about going to the States.

'Yes,' said Barr. 'We'd be off to the States tomorrow if only I could get a bit of a float.'

'You mean money?' And if people treated you as a lizard, wasn't that what you became? This was the first time Charles had met Barr, so he had no previous impression to measure the man against, but he surmised that as time went by he would increasingly acquire the characteristics people attributed to him. This was not Darwinism but it was in that great tradition.

'It'd take a damn sight more than a thousand quid.'

Olive came in from the kitchen, wiping her hands on a towel.

'Tom's had an offer from a cousin in New York.'

The thought of Guy being spirited away across the Atlantic was too much for Hannah, who turned to Charles and said, 'We'd never see him again.'

But once Charles could switch his mind away from how acquired characteristics could be picked up, he scented victory. What Barr and Olive had been rowing about he could only guess at, but it must be something to do with the offer he had made. Olive looked at him defiantly. She was hard and she knew what a bitch she was; she looked him in the eye, as much as to say, 'I don't care a damn what you think. Or anybody else for that matter. Does anything *mean* anything? This war and all those men dead and poor Tom left as he is. And me doing what I've done. It's a bitch world, but we're going to enjoy it. Tom and I are happy.' She said none of these things, but Charles had a feeling she might have done and what's more she was thinking of James.

What she did say was, 'You heard what Tom said. You standing there like that! Are you dumb?'

'Once Charles would have flashed back at her, but in his new mood of hope and reconciliation he turned away to look at Guy. He was not just a baby, he was a promise. Life! Life! Life! It did not matter what Olive's feelings were. Later, much later, he thought she could not be so inhuman as to have no feelings at all, but the way she had switched from being the possessive mother to money-grabber made her seem that way. No doubt Barr had talked to her straight. It was Hannah's view that Olive could think of only one thing at a time. For that moment, it was money and America.

The bank had put the money in a brown-paper wallet. Charles handed it to Olive, who took out the notes and counted them carefully, Barr watching over her shoulder. Hannah had picked up Guy and, pressing him to her bosom, she went to the window and gazed out, as Charles had gazed, at the roof-tops and the same black cat with white paws and a white shirt-front because she could not bear to witness what was going on. It had been her idea, money. Charles would never have thought of it himself, but now that the transaction was actually taking place she was sickened. It made Guy so much to be pitied.

'We want two thousand,' said Olive.

'I'll 'ave to give you the rest by cheque.'

Later when they were in the train on the way back to Cardiff and Hannah with Guy asleep in her arms, and the cot clothes, the little hamper with the feeding-bottle and the flasks of baby food around her, Charles said, 'They could never 'ave got Guy out of the country.'

'I just thought they'd smuggle him out and there'd be no getting him back no matter what the judge said in London.'

'As a matter of fact I'm not entirely convinced they're going to the States. But if they do go they need passports – and to get passports you need certain documents: her birth and marriage certificate, Guy's birth certificate no doubt. The moment the authorities realized Olive was travelling without her husband they'd want a written authority from Ewart.'

'How do you know all these things, Charles?'

'I keep my eyes open.' To himself he said, 'Resurrection', and the

255

wheels of the train took up the word, tripping it out rhythmically, Resurrection! Resurrection! Resurrection! across the green shires and into Wales.

Minsky was wrong about dying and when the weather warmed up he liked to sit out in the sun looking very intently into flowers. He held them close to his eyes and confessed he could feel himself hypnotized. The real world was lost and the flower world took over.

'Look, this little flower, what is it? I am not knowing names of flowers.'

'It's a sort of wild pansy,' said Charles.

'I am holding it so close the big two petals at the top are like a canopy. Now what colour would you say? Black? Purple? There is no exact word. The bottom three petals have lines and colour running out from the centre. So the little flower looks amazed; it is an amazed little creature with these blue-black lines running through a yellow field to where the stamens are being. It is like a temple and I am thinking of myself inhabiting this temple. It's crazy but it's harmless, isn't it, losing your eyes to a flower?'

Back home in Gloucestershire they called it heartsease. Charles could not remember whether they had any in the garden at 'The Lookout' and resolved that they would have lots of them. From now on it would be his favourite flower, just because of the name.

Minsky was happy because he had news from his relations in Eastern Europe. It looked as though they would be settling inside the frontiers of the new Poland, but not for long; they'd had enough of Europe and wanted to get away to America, and it gave Minsky pleasure to think how he could help them when currency could be transferred more easily. But the greatest development of all was that he was thinking of taking his son-in-law Frederic into the business, and that the boy was a good boy who was taking instruction from a rabbi with a view to becoming a Jew. Not that it was easy or in any way a foregone conclusion. The rabbis were very strict, and would not accept him if they had any doubts about his commitment. The fact that he had even set his foot on this path was a great comfort to Minsky. Charles could not possibly understand what a comfort it was.

'Because you see, my dear, how much we like to be a family who are sharing the same view of the world. With you it is so different.

256

What you tell me about the baby and getting him back, and the mother actually handing him over for money, is strange beyond my understanding. How can such things be? I wish no offence, Charles, but you are living in a world that throws out from the centre. I could be almost saying it is all explosive. I don't feel at home with such thoughts. I like to think of everything coming *into* the centre.'

One eye shut, Minsky was now peering with his other down the throat of a snapdragon. 'It is like a journey into China. I can see yellow and red streamers on all sides of the nostrils and jaws. The jaws gape. Smoke comes from the nostrils. No, it is fire and I am walking into a fiery furnace like a prophet of old. I am coming to no harm either. Oh, my dear, it is a whole world you can see in a flower. It is so small and weak a thing, but in it is a wonderful world just for the looking at. You think I've gone foolish?'

'No.'

'Look.' Minsky handed over the flower and made Charles look into it as he had done. 'Do you see the gates of hell opening to receive you?'

'I don't believe in hell.'

Minsky laughed. 'I think you do. Hell is what you have come to believe in these past few weeks. No? What is the place you think you've come out of?'

Charles was surprised. He had not spoken to Minsky of his state of mind when Guy had been so ill, but he now realized that Minsky, in spite of his own illness, had been thinking of him and feeling for him.

'Why are you so kind to me?'

'Kind, you say?'

'When I started out in business you lifted me up. There's been kindness on kindness. Now why, I ask myself?

Minsky was sitting near enough a rose-bush to lean over and pull one of the roses up to his eye for inspection. It was a fully-blown rose and he could part the petals and see the golden flurry of stamens. 'It was nothing.'

'I don't think there's anybody I owe as much to as you.'

'It is nothing. Let us talk of other things.' It was not just to divert the conversation that he asked more about the trip to Brighton; he was genuinely curious about the detail. All kindly and sympathetically meant but with detachment, like a traveller observing the strange ways of a tribe he had come across in the wilds. 'A thousand pounds in notes, you say. Five pounds a time. So two hundred notes. Very bulky. You'd have needed quite a bag. So! Strange of all is the change of heart. One day Mrs – '

'Paul.'

'One day Mrs Paul is determined to keep her son. The next she is ready to part with him for money. In the interval this man – who? Barr. He must have been very persuasive. Then he took a cheque. Why did he not ask for a banker's draft?'

''E knew my cheque would be good.'

Minsky took out a handkerchief to wipe the pollen from his nose. 'I am suspecting this story about going to New York is true. The great opportunity had suddenly come up and there was Mr C. White as a source of money to make it all possible. So he bullied Mrs Paul and she suddenly became afraid of losing him.'

Charles shrugged. The main thing was they they had got Guy back.

'Why do you call me Mr C. White? You used to call me Charles.'

'My dear, you are taking on a new dignity. I see that, and do not wish to be familiar. You are Mr C. White, a man who has come out of the fiery furnace.'

This annoyed Charles. 'I don't know why you make fun of me.'

'Fun? Me? No, but I think you should know that to the observer like me you have taken on a new dignity.'

'But I can tell from your tone of voice that you do not approve of this dignity.'

'Put it another way, Mr C. White. I have an affection for you because – I have not said this before – you remind me of my brother. Not in looks – in ways. He left home, taking his fiddle with him, and we had heard nothing for two years or even more when he wrote to us from Odessa. He was a tailor employing two men and two women, but he still played the fiddle because that was his real life.'

'I can knock tunes out of a 'armonium, but I wouldn't be able to do anything with a fiddle.'

'Not the point. Nathan married and had a son who was drowned swimming. Nathan never touched his fiddle after that. That's why you remind me of my brother.'

Charles could not understand. First of all, Minsky had said he had a new dignity; then he said he was like a man who had given up his fiddle. Minsky was speaking out of some strange world where similarities between quite different things were seen because they each related to some third factor which Minsky was well aware of but Charles was not. As much as to say to a totally deaf man that a fiddle and a harmonium were musical instruments, when he had no inkling of what music was and, to look at, the fiddle and the harmonium had nothing in common.

'I only mean that you are like my brother because you are so easily confused. What good did it do him to give up his fiddle? Why did you hand over two thousand pounds when you know the law would return the child to his father anyway? You and my brother are both men who like to make gestures, and that is what gives you dignity. Deep down, though, what does this gesturing mean?'

'Giving the money was no gesture. I'd 'ave given three thousand. Four. I'd 'ave bankrupted myself because I wanted that boy back in short order, away from that woman. I know the court would've given 'im back to 'is father anyway. But that takes months, years perhaps. What would've 'appened? Can you imagine it from the kid's point of view? First one mother looking after 'im. Then somebody else. And that story about going to the States might well be true; they could've wangled Guy out somehow. No, I was making no gesture. I was just stopping that bloody woman because of the damage she could do to 'er own son.'

Minsky was still busy with his flowers, picking them up, laying them down; love-in-the-mist, petunia, even a dandelion. 'If it turns out the way you say, some day the boy will go looking for his mother.'

'After a long time. Per'aps never.'

'Do you think when he is old enough his father will tell him about his mother?'

Charles was uncertain. 'Not a matter for me. Ewart will make up 'is own mind when the time comes. And it depends on circumstance. If there's another marriage and what the new wife is like . . . she would want a say, I reckon.'


It had seemed natural to take Guy back to Penarth rather than to Somerset. Charles sent Ewart a telegram from Paddington which Ewart did not see until the evening, but he cycled back into Bridgewater and caught the last train to Bristol where there was no connection for Cardiff until the following morning. There was a heavy shower and he arrived at 'The Lookout' in clothes so wet he had to sit in a blanket while his coat and trousers were hung in front of the kitchen fire to dry. He could not believe his luck; he had seen Guy, nursed him and crowed over him. How had the miracle been performed? Charles had not wanted to tell him about the money – it would place Ewart under too great a sense of obligation and that would be intolerable for both of them. But Ewart's questioning was so insistent that Hannah gave way and said that although she was quite sure the main reason Olive handed Guy over was because Barr wanted her to, it was also true that money had changed hands.'

'Money?' Ewart was incredulous.

Charles thought there was no need to give this reason; the attitude of Barr would have been enough in itself. Still, the damage was done.

Charles never confessed to Ewart how much money he had handed over for Guy. It was money he himself could ill afford, much more than his annual profit, but the very size of the ransom gave pleasure in itself. Two thousand pounds was what he would have called an *important* sum of money, and it was fitting that so important a matter as the recovery of Guy should be marked fittingly. He thought about the money infrequently as time went by, but he never regretted what he had done. If he had handed over, say, a thousand pounds it would have been demeaning. As for five hundred, that would have been to trivialize the transaction; he was not just recovering the son of Hannah's cousin, he was redeeming a more personal loss. Even to think of the loss in cash terms was blasphemy, but it would have been even more blasphemous if it had not required a real financial sacrifice. At the time he asked the bank for a thousand pounds, he did not know whether he had so much cash in hand. He had not. The bank manager had agreed an overdraft, which at one time he would have considered a step along the road to bankruptcy, but Minsky had taught him better. Sacrifice! he thought. Yes, he had made his little sacrifice and Ewart would not be allowed to contribute to it not by ten pounds, not by one pound, not by a farthing!

For Agnes the rescue of Guy gave pleasure on two counts; that he was back with those who loved him and that Olive had taken money for him. That said everything about the woman. For Agnes the pleasure came from seeing Olive in such a sharp focus, so unambiguously; she had no claim on whatever remnants of sympathetic understanding Agnes was capable of. Agnes believed there were too many attempts being made at sympathetic understanding – of the poor starving Germans, for example, who had lost the war – and was glad that one figure at least had finally lost any claim to hers.

She was so astonished by the news that her father had actually handed money over that she opened her eyes wide and began laughing in an exaggerated sort of way. 'Oh, no! You just can't believe it! How can a woman be like that? A man, yes. But a woman! A mother, I ask you! and then, of course, there's Barr. He'll make life hell for her. I shall think of them over in the States just tearing each other's eyes out!'

Charles was saddened to hear her talk like this. They ought to put bitterness behind them. They had all suffered, but they had come through; no, you could put it more strongly – they had won. So a smile on every face was in order.

He was now of an age when a man made his will, so he went round to D'Eath to talk about it and found the solicitor in an unexpectedly expansive mood which was not deflated even when Charles gave him the news that Mrs Olive Paul was presumably already on her way, with her lover, to New York. D'Eath ought to have snubbed him for talking about another client's affairs, but he was expansive because the divorce proceedings he was taking on Ewart's behalf had reached a satisfactory stage and he was already pencilling dates in his diary when he and Ewart would go to London to attend in the High Court. It was, he agreed, a nuisance if Mrs Paul had made herself scarce, but there was no real problem because the case was so straightforward. It might even be an advantage. At the same time, he must say he thought it strange that the news of the child's abduction and recovery should come almost casually from Mr White when it should have come from Mr Paul.

'It won't affect the outcome of the petition, but the court will have to be told. Mrs Paul must have known she could not have custody. Why do people behave so idiotically, Mr White?'

'It's the way men and women are. Instinctive. Even solicitors must know that.'

D'Eath looked coldly at Charles. 'But that is not what you came to see me about. You want to make a will?'

'A simple one.'

'Not too simple, I hope. Simple wills can be ambiguous. We

must go into detail. Apart from your wife, have you any special bequests?' He drew his notebook towards him.

The making of a will was an unexpectedly agreeable experience for Charles and he came to make a habit of it. Every two or three years he would take out the old will and revise it in the light of changing circumstances. He had long ago abandoned the idea of keeping a diary; he had tried for a month or so, but Guy's illness had put an end to the experiment; writing down his thoughts and experiences was too painful and, in any case, he became aware that what he wrote was not necessarily the truth. He could not resist exaggeration and fudging, qualities which he recognized when he read the entries over after an interval. But a will was different. Even to think of one was to take on immortality, a trivial kind of immortality no doubt, but nevertheless the only one possible for him. He was writing a little letter to posterity.

Now with D'Eath looking at him through those pince-nez, Charles realized he had not properly prepared for this, his first will and testament. He did not expect to die early because he came from a family who lived long – his mother was still alive and doing odd jobs in Gloucestershire; his father had been the exception, but he had died in a threshing-machine accident – so the decisions he had to take were not urgent. By a simple will he had meant one in which he left everything to Hannah, but it then occurred to him that she might give most of it to the Millenial Dawnists. If he willed something substantial direct to Agnes, there was no knowing what use she might put it to; she was incalculable. No doubt there was some Women for Socialism group she would want to prop up financially. And there was the child Guy, whom Charles had come to regard as a James figure. And what of Ewart? Was there any chance of him and Agnes coming together?

'All you've got to do,' said D'Eath after a long silence in which the two men stared at each other, 'is tell me what you want and I'll prepare a draft. You can always alter it.'

'I must apologize for wasting your time, Mr D'Eath. It's more complicated than I thought. I'll just go away and think about it.'

What a fool D'Eath must think him! Charles walked slowly back to his office hoping to come to some important conclusion. He could not think properly when walking because there were too many distractions – the display of cakes and bread in the baker's window, the shortness of a woman's skirt, sparrows pecking in the road grit under the very feet of horses, a cyclist running into the back of a car that had stopped abruptly. He just idled his way through the autumn sunshine, stopping to read the headlines in the papers at a news-stand, exchanging a word or two with an old customer who seemed as much on holiday as he was himself. And happy. Yes! Happy!

Ewart had brought his mother over from Somerset, and they had rented a terrace house off the Cogan Road. She was so shaken by the kidnap that she feared it would be repeated at any time, and although she wanted to be near her darling grandson and to have daily sight of him she could not face the responsibility of looking after him. So he stayed with the Whites, and Ewart hired a nanny with a boxer's face and hands who when she took him out never went without a police whistle. The expense could not be met out of a journeyman baker's wage, and it took Ewart back into Charles's employment on £5.10s.0d a week. He spent most of his time working on papers, accounts and contracts in a hut on the building site, going outside from time to time to chat with the foreman and to observe the shipping in the Channel. His presence down at Lavernock left Charles with the yard in town to supervise and with the time to drop into D'Eath's office for inconclusive interviews. Yes, he went in perhaps once a month to try some little problem on D'Eath. How did one set up a trust for the benefit of an infant, for example, and how much would it cost?


During the war ordinary time seemed suspended, but now it was moving again and Charles was older than he thought. In an album, he came across that photograph he had taken the day Olive and Ewart announced their engagement. It had browned, but how young and fresh they all looked! Olive held out her hand to show the engagement ring while Ewart, his arm round her, gazed at the camera with an expression on his face which Charles could only describe as fatuous. Agnes, in her long pinafore frock, looked sweet – a real holiday girl with her hands clasped behind her back and an impatient look as though she just wanted to dash off to the beach. Hannah had her chin up, more thoughtful than merry. But when Charles thought what had happened since he took that photograph from under his black hood, they looked innocent and timeless, caught in a never-ending springtime.

263

Of course they were innocent. How could they know what the future held? Innocent, fragile and now all, in some way, wasted by the years. How many years? How old was Agnes then? And Hannah? And he? How long had he and Hannah been married?

For their thirtieth anniversary Charles had the mad idea – mad according to Hannah – of driving to Ilfracombe in the Riley and staying at a posh hotel where they could have Cornish lobster and champagne for supper. It meant a thorough garage overhaul, new tyres and extra cans of petrol being strapped to the side. Hannah thought it was crazy to drive to Ilfracombe when it was not all that far, out there on the other side of the water. Charles did not know what she expected – that he should take her over in a rowing-boat? The steamers that used to ply before the war were not yet running. They could go by train, but Charles was determined to drive and drive he did. Up to Gloucester where he was tempted to make a diversion to see his mother but did not (they could look her up on the return journey), and down to Bristol and the West Country where they had a puncture in Bridgewater of all places – Ewart had talked about the town so much that Charles felt he knew it well – and while he replaced the wheel Hannah took some pleasure in asking whether he knew Mrs Dover-Davies's news.

'Deedee? Gladys Deedee! No.' Charles was sweating with a spanner in his hand.

'I met her at a Chapel raffle. She said that Mr Olleranshaw was now a widower and they were going to marry in time for the pantomime season starting in Bradford. Isn't that a peculiar way of thinking?'

'Theatre people aren't like us.' If James had been an actor he would have been in a different world, too

'But marriage is not a way of preparing the ground for a pantomime.'

Charles was more bothered by this information than he would have liked to admit. A little side-show on his life's journey had been closed. 'There must be some reason. Time on their 'ands before the show in Bradford, perhaps.' He wondered if they would talk about James and, if they did, what they would say. It did not matter. He was free. 'They're a good match. I can see them setting each other off.'

In Ilfracombe on the eve of their thirtieth wedding anniversary, Charles kissed her and said they ought to have run off to Bristol as he had wanted all those years ago, because that would have

264

broken the pattern he had been born into. Polly might never have entered their lives. Something quite u expected and wonderful might have happened: twins, even. He might have been a real financial success if he had not needed to fit into conventional business practice; he might have been a property millionaire. But life had been as it was and James was part of it.

'We are all part of God's great plan, Charles.'

'I just wonder about Agnes and Ewart.'

'So do I.'


Having given Guy his bath, Agnes was at that very moment dabbing him all over with a powder-puff while Ewart carried the zinc bath downstairs and emptied it. For all her impatience with him, she was softened by the intimacy which Guy's ablutions had aroused.

'He's so strong. I've got to take a real grip or he'd be off. Here, you take him. He's too heavy for me.'

Ewart tried to put Guy's nappy on, but he was clumsy and Agnes had to finish the job. Once in his nightie Guy, pink as a cooked shrimp and bright-eyed, lay contentedly looking up at them as much as to say, 'I'm comfortable. What about you two?'

But that is another story.

**Guildford Institute Library**
**Withdrawn From Stock**